PHILLIPA ASHLEY writes warm, funny romantic fiction for a variety of world-famous international publishers.

After studying English at Oxford, she worked as a copywriter and journalist. Her first novel, *Decent Exposure*, won the RNA New Writers Award and was made into a TV movie called *12 Men of Christmas* starring Kristin Chenoweth and Josh Hopkins. As Pippa Croft, she also wrote the Oxford Blue series – *The First Time We Met*, *The Second Time I Saw You* and *Third Time Lucky*.

Phillipa lives in a Staffordshire village and has an engineer husband and scientist daughter who indulge her arty whims. She runs a holiday-let business in the Lake District, but a big part of her heart belongs to Cornwall. She visits the county several times a year for 'research purposes', an arduous task that involves sampling cream teas, swimming in wild Cornish coves and following actors around film shoots in a camper van. Her hobbies include watching *Poldark*, Earl Grey tea, Prosecco-tasting and falling off surf boards in front of RNLI lifeguards.

 @PhillipaAshley

Also by Phillipa Ashley

**The Cornish Café Series**
*Summer at the Cornish Café*
*Christmas at the Cornish Café*
*Confetti at the Cornish Café*

**The Little Cornish Isles Series**
*Christmas on the Little Cornish Isles: The Driftwood Inn*
*Spring on the Little Cornish Isles: The Flower Farm*
*Summer on the Little Cornish Isles: The Starfish Studio*

**The Porthmellow Series**
*A Perfect Cornish Summer*

# A Perfect Cornish Christmas

## Phillipa Ashley

**avon.**

Published by AVON
A division of HarperCollins*Publishers* Ltd
1 London Bridge Street
London SE1 9GF

www.harpercollins.co.uk

A Paperback Original 2019

First published in Great Britain by HarperCollins*Publishers* 2019
2

A catalogue copy of this book is available from the British Library.

ISBN: 978-0-00-831615-0

Typeset in Birka by Palimpsest Book Production Limited, Falkirk, Stirlingshire
Printed and bound in UK by CPI Group (UK) Ltd, Croydon CR0 4YY

MIX
Paper from
responsible sources

FSC
www.fsc.org
FSC™ C007454

For John, Charlotte and James

# Chapter One

**Christmas Day 2018**

Brushing sleet from her eyes, Scarlett Latham hesitated over the sign on the door of the Smuggler's Tavern.

*Feeling lonely and lost? On your own on Christmas Day?*
*Join us for a free festive dinner.*
*No need to book! Just walk in!*
*Everyone welcome.*

Scarlett wrapped her arms around her body, trying to hug some life into her frozen limbs, but her thin party dress offered no protection from the biting wind.

The streets of Porthmellow were deserted as all the normal people of the Cornish harbour town prepared to enjoy Christmas lunch with their friends and families. In contrast, the windowpanes of the pub glowed with warmth and the sound of laughter and music drifted out onto the quayside. Scarlett looked at the sign again, teetering on the brink: step into the light, or stay out here in the sleet? The board's words were becoming fuzzy as her tears mingled with the wet snow, but she could still make them out.

Feeling lonely and lost?

A sob caught in her throat. She hadn't felt lonely or lost until two hours before. Now she'd never felt more alone in her life . . . She caught sight of her reflection in the dark glass of the outer door. It was even worse than she had thought: she was soaked to the skin in her Christmas Day finest, her mascara running down her face in rivers. Did she dare cross the threshold? What would people think?

She read the last line again.

<u>Everyone</u> welcome.

Some instinct deep inside propelled her through the tavern's entrance. It seemed bizarre to join someone else's Christmas festivities when her own had gone so spectacularly wrong. Maybe she wanted to prove that Christmas could and should be a happy time when people set aside their differences and enjoyed each other's company for a few hours. Or maybe she was simply afraid she'd otherwise freeze to death and be found huddled against a pile of lobster pots, covered in snowflakes, like the Little Match Girl.

The oak door creaked open onto a scene of warmth and light that was a world away from the frozen gloom of the deserted harbour. People in paper hats were letting off party poppers and blowing tooters in each other's faces. Crimson and green cloths covered the tables, which were laid for a Christmas feast, while tinsel shimmered in the glow from the fire. The smooth voice of Michael Bublé was crooning from the speakers, *'Tis the season to be jolly . . .'*

A gust of wind snatched the door from her hand and banged it shut behind her. In an instant, the cold was cut out and a dozen faces turned in her direction.

It was too late to turn back now, she'd stepped over the threshold. They'd be bound to ask questions, seeing how distressed she was, but was she ready to answer them?

An elderly man in a fisherman's cap decorated with tinsel hurried over to her. He was vaguely familiar . . . though her numb brain couldn't put a name to the weather-beaten features.

'Hello, my maid. Welcome to the Smuggler's Tavern. Have you come for the Lunch for the Lonely? You're very welcome, even if you've a strange choice of shoes for the weather.'

With a cackle of laughter, he pointed to her feet. Scarlett looked down too. Her new rabbit slippers, a gift from her sister, Ellie, were now a sodden mush of grey fluff, as if the unfortunate bunnies had met a sad end on a snowy road. Her Christmas tights had a spud-sized hole at the knee and the hem on her sequinned skirt was drooping.

'You must be freezing.' The old man's tone softened. 'Here, have my cardi.'

'I'm . . .' Scarlett was going to refuse, but realised that her teeth were chattering. 'It l-looks new . . . Don't you n-need it?'

Already taking it off, he pulled a face. 'No. Can't stand the bleddy thing. Unwanted present from my cousin. Does it every year. Same cardi, same colour, always the wrong size.'

He draped the cardigan, a sludge-coloured cable-knit with leather buttons, around Scarlett's shoulders. The warmth was instant and for a second, she felt comforted. Then she realised that the tooters had stopped tooting and she'd replaced Michael Bublé as the festive entertainment.

A man about her own age approached, a wary expression on his face. He was very tall, very blond and wearing a green sparkly jumper and an elf hat with pointy ears. He reminded Scarlett of the Big Friendly Giant. He was joined by a young woman wearing a Santa apron and an elderly lady in a glittery top and reindeer ears, holding a walking stick bedecked with tinsel. They were all smiling at Scarlett, with looks of pity on their faces.

The older man tucked the cardi tight around Scarlett's shoulders and pulled back a chair from one of the tables that was laid for Christmas dinner.

'Have a seat, love,' he said. 'I'm Troy, by the way.'

'Yes, and have some hot punch,' the younger woman added. Scarlett noticed that her apron had 'Sam' printed on it. 'It's non-alcoholic,' she told her gently.

That was it. Sam must think she was pissed.

'I – I h-have only had a couple of glasses of f-fizz,' Scarlett said. 'And some eggnog, but it tasted like sick so I chucked it in the c-camellias.'

4

Sam smiled indulgently. 'Would you like us to find you some dry shoes?' she asked.

The elf man produced a fleece and draped it over her knees as if she were in a nursing home. 'Another unwanted present,' he said, flashing her an apologetic smile. He held out his hand. 'I'm Jude.'

'I'm . . .' Scarlett's lips were numb. She tried to lift her hand, but couldn't.

Jude subsided like a sunken cake. 'Possibly bad timing. Maybe we can properly introduce ourselves when you've warmed up a bit?'

Scarlett nodded. Despite Troy's cardigan, she was still shivering and finding it hard to understand what people were saying to her. Her brain felt like the slush clinging to her slippers. She opened her mouth but it wouldn't connect to her thoughts.

'I'm Sam,' the kind-eyed, younger woman said, then pointed to her apron and rolled her eyes. 'But you must have guessed that.' She crouched down in front of Scarlett. 'You're wet through . . . What's happened to you?'

'I – I c-can't really s-say right now,' Scarlett stuttered, at a loss how to explain the havoc that had been unleashed on her family that Christmas morning.

'OK . . . Maybe you'll feel better when you've had something to eat,' Jude said gently. He pulled off his elf hat, as if out of respect, and revealed blond hair tied in a ponytail.

'Yes, why don't you stay for a hot meal, my love?' The elderly woman smiled at Scarlett. 'I'm Evie. You don't have to tell us anything you don't want to, my dear, but it would help us if you could let us know who you are?'

'Who I am . . .' A series of images flashed into Scarlett's hazy brain.

Her mum running into the scullery and refusing to come out. Her father standing outside the door, demanding to know what it all meant. Her brother, Marcus, shouting at Scarlett and her sister, Ellie, for ruining Christmas Day and Ellie, normally so calm, screaming back that it wasn't their fault. The house ringing with accusations, shouts, tears and denials . . . and Marcus's two boys in the middle of it all, pale-faced and terrified.

Heidi, Scarlett's sister-in-law, had threatened to take them out of 'this toxic situation' before screeching, 'And I would do if I hadn't had so much eggnog.'

Scarlett had rounded on her saying: 'It's bloody horrible, anyway.'

Then, to cap it all, the smoke alarm had gone off.

'Jesus Christ, the oven's on fire!' Marcus had bellowed. 'Get the boys out!'

He'd opened the oven door and clouds of smoke had billowed out from the cremated roast potatoes and pigs-in-blankets.

Ellie, of course, had then tried to calm everyone down and their mum had let out a wail from behind the door.

And Scarlett hadn't cared. She'd wanted her mother to suffer. How could she have done this to the family? To her father? To *her*?

She'd had to get away, knocking back a full glass of fizz as she went. What a mess, what a horrible mess. She had only just begun to get over her split from her boyfriend, Rafa, and she'd thought she could at least rely on her family for some solace and fun. More importantly, she'd wanted so much to make them happy, to give *them* something that showed how much she cared for them and appreciated the bond they shared.

Now it had all been blown to smithereens and some of the people she'd thought she knew and loved were strangers to her. Worse, some of them seemed to blame her for what had happened, as if *she* was the one who'd lied and cheated and lobbed a bomb into the family.

While the smoke alarm shrieked and her siblings argued in the kitchen, she'd slipped through the French windows into the grounds of Seaholly Manor. The cold had snatched her breath away and the sleet had felt like needles on her face, but she hadn't cared.

She'd fled up the lane, her party dress soaked within minutes, praying no one came after her. Her lungs were bursting by the time she reached the main road. A pick-up truck had passed her, slowing briefly before speeding up again when the driver saw a wet madwoman in a party dress and bunny slippers rushing down the hill into Porthmellow.

She'd been shivering uncontrollably by the time she reached the harbour, its Christmas lights twinkling through the grey haze of a winter noon. That's when she truly clocked that she might be in danger of hypothermia and that bunny slippers, a party dress and a stomach full of twiglets and Prosecco might not be the best protection against the worst the Atlantic could throw at her.

Reluctantly, she'd realised that the only thing to do was get to a pub or restaurant and call Ellie and ask her to walk down with some dry clothes and meet her . . . she hadn't taken her bag or her phone, so she'd have to beg someone to let her use their landline. She wouldn't call her mother; she couldn't bear to speak to her – and as for her father, how could she ever face him again?

'How's your knee, my maid?' Evie's voice reached her. It was gentle and soft, the voice of a mother to her daughter, and triggered a fresh wave of despair at what she'd lost.

Her gaze fell upon the red and bleeding skin beneath the hole in her tights.

Oh yes, she'd stumbled on the cobbles by the Fisherman's Institute. Just like when she was little and had tumbled, it hadn't truly hurt until someone had tried to comfort her. Now, it throbbed like mad. Everything had begun to hurt as the numbness thawed, her senses came back to life and the awful realisation of what had happened back at the manor hit her.

The gift – from Scarlett and her older sister, Ellie – was supposed to be the perfect present to her family. It was meant to fill their faces with delight and joy, not pain and anger.

She stared back at Troy, Sam, Evie and Jude, and the blur of faces behind them.

Evie patted her hand. 'Do you even *know* who you are, my maid?'

'I thought I did,' said Scarlett. 'But I don't any more.'

# Chapter Two

Scarlett took a moment to scan the sitting room at Seaholly Manor. Everything was running like clockwork. The floor was a sea of wrapping paper and packaging, coffee cups and champagne flutes, some containing the dregs of the Buck's Fizz they'd sipped while opening their presents.

The past few months of careful planning alongside Ellie were about to pay off.

Ellie appeared by Scarlett's side, a laptop in her arms. 'Auntie Joan would have approved, don't you think?' she murmured.

'Definitely,' Scarlett replied, taking the laptop from Ellie.

'I'll get us a drink while we set up.'

Ellie went into the kitchen and Scarlett connected her laptop into the TV. A ripple of excitement ran through her. Their plan to have the perfect family Christmas at Seaholly

Manor was all going according to plan and yes, Great Aunt Joan would surely have been proud of them. Sadly, she'd passed away in the summer, but Scarlett felt that the Lathams were honouring her memory in the best possible way by gathering at Joan's home for a couple of weeks.

Joan had been a very successful and flamboyant romance novelist, whose bestselling books had enabled her to buy the eighteenth-century manor in the sixties. She had loved company and was legendary for her parties, held in the lush gardens or on the beach at the bottom of Seaholly Cove. It was Joan who'd left the house to Scarlett's mother, Anna.

Scarlett, her parents, Marcus and his family all lived within ten miles of each other in Birmingham, although their busy lives meant they didn't get together as often as they probably ought to. As a rule, their father wasn't a great one for parties but he'd always been happy to make the journey to Cornwall to spend the holidays with his family.

Scarlett was also particularly looking forward to enjoying some time with her sister, who at thirty-eight was six years her senior. After spending most of her life travelling all over the world while working in bars and cafés, Ellie had moved into the manor in the early autumn as 'caretaker'. Scarlett was amazed how quickly she'd settled into Porthmellow life after her globetrotting lifestyle. Since returning to the UK, Ellie had found work as ship's cook with Porthmellow Sailing Trust and helped out at the Harbour Café.

The previous year had brought big changes for Scarlett too, and not in a happy way. She'd broken up with her ex, Rafa, which had knocked her confidence where dating was concerned, and she hadn't dated anyone since. The split was followed by the loss of a major client from the freelance copywriting business she'd built up over the past few years. Scarlett had written the copy for a large engineering company who made all kinds of screws and fasteners, and while it was hardly glamorous, they gave her a lot of work, from their website to press releases. However the company had been taken over by a giant American corporation who'd made lots of people redundant and slashed their budget, meaning she was having to fight hard to find new business in very uncertain times.

So she was trying hard to stay positive that New Year and a happy Christmas, surrounded by the family she loved, would kick off the fresh start.

Ellie walked in from the kitchen, a grin on her freckled face. 'Woo hoo! I've got a surprise for you.'

She handed Scarlett a glass of something that looked like a Minion who had been put through the blender. 'Here you go. Have a sniff of this.'

Scarlett wrinkled her nose. 'What is it?'

'Heidi's homemade eggnog,' said Ellie.

'Heidi made *eggnog*?' Scarlett exclaimed.

'Shh, she might hear you,' Ellie said, smirking all the same.

'I'm just amazed that Healthy Heidi would even think of touching anything alcoholic, especially when mixed with eggs.'

'She says it's healthier than the commercial variety, packed with protein, and she's added some secret ingredients.'

Scarlett pulled a face. 'Like what?' She put the glass to her lips.

'Powdered kelp.'

Scarlett swallowed a gulp of the yellow liquid and gagged. 'Yeugh.'

Ellie sipped hers and pulled a face. 'It's awful, isn't it?'

'Truly horrible, but I don't want to hurt Heidi's feelings. Can we chuck it in a plant pot?' Scarlett headed for a large aspidistra in the corner of the room.

'I don't think so. It might not soak into the soil and the plant will probably wilt on the spot. Quick, open the French doors.'

Scarlett took both glasses and stepped into the garden. The contrast in temperature with the cosy house made her chest tighten. Overnight, a cold front had blown in, coating the flagstones with a film of sleet. Her bunny slippers weren't ideal for venturing too far so she quickly threw the eggnog into a flowerbed and hurried back inside.

'Brrr. So much for this being the Cornish Riviera. Look at my bunny slippers.' She held up a foot to Ellie.

Ellie laughed. 'They are a bit soggy. Let me put them in front of the fire, while you get the laptop ready.'

'Thanks. You know . . . I'm starting to have cold feet in other ways. I'm a bit nervous now it's come to the crunch.'

'It'll be fine,' Ellie said, placing the damp slippers on the hearth tiles.

Even though all three of the Latham children were the wrong side of thirty, their parents still gave them stockings, although the 'fillers' had long since ceased to fit inside the actual stockings. They always contained small bottles of posh 'smellies', the latest book by their favourite author, chocolates and a 'silly' gift. This year everyone had received a pair of novelty slippers – even Marcus, who had groaned when he'd opened a pair of size eleven badger slippers.

Ellie was wearing fleecy alpacas, while Scarlett's feet were cocooned in the fluffy rabbits. They were ridiculously impractical and probably lethal on the polished boards of Seaholly Manor, but wasn't that the point of a stocking present? It had to be fun and, above all, *silly*. It was a stark contrast to Marcus and Heidi's gift – a subscription to a health and fitness magazine and app.

'I know you both want to turn over a new leaf,' Heidi had said, with a dazzling smile. 'But perhaps not today.' She patted her stomach. 'Even I'll be relaxing my regime. Might even treat myself to a smidge of Christmas pud. After all, we can work off all the fat and sugar with some hill training on our run along the coastal path tomorrow, can't we, Marcus?'

Marcus had almost snorted his Bailey's onto the rug. 'Um . . . Maybe not in these, eh, Heidi?' He held up his badger-clad feet and everyone had laughed. Even Heidi had managed a titter before remarking,

'Perhaps not, but you can *definitely* try out your new Christmas trainers tomorrow, darling.'

As Marcus sought refuge in the *Good Beer Guide* that Scarlett had given him, Scarlett hugged her sister-in-law. Over Heidi's shoulder, she and her father had exchanged a knowing glance. He was now the proud owner of a Fitbit, whether he wanted to be or not.

'Thank you, Heidi – and Marcus. I'm sure I'll be very grateful for the subscription in the new year,' Scarlett said. 'Aren't you going to try on your piglet slippers? Mum and

Dad spent ages choosing an animal to suit each of us. The piglet was my idea,' she said brightly. 'Fabulous, aren't they?'

Heidi's eyes narrowed behind her forced smile. 'Hilarious . . . but what made you think a piglet was appropriate?'

'Well, you know, you're so *not* a pig, are you? You're so slim and healthy and you never pig out . . .' Scarlett back-pedalled frantically. 'And, um, a piglet is very cute. And pink.'

'Cute and pink?' Heidi raised her perfectly arched brows.

Marcus glanced up from his book. 'I'd like to know whose idea it was to make me a badger.'

'Dad's, I think,' Scarlett said, moving to her father's side and perching on the arm of the chair next to him. 'Wasn't it, Dad?'

Roger waggled his feet. 'I shouldn't take offence, Heidi,' he said wryly. 'At least you're not an elephant like me.'

'That's something, I suppose,' Heidi muttered, eyeing the pink furry footwear with disdain before brightening up. 'Now, does anyone want to try my healthy Christmas cocktail? I got it from an Instarecipe and it's a superfoods version.'

Scarlett rubbed her hands together, trying to mollify her sister-in-law. 'Luvverly. Sounds delish.'

'In that case, I'll pour you an extra large one,' said Heidi, and scooted off to the kitchen.

As well as the stockings, their parents had given Ellie a tiny model Porsche along with some cash to help get her ancient car repaired. Scarlett had already received a contribution towards the new laptop she was now setting up next to the TV in the sitting room. They were very thoughtful presents, even Heidi's – she probably thought she was helping to save her sisters-in-law from a whole raft of health problems caused by addiction to Bombay Sapphire and Hotel Chocolat.

At least, Scarlett thought, she hadn't received *A Self-Help Guide to Dating and Relationships*, although it might have come in handy, considering her lack of progress since she'd split with Rafa. He'd been dark and handsome in the best Spanish tradition, a keen triathlete and a tennis player like his namesake. Maybe Heidi was hinting that Scarlett should take more exercise than the regular group swim sessions she enjoyed at her local 'baths' in Birmingham, although Scarlett went to the class as much for the social side as the workout.

There was one thing for sure. She had no intention of taking the plunge while in Cornwall. A toe-dip in the waters the day before had proved that was out of the question. These folk who did Boxing Day swims were barking, she'd decided.

Ellie opened the bottle of crème caramel liqueur that Scarlett had given her and topped up the empty eggnog glasses.

Scarlett connected the cable from the computer to the TV, surprised to find her fingers fumbling with the connectors. She was used to giving client presentations when pitching for a copywriting project but now the moment had come, she was nervous. She'd held onto the secret for over two months now and the suspense was killing her. It seemed like forever since she'd come down to Cornwall bearing the small box that had arrived from TreeFynder, a DNA testing company and ancestry website.

It had been Scarlett's idea to arrange the test, which had been billed on the site as 'The Ultimate Family Christmas Gift'. Her father, a retired civil engineer, had an interest in history and had often joked that the Lathams had Viking heritage. Marcus had often mentioned he'd be interested in finding out more too. It had seemed like the perfect celebration of the Latham family's close bonds and an entertaining way to spend Christmas Day. She and Ellie had both agreed that Auntie Joan, who'd loved her extended family dearly, would have been delighted at the gift.

Admittedly, the initial DNA test had been slightly gross. Scarlett and Ellie had had to spit into a pot and the test had required a surprising amount of saliva. She recalled the two of them standing in this very room all those weeks ago, reading the instructions with a mix of excitement and disgust.

'Can you imagine Auntie Joan's face, if she'd known we were spitting in her sitting room?' Scarlett had asked.

Ellie had laughed and held up the pot. 'Maybe we should rename it the spitting room.'

The results had taken about four weeks to arrive. The pots had gone off to TreeFynder.com and the results were posted online. They would reveal Scarlett and Ellie's heritage and be linked to other people around the world who shared their DNA, if they were registered with the same company.

It had taken everything for Scarlett not to look at the report, but it seemed like cheating if she knew the outcome ahead of everyone else, so she managed to restrain herself. She'd know everything in a few minutes, anyway.

'Hey, you two.' Her father, wearing a stripy apron, popped his head round the sitting room door. 'Are you ready yet with this "big surprise"?'

Anna followed him into the room. Their mother's face was

red from the heat of the kitchen. 'The suspense is killing us, isn't it, Roger?' she said. 'And as everything's under control in the kitchen for a bit, can we get it over with?'

Ellie nodded. 'Yes. You can round up the troops, Dad, if you don't mind.'

He rolled his eyes. 'It's like herding cats, but I'll do my best. What about the boys?'

'Oh, you can leave them in the snug with their games,' Scarlett said, aware that tearing the boys away from their Xboxes might be impossible anyway. 'Thanks for coming all this way for Christmas.'

'How could I miss it?' He put his arm around her. 'Especially with this big surprise you and Ellie have planned. You've been acting like a pair of kids for the past week. No idea what it is, though.'

'All will be revealed any moment.'

A few minutes later, Roger managed to get everyone – except the twins – gathered in the sitting room with a glass of fizz in their hands. Six pairs of eyes turned on Scarlett in expectation.

Her parents were sharing the love seat, while Marcus and Heidi occupied the larger of the two sofas. Ellie was perched on the edge of the small sofa, a smile on her face. Only she knew what was coming. Now it came to the announcement, Scarlett had a momentary wobble. What if the gift was an anti-climax after all this build-up?

'You've probably guessed that I've been up to something, and Ellie has been in on the surprise for a while. This present is especially for you, Mum, Dad and Marcus, but you'll be interested too, Heidi.'

Her parents exchanged glances.

'You'll love it, Dad,' Scarlett said, mentally crossing her fingers. 'You know how you've always said you must be a Viking?'

'Er . . . Yes . . .' Her dad looked a little confused. A quiet, thoughtful man with an engineer's precise mind, he wasn't given to effusive outbursts. However, Scarlett was convinced he'd be totally fascinated by all the data and details uncovered by the test.

Marcus snorted. 'What is this present? A custom-made helmet with horns?'

Heidi sniggered. 'Not planning on pillaging Porthmellow, are you?'

Their mum frowned. 'Am I the only one who's confused?'

'It's not a helmet,' said Scarlett. 'It's something even more exciting, and it's for everyone. Now we're going to find out if you really *are* a Viking, Dad. Ellie, are you set?'

'Yup.' Ellie held up her phone.

Scarlett tapped her keyboard and a page from the TreeFynder website appeared on the telly, complete with its tree logo and banner announcing:

### Discover your roots with TreeFynder!

She cringed at the cheesy copy on the ancestry website. Privately, she'd have loved to rewrite it all and get a new design done – as with most websites – but that was for another day.

Marcus and her parents sat back, intent on the TV screen. Heidi crossed her legs and smiled. 'Gosh, the suspense is killing me.'

'All will become clear,' Scarlett said dramatically, ignoring Heidi's sarcasm but slightly disappointed by the baffled expressions of the rest of the family.

She logged on and the screen flashed up a message:

**Congrats! Here is your Latham family tree!**

'A couple of months ago, Ellie and I decided to have our DNA tested, so we could find out our genetic roots, and we really will know if Dad's a Viking.'

Marcus let out a whistle. 'Now this is interesting. I've always wanted to do this.'

*Re-sult*, thought Scarlett in triumph. 'Right. Deep breath, because neither Ellie nor I have looked at the results. We thought it would be more of a surprise for everyone that way.'

'It's been so hard not to check out the site,' Ellie said.

'Without further ado, now we find out who our ancestors were. Ta da!' Scarlett declared and tapped her mouse pad. At the same time, Ellie clicked on her own results on her phone.

The silence could only have lasted a second or two, but it seemed far longer to Scarlett, already wound up to fever pitch after keeping the secret for so long.

Her mother spoke first. 'Um. This is very exciting, I'm sure, but what does it all mean?'

Scarlett had spent so long on the TreeFynder site, learning how to interpret the potential results of the ancestry test, that she'd forgotten the figures and tables on the screen would mean nothing to anyone but her and Ellie. The actual findings

19

were a complete surprise to her too, but she knew what they might mean in principle.

'Well, both Ellie and I have had our DNA tested, which of course tells us about the rest of our relations and ancestors – and yours.'

'Ah, I see.' Marcus leaned forward.

'How fascinating,' Heidi muttered, picking up a magazine.

'Obviously it doesn't cover Heidi, but it will show the boys' heritage too,' Scarlett said, hoping to win Heidi over.

Heidi let the magazine rest in her lap, her attention caught at last.

'Yes, can you please explain this to those of us still stuck in the Stone Age,' her father said.

'OK. Well, Ellie and I sent off a sample of our DNA to this ancestry site and these are the results of their analysis. This chart shows the areas of the world and types of people who are our ancestors. It says that I'm 60 per cent Iberian, 20 per cent Irish and 20 per cent other ethnicity. So – no Viking . . .'

Ellie held up her phone. 'I am! Mine says I'm 70 per cent Scandinavian, 15 per cent Irish and 15 per cent other ethnicity.'

'They're very different. Is that normal?' Marcus asked.

'According to the guidelines, siblings can have very different genetic make-ups. Dad's the Viking and Mum's obviously the Mediterranean one. I have a different mix of Mum and Dad's DNA to Ellie.'

'That's no surprise. You've always looked like Mum,' said Marcus.

'She certainly loves her Spanish holidays,' her father said drily. 'Now we know why.'

Their mother flashed a smile. 'Which reminds me, I must go and check on the potatoes.'

Marcus, Ellie and Scarlett exchanged wide-eyed looks, wondering how potatoes could have anything to do with Spanish holidays.

Anna got up, holding the tea towel she'd carried in from the kitchen.

Ellie groaned. 'Oh, don't miss the best bit. The potatoes can wait, Mum.'

'You won't say that when you get a plate full of blackened lumps for lunch.'

'I'll check them,' Heidi said, clearly looking for an excuse to get away from the family love-in. Actually, Scarlett didn't blame her on this occasion and it might be less awkward if she wasn't there.

'Are you sure you can manage?' Anna looked worried at the prospect of Heidi handling a tray of potatoes. 'They are roasted in goose fat, you know . . .'

'I'll cope somehow.' Heidi got up and patted her shoulder. 'You enjoy your *special* present, Anna.'

Scarlett wasn't sure if her sister-in-law was being sarcastic or not, but she let it drop. Their mum sat back down on the sofa, still clutching the tea towel.

'Now, here's the really exciting part . . .' She hovered the cursor over the Find Relatives menu. 'Who knows. We might find some long-lost second cousins on here. Maybe we're related to royalty, like Danny Dyer is.'

Marcus groaned. 'God, I hope not!'

Their father laughed.

'I don't think we're in line for the throne, Dad, but – oh look, we have a first degree relative on the site,' said Scarlett. 'What a surprise. *Not.*'

'That'll be me, of course,' said Ellie, clicking her phone. 'Because we're both registered on their database . . . Let's take a look. Oh, yes . . . oh . . .' Her voice trailed off. 'Oh.'

'What?' Scarlett asked.

'I think I'll go and help Heidi with the roasters.' Their mother was halfway out of the door.

'Mum, wait! Stay and see some more.' Scarlett couldn't conceal her disappointment. Then again, it was her father who loved history.

'Sprouts need putting on!' she shouted.

'This early?' Marcus laughed. 'Come on, Ellie, show us this relative-finder thing.'

'It, um . . . seems to have disappeared.' Ellie held up a black phone screen and aimed a look at Scarlett. There was desperation in her eyes.

'Don't worry, I can get it up on the telly,' said Scarlett, cheerfully.

'Wait!'

Ellie's cry was too late. The 72-inch screen flashed up a notification.

### You have a half-sibling on TreeFynder.

Marcus dived on it like a hawk. 'Half-sibling? What's that supposed to mean?'

Ellie couldn't suppress her gasp and exchanged a panicky

glance with Scarlett. 'That's wrong. It's not possible. We don't have any half-siblings.'

'It must mean sister or brother, of course,' said their dad. 'It can only refer to you and Ellie.'

It must refer to her and Ellie. Half-siblings. Scarlett went cold all over as the implications sank in like wet slush soaking through the bunny slippers. Ellie stared at her; lips pressed together. When Ellie had seen the results on her phone, she'd tried to stop Scarlett from sharing them with the rest of the family.

'It must be a mistake. Let's try again.' Faking a sigh of exasperation, Scarlett refreshed the page, hoping against hope it would miraculously show a different answer. But a second later, it flashed up the same horrible phrase.

**You have a half-sibling on TreeFynder.**

The words leapt out at Scarlett and seared themselves on her brain. She felt sick.

**Half-sibling.**

Their father frowned at the screen. 'I don't understand—'

'Scarlett's right. There must have been a cock-up.' Ellie got up and turned off the TV. 'I think they've mixed up our DNA with someone else's. It must happen a lot.'

'I doubt it,' Marcus said, 'I've heard these labs are very accurate.'

'Actually, I saw a programme that said there can be a big margin of error,' Ellie declared. '*Huge*.'

23

'Then why did you bother getting tested?' Marcus said sharply, treating both of them to a glare.

'Because we thought it would be fun . . .' Scarlett said. 'Didn't we, Ellie? Dad's always wanted to know if he has any Viking in him, and we thought it would be the perfect family present.'

'Obviously, it isn't,' Marcus said, narrowing his eyes at Scarlett again.

'Let's not worry about it now. We'll contact the site after Christmas and get our money back,' Ellie said, then sniffed the air. 'Hmm, what's that amazing smell? I think dinner must be nearly ready.'

'Mum's only just put the sprouts on,' Marcus muttered, his eyes straying to the laptop.

'Shall I get us all another glass of Prosecco?' Scarlett piped up, feeling as if she might throw up. She didn't want Prosecco and had no idea how she was going to eat Christmas dinner.

'But I don't understand,' their father insisted as Scarlett snatched up her laptop, intent on hiding it under her bed, as if that would make any difference at all to the results. The genie was out of the bottle now. Her hands were shaking.

'If your DNA test says you and Ellie are half-siblings, what does it mean . . .' Their father looked at them both. Scarlett hugged the laptop. Oh God, everything was becoming horrifyingly clear. Their mother's lack of enthusiasm for the DNA test, slinking out of the room when they tried to find their relatives. Oh, Christ on a bike, what the hell had she unleashed on her family?

'Nothing, because it's a computer error or a mix-up in the

lab. Don't worry about it, Dad,' said Ellie. 'Blooming rip-off! For all we know, TreeFynder doesn't even have a real lab and it's a couple of kids with a chemistry set in their bedroom. Let's forget it for now and have another drink. What do you all want?'

Their father nodded but seemed confused and quiet. Marcus, however, would not be silenced. 'But I'm still confused about exactly what the results mean,' he said insistently. Scarlett loved her brother, for all his faults, but at this moment would have happily wished him to evaporate.

'Marcus. There's no point having the conversation. Now, come on, let me get you a drink.'

As she looked at him, it hit her. Marcus and Ellie both had their father's thick dark curly hair. Scarlett was fair. Her mum had light brown hair that the sun bleached in summer, but Scarlett was blonde all year round, and almost wheaten in the sunny months. Her hair was straight and easily tamed, which Ellie had always envied but Scarlett thought was a bit boring compared to Ellie's bouncy curls. Her siblings had strong noses, ever so slightly 'Roman', according to Auntie Joan – which hadn't amused Marcus, but had made Ellie burst out laughing and start muttering, 'Hail, Great Caesar,' to him.

As they'd grown older, Ellie and Marcus had changed but had always at some point resembled their dad. Scarlett *never* had.

If that test was accurate . . . Scarlett felt as if she was about to suffocate and her stomach clenched. She had to get out, or she might be sick, but Heidi blocked the doorway, her

25

hands still in oven gauntlets. She'd obviously been there much longer than they'd realised.

'I'm *sure* this is all a mistake, Roger,' she said, looking at their father with pity. 'Because if that test is accurate, it means that Ellie and Scarlett can't possibly have the same father. One of them isn't your daughter.'

## Chapter Three

**Nine months later**
**October 1 2019**

'Ellie. Marcus here. I'm calling re: Christmas. I've got five mins between meetings so I thought I'd phone before you make any plans.'

Ellie's heart sank at the mention of Christmas.

'Hi, Marcus . . .' Ellie could hear phones ringing in the background of her brother's Birmingham office, in sharp contrast to the quiet of Seaholly Manor.

He launched in again, cutting her off.

'It may only be the start of October, but you know Scarlett likes to organise us all. Or *used* to. It's of no matter anyway, because we won't be coming to the manor for Christmas. Although after last year's catastrophe, I expect you've already worked that one out. I'm assuming that Mum and Dad won't be there either.'

She held the phone away from her ear, trying to rein in her irritation. Finding out that their family wasn't what they'd thought had been a hell of a shock for all of them, but Marcus had taken it very hard.

'I don't know what their plans are yet,' she said patiently.

'Whatever they decide to do – or not do – *we* definitely won't be coming down to Cornwall. We've booked a skiing chalet in Courcheval with some friends and we leave on the twenty-seventh. Heidi thought it would be good for the boys to get some exercise instead of lazing about, and besides, they're getting to the age where they'd rather be with their mates than hanging around with family in a draughty old house. And, to be honest, Heidi still hasn't got over the trauma of last year. None of us have—'

'Right . . .' Ellie interrupted his flow. He sounded irritated and guilty and her own patience was running out as fast as sand in an egg timer. Which reminded her of last Christmas. Heidi's face when Ellie had told her the eggnog tasted like sick. Ouch. Ouch. *Ouch*.

'Um, Els . . . Have you seen Mum recently? I've been worried about her.' Marcus's clipped tone lost its edge, instantly taking Ellie back to the unsure younger brother she used to know. He did love their parents dearly and had been especially close to their mother. Marcus and his dad hadn't always got on that well, but the bomb that Scarlett's 'Christmas gift' had lobbed into that relationship had changed the dynamics.

Marcus was finding it hard to believe his mum had had an affair, and even harder to believe she wouldn't admit to it. They all were, although Ellie's priority was to support both parents in trying to save their marriage, which until eleven a.m. last Christmas Day, had appeared to be long and happy. Scarlett had been and still was devastated and since then, Ellie had had to set aside her own feelings of shock and disbelief to support the others as best she could. Privately, however, she'd spent many sleepless nights worrying about its devastating effects on her family.

'Ellie?'

'Not since she came to stay a couple of weeks ago. I've spoken to her on the phone plenty of times. She called me from work. I've spoken to Dad, too.'

'And? Have they come to any decisions?'

'Not yet. They're still sleeping in separate rooms from what I can work out. Scarlett paid them a visit a couple of days ago.'

'I'm surprised they let her in the house!'

'Dad invited her . . . but Mum was there too. Marcus, how many times do I have to tell you that this mess isn't Scarlett's fault?'

'I know it's not totally her fault, obviously, but if she'd never bought that bloody test kit, none of this would have happened. She does have a tendency to put her foot in it, ever since she was a kid.'

'Don't blame Scarlett. This whole thing has hurt her more than anyone.'

'She's still not speaking to Mum, then?'

'Not really. She still sees Dad and phones him, but I don't think she and Mum are on speaking terms.' Ellie wasn't sure just how the revelations had changed Scarlett's relationship with their father, but she wasn't going to complicate things by voicing that to Marcus.

'Humph.'

'Marcus?'

'I still say that the test was wrong.'

'What? Both of them?' Ellie replied, shuddering at the memory of Scarlett's fresh disappointment when they took a private DNA test that proved she *was* 'only' Ellie's half-sister. Their mother had been angry and hurt but continued to insist there had to be a mistake.

'I wish none of this had ever happened. If Mum did – you know, with another bloke – then why won't she admit it?'

'I don't know, but it's obviously a deeply painful experience for her as well as the rest of us. Until, and if, Mum is willing to share the truth, how can you expect Scarlett – and Dad – to start understanding and forgiving her? We don't know any of the circumstances.'

'I suppose not . . .' Marcus said grudgingly. Ellie hated to see the turmoil the family was going through, but as the eldest, she felt obliged to try and keep the peace. Her travels over the years had also, she admitted, given her a slight distance – and a fresh perspective on family life. She'd seen a lot of unusual family set-ups while she'd worked and lived all over the world, enough to remind her that no one's circumstances were ever as smooth as they might appear.

The old grandfather clock struck the half hour, startling Ellie.

'Marcus. Can we talk about this later, please?' she asked. 'I have to go to work. Someone's off sick at the café and they want me for the lunch service.'

'The café? I thought you were working on a yacht.'

'It's a vintage sailing trawler actually, but it's the end of the season so I'm only helping in the office two days a week. I've started doing some shifts in the Harbour Café again.'

He huffed. 'Oh, well, I suppose you need a bit of money for extras and stuff. Lucky you don't have to pay a mortgage or rent.'

'Mum and Dad seem OK with the arrangement at the moment, and they've got enough on their plate without worrying about whether or not to sell this place. It's not good to leave old houses like this empty, especially over the winter. I'm keeping the place safe and secure until they decide what to do with it, and I'm doing the garden and small maintenance jobs.' Which took up a lot of her time, she could have added, not that Marcus would realise, because he didn't know one end of a screwdriver from another.

'They can't even decide whether they want to stay married, so I shouldn't hold your breath. Although if they do get a divorce, they'll have to sell the manor and you'll have to move out.'

'Sorry. What was that?' Ellie held the phone at arm's length, fuming quietly that her attempts to soothe him had obviously failed. 'I can't hear you, the signal's really bad down here.' She heard his tinny voice say something about 'being prepared for the worst' then banged the handset on the hall table. 'Oh no! Damn! I've lost you. Speak soon!'

She hung up.

Swearing under her breath, Ellie scooped up her car keys from the hall table. With a bit of luck, Marcus would be too wrapped up in his waste-management meeting to remember he'd called her landline.

As she drove, she thought back on her conversation with Marcus – it had renewed her worries about everyone involved, especially Scarlett. While Marcus had gone into a similar path of denial to their mother, choosing to blame Ellie and Scarlett for opening up a can of worms, Scarlett had taken the opposite and perhaps more understandable route: retreating from their mum and blaming her. Ellie understood this, even if she thought it wouldn't help the rifts to heal any faster, or encourage their mum to open up. Not only did Scarlett have to cope with the turmoil of their parents' estrangement, she also had to come to terms with finding out that her dad wasn't her biological father. Scarlett couldn't even begin to do that while their mother refused to be honest with them.

At least Ellie's work at the bustling Harbour Café, with its cheerful boss and quirky clientele, kept her mind off her problems for a while. She loved Porthmellow in all its moods, even on a foggy autumn evening such as this, with mist wreathing around the old clock tower and the waves slip-slopping against the harbour walls. With its cosy beamed interior, the café was at the heart of village life; bustling with locals and visitors from breakfast till teatime.

Twilight was falling by the time she walked out of the old building onto the quayside. It was almost completely dark when she reached the dead-end lane that followed a stream down one side of the steep valley to Seaholly Manor and then the tiny cove itself.

The bare branches of the trees lining the cove lane were spidery in the gloom. Some people might have found the manor spooky on their own, but Ellie had spent nights in some 'interesting' places around the world and ghosts didn't bother her. In fact, she wouldn't have minded a chat with Auntie Joan again, bless her. Ellie hadn't seen her that often, but it was enough to miss her witty, sharp conversations and anecdotes about famous authors. Joan had never been shy about relating her romantic adventures either. Their mother would probably have been horrified to hear what she'd shared once the girls were over eighteen. Even before then, they'd delighted in reading her novels, especially the ones in black and red covers that were written under another name that Joan kept in a chest in her room and didn't think they knew about.

Seaholly Manor had so many happy associations that Ellie felt she could never be afraid there. It was also unlikely that anyone would find their way down to the manor by accident, as it wasn't signposted from the road. Unless the burglars had a thing for first editions and filthy fiction, there was nothing worth nicking anyway. Still, on such a gloomy night, she was looking forward to getting inside and making up the fire before phoning Scarlett to see if she was OK.

The road levelled out and narrowed over the last few hundred yards to the manor. From nowhere, a shadow darted out from the bushes and across the road.

Ellie let out a cry and swerved to avoid the fox. A heartbeat later, there was a bang as the car slammed against the hedgerow. The seatbelt tightened across her chest and there was only silence.

It took a few seconds for Ellie to get her breath back. Gingerly, she flexed her wrists and hands and waited for any stabs of pain in her neck or back. The seatbelt had done its job, which was why she was out of breath, but otherwise she seemed to be OK. The car, however, probably wasn't. That sickening crash hadn't been the sound of metal hitting mere twigs. Like many Cornish hedgerows, this one had an earthen bank, reinforced with stones, at its heart.

The vehicle was at an angle, so she was able to open the door and swing her legs onto the tarmac. Her eyes adjusted to the dim light, the road lit only by a sliver of moon appearing now and then from behind the clouds.

She shone her phone torch on the front of the car. The bonnet was warped and the bumper was crumpled and pushed back into the engine.

'Oh f-f—' It looked pretty bad and she already guessed that the insurance company would write it off. That was all she needed. She also had the problem of what to do next, because she doubted it was driveable. She'd have to call out the local garage to tow it, if she could get hold of them. She was blocking the road too, not that anyone else was likely to use it.

The car wouldn't start, so she was about to phone the Porthmellow Garage when she heard the low rumble of another vehicle coming down the lane. Two headlights wavered in the gloom and her heart sank further.

They belonged to a Ford Transit of the kind Scarlett loved to call a 'kidnapper's van'. Hairs stood up on the back of Ellie's neck and she prepared to jump into the Fiesta and lock the doors. It stopped a few feet away, the door opened and a man got out. She didn't recognise him but she knew one thing: he cut an unnerving figure in the dark. He was over six feet, wearing a black leather jacket and built like the proverbial brick outhouse.

She debated whether to jump inside while she had the chance, but told herself to be sensible and assume he had a rational explanation for being on the lane. A wrong turn in the fog was surely more likely than him looking for people to abduct?

'Hello. Are you OK?' he called as he approached. His accent wasn't broad, but more importantly, his tone was concerned. Ellie let out a breath she hadn't realised she'd been holding.

'Yes. My car isn't though. I swerved because of a fox . . . It was instinct. That's why I'm blocking the road.'

'That doesn't matter, as long as you're not hurt. You're sure you're all right?'

'I'm fine, thanks.' Ellie gave him a closer look. 'Did you take a wrong turning down here in the fog? Porthmellow's the next road.'

He smiled. 'No, I meant to drive down here. I'm Aaron Carman. I've just moved into Cove Cottage.'

'Really? I had no idea . . . You weren't there yesterday when I went for a walk on the beach.' And no one had told her that a man was moving into the only other house for a mile around, and she'd have expected to hear about it on the Porthmellow grapevine. 'I'm Ellie Latham. I live at the manor house,' she added.

'Pleased to meet you, Ellie, but not under these circumstances. Actually, I only moved in late last night. I brought my own stuff in the van. I don't have much.' He tutted loudly at the Fiesta. 'Your car could be a write-off, you know.'

'I know.' She gritted her teeth.

'That's a shame. Would you like me to help you shift it to the manor?'

Ellie was more aware than ever that she was alone in the dark with a complete stranger offering to come to her house. On the other hand, it would be a lot simpler than calling out the garage in Porthmellow after hours.

'Um . . .'

'It's no trouble,' he said, moving closer and resting his hand on the bonnet.

Ellie looked up at him and a light bulb flashed in her brain. Those handsome features, the light brown skin, his upright bearing . . . 'Did you say you were called Aaron *Carman?*'

'Yes. Why? Has my bad reputation preceded me down here?'

Ellie smiled, despite her predicament. She felt on safer ground now. 'No. The opposite, in fact. You must be Troy and Evie's son? I'd no idea you were moving into the cottage. I thought you were in the army.'

He smiled. 'I was, but I'm out now. Long story. Now, come on, why don't you let me help you with the car?'

Her feeling of relief from knowing Aaron was unlikely to be a serial killer was followed by the minor irritation that he thought she couldn't handle the situation. 'It might be difficult getting it to start at all. Do you know anything about cars?'

'A bit. I was in charge of a tank-mechanic engineering squad in the army until recently. I've dug armoured vehicles out of ditches, so I think I might be able to get your Fiesta down to the manor.'

'Oh. OK . . .' Ellie silently cursed herself for underestimating him but also realised she was in no position to refuse his help. 'In that case, I'd really appreciate it. Thanks.'

Aaron helped her push the car off the road and then fetched a rope from the van before moving it ahead of the Fiesta. In no time, with Ellie at the wheel, he'd towed her the few hundred yards to the manor.

She unlocked the door and stood in the hall with him. The lights revealed him in his full glory. Though he had to be in his mid-forties, he was still a very good-looking guy, with an easy-going confidence that sat well with his military bearing. She could also see the resemblance to his mother, Evie, who lived in the town and was on the festival committee.

'I'll call the garage in the morning,' she said, wondering what to say next. She didn't want to seem forward but also felt she should thank him in some way. 'Erm, would you like to come in for a coffee, or are you too busy unpacking?'

'I'm not too busy for a coffee. Thanks. Better wash my hands first, though.'

'Me too.' She held up her grubby palms. 'There's a cloakroom here off the hall and that's the sitting room opposite. Make yourself at home. I'll be back with the coffee in a minute.'

Now the adrenaline of dealing with the accident was wearing off, Ellie was calming down. She scrubbed her own hands in the scullery sink and then made a pot of strong coffee. She really felt like having a whisky with it but decided against it.

A few minutes later, she was sitting opposite Aaron, both of them cradling mugs. He'd poured liberal amounts of hot milk into his and added a spoon of sugar. He certainly didn't need to watch his diet, Ellie thought, hardly able to take her eyes off his impressive physique. There was no way that anyone would fit on the love seat beside him. He must have been six foot three at least, and she could hardly miss the breadth of his thighs or the width of his shoulders especially now he'd taken off his jacket and laid it neatly on the back of a chair. Every time he moved, some muscle or other rippled.

He sipped his coffee and smiled. 'You know, I was a bit worried about stopping on the lane in the dark.'

Ellie laughed, slightly nervously, as she recalled her initial reaction to him. 'Why? Did you think I might be a serial killer?'

He chuckled. 'No, I thought you might think I was. I can come as a bit of a shock to some people.'

You can say that again, thought Ellie. 'I should have recognised your name at once. Your mum has mentioned you to me before but I was a bit shaken by the bump. How long have you been out of the army?'

'Not that long. I left a couple of months ago but recently decided to move here. I'm starting a new business . . . I'm my own boss. Do you know my mum and dad well?'

'A bit. I've got to know them better since I've been involved in the Winter Solstice Festival. Evie and Troy are on the committee, as I'm sure you know.'

'You'll never get away now. It's all I hear about from them. Have you lived here long?'

'Only since last autumn. This isn't my house. It belongs to my parents but I'm caretaker until they decide what to do with it. Maybe your mum mentioned it?' she asked, wondering how much gossip there was about her parents' situation. She'd told her boss at the café and a couple of colleagues at the sailing trust and there was bound to have been talk about the row that resulted in Scarlett's dramatic entrance at the pub on Christmas Day.

'I only hear the gossip Mum tells me in her emails and letters. A lot of it means nothing to me, but Mum loves keeping me up to date so I was always happy to hear it. Since I've come home, she's had a field day with all the latest Porthmellow scandal.'

Ellie wondered if he did know about the Lathams but was too polite to say as much. 'Your mum's lovely. So funny and kind. She must have missed you very much while you were away.'

'Maybe more than she'd let on. I joined up when I was eighteen and I've spent most of my time in REME.'

'REME? Sorry, you've lost me.'

'Royal Electrical and Mechanical Engineers. Basically, I helped to look after the army's equipment in all kinds of um . . . "interesting" places.'

Ellie winced. 'That figures. Sorry for asking if you knew anything about cars.'

He grinned. 'It was a perfectly reasonable thing to ask when confronted by a strange bloke in the dark. Bet you thought I was about to do a spot of mansplaining?'

'Nooo . . .' Ellie smiled. 'OK, yes, but now I cringe when I think of what I said.'

'Don't worry about it.' His deep brown eyes twinkled with gentle amusement.

So, not only gorgeous but a sense of humour, thought Ellie. 'Thanks,' she said, eager to move the conversation on to other topics. 'We do have something in common.'

'I'm intrigued.' He had a lovely voice, deep and, now she had time to listen more closely, with a definite trace of a Cornish accent.

'I've spent a lot of my life abroad too, and had some exciting times, though in far less dangerous places. I've been travelling and working in the Caribbean and Thailand and Australia ever since I left college.' Ellie didn't qualify that she was halfway through her degree at the time she left. It was ancient history now anyway, but lately the disastrous relationship that had made her abandon her studies had been on her mind. The man at the heart of that relationship had close links to the local area, and possibly still did.

She'd run away from heartbreak and nineteen years later, she often wondered if she'd stopped running since.

She and Aaron carried on chatting about some of the places they'd been to, and although he made light of his time in the services, Ellie guessed that his tours of Afghanistan and Sierra Leone had probably been very tough. He told her a little more about his plans to set up an events security business based in Porthmellow, which let her know that he was planning to stick around for a little while. In no time, half an hour had whizzed by and the chimes of the hall clock striking seven interrupted them.

'I'd better not keep you any longer. If I can help with the car repairs, let me know. I could do the work myself if you'd like. A mate has a lock-up in town. Either way, while we're both around, it would be great to get to know you better. I'll probably be up here a lot, borrowing a cup of sugar like my mum says they used to in the old days.'

Ellie laughed. She could imagine Evie Carman saying that. 'You're welcome to borrow as much sugar as you like.'

She waved him off at the door and watched the taillights of his van as it drove the last few hundred yards down to Cove Cottage. Ellie closed the door behind him and flopped down on the sofa. Finally, she poured herself a whisky, allowing the tangy warmth to make its way through her veins. The shock of the accident on top of a full day on her feet was wearing off. She felt physically exhausted, but her mind wouldn't let her fall asleep on the sofa as she often did. Her thoughts kept returning to the man who had occupied the love seat for the past half an hour.

Aaron was disturbing in every way and it wasn't only due to his sheer physical presence. As they'd chatted, the Cornish burr that emerged reminded her of his connections to Porthmellow, which were way deeper than hers. She'd found herself drawn to his quiet confidence, probably acquired from decades of being in command. He looked so at ease in her sitting room, but then he must be used to making himself at home anywhere, even more so than she was.

Yet she felt the need to keep reminding herself that she might not be at Seaholly for long and that he might move on soon if his new business didn't work out. Neither of them might have the chance to get to know each other that well.

The pang of disappointment was sharper than it ought to be, considering she'd only met Aaron a few hours ago. Then again, it was par for the course where her love life was concerned. Fleeting relationships and brief encounters had been the hallmark of her life. Maybe it was her destiny to drift in and out of people's lives – and vice versa – and never settle down. After all, the one time she'd wanted to spend her whole life with a man, it had ended in sorrow and chaos. She was already getting too comfortable at Seaholly Manor, a house she couldn't afford to keep in her wildest dreams. If her parents split up, they wouldn't be able to keep it either, so she'd better not get any more attached to it, and especially not to her attractive new neighbour.

The phone rang and Ellie dragged herself off the sofa. Argh, she'd meant to call Scarlett to see how she was. It was a good bet this was her now.

'Ellie? Have I woken you up? You sound sleepy.'

'No, Scarlett. I wasn't asleep. In fact, I was about to call you.' Ellie debated whether to tell her about the 'bump' and Aaron then decided to save it for now.

'Were you? Well, I thought I'd better get in first. I have a favour to ask you.'

'Um . . . yes?'

'Can I come stay at the manor?'

Ellie perked up, pleased to hear Scarlett slightly brighter. 'Any time. Of course, you know I'd love to see you. Have you decided how long you can stay over Christmas yet? Obviously, I'm hoping to see you before then, too.'

In the brief silence, Ellie heard the clock strike the quarter hour and the wind gusting outside.

Then Scarlett came on the line again. 'Actually, it's a bigger favour than that and I don't know how you're going to feel about it. Not after my last idea went so badly wrong.'

Sensing she might need the support, Ellie took the phone into the sitting room and sat on the sofa again. What the heck was Scarlett up to now?

'Shoot. This favour can't be that bad, can it?' She said it light-heartedly, because she knew she'd do anything she could to help Scarlett. She was half-expecting it to have something to do with their mum.

'OK. Deep breath and you can say no if you want to, but the thing is . . . would you mind very much if I moved in with you?'

Ellie stopped herself from drawing an inward breath. So, shocks really did come in threes.

'Ellie? Have you fainted?'

'No, of course not. You know you're more than welcome. I'd love to have you,' Ellie said, meaning it but also realising how she'd become used to having the run of the manor lately. 'What's brought this about? I thought you loved your flat in Brum.'

'I do – *did* – but I've been here a few years now and . . . things have gone downhill since Rafa and I split up.'

'It wasn't a vintage year for you, was it?'

'I don't care about him any more, the git,' Scarlett said defiantly, although Ellie guessed it was largely bravado. 'But I *do* care about my business. I was hoping to start working for another big client but they've decided they're cutting back because of "Brexit-related uncertainties" so that's not going to happen.'

'Oh no, I'm sorry, lovely,' Ellie sympathised. Scarlett sounded pretty down.

She heaved a sigh. 'I should know by now that these ups and downs come with the territory of being your own boss.'

'You'll make it up. You're a brilliant copywriter. I know you can do it. You've had a few setbacks lately so no wonder you feel battered and bruised.'

There was a pause. 'Yes, you're right, as usual . . . after Rafa and then Christmas I haven't trusted my judgement on all kinds of stuff. Men, people in general, and even looking for new work. My judgement feels skewed, as if I'm off kilter with the world a bit. Does that sound stupid?'

'Of course not, lovely. What happened would shake anyone's confidence, but you have to believe that you're still the same old Scarlett we know and love.'

'That's just it . . . the old Scarlett might not be enough . . .'

Ellie wanted to reach down the phone to hug her sister.

'But,' Scarlett's voice brightened. 'I *do* have one piece of good news on the work front. A rival screw manufacturer outside Exeter wants me to take on all their copywriting now I don't have a conflict of interest. They can't give me quite as much work as Rafa's company did, but it's too good an opportunity to turn down because let's face it, I do know a *lot* about screws. Of course, it's a long way from Brum but then I started thinking . . . Exeter . . . that's not too far from Ellie.'

Actually, thought Ellie, while admiring Scarlett's optimism, it was over a hundred miles away, but she didn't want to burst her sister's bubble.

'*And* my shitty landlord's hiked the rent on the flat just when I've taken a hit in revenue so I thought . . . 99 per cent of my work is done online from home and I can work for a couple of my existing clients anywhere. I can visit Eurofasteners from Cornwall when I need to. Then I also heard that one of my PR clients needs someone to write a customer magazine for a Cornish fashion company and so I said I was probably moving down here, which was a mad idea but I need to grab any chance I can these days while I have the nerve and it would be much more inspiring to write about clothes than screws all the time . . .'

'I get that,' Ellie said, still processing how to respond without deflating Scarlett's optimistic mood.

'Obviously, I won't earn as much as I did, but enough to contribute to all the household expenses and get by. The whole thing with Rafa last year and then the rent hike, well, they seem like omens to take a leap of faith rather than wallowing here.'

Omens, eh? Ellie marvelled at her sister's ability to rationalise. What had actually happened was that Scarlett had consciously – or otherwise – found two new clients that she could work for while living in Cornwall.

'Hun, if it's any consolation, I never really thought Rafa deserved you and, genuinely, you're better off without him.'

45

'Really? You never said that to me before.'

'How could I when you were so down about the split? Now you've told me yourself that you're over him, I may as well say what I think. He was way too full of himself and you're far too good for him, but that's history now. And I have no problem with you coming down here and I *totally* understand that you want to make a fresh start, but you're forgetting one thing. Mum and Dad might not keep Seaholly Manor for long.'

'I know that, so I called Dad earlier – I'm not asking Mum! – and asked if they had any immediate plans to sell, but he said neither of them had discussed it . . . Mind you I don't think they talk much at all these days.'

'I'm sorry, hun.'

'Yeah, well. Dad said it would take months or even years to sell the place even *if* they did decide to get rid of it, so he reckoned I should go ahead. Between us, I think Mum's hoping Dad will simply forget what's happened, but he won't and neither can I.'

Ellie heard the break in Scarlett's voice. Even with Scarlett only a few miles from her parents, it sounded as if there was no prospect of reconciliation on the horizon. 'I must admit it's not looking hopeful if they still have separate rooms after this long,' she said, deciding to be honest. 'I spoke to Dad last weekend and when I tried to ask how things were going, he almost bit my head off.'

'Did he say anything about a divorce to you?'

'I never got that far. I only tried to suggest gently they go see Relate and he told me to mind my own business and that he and Mum would sort it out on their own. Marcus tried to hint to them to have counselling too, and got the same response.'

'He said the same to me when I met him for coffee last week. He also told me that he doesn't blame me for the test. He was still Dad, but somehow, I can't help feeling that he's taken a step away from me. There's a distance between us that wasn't there before.'

'I'm sure that's not true!' Ellie was horrified at the thought of a growing rift between Scarlett and their father and hoped her sister was reading the situation wrong.

'He said it didn't matter who my biological father was, that I'm his daughter in every way that matters and that it was only a terrible accident that he'd found out, but when he kissed me goodbye, it was so quick, as if he couldn't wait to get away from me.'

'I'm sure Dad would never push you away and he's right; it isn't your fault,' Ellie said gently, yet she felt cold at the idea that their father might possibly be distancing himself from Scarlett, even subconsciously.

'But it's so strange looking at him now and knowing we have no *actual* connection, not genetically or even legally. He said he'd changed his will so that I'll inherit the estate equally with all of you. That was awful to hear, even if he meant it well. Just hearing him say it felt so weird. He didn't need to even tell me; it seemed such a formal thing to say.'

'Don't overthink it, hun. Of course, he loves you the same as he always did. You must believe that,' Ellie said, tiptoeing on eggshells.

'I suppose so, but I can't help wondering if it must have changed the way he sees me. Mum hasn't forgiven me for stirring things up, even if she is wrong. Whenever I'm around, she's so tight and closed – we both are – and I do feel angry with her.'

'Mum will have to accept that. If she's being awkward with you, it's because *she* must feel guilty. Has she given you any clue at all who . . . ?' In the nick of time, Ellie slammed the brakes on her next phrase. There was no way she was going to refer to any other man but her own father as Scarlett's dad. 'Who *he* might be?'

'She won't even admit to me or Dad that she had an affair, not even after the other tests we did.'

'It must be driving you mad. I love her, but it would be better if she told Dad the truth. Better for everyone, especially you, and if she *did* own up, perhaps they could start to move on. Of course you can come down here, as long as you know that one day in the not-too-distant future, we might have to leave again.'

'I know that, and if they do split up – and maybe they won't – I'll have to make other plans. Maybe if you want to stay in Porthmellow we can get a flat or a house together. If we keep saving up what we'd have had to fork out in rent, that would help. *If* you are staying, of course.' Scarlett's voice lifted hopefully.

It was happening again – temptation was being put in her way. The house, Aaron, the community and now Scarlett luring her to linger. Maybe Scarlett was right. This was an omen – a series of omens – that meant she should stay in Porthmellow.

'I don't know what my long-term plans are. I do like it here and I must admit that I'm very tempted to stay. I'd love to have you . . . as long as being in Porthmellow again doesn't stir up unhappy memories.'

Scarlett huffed. 'I won't be going into *that* pub again, that's for sure, and it'll be awkward to even be around the town to start with, but I thought I could see how things go and try to keep a low profile.'

'OK.' Ellie shook her head, a smile on her face. 'When are you thinking of coming?'

'Um. Two weeks' time?'

'*Two weeks?*'

'Actually, less than two weeks. I plan on coming down a week on Thursday. Is that OK? One of the neighbours has offered to bring some of my stuff down in his van when he visits his boyfriend in St Ives the following weekend. I can manage with what I can fit in my car until then.'

Bloody hell, Scarlett really did have everything worked out. She must have been thinking this over for a while. 'Yes . . . it's slightly short notice, but why not? Let me know what I can do to help.'

Ellie spent a while making more arrangements and then put down the phone. She went into the kitchen to cook some supper, realising that she was now starving. Even after a day at the café, she found it relaxing to slice a few mushrooms, grate some Gruyère and whip up an omelette.

While she chopped and cooked, her mind worked overtime on the latest surprise this day had delivered. Having her sister around would be different. It could be a lot of fun but it would also cause disruption. She'd become used to her own company, and she and Scarlett did argue sometimes, but Scarlett was obviously hell bent on this plan. Ellie had been reminded of how much her sister had been affected by the revelations on Christmas Day. Finding out her father wasn't her biological dad must have left an enormous hole in her life, and their mother's continued state of denial and unspoken anger with her daughter wasn't helping at all. In one fell swoop, Scarlett had lost both parents to some degree. This change in lifestyle might be her way of getting through it.

And all of this happened just after the split with her boyfriend and the loss of her core client. It was no wonder Scarlett felt her world had been turned upside down. Whether moving almost three hundred miles to a new home that might only be temporary was a good idea, Ellie wasn't sure.

There was something else. Scarlett had listed her reasons for moving as if it was the most rational decision in the world, but Ellie had a powerful feeling that she hadn't heard the full story yet. And as for 'keeping a low profile' after her dramatic entrance at the Christmas lunch . . . in a place like Porthmellow, there wasn't a snowball's chance of that.

# Chapter Four

'Hello! How was the journey? I was worried you might be held up by the road works on the motorway.'

Scarlett's spirits lifted as Ellie met her on the drive of Seaholly Manor. It had been a long journey but Ellie's welcoming smile more than made up for it.

'It was OK until the mist came down. Look at it. It's like something out of the *Hound of the Baskervilles*!' Scarlett tried to make out the house through the October mist, which hung in wispy threads among the tree branches and seemed to press on the roof of the manor. Although it wasn't as sharply cold as it was in the Midlands, the damp clung to everything, leaving pinpricks of moisture on her teddy coat.

'It's a real pea-souper that rolled in after lunch. I don't think it will clear until morning,' Ellie said.

A shiver ran through Scarlett, and not for the first time since she'd handed back the keys to her flat and said goodbye to the neighbours. She'd shed a few tears as she'd driven out of the city suburbs, past her favourite balti restaurant where the owners didn't even need to take her order they knew her so well. She would miss the Victorian swimming 'baths' where she ploughed up and down twice a week and the park where she met up with her friends for a coffee in winter and a picnic in summer.

Seaholly Manor was isolated, and so far from her parents and Marcus. With dusk approaching on a gloomy autumn evening, she was half-tempted to turn the car around and head back to the bright lights of Brum.

Oh God, what had she done?

As if reading her thoughts, Ellie gave her a hug. 'Come inside. I lit the fire in the sitting room as soon as I got in from work, and the kitchen will be nice and cosy too.'

Scarlett dragged up a smile. The lamplight glowed from the window of the sitting room. That was cheery at least.

'Is your car fixed, by the way?' she asked.

'Oh, it's er . . . at the garage in town. We're waiting for a part.'

'What a pain. How do you get to work?'

'I walked over the coast path. The fog wasn't as bad then, though I definitely wouldn't try that path in this murk. Come on, I'll give you a hand with your stuff.'

After abandoning Scarlett's luggage in the hallway, they sat at the kitchen's oak farmhouse table. The warmth from the Aga enveloped Scarlett and sparked another memory: of last Christmas Day when she'd stepped into the Smuggler's Tavern's Lunch for the Lonely.

However, with Ellie chattering away about the latest local

gossip while she made them both hot chocolates, she soon perked up. She had to face the locals again sometime and it wasn't as if the people at the pub hadn't been friendly. In fact, they'd been *too* friendly. Which could be both a good and bad thing. Good for finding out gossip about her real father; bad for stopping it from spreading.

Scarlett had always prided herself on being honest with Ellie, so she felt doubly guilty about being economical with the truth this time.

Yes, the lease was up on her flat. Yes, she was struggling with the rent and, yes, she did want to make a fresh start. What she'd left out was the part about how she'd discovered that her 'biological father' was – possibly – from Porthmellow and she desperately wanted to know who he was.

His identity had occupied her thoughts since last Christmas and she'd been listening out for any clue from her mother, not that her mum had even admitted she might have had an affair. Scarlett had worked out when she must have been conceived, and from old photos in a family album had pieced together that her mother had been staying with Auntie Joan during that time. So the 'deed' was very likely to have taken place in Porthmellow.

Plus, there was another, more compelling clue to her origins. When she, Ellie and their mother had been sorting through Joan's stuff, Scarlett had found a postcard with a message that had struck her as weird. It hadn't meant that much at the time, but had taken on much greater significance since, and Scarlett couldn't recall the exact words. She'd meant to show it to her mum at the time, however, in the chaos of sorting out her auntie's vast collection of books and papers, she'd forgotten about it. Of course, she could be clutching at straws and probably was, but once the idea that the postcard might be related to her mum's affair had formed in her mind, she couldn't get rid of it.

She lay awake at night, trying to envisage what her biological father might look like. What kind of a man was he? Not the most upright kind, if he'd had an affair with a married woman . . . unless he hadn't even known her mother *was* married? Had it been a full-blown affair, or only a one-night stand? Did he have a family of his own now, or even then?

If he did, that meant she would have half-siblings she didn't even know about. In fact, it was more than likely she *did*.

The questions constantly pecked at her mind. Was he short, tall, fat, skinny? Did he even look that much like her? Despite having half of his DNA, she could easily resemble her mother with very little trace of her father.

Was he even alive? Scarlett had asked herself that one many times, but hated to think of it. It made her go icy, because that meant she would never know him at all.

Perhaps that's why her mother refused to say who he was, or even admit what she'd done – because she knew the man was dead, and there was no point trying to find him? Or if he was alive, her mother might be protecting him and his family because he was someone they knew . . .

Night after night, she'd tormented herself with all these questions, and no matter how hard she tried to accept that she might never know, she found it impossible.

In her calmer moments, she had considered her mother's

feelings, even if she'd never told her that. What had it been like to keep this secret all these years? If, of course, her mother *had* even known that the mystery man was her father . . . she might have assumed that Roger Latham really was Scarlett's dad.

Despite trying to put herself in her mother's shoes, as Ellie had suggested, Scarlett was finding it hard to accept Anna's complete denial of the facts. No amount of persuasion or pleading from Scarlett in private would tempt her to say anything. However, Scarlett had seized on the idea that her dad might be Cornish, and that, combined with her troubles with Rafa and loss of business, had helped her decide to make the move to Porthmellow.

Ellie, bless her, hadn't hesitated – OK, only a *teeny* bit – to say she could share Seaholly Manor with her. Scarlett knew she would have to come clean at some stage but until – and unless – she knew her hunches were right, she didn't see much point in stirring up more trouble.

'Here you go. Come on, let's have these in front of the fire.' Ellie handed Scarlett a steaming mug topped with a whirl of clotted cream and cinnamon. Scarlett took them into the sitting room where the flames glowed in the hearth and a tang of woodsmoke hung in the air. Ellie followed soon after with a plate of mince pies.

'Not too soon, is it? Honestly, people would eat them year-round if we made them. We had some left at the café so I took them home. It's definitely not too early for the customers but the damp and fog kept many people indoors today.'

Scarlett took one of the sugar-dusted pies. 'It's never too soon for a mince pie.'

Once she'd finished her mince pie and unwound a little, Ellie helped her take her bags upstairs.

'I put you in Auntie Joan's old room. I hope that was OK?' Ellie said. 'It's the biggest and it's had a new bed and a bit of a makeover since she passed, but some of her stuff is still here. It won't upset you, will it?'

'Of course not. I love being surrounded by her treasures. I'm glad Mum and Dad decided to keep her dressing table set and knick-knacks. Are you sure you don't mind? Don't you want the biggest room?'

'They're all pretty spacious and mine is closest to the bath-room. You can even get a glimpse of the sea on a clear day,' Ellie said.

'I don't feel so bad, in that case.'

'I'll leave you to unpack while I put some dinner on.'

'I don't want you waiting on me hand and foot,' said Scarlett.

Ellie put on a stern face, which funnily enough reminded Scarlett a hell of a lot of Auntie Joan – minus the perm and pearls of course. 'Actually, after tonight I was hoping you'd be waiting on me. You'll be wishing you were Cinderella when I give you the household rota.'

'Better enjoy tonight while I can, then,' Scarlett said with a smile, thinking how happy her sister seemed. Living in Porthmellow really suited her.

'Better had.'

The stairs creaked as Ellie jogged back downstairs. Hearing the clang of pots and pans and Ellie humming in the kitchen below, Scarlett drew the curtains and sat down on the bed. Her pulse quickened as she looked around the room. Auntie

Joan's dressing table was a 1950s mahogany affair and Scarlett knew that its drawers held treasured reminders of her. Joan had been her mother's auntie, so Anna had been in charge of deciding which possessions to keep or give away. Most of the book collection was downstairs in the floor-to-ceiling fitted bookcases that lined Joan's study, but a few were kept here in Joan's bedroom in an alcove full of shelves.

Taking a deep breath, Scarlett crossed to the shelves and scanned them. Inside one of these books was the postcard that she'd been waiting to examine ever since they'd sorted through them the previous summer.

Although she couldn't remember the *exact* inscription, she knew it had something to do with a 'special night' or a 'memorable night' and had been addressed to her mother, with love and kisses at the end. It was definitely more than a friendly card, or she'd thought so at the time. However, even though the card had struck her as odd, she'd dismissed it from her mind until her parentage had been called into question.

Whilst hunting for it felt disloyal to her dad, who she loved dearly, she couldn't let the chance to know about her roots pass her by. There was a yawning chasm in her life story that no amount of reassurance or denial could fill. She couldn't rest until she'd found the truth and now that she had an opportunity, she was filled with nervous excitement and dread.

She tried to calm down. She was searching for a book with a distinctive cover of painted seashells and a starfish. She ran her finger over the shelves, looking for the slim volume. *Treasures of the Cornish Seashore.* Or something like that.

It had been on the bottom shelf, if she remembered rightly,

when they were sorting out Joan's things. A faded softback from the 1970s with the postcard of St Ives inserted – hidden? – in the centre.

She gave the bottom shelf a closer inspection, sure she must have missed the book, but still couldn't locate it. Frowning, she checked the middle and top shelves; the alcove was narrow so it wasn't likely she'd missed it, but she was tired after the drive . . . On her third careful pass over every spine, she had to admit defeat. Damn, she wanted to pull out every book just to make sure. Had she completely misremembered the title? There were guides to flowers and birds and rocks and minerals, but no treasures of the seashore.

The book definitely wasn't on the same shelf as before.

She felt completely deflated, and had to remind herself that she hadn't moved all this way only to track down a postcard.

She was about to double check all the shelves again when she heard the front door open and Ellie's voice.

'Hi! It's horrible outside. Come in, quick.'

Scarlett crossed to the bedroom door, which was open a little way. She put her ear to the gap, intrigued by the fevered edge of excitement in Ellie's voice. Ellie laughed and then the front door closed and a man's voice could be heard.

'I saw the car. I'm not stopping, because you have visitors, but I wanted to say that I've finally got hold of the new door panel for your car.'

Scarlett listened even harder. Wow. Ellie and her mystery man both sounded like dogs with two tails. They were obviously very happy to be in each other's company.

'Scarlett!'

At the sound of footsteps trotting upstairs, Scarlett shot back towards the bed and unzipped her bag.

'Are you decent?' Ellie asked at the door.

'Course I am. Just unpacking. Come in.' Scarlett pulled out some stuff and tossed it on the bed.

Ellie stepped inside.

'Aaron's here. He popped in to update me on my car. He lives down by the cove. He can't stay long but do you want to say hello?' Ellie lowered her voice. 'Don't worry, he's not one of the lonely lunch people. In fact, he's almost as new to Porthmellow as you, and I thought it might be a good idea for you to meet someone who isn't part of the establishment.'

'Sounds like a good idea. I'd love to meet him.' Scarlett gave Ellie a knowing look. 'Aaron, you say?'

'Yes. He's Troy and Evie's son. They were at the pub on Christmas Day, actually, but don't let that bother you.'

'I look a bit of a mess after the journey,' Scarlett said, indicating her old jeggings and hoodie.

'Oh, Aaron won't care. That doesn't matter. We're all casual round here, you know that.' A frown creased her forehead. 'Besides, doesn't look as if you got very far with the unpacking.'

'No, I only just started. To be honest, I was knackered and lay on the bed and chilled out,' Scarlett said, feeling guilty for fibbing to her sister. 'There's loads of time for sorting my stuff tomorrow.'

'True. Do you want to stay up here and chill out, then?' Was that a hint of disappointment in Ellie's voice, or did she want to be alone with this new guy?

Scarlett decided she wanted to see him, anyway. 'No way. I'd love to meet the new neighbour.'

Ellie beamed. 'Come on then, let's unleash you on Aaron.'

Whatever Scarlett had been expecting from Aaron, she wasn't prepared for the gladiator of a man sprawled over the love seat in the sitting room. He looked perfectly at ease there, as if he'd been in the house numerous times before. So, thought Scarlett with secret amusement, not such a 'new guy' after all, and yet Ellie had never mentioned him.

'This is my sister, Scarlett.'

'Hi. I'm Aaron, Ellie's wicked new neighbour,' he said, eyes glinting mischievously. 'Your sister thought I was a serial killer when we first met on the lane in the dark because my Transit has no windows.'

'I wish I hadn't told you that!' Ellie burst out. 'Anyway, I thought you were a kidnapper or a burglar, rather than a serial killer.'

'Scarlett,' Scarlett said, holding out her hand and laughing. 'Ellie's wicked younger sister. It's my fault she thinks anyone with a van with no windows is a kidnapper. Just one of my little jokes,' she added quickly in case Aaron thought she'd once been abducted herself.

With a grin, he shook her hand firmly but briefly and sat down again. 'To be fair, no one had told Ellie that I was moving into Cove Cottage. I only decided myself a couple of weeks before.'

'Me too,' Scarlett said.

'Ellie did warn me you were moving down here.' He sucked in a breath. 'Brave.'

'Really?' Scarlett asked. 'Why's that?'

'The locals.'

She smiled. 'Are they that scary?'

'Some . . .' he laughed. 'I was born and brought up in Porthmellow myself until I joined the army. I'm a vehicle engineer.'

'Ah. So *you've* been helping Ellie with her car,' Scarlett said innocently.

'Trying to. It's been in a mate's lock-up in town for almost two weeks but I finally got the part last night. Should have it back on the road tomorrow.'

'That will save you from giving me a lift into town,' said Ellie.

'It's been no trouble. I have to go up and down to town most days anyway – which reminds me, will you be going to the festival planning meeting next week?'

Ellie nodded.

'Mum and Dad have roped me in to help with the Solstice Festival,' Aaron said, exchanging a glance with her. 'They've been on the main committee from the start so I can't say no.'

'What's the Solstice Festival?' Scarlett asked.

'It's a Christmas festival mashed up with old Cornish pagan traditions. First time we've had one in Porthmellow,' Ellie explained.

'Sounds like fun,' said Scarlett.

'It should be. It's meant to be a quirky celebration of the passing of the shortest day. The sailing trust did tours of our new boat at the summer food festival and it went so well, we're going to repeat it at the solstice event and decorate it

61

with fairy lights and dress up as pirates. You'll have to come aboard and have a tour.' She directed this at Aaron.

He held Ellie's gaze a millisecond too long. 'I wouldn't miss it for the world.'

Scarlett narrowly avoided blurting out that they should get a room. Ellie was transfixed, her eyes lighting up, and Aaron seemed equally mesmerised. Wow, so Scarlett had walked in on a blossoming romance between her sister and this admittedly sexy hunk of a bloke. Ellie wouldn't be thanking her for cramping her style. Maybe they were already sleeping together and now she'd be in hearing distance of it all. Ouch.

He turned his attention to Scarlett, perhaps realising that he'd been ignoring her in favour of Ellie. 'Do you know my mum and dad? They're Porthmellow stalwarts. Born and brought up here; lived here all their lives. My dad, Troy, still helps out the harbour commission and he always wears a fisherman's cap. My mum, Evie, has recently had her knee replaced so she has a pink walking stick.'

'Scarlett hasn't been down to Porthmellow since last Christmas,' Ellie put in hastily.

'OK. Sorry, I tend to assume everyone knows my mum and dad.'

But the penny was dropping for Scarlett. The elderly man in the fisherman's hat and the lady leaning on a stick. Troy and Evie. Of course. Even though Scarlett had been in a terrible state and half-frozen, the names of the people at the Smuggler's Christmas lunch were imprinted on her mind. She realised she'd have to see them sooner or later. Everyone, especially the Carmans, had been so kind to her. Once she'd warmed up, the pub landlady had called Ellie who'd arrived with a coat and warm clothes to escort her home. Scarlett had apologised profusely and said there had been a bit of family tension, which combined with too much fizz on an empty stomach had led to her needing some space.

'Actually, I think I might have come across them,' she replied.

'I doubt you'd forget them. They're a real pair of characters.'

Scarlett smiled politely. 'I'm sure I'll get to know them better now I've moved in here.'

'Do you plan on staying long?'

'As long as Ellie will have me.' Scarlett didn't want to commit Ellie to anything in front of Aaron. If her hunch was right, Ellie fancied him like mad, but that might be as far as the attraction went. Ellie could only have known him for two weeks anyway. 'What about you?' she asked, figuring this was a good opportunity to ask about his plans on her sister's behalf.

'A few months at least. More, possibly. I'm trying to see if I can set up a security business with a friend from the army. We have a couple of private clients down here and a contract for several events already, starting with the festival.'

Scarlett laughed. 'Expecting trouble, are you?'

'Oh, I'm sure the seagulls can kick off big style.' He grinned. 'But security is something the organisers have to take very seriously, even though it's not usually a problem. Mum and Dad have said that they're not expecting it to be anywhere near as big as the summer food festival so my team probably won't have much to do.'

'Even so, it might be more work than you think,' Ellie said.

'Yes, and my parents will make sure I don't slack.' He glanced at his watch, a chunky rubber affair with a tonne of dials. 'I'd better go. I've got a meeting with a potential client this evening. Maybe we'll see you both down the Tinners' tomorrow? A bunch of us are meeting up there for a few drinks. Could be a great way for Scarlett to meet the locals?'

'Sounds good,' Ellie said, adding, 'if it's OK with Scarlett?'

Scarlett nodded. Even though she wasn't hugely looking forward to meeting the Christmas Day lunch gang again, she didn't want Ellie to miss out on the chance of seeing Aaron, even if it was in a group. 'Sure. I'll drive if you like, Ellie.'

'If you don't mind.'

'No problem.'

'Great. Sorted.' Aaron got up and Scarlett decided to make herself scarce while they said goodbye.

'I ought to finish my unpacking. Nice to meet you, Aaron. See you tomorrow night.' With a smile, she headed for the stairs, intent on leaving Ellie to see him off the premises. She caught a snatch of Aaron saying something she couldn't quite make out and Ellie replying, 'Oh, I promise to let you know if either of us need you.'

Scarlett closed her bedroom door to give them some privacy. Nevertheless, while she unpacked her clothes, she could still hear laughter and the rise and fall of animated voices for a few minutes until the front door shut again.

Ellie obviously had a tank-sized crush on the guy and Scarlett didn't blame her. But even if her sister hadn't fancied him, she wouldn't have dreamed of going after Aaron. She had enough on her plate looking after her new customers, and trying to build up the business.

She had another moment of misgiving, wondering if she should have come to Seaholly at all. The vanishing postcard and arrival of Aaron had been a sobering wake-up call. She'd been so wrapped up in her own insecurities since last Christmas, it had blinded her to her family's worries. She should have thought more carefully before landing on Ellie, but now she was here, she had to make the best of things while trying not to disrupt her sister's life. Scarlett was sure that the clue to her heritage lay in Porthmellow and she could still look for her father without the postcard, though it was going to be a whole lot harder. It could have been thrown out, of course, or her mum might have moved it.

On the upside, perhaps some of the older locals who'd known Joan might remember her parents visiting – particularly her mother. The pub might be a great place to start her quest to find out more about her father.

# Chapter Five

The Tinners' Arms was the newer of Porthmellow's two pubs; new being only two hundred years old rather than four. The solid granite tavern, built for workers in the nearby mines, was situated on the opposite side of the harbour to the whitewashed Smuggler's Tavern, the scene of Scarlett's Christmas Day meltdown. Like its 'rival', it was one of the main social hubs of the town and even on a dark October evening, was surprisingly busy with locals.

'Oh, look. The festival committee is in here. You can meet everyone all at once,' Ellie said as they walked inside.

'What?' Scarlett followed Ellie's gaze with a sinking feeling. The group of people squashed around tables by the fire turned their collective gaze on her and an unpleasant memory flooded back. 'Oh my God, no. Aaron didn't mention they'd all be in here. There's loads of them.'

She tried to turn around, but Ellie was right behind her.

'Don't worry,' she soothed, ushering Scarlett further into

the dim interior. 'It's only Sam Lovell and her sister, Zennor, and her fiancé, Ben. They're all lovely. So's Drew, my boss, and his partner, Chloe.'

'Oh, so not *many* people then!' Scarlett whispered as they queued at the bar. 'And you forgot the elf man!'

'What do you mean?'

'That guy. The tall one with the surf-dude hair. He was in the pub when I rocked up on Christmas Day, along with Sam and Evie and her husband. They all were.'

Ellie gave their drinks order before replying. 'So?'

'*So?* Have you forgotten I was wearing a pair of bunny slippers and acting like a crazed escapee from a maximum-security institution? This is a terrible idea. The elf man covered me in his fleece . . . like a pensioner or a poorly hamster.' Scarlett stifled a groan of shame.

Ellie glanced again at the elf man. 'Oh, you must mean Jude Penberth? He's not a surfer, as far as I know, but it's just like him to help you out. He's lovely, and as I've said before a dozen times, there's no shame in having asked for help. They know you were very upset. They won't judge you. Sam's had problems of her own.'

'Really? Like finding out her father isn't her dad after all and running off to a bunch of strangers in her slippers?'

'*Much* worse,' Ellie said quietly. 'Sam's father left the family when she was little. Then her mother died, leaving Sam to look after Zen and her brother, Ryan. Ryan tried to rob some of the villagers and did a runner for over a decade. He's back now, though, and if he can come home to Porthmellow, I'm sure you can. It's not as if you did anything wrong.'

Scarlett looked at Sam and winced. 'Well, I suppose if you put it like that . . . mind you, I feel even worse now for making such a fuss.'

'It was a shock.'

Ellie's eyes widened. 'Oh my, Gabe Mathias is here too. We're definitely not leaving.'

'Gabe Mathias? What? *The* Gabe Mathias, the TV chef?'

'Yes, he's Sam's partner.'

Scarlett saw a tall, tanned and very handsome man rejoin the group of committee members.

Ellie handed her a glass of Pinot Grigio. 'Come on, you know you'd love to meet him. He's a sweetheart, too.'

'Everybody seems to be in this town.' Scarlett sipped her wine sedately, determined to show she could be restrained around alcohol.

'Er, not quite. But this bunch are all right. All you need to do is smile and say hello. Everyone knows you're sane normally.'

Scarlett almost choked on her wine. 'Thanks!'

Despite her misgivings, she decided that she'd better get the introductions over with. Fixing a smile on her face, she followed Ellie. This was going to be like taking a plunge into an unheated pool and Scarlett decided it was best to dive straight in, live with the pain and get used to it. It was better than bumping into each person individually over the next few weeks and having to go through the whole excruciating, 'Yes, it was me,' 'Yes, I'm fine now,' 'Thanks for being so kind,' over and over again. More importantly, if she wanted to have a chance of discovering some clues to her biological father's identity, she was going to have to bite the bullet and swallow her pride.

The gang around the table was an eclectic mix. Sitting next to Troy and Evie Carman were Ben and Zennor, a gawky young couple in goth make-up, matching purple hair and biker leathers who were intertwined like vines. You couldn't slot a beer mat between the festival chairperson Sam Lovell and Gabriel Mathias, whose arm was draped around her shoulder. At the end of the booth, Scarlett recognised a ponytailed older guy as Drew, Ellie's boss from the sailing trust, and his partner, Chloe, whom Ellie had said was a London events organiser. Apparently, she was over fifty, but Scarlett thought she looked at least ten years younger.

Then there was the elf man, perched on a barstool, minus his hat of course, his tousled blond hair brushing his shoulders. She was determined to act naturally and do everything she could to prove she wasn't always as weird as this lot must think she was.

'Oh look, there's Aaron.' She pointed to the man carrying a tray of drinks from the bar to the committee table. Ellie's eyes lit up. Aaron mouthed hello and nodded to the group, signalling that she and Ellie should join everyone.

'Come on.' Ellie led the way and all heads turned in their direction.

Aaron put the tray on the table. 'I've invited Ellie and her sister to meet everyone. If we're nice to Scarlett, I thought we might have another new recruit for the festival team.'

'Um. I'm not sure I'd be of any use . . .' Scarlett began, trying not to live up to her name as she came face to face with her rescuers.

People smiled and nods were exchanged. 'Hello, Ellie. Hi, Scarlett.' The chorus of greetings was warm and friendly.

Troy, wearing his cap minus the tinsel, peered at her. 'Eh. You're the maid who wandered into the pub on Christmas Day. We were proper worried about you until Ellie came to take you home.'

His wife nudged him. 'Troy. That was ages ago, she won't want to be reminded of that tonight. She was just having one of those days. We all do.'

Evie was spot on. Scarlett summoned up the biggest grin she could find. 'I'm fine now and you'll be pleased to know I'm not wearing my bunny slippers.'

Everyone burst out laughing.

Troy chuckled. 'Pleased to see you have a sense of humour, maid. It'll stand you in good stead around here. Jude, stand up and give one of these ladies a seat.'

'No need, because we have to go soon.' Drew pulled out his chair.

'It's nothing personal. We promised to babysit my grand-daughter,' Chloe said. 'Hopefully we'll see you again soon, if you've moved into Porthmellow?'

'I'm sure you will,' Scarlett replied, keen not to wash any more of her dirty linen in public.

Sam and Gabe began to chat to her. Sam was funny and kind, and being close to Gabe Mathias was no hardship, as he was even more gorgeous in the flesh than on the TV. Wait until her friends back in Brum heard about it . . . when she eventually returned there – *if* she did. Looking around the pub, surrounded by strangers – apart from her sister – she had a panicky moment. She hadn't really thought of any plans beyond moving in with Ellie and hunting for her real father. It was ironic that before the momentous events of the previous Christmas, she'd been the queen of forward planning. The revelation about her parentage had changed that, and perhaps made her live for the moment more. Soon, the talk turned to the festival and Scarlett was very happy to have the focus shift away from her.

As Aaron had briefly outlined, the event was to be a joint Christmas and solstice festival, which brought together the traditional and pagan elements of the season, celebrating the passing of the shortest day and the festivities to come. It was scheduled for the night of the twenty-first and Scarlett was surprised to hear that several thousand people were expected. She loved visiting the German Christmas market in her home city, and though this event was on a toy-town scale compared to that, it sounded charming. There would be street entertainers, a solstice parade with people in fancy dress led by fire-eaters. The town band would be playing festive music and stalls would sell gifts and seasonal food. Gabe was doing a cookery demo of festive grub.

'We're always looking for more volunteers,' Evie said. 'If you wanted to help.'

Troy tutted. 'Eh, don't rope the girl in. We've only just met her.'

'It's OK. I'm not sure how I can help, but I'll be happy to lend a hand if you like.' Scarlett decided that this was another way to show she was prepared to be a good citizen. And probably also a good way to find out more about her father.

'I'm sure we can find you something,' Sam said. 'When you've settled in, let Ellie know if you want to join in, or give one of us a call.'

A few of the younger committee members went to the bar, and Troy vanished to the loo, leaving Scarlett next to Evie, while Aaron, Jude and Ellie chatted.

Evie shuffled closer. 'Are you feeling any better these days?' she asked in a low voice. 'Ellie's told me that your mum and dad are still having a few problems, not that she's shared the details – or that it's any of my business.'

Scarlett baulked at the open mention of their issues, however, Ellie had had to make some excuses for her behaviour the previous Christmas. Evie was so sweet and genuine that Scarlett didn't mind too much. She was determined to be cheerful and show her festive meltdown had been a one-off, and besides, this was an opportunity to make a few enquiries of her own.

'It's OK, and you're right, Mum and Dad are going through a difficult patch . . . um, do you know them well?'

'Not very well. Obviously, your auntie Joan was a stalwart of the village. Such a clever lady. I loved her books.' Evie winked. 'She used to give me a signed copy when a new one came out, even the racy ones. Did you know about those?'

'Joan didn't think Ellie and I knew, but we found the copies hidden away even before she died.'

'She was one of a kind, was Joan. So refined and ladylike but with a wicked sense of humour, and very open-minded.'

'Hmm . . .' Scarlett replied, wondering if it was an open secret that Joan had been having a relationship with her 'handyman'. 'We all loved her to bits and miss her a lot, especially my mum . . . she used to spend a lot of her time here, particularly when we were young.'

'No wonder. Seaholly Manor is a beautiful place.'

'Mum found it peaceful and soothing. With my dad working away such a lot, she liked to bring us here for holidays when we were little . . . and she used to come with Ellie before I was born.' Scarlett felt like she was treading on wobbly stepping stones, not sure if she should venture any further. 'Do you remember those days? Mum says they had a lot of fun.'

'Gosh, I remember the parties, not that I went to any of the wilder ones. Me and Troy were too busy bringing up Aaron and Gemma. I was Joan's age, so still a lot older than your mum, obviously.'

'Wild parties?' Scarlett gave a laugh. 'That doesn't sound like Auntie Joan,' she joked, knowing her great-aunt had loved entertaining but intrigued to know what Evie meant by 'wild'.

'Oh, she had a few at the manor with her arty friends from London, authors and artists and such like. She'd host them and invite all and sundry from the village . . . I could have gone, but they weren't Troy's scene, as you can imagine. They went on late. Joan's friend – Lawrence Guise, the gardener – said Joan would stay up until late but the younger ones would party 'til dawn on the beach in the summer.'

'Sounds like a real blast.'

'I do think some turned a bit on the lively side . . . you know, wacky baccy, skinny dipping and shenanigans in the dunes . . .' Evie's eyes glittered with mischief. 'Like I say, I only heard the gossip. You should ask your mum about it all. I'm surprised she hasn't told you more about it already.'

'She probably didn't want to be a bad influence on us,' Scarlett replied, dying yet dreading to hear more of the juicy details.

Evie giggled. 'Oh, go on. I bet you've done some stuff you don't want to tell her.'

Scarlett smiled. 'We all have to have a few secrets, don't we?' She tried to make it sound light-hearted, but she felt disturbed by Evie's revelations. Had her mother been involved in some of the 'shenanigans'?

'I doubt very much she'd have been involved, with you little ones to look after, and anyway, I don't think Joan had that many really rowdy dos after the seventies. She was growing out of all that herself.'

Troy arrived back from the gents.

'Sorry I've been a while. Pickled herrings for lunch. I love 'em but they play havoc with my digestion.'

'That's way too much information, Troy!' Evie cried. 'I think we should be getting home. My knee's stiff. I had a new one in the summer,' she told Scarlett. 'Come on, you old devil. Take me home.'

Ben and Zennor left the pub along with Troy and Evie, and shortly after, Sam and Gabe finished their drinks and went home too, which left Ellie and Scarlett alone with Aaron and Jude.

Scarlett wasn't sure how much she'd really learned about her mother's past other than that Joan's parties were even 'wilder' than she'd imagined, by the sound of them. Short of asking Evie straight out if she'd known if her mum had shagged anybody local, she couldn't see how she was going to get that much further forward.

With the departure of some of the others, Jude had moved from the stool to the bench seat next to her. While Ellie and Aaron chatted away like old mates, Jude was much quieter. Scarlett had only met him once before and the previous occasion had hardly been conducive to small talk.

Scarlett was gradually adjusting to seeing him minus his ears and thinking of him as an ordinary bloke rather than the elf man who'd rescued her. However, 'ordinary' perhaps wasn't quite the word for him. His hair was thick and bleached into many shades of blond by the sun, but his eyes were his most striking feature by far. They were green, but not some common or garden hazel colour but *actual* green flecked with amber. So maybe he was one of the elf people after all. Scarlett stopped herself from laughing just in time . . .

'Everything OK?' he asked.

'Why?'

'You were away with the fairies for a moment there.'

She almost choked on her gin. He could read minds, too. She laughed. 'Sorry, I was only thinking how strange it is to be here in Porthmellow after all that's happened.'

He thought before replying. 'Tonight must have been a baptism of fire. It took some guts to walk in with us lot here. Assembled Do-Gooders of Porthmellow.' He added a gentle smile and Scarlett, expecting to be embarrassed at the reference, instead felt relieved that he'd mentioned it in a low-key and humorous way that she could live with.

75

'I never thought I would come back, to be honest. And there's nothing wrong with doing good. I just didn't expect to be on the receiving end of it.'

'There's no shame in needing help. Ellie said you'd had a bit of a family crisis on Christmas morning. Please, you don't have to tell me any more. Unless you want to, of course, but I'm guessing you'd rather forget the whole thing?'

'Walking into the pub in my slippers, yes. Unfortunately, the other stuff is more complicated.'

'Things always are.' Jude had a wistful look in his eye, then he smiled. 'Your glass is empty. Another one?'

'I'll have a small G&T, thanks, but let me pay. I insist.'

Jude nodded. 'OK.'

Aaron and Ellie still had half-full glasses, so Scarlett went to the bar and returned with Jude's half a bitter and her gin. They chatted about her job and she told him some of her plans.

'Did Ellie tell you Zennor and Ben run a graphic design company? They might need a copywriter. It's worth asking them. Probably only small clients, but still.'

'Any new client would be good, but I'd feel awkward about approaching them for work when I've only just met them . . .'

'They wouldn't mind at all. I'm not sure they're swamped with top copywriters like you in Porthmellow.'

Scarlett searched his face for any sign of irony but decided he was being serious. Once upon a time she'd have had no qualms about chatting up a potential new client immediately, but her foundations had been rocked in so many ways lately that she was no longer so confident. She felt she needed to get her feet under the table in Porthmellow first. 'I'm not sure there *are* any top copywriters here, even now.' She smiled. 'I'll definitely get in touch when I've settled in. Thank you.'

'No problem. I'm sure they'd be delighted to have you.'

Jude seemed to glow with pleasure. Despite his eyes, there was nothing fey about the rest of him. He wore a long-sleeved T-shirt over dark chinos and a leather bracelet with a silver clasp. He was about her age, she guessed, and striking rather than gorgeous in the way of Gabe, Aaron or Rafa. Yet Scarlett wanted to look at him, and looking at him gave her pleasure. It was silly, but she felt that he had an inner luminosity. Unless she had her gin goggles on, of course. She pushed her glass away, deciding that she was at a stage of pleasantly relaxed and didn't want to tip over into the dangerous area of wanting to tell him her life story.

'So, what do you do in Porthmellow?' she asked, resisting the urge to ask if it involved casting spells.

'Not a lot, according to some people.' His lips tilted in a smile. 'Actually, we have something in common, because I'm in the writing business too.'

'Please don't say I'm not the only copywriter in the village?' Scarlett wasn't joking. She couldn't handle the competition.

'No, I don't write copy, although I do contribute to magazines. I write about natural history. Wildlife, plants and flowers. I'm a forager.'

'A forager? As in picking plants to eat?'

'Flowers, plants, wild seafood, fungi. Anything and everything you can make into a meal or drink. I run foraging and wild cookery courses and I've published a couple of books on the subject. I also teach part-time at the local college.'

77

'Wow. You're the first forager I've met. How did you get into that?'

'I'm from Porthmellow. Mum and Dad still live here. I have a PhD in Botany and I worked for a university in London for a while but, well –' he hesitated a little too long before continuing – 'let's just say I couldn't keep away from the bright lights of Porthmellow. I must be getting old, longing for a quiet life.'

'You don't look that old!' she blurted out, but immediately regretted the personal remark. 'Sorry!'

'I won't see thirty-six again,' Jude said solemnly.

'Still very young,' she replied hastily, also suspecting there was more to his return than he'd admitted. She'd only just got to know him, so she certainly wasn't going to pry. 'So, you're Doctor Penberth. I'm impressed,' she said, shifting the focus to his unusual job.

'Yes, and actually,' he said solemnly, 'I do prefer people to use my title unless they know me very well.'

Scarlett was floored. He hadn't seemed pompous but perhaps she'd misread him. 'Oh, erm . . . I see . . .' she floundered, not sure how to react.

Suddenly his stern expression melted into a grin. 'I'm joking. I only use the doctor thing for occasional academic stuff; conferences and so on. Jude will do fine between us.'

'You – you . . .' She dissolved into laughter, her cheeks warming at being taken in.

'I shouldn't have teased you. I'm sorry.'

'It's fine.' She laughed. 'I should have guessed you were joking.'

A burst of laughter from across the table caught her attention. Ellie and Aaron were very close. It seemed like they were all getting on well together.

Jude sipped his pint and replaced it on the table. 'Um . . . talking of work, you might see me foraging in the grounds of the manor. Your auntie Joan was very kind and let me collect plants from the gardens, and I carried on picking them after she passed away. Ellie said it was OK to continue, unless the place is sold, obviously.'

'There are no plans for that at the moment,' Scarlett said. Jude was another local who seemed to have been friendly with Joan, but Scarlett had never come across him on her visits – she'd definitely have remembered him. 'So this foraging . . . do it a lot, do you?'

She'd made it sound vaguely disgusting and a bubble of embarrassed laughter rose in her throat. Jude made her want to laugh and she hadn't felt like that very often lately but she wasn't sure he would share her sense of humour.

'Actually, yes, I do.' He smiled wickedly and Scarlett revised her opinion of him upwards yet again. Maybe he'd get her jokes after all. 'You don't mind then?'

'Not if Ellie doesn't. You can forage as much as you like. Not that it's our place, anyway. As you probably know, it's my mother who owns the manor now, but I'm sure she won't mind either.'

'Yes, I knew that Joan had left it to your mum.'

'Did you know my aunt very well?'

'Not as well as you, obviously, but I saw her at least once a week or so when I was foraging in her grounds.'

Scarlett giggled again. 'Oh, I'm sorry. I know it's juvenile of me, but foraging is such a funny word. It sounds a bit . . .'

'Pervy?' Jude suggested, with a glint of amusement.

'Well, kind of.'

'It does sound weird to make a living from collecting wild food. I'm convinced that a few of the locals think I'm some kind of wizard, brewing up potions from the hedgerows, but you would be amazed by all the wonderful things you can find by the seashore, woods and even in your own backyard.'

'I'm sure I would. Though there wasn't much to forage in my backyard in Birmingham.'

'Ah, but that's where you're wrong.' Jude's glow was back. 'You can find all sorts in parks and gardens. Birmingham's renowned for its parklands. Like chickweed, for instance. You can find that all year round and it's very tasty in salads or in a dip.'

'Really? I'd no idea . . .' Scarlett thought of the bare branches of oaks around the manor and the russet bracken on the moorland, wondering what there was to actually forage. 'But are there really that many edible plants around at this time of year?'

'You'd be surprised,' said Jude with a smile. 'There are still plenty of nuts and green leaves at this time of year if you know where to look, especially on the coast. I also have blackberries and bilberries in my freezer and a great stock of cherry brandy ready for the Solstice Festival. I could show you some of the things you can find around the manor, if you like, the next time I come over? Ellie too,' he added quickly.

She hesitated. It had been a long time since she'd agreed

to go out with a guy, not that hunting plants was a 'date', but actually, that might be exactly why she should say yes: the invitation seemed genuinely innocent. 'OK. I'd like that. And I'm sure Ellie would,' she tagged on hastily, though she guessed Ellie might decide she was too busy with Aaron . . .

Jude's pleasure showed in his eyes. 'Great. I'll give you my number so we can arrange a time?'

They talked about Cornwall for a while longer, Jude's passion for nature and his birthplace lighting up his face and his voice even more. Once or twice he mentioned his time in London but it was obvious that he'd missed his homeland during his botany PhD. When Ellie signalled that it was time to head home, Scarlett was surprised how disappointed she felt to have to go, especially when compared with the dread she'd experienced when she'd first walked in.

They got up and said their goodbyes.

'You'll call me, then,' Jude repeated as she was about to leave.

'Yes. Soon as I've asked Ellie.'

'Great.' He pushed his hair out of his eyes and Scarlett had a strange feeling in the pit of her stomach. There really was something extraordinary about Jude Penberth, but she couldn't quite put her finger on it.

# Chapter Six

'Y ou have to tell me if I'm getting in the way. Or if you want me to move out.'

Ellie hid her smile as Scarlett rested the back of the chair against the café table. Scarlett had come to pick Ellie up from work, and was helping her clear away after closing time. Ellie was in charge while the owner, Tina, had a hospital appointment. As it was half-term, the café had been very busy and Ellie felt knackered, so she was glad to have Scarlett's help to pack up.

'After you've only been here a week?' Ellie asked, amused and touched by Scarlett's eagerness not to get in the way of her lifestyle.

'Well, I won't want to leave, obviously, but if you need me to make myself scarce one evening so you and Aaron can . . . you know . . . you must tell me.'

'It's early days with Aaron,' she said, slightly alarmed by how keen Scarlett was to pair her off. She was ready to admit that she and Aaron had been flirting with each other, but hadn't quite realised the impression they were giving to people around them. 'We've only known each other for a few weeks,' she said, as much to remind herself not to let her feelings run away with her, as to put Scarlett off the scent.

'Oh, come on. You two are practically glued together whenever I see you. I reckon he exaggerated the damage to the car, so he could spend more time with you.'

'That's crazy,' Ellie insisted, but had to admit that the very idea of Aaron made her grow shivery. She hadn't felt this way about a man since she was a student – and look how that had ended.

Scarlett rested the final chair on the table. Aside from locking up, they were almost ready to go. 'You do like him, though,' she said.

Ellie decided she might as well be honest. 'Yes, I like him. A lot. Who wouldn't? He's gorgeous and helpful.'

'And he's been serving his country. He's a genuine real-life hero.' Scarlett came over to her, grinning wickedly.

'He is, but apart from *that* I don't know an awful lot about him. Obviously, his mum and dad worship him and it seems as if he's been dedicated to his army life. I think his job's been all-consuming for him. I guess that kind of lifestyle couldn't be any other way.'

'Even if he's been in the forces, there must have been some time for, you know . . . Has he talked about any other women – or men?'

'He mentioned a female officer from a different regiment

who he was involved with for a few years, but he said it was very difficult to maintain a relationship when they were both posted to different locations.'

'I suppose it must be. But he's home now and I bet he wants to put down some roots.'

'Who knows?' Ellie said, reminding herself not to get her hopes up. 'He'd like to make a go of the security business, but these days, nothing's certain, is it?'

'You can say that again. I'm grateful for every job I get because I never really know if it will be my last. We live in interesting times, but it's a good sign if Aaron's trying to settle down here. Is the fact he might not stick around stopping you from taking things any further?'

Ellie laughed, hiding her discomfort at Scarlett's probing. 'I don't know. Maybe. Though if he knew my track record, he might keep well away. I've hardly put down any roots myself, even tiny ones.'

'Apart from in Porthmellow.'

Ellie returned a high chair to the alcove. 'True,' she said, and walked back to Scarlett. 'But really, we hardly know one another yet. He's charming, he's fun and, I'll admit it, he's hot. But beyond that, who knows?'

'Aaron can't be that bad if he's Troy and Evie's son. There's no gossip going around, is there? No rumours of skeletons in his closet?'

'Not that I've heard, but you know yourself how secrets can surface. None of us really know our families, do we?'

Scarlett sighed. 'I did, once upon a time . . .' she said wistfully. No matter now often their father had reassured her he

84

loved her, Scarlett had told Ellie, she still felt like the very foundations of her existence had been shaken.

Ellie patted her arm. 'Come on, lovely, let's finish up here, nip into the Co-op for some supplies and then get home in front of the fire. I'm done in after a day dealing with wild kids high on Hallowe'en cookies.'

After picking up some groceries, Scarlett drove them to the manor. Ellie tried not to tense up or reach for the grab handle as Scarlett whizzed around the steep bend out of Porthmellow in the dark. It was only a five-minute journey by road, but it was a white-knuckle ride at the hands of Scarlett, who, Ellie pondered, might possibly turn out to be the daughter of The Stig. Scarlett didn't indicate until it was almost too late, and made a sharp turn down the lane that caused Ellie to let out a squeak and Scarlett to protest: 'It wasn't that scary! I had plenty of time.'

Ellie closed her eyes as Scarlett barrelled down the lane, hoping that Aaron – or anyone else – wasn't coming the other way. She heaved a silent sigh of relief when they arrived at Seaholly Manor.

Once the trauma of the drive had worn off, she reflected how lovely it was not to have to come home alone to a dark house, and that some company was very welcome now the days were so short. Knowing that someone else was in and out of the house while Ellie was at work was comforting, too.

However, she had to admit that, much as she loved her sister, sharing her space after having free rein at the manor had been trickier than she'd anticipated. She hadn't realised how much she'd like to spend time with Aaron Carman when she'd agreed to let Scarlett move in.

Scarlett was as good as her word when it came to contributing to the household expenses, which was very welcome. As energetic and optimistic as ever, she'd wasted no time in turning the study into the hub of her business. Over the past week, she'd upgraded the broadband package and installed a landline extension – which was good because she was on the phone a *lot*, either to customers, or her mates.

After a stir-fry cooked by Scarlett – another bonus of having a housemate – Ellie opened her own laptop to check on some information from the sailing trust. There was a group email from Skipper Drew to all the team, including the mate and the marketing manager, discussing their stall for the Solstice Festival. The trust operated two vintage sailing trawlers and took groups of adults on day trips and holidays around the South West. The previous spring and summer had often seen Ellie at sea, cooking for the crew and guests, but there would be no more trips until Easter. Nonetheless, the festival was a great opportunity to let visitors know about their work.

She explained to Scarlett that the trust planned on selling gift vouchers for sailing courses and days out as the perfect Christmas present. Ellie was also involved in the Harbour Café stall, preparing mince pies and pasties, mulled wine and hot chocolate.

'Evie and Sam said I could help out if I want, but I'm not sure how,' Scarlett said. 'I feel a bit like a spare part at the moment.'

'They're probably waiting for you to offer your services,' Ellie said, keen to encourage Scarlett to find a new focus to take her mind off everything. 'Maybe you can help with the copywriting and PR?'

Scarlett perked up instantly at the scent of a new business opportunity. 'Excellent idea . . . Jude said Zennor and Ben have a graphics company.'

The phone rang. 'I'll get it,' Scarlett said. She was gone for a while. She'd closed the door to keep the room warm so Ellie could only hear snatches, but when she walked back in, Ellie could tell she was downcast.

'That was Mum,' she said.

Ellie winced, wondering how the conversation had gone. 'Is she OK?'

'Yes, but she wants to come down for a visit.'

Ellie screwed up her face. 'Uh huh. That sounds ominous. Did she say why?'

'Only that she wanted to talk to us face to face.'

'Shit, I bet she wants to sell this place. Oh no, I hope they're not splitting up!' Ellie blurted out.

'Can you blame Dad if he wants to make a break?'

'Don't say that, Scarlett,' Ellie said, exasperated and worried about their parents. Like any couple, they'd had their moments, not helped by the fact that their father was a quiet man, who liked to spend his time with his books or in his shed. He'd never left her, or as far as she knew, her siblings, in any doubt of his deep love for them but, like most men of his age, he wasn't given to showy displays of affection. Their mother was a loving, practical and energetic woman, as you'd expect from someone with three children, a teaching job and a husband who worked away a fair bit. They had seemed to work well as a team, and despite the odd row, had appeared to respect and love each other dearly.

Now, Ellie wasn't sure if she'd missed troubling undercurrents that her mum and dad had carefully hidden from all their children.

'If they have decided to get a divorce, we can't do anything about it,' she said briskly, hiding her concerns. 'When does she want to come?'

'Early next month. She said she and Dad need some space – some physical space away from each other – and she hinted she might stay on here for a while.' Scarlett paced around with the phone. 'I'm not sure I'm ready for that, to be honest. I try to stay calm but keep wanting to ask her about – *him*.'

'I can understand that, but this is Mum's house,' Ellie pointed out. 'It's more than reasonable if she wants to move in here for a while. You'll have to try and get along.'

'It's easy for you. You're calm, you get on with everyone. Sometimes I think you're a saint.' Scarlett flopped down on the sofa, the movement transporting Ellie back twenty years to the moody teenager phase that Scarlett had gone through when Ellie first left for university.

A *saint*? Nothing could be further from the truth, thought Ellie. 'You're wrong. I'm not that calm, and I try to get on with everyone. You have to, when you work with customers all the time. But I don't think that my way is the best, or suits everyone. Avoiding conflict isn't always a good thing, I promise you.'

Ellie thought back to her sudden departure all those years

ago. Scarlett must have missed her badly when she went to university, so goodness knows how she'd felt when Ellie left the UK altogether halfway through her degree. She must have been devastated, her parents too. She didn't think Marcus had been affected; he was preoccupied with his cars and sport.

'You don't seem to run away. You seem to take stuff on and get on with it, whatever the circumstances,' Scarlett said.

'I've done plenty of things I'm not proud of.'

Scarlett was intent on Ellie, her attention piqued. Ellie was already wishing she'd kept quiet.

'Like what?' she asked.

'Like things I don't want to admit to.'

Scarlett laughed. 'You haven't robbed a bank, have you?'

Ellie studied the rug. Scarlett had no idea. 'Nothing *illegal*,' she said quietly, already regretting letting the conversation get this far.

Scarlett sat bolt upright. 'Oh my God, what were you up to out in Thailand?'

'Managing a bar. Nothing else.' Ellie's voice quietened. 'But we all make mistakes.' She paused. 'Even saints,' she said ruefully, quickly softening the comment with a smile.

Too late. Scarlett had sensed a secret and wasn't about to let it lie. 'What d'you mean, make mistakes?' She touched Ellie's arm lightly. 'Hun, you know you can tell me anything.'

Ellie had already said too much. Or perhaps it *was* time to get something off her chest that had been weighing on it for a long time. Scarlett deserved some honesty from one member of the family, at least. 'I did something I *knew* was wrong. I was young and green, but I still knew it was wrong, deep down, and I shouldn't have done it.'

Scarlett bit her lip and leaned forward. 'You've got me worried now.'

'There's no need to be *worried* . . . but maybe we should have a heart to heart and be totally honest with each other.'

Scarlett touched her arm again. 'Ells?' she murmured.

'Remember when I dropped out of uni when you were in the sixth form?' Ellie asked.

Scarlett frowned. 'How could I forget? Mum and Dad hit the roof. I was amazed because you'd always been such a nerd until then.'

Ellie thought back to the earnest young English student she once was, passionate about Keats and her hatred of DH Lawrence . . . she gave it up for a life of travel and working in bars and kitchens, and it seemed a century away now. 'You all thought I'd just got bored and wanted to see the world. Mum and Dad thought I'd got in with a crowd of hippies.'

'I was angry that you left me. That was selfish of me, but it was such a shock that sensible Ellie had dropped out. I thought you'd had a meltdown and finally rebelled after all the swotting and work.'

'I didn't dare tell anyone the real reason, especially not Mum and Dad.' Ellie took a deep breath. 'I was seeing my tutor. My married tutor.'

Scarlett was wide-eyed. 'Oh my God, Ellie, I'd no idea you were having an affair!'

Even these days, Ellie thought, infidelity still had the power to shock. It should do, it caused long-lasting hurt and damage that never really healed.

'I wouldn't call it an affair, as such.' Ellie forced herself to go back to the end of the spring term in her second year at Plymouth Uni. 'Professor Mallory, or Julian as he'd asked me to call him, was a lot older than me, and brilliant and sexy and sophisticated . . . and at the same time, he also seemed to "get" me. I'd chosen to study a paper on Anglo Saxon poetry that no one else had. He was an expert on it and gave me a one-to-one tutorial.'

'Wow . . .'

'Yeah, don't look like that at me. It seemed normal at the time. He made me coffee afterwards and we started talking about all kinds of stuff. He'd been born in West Cornwall and we got talking about Porthmellow and Auntie Joan. He'd heard of her, you know, and he even knew a couple of the authors she was friends with. I expected him to dismiss her books as trash, but he was actually quite nice about them. He'd read a couple because they were set in Porthmellow and he was brought up not far from the town.' Ellie broke off, remembering Julian's comments that she should write a novel of her own. She'd felt flattered and believed he meant it at the time but she'd never acted on it, of course. Life had taken a different course, sweeping her as far away from literature as possible.

'This doesn't sound as if it's going to end well,' Scarlett said gently.

'No . . . but at the time, it felt as if we – me and Julian – were meant to be, or so my twisted logic went. I suppose I was dazzled

91

and felt that we had a genuine connection, but that's no excuse. I was madly in love with him but then I got ill. Remember how low I was over the Easter vacation, and then I missed the start of the summer term and was struggling to catch up?'

'*Low*? You had glandular fever, Ells! You were wiped out for most of the holiday. Mum told us to keep away from you in case we caught it, but I came in to see you anyway. It was Marcus who was terrified of catching it. It's the kissing disease, he said, so you must have been snogging loads of people.'

'Only one,' Ellie said. 'And that was after I'd recovered.' The glandular fever had knocked her out for the whole Easter vacation and its effects had lingered into the next term, making her fatigue easily.

'Julian was really supportive. He made sure I got help from the uni health service, he allowed me extra time to hand in essays and he offered me some extra tuition.'

'Oh Jesus, Ellie. You were only nineteen!'

'Nearly twenty.'

'How old was he?'

'Thirty-nine.'

'The creepy perv.'

'He didn't look it. He was gorgeous – and come on, I was young but I wasn't totally naïve. I'd had relationships with a couple of guys before then.'

'Not married ones, or ones twenty years older!'

'I was well aware that Julian was married with a young child. But he said . . .' Ellie felt the guilt and pain flooding back. 'He said he and his wife were considering a trial separation and had only got married because she was pregnant.'

92

'I still say he's a perv,' Scarlett sniffed in disgust.

'Julian said they were totally unsuited and that she'd been seeing one of his colleagues, and I *did* see her flirting with one of the other tutors. I've no idea if there was anything more to it, but I had such a massive crush on him and he'd been so kind and trustworthy and reliable in every other way, that I believed him. Or rather I *wanted* to believe him. I'm not a victim. I take part of the responsibility – then and now.'

'Well, you shouldn't take responsibility because he was obviously a manipulative shit. How could he do that to you?' Scarlett burst out, as if she'd like to get hold of Julian right that second. Ellie couldn't help but be touched at the way Scarlett wanted to fight her corner now, even after all these years.

'Auntie Joan would have said it takes two to tango. That's why I don't want to be so hard on Mum. She might have had a fling and now regret it deeply, like me.'

Should Ellie tell Scarlett the rest of the story? The part that still, even now, made the backs of her eyes sting with suppressed tears and made her wonder, almost every day, what might have been. Should she tell Scarlett that if things had been different, by now, Ellie would have had a grown-up child? Judging by Scarlett's open mouth, Ellie had already shocked her enough. The part about the baby that Ellie had lost could stay hidden for a while longer, possibly forever.

Yet Ellie desperately wanted to blurt out how shocked she'd been when she'd found out she was pregnant and Julian had offered her the money for a termination and some extra cash too, if she 'was prepared to be discreet'. She'd fled her halls of residence, devastated when she realised that he'd no intention of supporting the baby and was only terrified that his wife might find out.

She'd had the termination, thinking it was the right thing at the time, for her, for Mallory's family, for her future, and yet . . . she hadn't been able to stop herself from thinking 'what if' ever since. In the immediate aftermath, she'd been exhausted and traumatised by the whole affair. After the abortion, a couple of student mates had looked after her and accepted her story that she'd had a drunken one-night stand with a random guy. She'd recovered physically, but the mental scars lingered to this day. She hadn't told Julian she'd had a termination because part of her wanted him to suffer the way she was, by making him worry that she might tell his wife.

She also hadn't wanted to go back to uni, or go home and admit she felt like a failure. She didn't want anyone seeing her distress and forcing her to explain why. So, she'd put on a mask of bravado, told her family and her uni friends she was bored with the course, that it wasn't for her and she wanted to see the world.

It was hard to say if she regretted not having her baby. She'd had a wonderful time travelling, met some amazing, generous and fascinating people who she might never have known if she'd finished her degree and ended up teaching as she'd once planned.

Lately, though, her wandering had been replaced by wondering. What if she'd kept her baby and made a life with him or her? She'd now be the mother of a teenager. Now, approaching forty, she was hardly past it but her chances of having a family were diminishing . . . Unbidden and unexpected, tears clogged her throat.

'Ellie.' Scarlett was at her side, hugging her. 'You should have reported him,' she declared. 'Taking advantage of a student in his care. What he did was totally inappropriate and in effect, he forced you to quit. That's disgusting. He should have left, not you!'

'Maybe I should have, but would anyone have believed me? Even if they had, I was ashamed – so ashamed, I can't tell you. I didn't want everyone staring at me in lectures, pointing their fingers and sniggering. "Oh look, that's the one that shagged Professor Mallory, but then I always thought Ellie was a bitch. Flirting with him in tutorials, no wonder she got the best grades for her essays. She must have been screwing him for months – and him with a child too. Cow."'

'Ellie. Please, stop this.'

Ellie was shaking. She'd no idea why the bitterness had surfaced now, but that was the trouble with lifting the lid on bad stuff after so much time. No wonder her mum refused to admit to her own affair – she must be terrified of unleashing further chaos and misery on the family.

Scarlett's eyes were bright with tears, but Ellie wiped hers away, feeling drained after finally telling Scarlett about Mallory.

'I'm sorry. You're the first person I've told about how I really felt.' Or part of how she felt. 'I know you care and you're angry for me, but please, can we move on from it now?'

'Thanks for telling me. I'd no idea and I'm very, very sorry.'

'It was a long time ago and I've put it behind me. I've had a fantastic life; probably far more exciting than if I'd stayed at uni. Let's look to the future. We're both ready for new adventures.' She smiled at Scarlett; her heart full to the brim. Her sister was loyal and caring, and she was very thankful for that.

Scarlett let out a sniff. 'Yeah.'

'Even if they might be temporary adventures?'

'I hope not. I'd like to stay here a while,' Scarlett said.

'Me too. Porthmellow and this house have started to really get under my skin.'

'And Aaron is here, of course.'

'We'll see.' Ellie smiled to herself.

'I don't think he's a Professor Mallory,' Scarlett said.

'Neither do I. Mind you, I've been wrong about men before, but I get a good feeling about him. So, what do *you* want from being here, Scarlett? What kind of adventure?'

'Not the romantic kind, if that's what you mean.'

'Not even if it involves Jude Penberth?'

'Especially not Jude Penberth, though I'd be lying if I said I didn't find him intriguing. His eyes are mesmerising.'

Ellie laughed. 'You make him sound like Derren Brown.'

'Eeek. Nooooo.' She sighed. 'I like Jude, but he isn't my priority. Work is, and most of all . . . I wish I knew who my dad was. You don't think that's why Mum's coming down here, do you? To tell us who he is? Maybe she thinks that Seaholly is the right place to tell us.' Scarlett sounded hopeful, but Ellie wasn't so sure.

'It's certainly a peaceful place with happy memories . . . She might want to have us on our own so she can talk properly.'

'Hmm. Perhaps we're finally going to get some answers.'

Ellie thought back to the conversation with her mother. Scarlett might have a point, but Ellie had an even stronger feeling that their mother wasn't going to reveal her secrets so quickly, and that Scarlett's wait for answers might be far longer than her sister was expecting or hoping. After what had happened at Christmas, she wasn't even sure that delving any further into the unknown was a good thing. It could make things a lot more complicated for everyone.

# Chapter Seven

'Hello. Are you still up for a bit of foraging?'

Jude Penberth beamed when Scarlett opened the door to him later that week. She'd almost given up on ever hearing from him again, and thrown herself into her writing, but the previous evening, he'd pinged her a WhatsApp message with an apology that he'd been bogged down in the final proofs of his new wild food book.

Wow. The dodgy lighting in the pub hadn't done him justice. In daylight, his shoulder-length hair gleamed with rich tones: honey and cinnamon glinted in the autumn sun. His skin was burnished. It was as if delicious foods had infused him. He was almost edible and she had to resist the urge to reach out and touch him. And possibly taste him.

Now, that *would* have been weird.

She shook away the disgraceful idea. 'How could I refuse an offer like that?' she replied with a friendly smile, pleased that Jude didn't actually have the second sight or magical powers capable of seeing into her mind.

Scarlett had opted for jeans, her green and allegedly 'Cornish hurricane-proof' mac, and Ellie's wellies.

Jude was in walking boots and a dark blue waterproof, good quality and probably very expensive, but well used. He picked up a large blue rucksack from outside the door and shrugged it onto his shoulders.

'That's a big one,' Scarlett said.

'I'm sorry?' Jude looked nonplussed, as well he might.

'I meant your backpack is huge,' Scarlett gabbled. 'It must have a lot of stuff in it.'

'Ah well,' he replied with a serious expression. 'You'll have to wait and see, won't you?'

Scarlett cringed at her unintended innuendos but thankfully Jude took it all in good part. 'It's full of kit for our foraging expedition. I suppose I could have driven round but I'd much rather walk as it's not far via the coast path. My place is right on the harbour front.'

'Oh really?' Scarlett said, happy to hurry on from her faux pas. 'Which one?'

'The pale blue fisherman's cottage near the Net Loft restaurant.'

'I think I know it. Is it next but one?' she asked, picturing the blue cottage near to Gabe Mathias's stylish bistro, with its balcony overlooking the boats. It seemed to fit perfectly with Jude's personality: modest but attractive.

'I bet the aromas drive you mad. I'd love to eat there . . . maybe I can treat Ellie,' she said, trying not to fixate on Jude's face and body. Or she could take their mother there, if peace broke out between them. Her sense of nervous anticipation about the visit had heightened, which was one reason why she'd been looking forward to today as a distraction.

'I supply him with a few local sea veg and herbs from time to time when I can gather them. Foraged and seasonal foods are really popular with his clientele.'

'They're very trendy at the moment. Um . . . do I need to bring anything today?' Scarlett asked, thinking what a very pleasant diversion Jude was.

'Just yourself and a good appetite.' His gaze travelled to her feet. 'Erm. I'd suggest walking boots if you've got any instead of wellies though, as we might be doing a bit of climbing.'

'Climbing?'

'Only a bit of scrambling. Nothing dangerous, I promise, so you'll be fine.' He gave a reassuring smile.

After she'd found her boots, they set off towards the far end of the grounds of the manor by the stream that ran down the valley and spilled into the cove. The early November day was the kind that lured you into imagining winter wasn't around the corner, and laughed in the face of the fact that Christmas was less than eight weeks away. The granite manor was softened by the morning sunshine and crows cawed in the trees, competing with the seagulls wheeling overhead. Now the leaves had fallen, there was a better view from its upper floors to the sea, particularly from her room. She thought how lucky she was to have such a bolthole to escape to, and wondered again how long she might stay.

She missed her friends, but the list of reasons to linger was growing.

As she walked alongside Jude, she was struck by the contrast of the peace around her with the city, which would be packed with shoppers, Christmas pop songs blaring out and huge Christmas trees reaching up to the atrium in the malls. Here, there was only the distant sigh of the sea and the wind and birds. Porthmellow's Christmas lights hadn't even been switched on yet, although its tiny shops had their own charming displays. And while she would miss going for a meal and drinks in the Mailbox with her friends this year, the community events and festival would doubtless have a quirky charm of their own.

'Hang on a sec.'

Jude paused by the hedgerow and shifted a clump of leaves.

Scarlett perked up. 'Anything?'

'No. Thought it was a scarlet elfcup.'

'An elfc-cup,' she spluttered, fighting back giggles. 'Are they really a thing?'

'Yes, bright red, and very tasty, but alas . . .' He picked up a crumpled bag of Walkers Ready Salted. 'This is only a crisp packet. Let's move on.'

Still bubbling with glee at the idea of Jude sipping from an elfcup, she followed him down the path.

'It seems a funny time of year to go foraging,' she said, wondering, despite what he'd said in the pub, how they could possibly cook up a meal from weeds and toadstools, even if an elfcup did materialise. 'Is there really anything worth collecting?'

'November isn't the ideal time of year, but there will still be plenty of interesting plants to find in the valley and down by the cove.'

'How do we know what's edible? I mean, what happens if we pick up a poisonous mushroom or some deadly nightshade?'

'Then we'll probably be found in the woods by some dog walker and the whole of Porthmellow will come to the wake,' he said in a gloomy voice.

Scarlett emitted an actual squeak. 'That won't really happen!'

'There's always the possibility. People have become seriously ill from eating the wrong type of fungi or berry or even worse . . .' Jude's tone was still grim, but then he smiled. 'Which is why you need to go with someone who knows what they're doing. To start with, at least. You don't want to be playing Russian roulette every time you put something in your mouth, now do you?'

Scarlett felt heat rush to her cheeks. She definitely didn't trust herself to reply.

'I can't imagine ever being confident enough to gather anything more exotic than a blackberry.'

He handed her a small field guide. 'This will help for now. It's what most foragers use.'

The little guide called *Free Foods* was obviously well-thumbed and read.

'I'd have brought you a copy of my book if it was ready . . . though it's actually aimed at older kids as well as adults.'

'Older kids?' She laughed. 'Sounds about my level.'

He seemed relieved that she wasn't offended. 'Well, I'm

hoping it'll be available for the Solstice Festival. I can bring you a copy as soon as I get one, if you'd like it?'

'Only if you sign it.'

'I'd love to. Shall we start around the grounds of the manor?'

She smiled. 'Yes, I'd love to know what's lurking in my own backyard.'

He laughed, and she relaxed a little more. This could be a fun day and she sorely needed that. 'OK. Here are the golden rules of foraging: get the landowners' permission if it's private land and only ever take what you need and what you recognise. Shall we make a start? I can see some lovely Alexanders over there.'

Fascinated, Scarlett followed Jude to a far corner of the gardens where a clump of bright green leafy plants was growing on a sunny bank. They looked like any old weed to her, but Jude crouched down beside them and pulled a small knife from the side pocket of his rucksack.

Scarlett knelt down next to him as he cut off the base of one of the plants and held it out to her. 'Alexanders are a forgotten vegetable that only grow by the coast. They're a wonderful winter green.' He smiled at Scarlett, clearly amused by her sceptical expression. He cut off the base of the stem and stripped a few stringy pieces from it before handing it to her.

'You can eat the leaves as a salad, and the stem is great in a stir-fry. Here, try some.'

Used to buying her fresh food from the local Tesco, often pre-washed and chopped, Scarlett hesitated.

'It's fine. I promise.'

She bit off a chunk of the Alexander's stem. It had a satisfying crunch and a slightly peppery taste. She chewed it. It wasn't bad at all; in fact, it was fresh and tangy.

'Mmm. It tastes like celery, only stronger,' she said.

He smiled. 'Exactly. Before celery was commercially available, people would use Alexanders all the time. They grow all year but they're much nicer now, before they flower.'

Jude cut some more leaves and added them to the smaller canvas bag.

'Let's move on, I'm sure we can find some sea beet as we walk towards the cove.'

Jude scoured the hedgerows and banks, as curious as a wild bird, darting this way and that. In no time, he'd pounced on another patch of humble-looking green plants. It was a very 'mindful' experience, immersing yourself in the natural environment, focused only on the best plant. She could see why he enjoyed spending so much of his time doing it.

'Aha!' he declared, as if he'd found a nugget of gold. 'Here we go. *Beta vulgaris subspecies maritima*.' He cut the base of the emerald green plant and offered out the shiny clump of leaves to her. 'This is exactly like chard or the perpetual spinach you can grow in the garden. You can eat it raw, but I think it will be much nicer with our main course.'

Her stomach rumbled as she examined the leaves. She wished she'd had more than a slice of toast as all this talk of food was making her hungry. 'Um. It looks delicious and very healthy, but won't we need something more substantial for a meal?'

'Yes. That's why we're going down to the cove. Eventually.'

As they walked further up the cliff, Jude homed in on plants nestled in the hedgerow or behind bushes and beckoned her over to crouch next to him. She might still be young, but years of slouching on the sofa with a laptop balanced on her knees hadn't helped her flexibility. Her thighs were killing her and it was all she could do not to utter a granny-ish 'ohhh' as she got up and down.

'Wow. I can see that foraging keeps you fit,' she said.

'It's healthy in all kinds of ways. You're out in the fresh air, away from a screen, you can end up walking miles and, as you've seen, it's better than a gym workout. What's more, the food you get at the end of it is healthy and fresh and hasn't spent days or even months in transit.'

'Healthy unless you pick the wrong kind of mushroom, of course.'

'True.' Jude grinned. 'Come on, autumn is fantastic for finding fungi. I'll show you some of the best types. In fact, they're going to form a major part of the dish I'll cook you.'

By the time she'd reached the top of the hill, Scarlett was puffing hard. She could see the castle on St Michael's Mount to the west, the wavelets lapping at the base of the island. To the east, the pastel cottages of Porthmellow tumbled down the hillside, fishing boats crowding its double harbour.

Jude had stopped at the top to let her catch up.

'I think we can take a short cut to the cove, if we're careful,' he said. 'There's a narrow path down the side of the cliff. It might be a bit steep in places but it's safe enough.'

Deciding to trust him, she followed through the gorse, pushing aside the scratchy branches until halfway down to the beach the path seemed to peter out completely. She had no shame at all in accepting a helping hand to clamber down an almost sheer ten-foot drop to the beach and let out a breath of relief when her boots sank into the shingle of the cove. From there it was a thigh-busting, lung-sapping scramble over the shingle and onto the beach proper. The tide was out, exposing silvery sand glistening in the pale autumn sun. An oystercatcher pecked around the tideline with its bright orange beak.

He slipped the backpack from his shoulders and rested it against a rock. He took out a deep metal pot and a bottle of wine, which he popped into a rock pool to chill.

She brushed sand from her hands. 'I love it here,' Scarlett said. 'No wonder Auntie Joan never moved.'

'She said that Cornwall was in her blood. You can definitely tell that from her books.'

'You read her romantic fiction?'

He frowned. 'Are you surprised?'

'No. OK, yes. Her readers were mainly female and some people do like to dismiss that kind of book as trashy.'

'I loved her descriptions of the landscape and enjoyed spotting places I like in the books. They were addictive too. I always wanted to know what would happen.' A smile lifted his mouth. 'Though I can't say that I've ever met anyone like some of her heroes. Not in Porthmellow, anyway.' His eyes twinkled with amusement.

'No, but I suppose she must have based them on someone, even if they were an idealised version of people from real life. Although I'm not sure I'd like to meet some of her heroes either. Dirk Masterson is one that springs to mind, and the Wicked Earl of Trewarren. I'd have probably had to give both

106

of them a punch on the nose, no matter how broodingly handsome and tormented they were.'

Jude laughed. 'They're certainly a lot to live up to.'

'I'd rather you didn't try,' she said emphatically.

He wiped his forehead with his palm. 'Phew. Good. I don't suppose they made their heroines pick their own lunch from the hedgerow either. Come on, let's collect some mussels.' His confident tone slipped. 'Unless you're allergic to seafood?'

'No. I tend to see food, and I eat it.'

'Ho ho,' Jude said.

'Sorry. Terrible, terrible joke.'

'It is. But at least it means you're going to love my mussels.'

Scarlett managed to keep her response to herself. Gosh, she was doing well today.

Jude showed her the best places to find the shellfish and soon they'd filled his pan with gleaming purple-black shells. They took them to the backpack and he pulled out a portable gas ring, small chopping board and knife, and plastic bowls. Scarlett laid them on a flat rock that was perfect for a table.

'It's like Mary Poppins' carpetbag,' she said as he dug out a pot of double cream and added it to the other ingredients.

First of all, he cleaned, sliced and fried the mushrooms with some of the herbs and tipped them into two bowls, with a splash of wine and cream. Scarlett helped him wash and check the mussels, making sure they were all tightly closed. Then he popped them into the pan along with the wine and put the lid on. Soon they were bubbling away. He poured the rest of the wine into their glasses.

Scarlett tucked in, admittedly a little warily at first . . . How long did it take for the effects of mushroom poisoning to kick in? The wine helped though, and soon she and Jude were laughing and learning a lot more about each other.

'Have you always lived in Porthmellow?' she asked.

'Yes, my whole life. My parents still live just outside the village in the Granary.'

'Not sure I know it.'

'It's tucked away up on the hill. They used to have a restaurant in St Ives, but they've always lived here. They're semi-retired now and have a street-food business, selling fresh seafood. You'll see them at the Solstice Festival.'

So, the Penberths were Porthmellow stalwarts too. If they were friendly with Joan, maybe they'd met her mother in the eighties too and might know who she'd hung around with. Not that Scarlett could possibly think of a way of bringing the subject up at this precise moment. 'Did you get your love of food from them?' she asked. The smell of the seafood was driving her mad.

'Partly, but I was more fascinated by where the food came from. Mum said I should have had webbed feet, I spent so much time in the sea or rock pooling. I used to bring all kinds of creatures home in a bucket.'

Scarlett pictured him as a small blond boy, knee deep in a pool with a bucket and net.

He lifted the lid off the pot. Scarlett's stomach rumbled loudly.

'Sorry,' she said.

'Nothing wrong with working up a good appetite. Luckily

I think the mussels are ready. We'll just wilt the leaves on top of the pot.' He added the sea beet, Alexanders and plantain, let them wilt for a minute and then opened the bubbling pot. The smell was divine: fishy, herby, winey. Scarlett was positively drooling. She helped him transfer the shellfish into their bowls, discarding any that hadn't opened. Finally, Jude produced his final surprise from the backpack – a small crusty baguette from the Porthmellow Bakery.

Scarlett perched on a smooth rock, with her bowl balanced on her knees, dipping the bread into the delicious broth.

'The mussels were to die for. I've never had anything so fresh and tangy.' She wiped the last of the juice from her plate with a piece of bread.

Jude gave a smile of quiet pride. 'Glad you like them. This is one of the best places for them on the whole coast. One of my first memories is of coming down here with my dad and your auntie Joan once. I must only have been around four or five but I remember your mum was staying too.'

Scarlett almost choked on a crust. 'Oh. R-really?' she croaked, when she'd finally swallowed the bread.

'Yes. Obviously, I was only tiny but I do remember it was a hot day and I was paddling around the rock pools. Joan had given me a new fishing net and I was so excited . . .'

'Was my dad there too?' she asked, nibbling a piece of bread.

'I don't remember him being there but like I say, I was very young.'

'Dad was probably working abroad. He was a civil engineer until he retired and he often had to go on foreign trips,' Scarlett said, admiring Jude while they talked. He was one of those Peter Pan types who probably never aged. Even his outdoor lifestyle hadn't added too many lines to his face yet, but had given him a subtle golden tan.

'I'm afraid at that age the net was more important than the grown-ups, though I could hardly lift it in and out of the pools. Dad helped me find a crab and we looked at it then put it back in the water. I can see it scuttling off now with all its legs.' He smiled. 'That was the day when I realised I wanted to spend my life working with nature. Even then, I knew I could never go off to an office every day like my parents.'

'Oh yes!' Scarlett said enthusiastically. 'I always liked reading and anything to do with words. I drove my parents mad for books, and I talk too much. So if I start going off on random tangents, or talking to myself, you know why.'

He laughed. 'Some people think my obsession with plants and nature is weird.'

'I think it's brilliant. You remind me of Dickon from *The Secret Garden*,' Scarlett blurted out.

'Dickon?'

'The boy with squirrels in his pockets.'

'Right . . .' Jude screwed up his face.

Scarlett coloured but rattled on. 'Yes. They were called Nut and Shell. I know it's probably not the best guide to squirrel conservation but it struck a chord with me.'

Jude laughed. 'I haven't read it, but now I want to.'

'There's an old copy in the house if you want to borrow it. It's a children's book, but it's so beautiful.'

'I think I've seen the film. Why not?'

He sounded genuinely keen. Scarlett unwound even more. Jude didn't think she was weird, then, despite the stuff that often spilled out of her mouth straight from her brain. It must be a good sign if she felt relaxed enough to babble on in front of him.

'I told you I could be random,' she said.

'I like random. I like different and diverse, so be as random as you like. After all, I'm the weirdo who asked a woman he'd only just met to come and pick weeds and dangerous mushrooms.'

'Well, so far I've survived.' Scarlett laughed. Jude was such a change from Rafa or any of the other guys she'd been out with. She felt refreshed when she was with him. She was also intrigued to know more about his relationship with Auntie Joan and surprised that he had – sort of – met her mother.

'Jude. You probably already know some of this but I wanted to tell you that Mum and Dad are going through a bad patch at the moment. That's why I was, um . . . slightly upset in the pub on Christmas Day. I know I said that we'd had a family row and everyone accepted that, but something more happened that I don't want to talk about now. It was partly my fault and the family are still suffering the consequences.' Had she ruined the moment by mentioning the horrible events at the lunch?

'You don't have to say any more. No family is perfect, believe me.' He stood up. 'Least of all mine. I've often wondered how or why my parents are still together. Maybe that happens in most long-term relationships. Who knows what really goes on?' He paused before rubbing his arms. 'Shall we pack up? I don't know about you, but I'm getting cold.'

Scarlett wasn't that cold, but sensed that Jude wanted to put an end to the conversation. She was relieved, too, and vowed to steer clear of any more allusions to the past. Even so, his comments occupied her thoughts as they walked home, sticking to the safer topics of Jude's work and her own. They laughed at the very different subjects of their writing and the atmosphere had lightened by the time the manor house came into view again. Jude was talking about the festival.

'I've been to the summer food festival a couple of times while we stayed with Joan,' Scarlett told him. 'Obviously not this year's though.'

'That was huge. They pulled out all the stops for the tenth anniversary and it was such a success, they decided to try a winter event on solstice eve and combine it with a more traditional Christmas festival.'

'Aaron and Ellie have been talking about it. It sounds different, that's for sure.'

'Oh, it'll be different, if you've never seen a solstice festival before. I often go to the Montol night in Penzance. Obviously, it's a great excuse to party, just like so many pagan festivals, but it's great to see so many people entering into the spirit of things. The costumes are something else.'

'What kind of costumes?' she asked, even more intrigued than before.

'Weird and wonderful ones. Animals, people dressed in "mock formal" – a kind of goth version of formalwear –

devils, green men, folk icons. Porthmellow's version won't be as big as that, but we'll have fire-eaters, jugglers and a parade. All the Christmas lights will be on around the harbour too.'

'I never made it to the Montol festival but I used to love spending Christmas down here . . . Mum and Dad liked to visit the illuminated gardens and grand houses. We used to leave our shopping until the last minute so we could get our gifts in the pannier market in Truro.'

'I've had a stall there a couple of times to promote my books and talks. Um . . . can you surf? The sea's still warm, you know.'

Scarlett burst out laughing. 'I can fall off a surfboard brilliantly.'

Jude laughed softly.

'I used to go bodyboarding with Ellie and Marcus when we were kids, but not lately. I do like swimming though. I went swimming twice a week back in Birmingham, but that was in the local pool. I need to start again or I'll be the size of a house with all this lovely food.'

His eyes sparked with interest. 'You should wild swim.'

She wrinkled her nose, remembering the iron-grey waves breaking onto shingle in the cove. 'At this time of year? It's November. I can't imagine even sticking a toe in!'

'Yes, but the sea is the same temperature in May as now. The water's relatively pleasant. It's the getting out that's trickier, but you can wear a thin wetsuit if you're bothered. There's a Porthmellow wild swimming group I join occasionally, so you could give them a try. They're an eclectic bunch and they meet at least once a week, year-round . . . and then of course they organise the annual Boxing Day dip.'

'I've seen that advertised but, funnily enough, I've never fancied it after all the turkey leftovers,' Scarlett said, picturing herself shivering as she poked a toe in the surf. She'd probably *look* like a plucked turkey.

Jude laughed. 'It's awesome. We get the swim over before lunch then we all head to the pubs to warm up. It's a laugh and it raises money for the Fisherman's Institute too. There were almost a hundred of us last year splashing around off the beach below Clifftop House. Gabe lives there now. Go on, sign up for it. You'll enjoy it.'

'Well, I suppose it has to be better than last Boxing Day,' she said. 'Can I think about it?'

'Of course, but I promise you, it's a lot of fun. You'd love it.'

Hmm. She parked the idea for the time being and they walked on in silence for a short while, all the talk of Christmas plans having thrust her back to the previous year in a disturbing way. After Ellie had brought dry clothes and walked her home from the pub, Scarlett hid in her room while her parents argued. Marcus, Heidi and the boys had kept to the snug and driven off from the manor with hardly a goodbye on Boxing Day morning. Her parents had subsided into stony silence and left the day after too, together – Scarlett could only imagine their journey home – but her father had immediately moved into the spare room and since then they seemed to have lived almost separate lives.

She didn't know what their plans were this year, so perhaps

that's what her mother wanted to talk about: whether she could stay at the manor for Christmas – or longer? It was possible that her mum could move there permanently, if she could afford to keep the place. Both her mum and dad were retired and had pensions but Scarlett didn't know if they could afford to run two households . . . maybe if she and Ellie stayed on and they all contributed it was possible.

Things would be *very* tense with the three of them in the house. Which made Scarlett more determined to give serious thought to finding her own place in Porthmellow.

They'd reached the manor and Jude seemed distracted by something large with a lot of legs that was crawling over the drive. Scarlett debated whether to ask him to the pub – or something – to avoid parting without making arrangements to meet again.

As the beetle he'd been observing scuttled into the bushes, Jude turned his attention back to her. He scuffed the gravel with his boot before meeting her eyes. 'Of course, you don't have to join the swimming club . . . if you want to go wild swimming, I could take you. It's safer than swimming alone, but I'd understand if you preferred to go out with a group first.'

'I'm not sure—' Scarlett started.

'No, of course not. Stupid idea.'

'I want to come swimming but I'm not sure about . . .' *Getting my kit off in front of you, my wobbly bits turning blue with cold . . .* She hated to admit that her body confidence had taken a hit since the break-up with Rafa and that joining a few female mates at the local pool was different to stripping off in front of a fit hunk like Jude. 'I don't have a wetsuit,' she said, limply.

'Oh, that's easily solved. I can find you one from somewhere. I can get a hire suit from the local surf-hire place. They owe me a favour.' His expression brightened, and his enthusiasm infected her.

'I guess if I can wear a wetsuit, it might be OK.'

'I wasn't expecting you to go natural. You'll *love* it, I guarantee it, and I know exactly where I can take you for your first time.'

Scarlett couldn't stem a giggle. 'Well, if you put it like that.'

'Argh!' Jude did a face-palm. 'Jesus, no. I didn't mean it like that. Talk about you spouting random things, what am I like?'

'It's f-fine,' Scarlett said through her laughter. 'I know what you meant.'

'Yeah, well, I wouldn't blame you if you decided to pass, after that comment. We can go down to the main beach, where there are lots of people. But I was thinking of a kind of secret cove I know where it would be just us.'

She raised her eyebrows.

'I'm digging an even deeper hole, aren't I? Look, let's set a date and you can decide where. I'll bring a wetsuit. I think I can guess your size.'

'Really?' She cringed.

'Yes.' His face fell again. 'Argh. I'd better get out of here before I really drop myself in it. I'll call you with the details.'

'Thanks for the lunch,' she said, still stifling laughter.

'You're welcome,' Jude called, and then he hot-footed it in the direction of the coastal path back to Porthmellow.

Scarlett went inside, but watched him from the safety of her room for a while, his head emerging now and again above the hedges on his way to the cliff top before disappearing again. She couldn't stop grinning at his unintentionally funny comments. It made a change for someone else to put their foot in it. More deliciously, she had a glow that had been missing for a long time after being in his company. Jude was gorgeous and intriguing, and she didn't the least mind the sound of heading to a 'secret' beach with him. It seemed like the perfect opportunity to get to know more about him and his family – even if she did have to take the plunge into cold water to do it.

# Chapter Eight

Ellie flipped over her desk calendar, marvelling at how fast the first week of the month, and the whole turbulent year, had raced by. She was alone in the front office of the sailing trust, sorting out some admin, when Aaron walked in off the harbour front. Immediately, her mood leapt, and it was impossible to stop herself from grinning like an idiot.

He slid her car keys over the desk with a smile. 'Well, Ms Latham. I'm pleased to report that your car has passed its MOT.'

She blew out a breath. 'Thank you, Mr Carman. I call that bloody amazing.'

'You still doubt my skill with a spanner?' He turned down the corners of his mouth, making Ellie suppress a laugh.

'No, not at all. I just thought the patient was terminal, but you've obviously worked a miracle, otherwise there's no way it would have got through. Now, how much do I owe you?'

'Nothing.'

She shook her head. 'I can't have that. I pay my way.'

'OK. I can show you the invoice for the parts, though I got them at cost. The labour is free.'

'Come on, you've spent hours of your time on that rust bucket of mine.'

'OK, if you really insist on paying me, how about a bit of bartering?'

Aaron leant on the counter. He had a very cheeky glint in his eye. Even though she was on her own, she lowered her voice. 'Bartering? What with?'

'What about dinner?'

'You want me to cook you dinner?'

'Not really, but you keep insisting that you want to repay me somehow. It was only an idea.'

'It's a good idea,' she said, realising with a nervous thrill that she was being asked out on a date, albeit one where she had to cook.

Aaron became more serious. 'Look. Let's not dance around the issue, I'd love to see more of you so why don't you come over to Cove Cottage for dinner? Honestly, you don't have to cook. I'm not up to professional standards but I can rustle up some grub.'

'Hmm,' Ellie sighed and rubbed her chin. 'I tell you what, as we're grown-ups. Why don't we go halves? You provide the main course and I'll bring dessert and the wine.'

'You drive a hard bargain. Shall we try for next week sometime?'

Aaron left the office, whistling some jaunty tune. Ellie had trouble concentrating on her work for the rest of the day, she was too busy wondering where the dinner might lead. She had known Aaron for almost a month now and they'd spent many hours in each other's company without anything going beyond a look or accidental touch.

When she got home, she confessed to jitters about the date to Scarlett while her sister rustled up a stir-fry.

'I obviously said yes, of course, but I keep thinking, you know . . . gorgeous lovely guy moves next door and is immediately attracted to you? It all seems too good to be true.'

'Oh, Ellie, that's how people meet. Randomly. Auntie Joan always said that her books weren't about happy endings but happy beginnings. Two adults can meet and have a great life together, you know. It happens.' Scarlett broke off to tip the chicken and noodles onto plates. 'Even if our parents are having a hard time . . .' Scarlett's words faded and she was silent for a while but Ellie could imagine the cogs of her sister's mind turning.

At this early stage, Ellie mused, it might be crazy to think about settling down with someone, long-term commitment, a family even, but she'd grown to think that Porthmellow could be her forever home – and what a great place it would be to bring up children. She didn't need a partner to do that, of course, but Aaron was kind and principled and seemed as if he might make a good father.

Damn. What was wrong with her? She hadn't even kissed him, let alone got onto any of the stuff that might lead to making babies.

Laughing at her leaps of imagination, she carried their trays into the sitting room to have dinner in front of the fire.

Ellie was starving so she dived in straightaway, but Scarlett's fork hovered over her plate. 'This may sound like a funny question,' she said, 'but do you know much about Jude Penberth?'

Ellie was mid-mouthful so had a few seconds to consider the question. 'Not loads . . . why do you ask?'

'No reason in particular, only he mentioned that he used to come to the house and see Auntie Joan from time to time.'

'I knew that. Joan liked him because he shared her love of nature. I think she knew the family pretty well, but then that's no surprise as they've all lived in the area for donkey's years. Everyone knows everyone round here.'

'Yes, I suppose so,' Scarlett mused. 'I had the impression that his dad knew Joan well, and Jude was talking about Mum, too. Apparently, she was down here for a visit when he was a little boy. He didn't say you and Marcus were here, or Dad.'

'When was this?' Ellie asked.

'Jude says he was about four years old, so I think you would have been around five and Marcus must have been a baby.'

Ellie was intrigued. 'Maybe Dad was looking after us,' she said, then kicked herself when she realised where the conversation might be heading.

'Jude didn't give any details because he was way too young to be interested in what the grown-ups were doing but he *did* remember Mum being here.'

'And?' Ellie asked, now convinced that Scarlett's brain had been working overtime.

'I had been wondering if my dad – my biological father – might be from around here.'

Ellie's antennae twitched. This was a new tack from Scarlett. Where had it come from? She suspected it had to be linked to what Jude had told her. 'What makes you think that, lovely?'

Scarlett shrugged. 'It's probably me putting two and two together and making a hundred. It's only something Mum said, during one of our heated conversations about the DNA test. It doesn't mean anything on its own, but then I remembered something I found when we were sorting out Auntie Joan's books and other stuff. I didn't take too much notice at the time, but added to what Mum said . . .'

Ellie gave her some space, although her stomach had tightened. 'What did she say?'

'That Dad wasn't blameless in the whole thing and he should look at his own conscience. Trouble was, she didn't say why he was to blame, or what he should be guilty about. She clammed up and told me I was reading too much into her words.'

'OK. That could have meant anything,' Ellie said, abandoning all hope of eating her food while it was even lukewarm.

'It could, but then I remembered the *book*.'

'What book?'

'*Treasures of the Cornish Seashore*.'

'Um . . . You've lost me now.'

'It was in the alcove in my room – I mean, Joan's room – and it had a postcard between the pages,' Scarlett explained carefully, as if Ellie was a toddler. 'I've looked for it all over the room but I can't find it.'

'Maybe Mum took it? If it meant something to her. What did this card say?'

'I can't remember the exact words. Something about a special night . . .'

Ellie's eyes sparked with interest. 'Who was it from?'

'I don't know. It had her name on it and there were initials scrawled at the bottom. An M or possibly an H. Like I say, I can't remember every single word.'

'So, it could have been any number of people,' Ellie said gently, slightly worried that Scarlett was fixated on this post-card as if it was a vital clue in a murder mystery. She'd be interrogating her mother or the locals about it next when the card could be completely innocent and from anyone.

'Maybe.' Scarlett scooped up a forkful of noodles. 'You could be right. I'm probably reading far too much into random stuff. Come on, let's stop going on about it and eat our dinner before it goes cold.'

Ellie bit back a caustic reply and returned to her food, wondering if she could bear to eat it cold or if she should warm it up in the microwave. The day, which had started so promisingly with her chat with Aaron, had ended on a disturbing note. With their mother's visit only a few days away, Ellie sensed trouble brewing.

Scarlett was now flicking through the TV channels while finishing her dinner, but Ellie wasn't fooled. If there was one thing she knew about Scarlett, it was that once she had her teeth into something, nothing would stand in her way.

# Chapter Nine

'So, what do you think about this headline for my client's new brochure on the Jumbo fastener?' Scarlett asked, wandering into the kitchen where Ellie was opening and shutting drawers like a madwoman. 'It's the biggest one they've ever produced.'

Scarlett's swimming trip with Jude and hunt for the book had been put on hold as she'd been chained to the laptop for most of the past week, working on a suite of literature for her new Exeter-based customer, Eurofasteners.

'Hmm? Where are my bloody keys?' Ellie exclaimed, rooting through the cutlery drawer with one hand and holding a piece of toast in the other.

'In the dish on the hall table?' Scarlett suggested.

'That's where they *should* be.'

'I might have an idea,' Scarlett said. '*If* you give me your opinion on this headline.'

Ellie swung round, crust in hand. 'OK, shoot. Anything to find my keys.'

'Are you ready?'

'Yes!'

Scarlett read from the brochure design on her iPad: 'Jumbo Fastener: the massive screw you've been looking for!'

Ellie was stunned into silence, then she burst out laughing. 'It's brilliant, but you can't use that.'

'I don't see why not.'

'Scarlett. If you get that past the client, I'll eat Troy Carman's cap.' Ellie had tears of laughter in her eyes. 'Now, where are my keys?'

Scarlett sniggered, delighted to have got the reaction she wanted from Ellie. 'I think I saw them on the coffee table in the sitting room. I'll find them.'

She scooted off in search of the keys and took them back to Ellie in the kitchen.

'Thanks, lovely. And you've reminded me. Zennor Lovell popped in the café yesterday afternoon for a vegan tray bake. She asked me if you had "any spare copywriting capacity". She and Ben have been asked to quote to design a surf shop website.'

'Surf shop? God, I would *love* to work on a campaign like that.'

'Great. Can you call her asap? I got the impression it was urgent.'

'Sure. I kept meaning to make contact with them anyway,' Scarlett said, remembering Jude's encouragement in the pub. 'But I've been embroiled in sorting out other customers. I'll call her straight after breakfast.'

'Cool . . .' Ellie gave her a hard look. 'Are you sure you're

125

OK here on your own all day? It's a big change, running a business from an isolated place like this.'

'It's fine. I'll manage. I'm busy with this fasteners brochure today and if I can get this surf job, I'll be building up some good business.'

'OK. Be careful if you do go into town. It's a spring tide and some big waves are blowing up. Don't go down on the breakwater!'

'Yes, Auntie Ellie,' Scarlett said meekly, then ducked to avoid a toast crust that went whizzing past her ear.

As soon as Ellie had left, Scarlett called Zennor and arranged to go into Porthmellow to their studio, ZenBen Designs.

Scarlett took her coffee mug back inside the study. She called her father and asked him how he felt about her mother coming to Seaholly for a break, but he cut the conversation short, saying 'she must do as she thinks best'. Scarlett's optimistic mood took a nosedive. The conversation was typical of their interactions since Christmas. Her dad had never been effusive but she'd always loved their talks in his shed about his latest project, or history, or books. She'd felt his love as an unseen but strong foundation underpinning her whole existence.

Now, she was sure a crack had opened in their relationship and hated to face up to the possibility that those foundations had finally been shaken by the knowledge that she wasn't actually his child.

She hadn't been able to tell if he was upset or relieved that Anna was going away, and maybe that was another sign that she didn't know him as instinctively as she once had.

After wiping away a few tears, she pulled herself together and drove down the hill towards Porthmellow, trying to focus on the inspiring surroundings. The pretty pastel cottages and colourful harbour cheered her a little and reminded her how lucky she was to live in such a beautiful place. Even the waves crashing over the breakwater seemed exhilarating and the rain lashing the windscreen was almost romantic. After all, she could never have worked for a surf shop in Birmingham.

She parked behind the harbour and had to hold tightly onto the car door to stop it slamming against the vehicle next to her, and the ticket was nearly torn from her hands. She had to pull her hat down over her ears and could feel the wind tugging at the pompom.

The studio, in a side street behind the harbour, had once been an old petrol station and the lone pump still stood outside, now restored by Ben, according to Zennor. The two of them seemed to be impressed by Scarlett's portfolio, so they went on to discuss the surf shop website. She left with some roughs of the design and promised to send a quote for the job by the end of the day. She soon realised that she couldn't charge them as much as she had her city centre clients, but it was still a job well worth having and a lot more exciting than industrial fasteners.

As she made her way from the studio, she saw that huge wooden sleepers had been fixed across the entrance to the inner harbour where dozens of fishing vessels and yachts were packed like colourful sardines. The outer harbour, usually full of craft, was empty, and no wonder. The swell was massive, with waves slapping against the walls and crashing over the end of the stone breakwater where a yellow sign had been chained to a groyne, saying: *Breakwater closed. Danger of death in breaking seas.*

Ellie hadn't been exaggerating then.

Scarlett sank her chin down into the funnel neck of her coat. Rain tinged with salt spray stung her face. She wished she'd brought her gloves, because even in the short distance from the car park to the design agency, her hands had become wet and cold. Fishermen in yellow waterproofs were working on their boats, while a few locals scurried in and out of the harbour-front shops and cafés.

She'd just passed Gabe's restaurant when the leaden skies opened and unleashed a cloudburst. Driven by the gale, the rain soon soaked her coat and hat. She broke into a jog, her boots slipping on the cobbles. She wished she'd brought her waterproof, but she'd wanted to look a bit more stylish for her meeting.

'Scarlett!'

A door opened behind her and she skidded to a halt. 'Do you want to come in?' Jude called from the doorstep.

Scarlett didn't need asking twice and she dashed back to the blue cottage.

'Quick,' he said, and she almost fell inside.

She was breathing heavily from her dash around the harbour but it was the sight of Jude, barefoot, in jeans and a thin sweater, that really took her breath away. His hair was already damp and his sweater clinging to his chest, simply from calling to her from the doorstep of the cottage.

'Thanks. I'm so wet!' she said, then instantly felt her cheeks grow hot. 'I mean, I'm dripping all over your floor.'

Jude laughed. 'Take your coat off. I'll put it to dry in the kitchen.'

Scarlett handed the soggy coat over and went into the sitting room. Its uneven, whitewashed walls and the instant cocoon of heat from the fire reminded her of the Smuggler's Tavern. She'd felt the warmth envelop her that day too, not simply the heat of the room but the welcome she'd been given. It was hard to believe it was almost a year ago.

Jude came back in, raindrops twinkling in his hair. Scarlett licked her lip and tasted salt. She was trying not to stare at his tanned feet. They were nicely shaped for a man, and he wore a pewter toe ring.

'Coffee? Something different?' he asked.

She dragged her eyes away from his feet before he thought she was a pervert. 'Sorry?'

'I'm asking if you'd like coffee or something a bit different?'

'How different?'

'Pine-needle tea?' he said.

'Pine needles?' Spotting the glint in his eye, she pointed a finger at him and winked. 'You're winding me up. There's no such thing as pine-needle tea, unless you're a hobbit, I guess.' Or an actual elf, she thought.

'Maybe I am.' He smiled. 'Wait and see. I'll make some, but don't feel obliged to drink it. Why don't you warm up in front of the fire?'

Scarlett toasted her chilled hands while Jude was busy in the kitchen. She took the chance to peek around his home. The cottage was tiny, almost like a doll's house with its pastel exterior and diminutive front room, but also cosy and stylish

129

with rugs on the scrubbed boards, a slate hearth and modern furniture. The alcoves either side of the hearth were lined with books and there was also a delicious aroma coming from the kitchen.

Scarlett heard the kettle boiling and ventured over to the bookcase. There were a few family photographs on a little table by the hearth. She picked up one of Jude with two older people who were obviously his parents. You couldn't mistake his father: a middle-aged, bulkier but still handsome version of Jude. His mother was slight, but had her son's fair hair and fine features. A pang of regret and, yes, envy struck her. Jude knew for sure these people were his flesh and blood, whereas she had only half her story.

'Hello.'

Startled, the frame almost slipped through her fingers. 'Oh!' She managed to rescue the picture and gripped it tightly.

'I'm sorry. I made you jump.' Jude had a tray laden with two mugs and a plate of biscuits.

She reddened with guilt. 'I hope you don't mind me looking at the photo of you and your parents.'

'Course not.'

'Is it recent?'

'Couple of years ago. Mum's fifty-fifth birthday. It was taken down in Seaholly Cove, actually. We'd called in on your auntie Joan on the way. She wasn't too well, even then.'

'Poor Joan.' Scarlett replaced the picture on its table, feeling melancholy.

'I'm sorry if I've upset you.'

'You haven't. I loved Auntie Joan and I miss her, that's all . . .'

He put the tray on the table. 'I think I have an older photo of her, if you'd like to see it.'

'I'd love to.'

'Hold on.' He went to the dresser and opened the cupboard. He pulled out a small photo album and sat next to her on the sofa. 'Old school,' he said with a grin, turning the plastic pockets of the album, each of which held a print. Scarlett would have been happy to look at all the photos, but he flicked the pages too quickly and about two thirds through, settled on one.

He pushed the album across to her lap. 'There you go.'

Scarlett felt she'd leapt into the past. She was choked with emotion. Auntie Joan, over thirty years before, a striking woman in her fifties; Hayden Penberth looking handsome and chiselled and not unlike how she imagined Dirk Masterson, Joan's eighties hero. He had his arm around Jude's mum, who was wearing a strappy dress and floppy hat. She was holding Jude's hand while he clutched a fishing net in the other. He squinted into the sun, a cheesy grin on his face, the light shining on his pale mop of hair like a halo.

Next to Mrs Penberth stood Scarlett's mother, smiling, a stripy beach bag at her sandalled feet. Obviously, Scarlett had seen old photos of her mum before, but in this one, she looked like a French film star, blonde and slender in denim shorts and a white bikini top. She'd regained her figure despite having Ellie and Marcus.

'Who took it?' she asked.

'Dad was into photography and he was always using the timer for family photos, or to take pictures of me and him on our walks. No selfies then.' He smiled. 'I only have hazy memories of the day.' He peered at the picture again. 'God, look at my hair!'

'You look very cute. And the, er – trunks are funky. Postman Pat?'

He tried to grab the album, but Scarlett kept hold of it, so he shrugged. 'I was only five or six. Postman Pat was cool then.'

She giggled. 'I'll take your word for it.'

He pulled a face.

'It's a lovely photo and it's nice to see Auntie Joan. Thanks.' She laid the album on the coffee table. 'Is this the tea?'

'Yes. Try some. It's an acquired taste but it's warm and wet.'

She blew the steam from the pale-yellow liquid and sipped, trying not to think of what it reminded her of. Hmm. Well, it was different, a little like green tea but with an herbal tang.

He smiled. 'I won't be offended if you don't like it.' He pushed the plate towards her. 'Have a biscuit. They're Cornish fairings, and go well with the tea – or take the taste away.'

She sipped again and smiled politely. 'Thanks. Did you make them?'

'No, they're from the village bakery. They do it so much better than I would. I do enjoy cooking though. It's great to see people's faces when you show them just what can be done with a few "weeds".'

Scarlett was amused because Jude could have been talking about her. She sipped some more tea, wondering how much she needed to get down her for politeness' sake, and followed it up with a large crunch of spicy fairing.

He seemed to be enjoying his own tea far more than she was and while she nibbled away, he asked her: 'I was wondering . . . tell me if this is cheeky, but if you don't have other plans, would you like to help me on my stall at the Solstice Festival?'

She almost spluttered biscuit crumbs over herself. '*Me*?'

'If you're busy or don't fancy standing out in the cold – and possibly a howling gale – for hours, then I'd understand.'

He was so earnest, she almost laughed out loud. 'Wow. You're doing a great job of selling the idea.'

He winced. 'I can see that.'

Scarlett had to hide a giggle again. So quietly confident one moment, Jude did dig himself into a hole from time to time. She liked his self-deprecation, which was in stark contrast to Rafa, who'd never betrayed a chink of vulnerability unless it suited him. Then again, that was the world she used to inhabit, where appearances and spin were everything. It was a side of the business she'd never felt comfortable with.

'If you think I won't get in the way, of course I'd love to help you on the stall. I ought to check with Ellie first in case she might have been thinking of asking me but, to be honest, I think she's going to be with her workmates from the sailing trust.'

'OK. It'll be great to have some company. It can be lonely and boring standing behind the stall on my own. I'm fine leading foraging trips or teaching my students, but flogging my wares is way out of my comfort zone.'

'Well, obviously I'm in my element selling other people's products in print, but I'm not a natural when it comes to speaking to the public. I cringe when I have to tout for business or set prices, even after so many years working for myself. I've had to toughen up, but it doesn't come naturally.'

'Then we can cringe together and if it all gets too horrific, we can slope off to the pub – which is what I had to do after one event when I'd had precisely three pensioners and a Labrador all evening.'

'I'm sure that we'll get more than a Labrador. OK, it's a deal.'

'Before that, do you want to arrange a time for a swim? Obviously not in this storm, but I'll keep an eye out on the forecast for some calmer conditions later this week?'

'That would be lovely.' Scarlett put her mug down, rather proud she'd managed half the contents. 'I ought to be getting back to the manor to do some work. Time's running out on the car park too.'

'You don't want Foxy Seddon after you. She's the traffic warden from hell.'

'Ellie warned me she's a demon now she's back from maternity leave.'

Jude stood up but before Scarlett could move, there was a knock at the door followed by a sharp rap on the window. A man and a woman appeared through the glass, both in waxed jackets.

'Oy! Let us in, son!' the man shouted, knocking on the glass again.

He got up. 'It's Mum and Dad. I didn't know they were coming.'

'I'll go then,' Scarlett said, torn between wanting to get

away and curious to meet the man from the photos, and his wife.

Jude let them into the sitting room before she could get away.

'This is a surprise,' said Jude. 'This is my mum and dad, Fiona and Hayden.' There was a taut edge to his voice and Scarlett felt that a coolness had blown into the cottage along with the Penberths. 'This is Scarlett Latham, Joan's great-niece,' he said.

Scarlett needed no introduction to recognise Hayden. He was, she supposed, still handsome, with his tan and thick grey hair. If you were sixty, that was. Fiona had changed her hair colour from the beach photo, but had the same warm smile for Jude.

'I've heard so much about you and I've seen you around town,' Hayden said. 'You're every bit as gorgeous as your namesake.'

Scarlett frowned. 'My namesake?'

'Scarlett O'Hara. *Gone with the Wind*. A true femme fatale.'

For a second Scarlett actually thought he might lift her hand and kiss it, which filled her with horror.

Fiona Penberth rolled her eyes. 'Pack it in, Hayden. You're embarrassing them.'

'Course I'm not. No woman minds being compared to Scarlett O'Hara, now do they?'

'Nice to meet you,' Fiona said. 'Ignore my husband. I do.'

Though eager to get away, Scarlett smiled. 'It's lovely to meet you both. I'm sorry I have to rush off.'

'Oh dear, something we did?' Hayden pouted. 'Well, I hope

135

this isn't the last time we'll see you. Jude says you've moved in to the manor, I hope we bump into each other a lot more. If Jude has his way, I'm sure we will.'

'Hayden, don't,' Fiona chided.

He held up his palms. 'Just my little joke.'

'Well, I don't see anyone laughing,' she said acidly.

Scarlett was now desperate to escape. 'Would you mind getting my coat, please?' she said to Jude, hardly able to hide the plea in her voice.

'Of course. You wait here while I see Scarlett out,' Jude told his parents firmly.

With a hurried 'bye,' Scarlett escaped to the hallway and seconds later Jude brought her coat from the kitchen. 'It's a little drier than it was. I had it hanging over a chair.'

She pulled it on while he lingered by the door. She wanted to get away from Hayden, but not from Jude. On the doorstep, he whispered, 'Sorry about Dad. He thinks he's being funny.'

'Don't worry. It seems to be a parent's job to embarrass their kids.'

Jude nodded. 'That's one job Dad excels at. I'll message you about the swim.'

'Great. Thanks for the tea and biscuits. See you soon.'

A moment later Scarlett was back in the deluge. Pulling up her hood, she jogged back to the car park, getting even wetter in the process but deciding it was far better than being stuck in the middle of a Penberth family dispute. Poor Jude, having to deal with his dad's cheesy comments and his mum's obvious disdain.

She set off for home, wipers swishing furiously to try and clear away the lashing rain. Twigs and leaves littered the road, and on the track down to Seaholly she had to stop and remove a branch from the road. Once safely inside, she texted Ellie to warn her to watch out for debris and to say her meeting at the design company had gone well.

She took some buttered crumpets back to the study for a working lunch and made a start on an article for an industrial journal about the merits of the Jumbo Screw. With the wind whistling around the eaves and the sea grumbling in the cove, it was hard to focus. Her unscheduled visit to Jude kept coming back to her. It had been lovely until his parents – specifically his father – had arrived. Jude was relaxed and warm until then, and it had been worth enduring the pine-needle tea to spend more time with him.

Once Hayden and Fiona had arrived, the atmosphere had definitely soured. Then again, maybe she was being too harsh on his dad.

## Chapter Ten

While Scarlett went into town to stock up for their mum's arrival later in the day, Ellie decided to sod cleaning the manor and call in on Aaron. She intended to pay him cash for the extra parts he'd had to buy for the car to get it through its MOT, and had the notes in an envelope in her jacket. She was also acutely aware that as yet they hadn't set a firm date for the dinner she owed him and this seemed like the perfect opportunity.

She found him chopping wood for the fire in the woodshed next to the cottage. Judging by the pile of neatly stacked logs, he'd been working hard, and despite the cool morning was stripped down to a khaki T-shirt that looked to be army-issue. She allowed herself a few moments to luxuriate in the sight of him splitting the wood, before she announced her presence.

'Hi there. Looks like hard work.'

He turned, the axe still in his hands, sweat glistening on his muscular forearms. He was a very fit guy, she thought, as desire stirred powerfully in her body. Something had to happen between them sooner or later. Maybe he was waiting for her to make the first move. She hadn't been shy in years gone by on her travels – so why hadn't she moved things forward? Was it because, she dared to whisper to herself, she knew that this time – this man – was different? More serious, and if she took the plunge, it would be much harder and more painful to get over?

'It has to be done. I've run out of logs.'

Ellie walked through the dust motes eddying in the sunbeams penetrating the shed walls, inhaling the scent of freshly cut wood. She was transfixed by the sight of him and powerfully aware of a switch flicking inside her. There could be no going back.

He frowned, mistaking her fascination for something else. 'Something wrong?' he said, his deep voice resonating in the small space.

'There's sawdust in your hair and on your face.'

He hesitated only a moment before laying the axe on the ground. 'What are you going to do about it, then?'

'What am *I* going to do?'

'Yeah, Ellie. You.'

So he had been waiting for her. She didn't want to wait any longer for herself.

She reached up to his hair and brushed the dust off his close-cropped curls.

Fluidly, the next moment, his hand was on her back, gently nudging her against his body. She slipped her arms around him, her fingers resting between his shoulder blades and lower back. She felt the heat of his skin beneath his T-shirt. The scent of the freshly cut wood mingled with the dust and his masculine scent, filling her senses.

She wasn't sure who kissed who, but the kiss was long, lingering, hot and sweet.

'Wow. That was unexpected,' he whispered, still holding her.

'Not that unexpected,' she said, feeling liberated. 'I couldn't wait until our dinner . . . but I wanted to talk to you too, before then.'

'Sounds serious.'

'Neither of us may be here – in Porthmellow – for long. Or at least, we can't say. You've said you need to see how the business goes and, let's face it, you're a nomad like me.'

His smile faded. 'Are you trying to tell me you have plans to leave already? If you do, I'd rather know.'

'I don't have plans as such, but Mum's coming down here later today and says she wants to talk. For all I know, it could very well be about selling the manor.' Ellie let go of him but stayed close. Her words were a warning to herself; she mustn't start to think about putting down roots, especially with Aaron, when the future was so uncertain.

'I'm more than prepared for change and uncertainty. That's been my whole life in the forces. I'd like to stick around here too, especially as my own parents aren't getting any younger and I like being closer to my sister and her family too – but it'll depend on the business.' He hesitated before continuing with studied casualness. 'Do you have plans to travel again if your parents do sell?'

140

'I don't have firm plans about anything.' *Except I want to sleep with you*, she thought, a current of desire jolting her with such force it scared her. 'I – well, I don't want to give either of us any expectations.' She was trying to convince herself as much as anything, after her recent thoughts about her future.

He held her again. 'The only expectation I have is of kissing you again and enjoying it more than any kiss for a very long time.'

'Have you done a lot of kissing lately, then?' she asked lightly, terrified of how much his answer mattered. Until now she hadn't really thought there might be someone else, and she would never ever get involved with someone who was committed elsewhere. Not after Mallory.

'Not really. I wouldn't say I fancied snogging any of the squaddies in my unit.' He touched her cheek with his thumb. Every nerve ending zinged with life.

Her phone buzzed.

'Sorry. I have to get this. It's Mum.'

He let her go immediately and nodded. 'Of course. I'll give you some privacy.'

Ellie didn't object. After a brief conversation, she put her phone away.

'Everything OK?' he asked.

'Yes, but I have to go right now. Mum's already at the manor. I'm sorry. I – this isn't an excuse. I do really have to go.'

'That's a shame.'

'It really isn't a cop-out. I would stay . . .'

Aaron rested his hands on her shoulders. 'I believe you. Thousands wouldn't.'

'You . . . you're winding me up?'

'A little.'

He brushed her lips with his. 'Go on, before your mother suspects what you've been up to.'

'Hmm. She might be able to tell by my face. Parents are adept at putting two and two together.'

'In this case, they'd be right.'

Hiding a blush, Ellie reluctantly broke contact with him. Her skin sang with the memory of him all the way up the path to the manor. She had to stop just out of sight of the house and take a breath. A few seconds to pat down her hair and try to come down to earth, while already knowing that was impossible . . . and what's more, she'd totally forgotten to pay him for the car, which had been her main reason for going to see him in the first place.

'Gosh. You look *very* red in the face, Ellie.'

Anna kissed Ellie on the driveway of Seaholly Manor. Ellie might have replied that her mother looked tired and drawn, but she wouldn't have dreamed of it. Oh dear, she already knew this visit was going to require a lot of tact and careful handling, and not only from Scarlett.

She smiled warmly. 'It's the cold, Mum. I've been down to the cove. Breath of fresh air.'

Her mother gave her an even closer inspection. 'Yes. You look well. It obviously suits you down here.'

'I do like it,' she said, thinking about Aaron's kiss and realising they still hadn't tied down a date for dinner.

'There's something about the place. Invigorates you, changes

142

you . . .' Anna, normally so practical and no-nonsense, glanced around wistfully.

'How are you, Mum? If I dare ask,' Ellie said as gently as she could.

'OK, in the circumstances, I suppose. If you mean how's the situation with your father . . . things are still the same as they have been since New Year. We're living in a kind of limbo, only speaking to each other when it's essential. He's stopped asking me about – you know what.' She glanced at the house. 'Scarlett not here?'

'Soon. She went into town to get some shopping for your visit, and to see some new clients. You might know them? Zennor Lovell and Ben Blazey run a design agency,' she said, trying to break the ice with some general chit-chat.

'Those two goth types? Are they even out of school yet?'

'They're in their mid-twenties and engaged now.'

'Good grief. I'd no idea they were getting married.'

Ellie drew her closer. 'Shall we leave your bags in the car for now? Plenty of time to unpack later. I'll make you a cuppa.'

Their mother nodded. 'Sounds wonderful. I'd forgotten how long it takes to get here.'

Elle smiled to herself. If she had a pound for everyone she'd heard say that in the café or on the boat, she'd be able to buy the manor. She let her mother go into the house ahead of her, reminding herself again that Anna was the owner.

'Is it OK that you're in the smaller room for now? Scarlett has moved into Joan's old bedroom.'

'It's fine.' Her mum looked around the hallway, her keen eyes not missing a detail. 'Are those hydrangeas from the garden?' she asked, walking to the hall table where Scarlett had arranged a vase of the faded blue and pink blooms and added some holly twigs.

'Yes, they're the last though.'

Her mum nodded. 'Shame.'

'Do you know how long you'll be staying?' Ellie asked.

'Not yet. But I won't get under your feet. I want to talk to you.'

'So you said.' Ellie's skin prickled in an unpleasant way.

'I'll wait for Scarlett, if it's OK, so I can get it all over with in one go.'

'Yeah, sure. We'll take things at your pace.' Ellie hugged her mother again, sensing the tension in her slight frame. 'Mum, we both know that things must have been horrendous for you and Dad. Whatever you want to say to us, we're here for you,' she said, wondering if the same was really true for Scarlett. 'You go and chill out in the sitting room and I'll make the tea,' she added.

She made the drinks, wondering what bombshells were about to land in their lives now. It was hard not to feel very apprehensive about what might be coming. If it was about selling the manor, she'd have a hard job hiding her disappointment. She'd settled into life at Seaholly and in Porthmellow far more deeply than she'd realised, especially since the arrival of Aaron had offered new possibilities that she was already pinning far too many hopes on – especially after that kiss. She was becoming like the limpets in the cove, firmly attached to her tiny patch of rock. However, the greater good of the family mattered more.

She'd texted Scarlett before she'd even put the kettle on, hoping that she would be in a calm and tactful mood, at least until their mum had settled in. It would be horrendous if they started off with a row the moment she walked through the door. Ellie added some homemade mince pies to a plate, hoping that a cuppa and bite to eat might give everyone a little while to take stock before any serious discussions took place.

She carried the tray into the sitting room where Anna was standing in the French windows, gazing out over the gardens.

Her face lit up when she saw the tray. 'Oh, what a welcome sight. I'm starving. You always did make wonderful pastry, right from when you were little. Remember I used to let you make all the mince pies and the Christmas cake?'

'I do. I made a massive batch at the café and brought plenty home. They go down a storm warmed up and served with clotted cream.' Ellie's mood relaxed a notch, although the praise made her wistful for a time when things had been 'normal' for the Lathams.

'I bet. You love your jobs, don't you?'

'I never thought I'd be so content in one place, but Porthmellow has seeped into my blood. The people are . . . interesting, but I do like them.' At some point, she would have to let on about Aaron, she thought.

'This place and the people have a way of capturing your heart. Sometimes it's hard to let that go.' Her mother allowed herself a smile then rubbed her hands together. 'Come on then, let's try these pies to see if they're up to your usual standards.'

'Cheek!' Ellie said, batting her arm.

For half an hour there was an easing of the tension while Ellie and her mother caught up on gossip and news from home and Porthmellow. Ellie made a second pot of tea and they'd almost exhausted the subjects of her mum's journey and how Marcus, Heidi and the boys were when she heard Scarlett's car arrive.

Anna put her mug down, an anxious look on her face.

Ellie met Scarlett in the hallway and took the shopping bags from her. 'She's here, then,' Scarlett said.

'Yes. She's in the sitting room. Shall I take the food?'

'I'll help. I need a few minutes to calm down.'

Ellie popped her head around the sitting room door with a reassuring smile for her mother. 'Won't be a mo. Just need to get the fresh food away.'

Scarlett put the milk and butter in the fridge. 'Has she said anything yet?' she whispered.

'Not about Dad. We've only shared the gossip about home so far.'

'Hmmph.' Scarlett leaned back against the worktop.

'She's anxious enough about seeing us, lovely. Please give her a chance.'

Scarlett pouted then nodded. 'OK.'

Mentally crossing her fingers, Ellie followed Scarlett into the sitting room.

Anna stood up and they exchanged kisses. Ellie was now stiff with tension.

'How are you? Was the journey awful?' Scarlett asked, sitting opposite their mother.

Ellie tried to stay calm as Anna briefly told her younger daughter what she'd already told Ellie, however, she knew that the moment when they discussed the elephant in the room couldn't be far off. She went to make Scarlett a hot chocolate and steady her own nerves before she returned to the sitting room.

Their mother was on her feet in front of the fireplace, examining one of Joan's Staffordshire china dogs, which sat like china sentinels on either end of the mantelpiece. No one would have even dreamed of removing them now their aunt was gone; they seemed so very Joan. Was this the moment their mother would break the news that she wanted to sell Seaholly?

'It always seemed a strange thing to me, to have spaniels sitting on your fireplace, but Marcus loved them when he was young. I could never bear to part with them.' Anna re-positioned the dog in its place and turned back to Ellie and Scarlett.

She clenched her hands together.

'Before you react to what I'm going to say, I want you to know that I've thought long and hard about telling you this.'

Ellie glanced at Scarlett, who had a mince pie halfway to her mouth.

'Don't look so terrified, girls.' She smiled at them and Ellie was cast back twenty years to an image of their mother, younger, holding down a job as an art teacher, hosting parties and fundraising for the local hospice, all while bringing up three children.

'Mum?' Scarlett abandoned the pie on the coffee table.

'I think you might have an inkling as to what I'm going to say. That DNA test . . . I may as well tell you that I didn't want to believe it at first. It seemed ridiculous to me, but over the past year, I've had to come to terms with the fact that there might be a *tiny* possibility that . . . that . . . it could be accurate.'

Scarlett stifled a gasp with her hand.

Ellie bit her lip, desperately trying to suppress any sign of shock or negativity. Admitting the test was correct must have been a *huge* hurdle for their mum to get over. She and Scarlett had always accepted that the test was accurate, but hearing their mother finally admit it . . . well, it was like the first moment they'd seen the results all over again.

'Mum? Are you OK?' she said carefully. 'Do you want to sit down?'

'I'm fine. I've rehearsed the words a hundred times but now I'm here, I find that none of them seem right. That test, it must be correct. I was in shock at first, then denial, but there is a chance that your father, well, he might not be your *actual* dad . . .' She looked at Scarlett. 'I'm so sorry, darling. I've let you down and I've allowed you to suffer. I'm sorry.'

Their mother burst into tears.

Scarlett choked back a sob.

Ellie didn't know who to go to first. 'Come on, sit down, Mum.' She ushered her mum to the sofa and sat her down. She passed her a box of tissues.

Scarlett finally looked up, her face white. 'Who is he?'

'I don't know,' her mum replied.

'You must do!'

'I don't.'

'How? *How* can you not know? I don't believe it!'

'Scarlett. Stop it!' Ellie was sharp, but she had to be. 'This is hard for you, but it must be almost impossible for Mum. Give her some time.'

'She's already had time . . .'

Anna wiped her eyes. 'Scarlett, love, I don't blame you for being angry and confused but I can't tell you who he was – is. I genuinely thought it was impossible that you were anyone else's daughter but your father's. I'd almost made myself believe that it – the mistake – never happened. It was only once; a moment of madness, and I'd had a lot to drink. And it couldn't have been *him* . . . it just couldn't.'

'Why did you think it was impossible? Who was he?'

'It was at a party . . .' Her voice hardened. 'Look. I don't want to talk about it and it won't do any good to rake over the details. I can't even remember the exact date now, but I've regretted it every day since. There was no need for anyone to know what had happened, and I was never going to tell any of you because that would only have blown the family apart.'

'It *has* blown the family apart,' Scarlett burst out. 'Don't you think I regret ordering that test every day, too? But you owe it to me to tell me who he was. I know pretty much exactly *when* it happened, that's obvious to anyone. I think I'd remember if I'd had an affair with another man and got pregnant!'

Horrified at the shouting match, Ellie leapt in. 'Scarlett! That's enough. This isn't helping anyone.'

'It's OK, Ellie. You can hardly blame her for being upset,' her mother said.

Scarlett ignored Ellie. 'Why didn't you admit the test was right at Christmas? Save us all a lot of misery. And what about Dad? What does he have to say about it?'

'He doesn't know yet. I thought I owed it to you to tell you first, especially you, my love.' Her eyes threw a plea to Scarlett.

Ellie was shaking with shock herself, but had to take charge or this situation would get even worse, and words would be flung that could never be taken back.

She reached out to touch Scarlett's hand, but Scarlett snatched it away. Ellie felt sick. This was even worse than she'd imagined. They finally had an answer from their mother but it had only opened up even more questions.

'Darling. I came here to tell you something I'm not proud of, that I have wanted to forget – deny – for over thirty years. I haven't even admitted it to your father. Though I ought to and I will when I go home, no matter the consequences. What I wish you'd understand is that there are two sides – many sides – to every story. I'm not seeking to excuse what I did, but your father . . .' She clammed up.

'What did Dad do?' Ellie jumped in.

Scarlett let out a snort. 'Yeah, blame Dad.'

Ellie flashed her a warning look. 'Go on, Mum,' she encouraged.

'It's more what he *didn't* do, but this is no time to lay blame. It's between me and him. I've told you all I can and I'm sorry that I can't give you any more answers. All you need to know is that your dad – Roger – has loved and cared for you all his life. He's told you that you are his daughter as far as he's concerned, and that's all that matters. You both need to try and come to terms with that.'

'I have been trying,' Scarlett muttered. 'I love Dad and I still love you . . .' The catch in her voice showed that she was on the verge of tears and desperately trying to hold it together. 'But I can't help wanting to know *more*.'

'There's no point, my love,' Anna murmured. 'There's nothing to tell, nothing worth knowing. I was drunk, I did something I regret that I can barely remember. I never thought it would have any consequences, but I was wrong.' She got up. 'I'd like to go up to my room now. I need some time to myself.'

Their mother brushed her hand over Ellie's. Scarlett sat with her arms folded, obviously too upset to say any more.

Ellie wished she could split herself in two and comfort them both. 'I'll come up with you, Mum.'

Anna patted Ellie's hand. 'I think Scarlett needs you more.'

# Chapter Eleven

The atmosphere had been taut as a wire since breakfast, with Scarlett fleeing to the study with a sudden enthusiasm for her screw article. Their mother had gone for a walk for much of the morning, giving Scarlett and Ellie the chance to talk alone.

Ellie had brought a mug of hot chocolate into the study for her. 'I'm glad Mum's finally admitted something happened, but why won't she say who he was?' Scarlett said, accepting the mug and thinking again how lucky she was to have Ellie back in her life. She didn't know how she'd have coped with recent events if her sister had still lived on the other side of the world. 'Thanks for the chocolate.'

'You're welcome, hun. It must have been a huge step for her to even admit she'd had an affair – or had sex, or whatever happened – and I think it's too much for her to talk about the details. She might actually have blanked them out and can't remember him.'

'I don't believe that. I've had the odd occasion when I had the wine goggles on but I've never been too pissed to remember who I slept with.'

'What if she remembers doing it, but doesn't *know* his name? She mentioned a party . . . they might have been smoking stuff,' Ellie said reasonably.

'Maybe.' Scarlett shuddered. 'It's not the best, is it? Imagining your own mother high and having sex with a random stranger.'

'No, but if we judge her and push her, we're only going to make things harder for her and we might never find out the full story, if she actually has a story to tell. Look, I don't have to work this afternoon, so why don't we all make the Christmas cake together, like we used to? It will give us some time with Mum, without all the questions and recriminations. You never know, she might open up if we back off?'

They'd always tried to wait until Ellie was on a visit home to make the Christmas cake. Everything she was saying made perfect sense, but it was hard for Scarlett to be rational and reasonable in her current state of mind.

She nodded. 'OK, and thanks for trying to keep the peace.'

She and Ellie popped into Porthmellow for more ingredients. The Christmas lights were being put up in the streets and across the harbour ready for the switch-on later in the month. Scarlett felt a frisson of excitement that the festive season was on its way, but it was tinged as always by the knowledge that this year would be very different. However, hunting down dried fruit, mincemeat and a bottle of brandy in Porthmellow's only supermarket cheered her up. This afternoon would be an opportunity to soothe troubled waters, for a little while at least.

When Anna returned from her walk, she seemed to brighten up when Scarlett mentioned the baking session. They all set to in the kitchen, taking it in turns to weigh, whisk and stir the cake mixture. Ellie also rustled up some pastry for mince pies, which Scarlett filled with mincemeat. Flour flew and there was even laughter. Scarlett felt the much-loved family ritual added a tiny bit more glue to the bonds that had weakened between them.

'We always loved doing this,' Scarlett said.

'Well, it should be the first Sunday before Advent, but none of us has ever cared about that. We had to fit it in when Ellie was home for a visit.' Anna was cutting up greaseproof paper to line the cake tin. It was an old one that had belonged to Auntie Joan and was indestructible. Joan had once said her own mother had handed it down to her, so goodness knows how many cakes it had seen over the years. The mince pie tins were equally ancient, rigid, with scallop shapes in the bottom.

They'd kept the vast majority of their aunt's kitchen equipment, and the pretty copper jelly moulds and stoneware jars still decorated the dresser. They'd tried to leave as many of her things as they could, apart from her clothes and some of the books, which had gone to the charity shop. Even as she weighed and sifted, Scarlett couldn't help thinking of the memories this house held – and of *Treasures of the Cornish Seashore*, with its mysterious and troubling message inside.

When they were almost ready to tip the mixture into the tin, the landline rang out.

'I'll answer it.' Ellie wiped her hands on a tea towel and almost galloped into the hall.

When she walked back into the kitchen a few minutes later, Scarlett noticed that her eyes shone with happiness.

'Let me guess who that was—'

'Actually, it was Drew. He wants to offer me a new contract as ship's cook next spring,' Ellie said. 'So you were wrong, Scarlett.'

Anna gave them both a sharp look. 'Wrong about what? What am I missing here?'

'Ellie's new man.' Scarlett winked theatrically.

Ellie squealed in protest. 'He's not my "new man"! We've only known each other a few weeks. He – Aaron Carman – is a friend,' she explained to her mother. 'He's the son of Troy and Evie; you know them.'

'I do, but I thought their son was in the army.'

'He was until very recently. He's left now and is hoping to start up a security business in the area. Actually, he's renting Cove Cottage.'

'Ellie ran into him on the lane. Literally.' Scarlett tittered.

'*Actually*, I ran into the wall. Aaron and I didn't make contact.'

'Not yet.' Scarlett dipped a teaspoon in the cake mix.

Ellie ignored her. 'He towed my car to the manor and got it fixed. He, um, used to look after tanks in the army.'

Her mother smiled broadly. 'He sounds like a useful bloke to have around. I vaguely remember him as a teenager. Seemed a nice lad, and the Carmans are salt of the earth. Is he really only a friend?'

'For now. Like I say, he's only been here a few weeks. I don't even know what his longer-term plans are.'

155

'None of us do.' Scarlett licked the teaspoon and sighed.

'Scarlett, will there be any of that cake mix left by the time you've finished with it?'

'And you'd better not even think of double-dipping,' warned Ellie.

Scarlett pouted. Suddenly, they were all back to their teenage years, teasing each other, Scarlett impulsive, Ellie trying to be the 'grown-up' sister, their mother trying to keep them in line with good-natured exasperation – and trying to delve into the details of Ellie's love life. At least Jude hadn't come onto Anna's radar, not that *he* was a love interest yet, although, if Scarlett was reading the signals properly, the wild swimming trip might change that very soon.

# Chapter Twelve

Scarlett was right, Ellie *had* thought it might be Aaron on the phone. While she wasn't thrilled with all the talk about him, at least while she was the focus of attention, other subjects were off the menu. She'd enjoyed the temporary return to normality while they'd been making the cake.

It seemed as if their lives had become even more tangled within the space of a few short weeks, with Aaron's arrival and their mother's revelation.

Then there was Scarlett, who seemed to be getting very cosy with Jude Penberth, not that that was a bad thing. It was probably a good thing for her sister to have another focus. Just as long as that relationship didn't go belly up. The last thing Scarlett needed right now was to have her heart broken all over again.

She loaded the dishwasher while Scarlett and her mum transferred the cake mixture to the tin and dotted it with cherries and almonds. The pies were already baking and wafting comforting aromas through the house. She was thinking about washing up the items that couldn't or wouldn't fit in the machine when her mobile buzzed in her apron. Her hand hovered over her pocket and Scarlett shot her a knowing glance.

Whoa, if a text had the ability to make the blood rush, what would seeing him in the flesh do to her? With her back to Scarlett and her mother, she pulled the phone from her apron pocket and glanced at the message.

**Any chance of making that dinner date asap? I'll cook?**

Ellie shut the dishwasher. 'Popping to the bathroom,' she muttered, but the others were intent on decorating the cake. She took the chance to escape to the cloakroom off the hall. Her fingers were still floury but she didn't want to wait.

**I owe you one, so I'll cook.**

She rinsed and dried her hands while waiting for the reply.

**Let's go halves. You provide the dessert.** 😉

Winking smiley. Wow. Ellie's thumb hovered over the keyboard. She was hot under the collar and it hadn't been caused by the heat of the Aga.

**OK. When?**

**Weds night?**

Ellie replied with a **Looking forward to it** and one kiss. God, was that too obvious? But then she'd be naïve to think that Aaron was only inviting her over for a tiramisu or an apple crumble. She pictured him in the cottage sitting room, firelight glowing, pulling her down onto the sofa. Taking off his shirt and revealing that army-honed body. The thought sent a jolt of lust through her. In her fantasy, he started to take off her top and undo her bra— Arghh. She didn't need to dwell on that part too much, there was nothing honed about her these days.

'Ellie!'

'Shit!' The phone clattered onto the Minton tiles.

'Ellie, we've put the cake into the oven. Are you OK?'

'Yeah, sure. Dropped my phone.' She checked the screen; miraculously it seemed to have survived without any damage.

'You were on your phone in the loo? Yuk.'

'Yeah, like you never do it.' Ellie opened the door. 'Actually, I'd finished and was washing my hands.'

'That's too much information.'

'Then you shouldn't come knocking on the door of the bathroom.'

'We wanted to ask you about the Aga. Have we put the cake in the right place? You're always saying it's temperamental.'

While they finished clearing away, Ellie could not stop her thoughts wandering back to her upcoming date with Aaron. Never mind Scarlett getting her heart broken – it was Ellie herself who needed to be wary.

## Chapter Thirteen

A few days later, Scarlett pulled off her wetsuit and pulled on her sweatshirt as she got changed under Jude's surfer robe, which was still warm from his body. Her own was tingling all over after her swim in the sea, but he'd been right, the water was surprisingly bearable even though it was the middle of November. She was so glad she hadn't chickened out of the trip, and not only because it was an excuse to escape the taut atmosphere at the manor.

While the baking session had created a brief truce, it was only a temporary respite from the tension simmering between Scarlett and her mother.

Jude had chosen a glorious day and driven her to a remote cove in the far west. She'd wondered where the heck they were going when he'd parked in a lay-by and led her over a stile and between two houses. After what seemed like miles, the path had zig-zagged steeply down and the sea had come into view. En route, Jude pointed out plants and took out some binoculars so that Scarlett could spot some choughs, the red-legged, red-beaked crows that even she knew were very rare. Then, almost out of nowhere, the cliff edge loomed. The final approach was another scramble down rocks, so they'd thrown their rucksacks onto the powdery sand and clambered after them.

They were alone on the beach, with only a turquoise sea crashing onto the sands. With a clear blue sky above them, the view was idyllic despite it being November. Jude had gone into the sea in only his board shorts, and she hadn't even tried not to ogle his lean body. She was pretty sure he had an all-over tan too, and suspected he might normally do most of his wild swimming in the nude. That thought made her physically tingle and heat race to her cheeks, and she'd forced herself to refocus on wriggling into the wetsuit he'd loaned her, a thick steamer type that wrinkled around her knees and ankles. They'd swum in a deep pool created by a sandbar, and although she felt like a seal, bobbling around in the squidgy neoprene, it had been a huge treat to swim in the open air. Finally, they'd raced towards the open sea – or in her case, waddled – for a quick dip in the waves.

Now she was glad to put her layers back on and join Jude by the campfire he'd made up in a pebble hearth with drift-wood and dried seaweed. When he'd taken a box of matches from his bag and shielded the flame before lighting it, she'd laughed out loud.

'I thought you might have rubbed two sticks together or something.'

'I'm not Bear Grylls, you know.' He rolled his eyes then

smiled. 'I could use a flint, but it could take a while. I'm guessing you'd like to warm up.'

'If anyone told me a few months ago that I'd be sitting by a fire on the beach after going swimming in November I wouldn't have believed them.' She was also amazed at how relaxed she felt in his company, even after the awkwardness of donning – and peeling off – the wetsuit with him next to her.

'The bonus is, of course, that we have the beach to ourselves.' He got out the tiny stove and quickly boiled up some water and made steaming mugs of coffee.

'I brought something, actually.' Scarlett produced four of the mince pies that they'd made alongside the Christmas cake. 'We all had a baking session at the manor.'

'Excellent.'

They ate a pie each with the coffee, while Jude heated up some soup from his flask. Scarlett was ravenous after the trek and the swim. She polished off her share of the soup, sipping it from an enamel mug and dunking hunks of bread, then ate a second mince pie. The flames crackled and flickered, a pleasing splash of colour now the skies had turned greyer.

Jude frowned at the horizon. 'I suppose we ought to be getting back before the next front blows in. I'd rather not be caught out in the rain.'

Scarlett didn't like the look of the slate-coloured band of cloud, either. 'No. I've had enough of a dip for one day.'

While Jude doused the fire, she packed away her kit and helped him tidy up so they left no trace. On the way back, they picked some more Alexanders and sea beet, some for Jude and some for Scarlett to take home for a winter salad.

'Mum won't believe I've foraged these,' she said, momentarily forgetting that she and Anna were at odds with each other. She was also seized by the urge to ask him more about his parents' relationship with her mother, but this didn't seem to be the right time, so she tried to focus on enjoying the moment.

She felt pleasantly tired, all her limbs relaxed as if she'd had a large glass of wine, even though she was stone cold sober. She wasn't quite sure how she'd find the energy to trek back to the parking space, but she was sure that Jude's company would be a big motivation.

He peered over to the far end of the beach. 'Now the tide's almost fully out, I think we could make it along this beach and round to Sennen and then we'd have a quick route back along the road. It would cut half an hour off the walk,' he said. 'If you're up for a little light scrambling over those rocks at the bottom of the headland?'

'How light?'

'Very. Really, we only have to negotiate a few rock pools. While the tide's still retreating, it's perfectly safe.'

Perfectly safe. He had no idea. She wasn't afraid of being cut off but she was in very great danger of falling for Jude Penberth, with his all-over tan and his mesmerising eyes and his love of nature.

'OK?'

'Yes.'

'There's no need to worry. We won't be cut off.'

They walked along the beach to the rocky stacks at the end, the waves crashing in like endless, distant rolls of thunder. When they reached the rocks, Scarlett couldn't see a way over them at all; they looked like an impenetrable wall of giant teeth. But Jude picked his way between the rock pools, showing her a tunnel they could squeeze through. He pointed out some of the creatures in the pools, crabs and anemones. She simply couldn't stop what came out of her mouth next.

'Jude, have you ever come across a book called *Treasures of the Cornish Seashore?*'

He hesitated. 'Yes. Of course. It's a bit old school but one of those little guides you used to see in all the bookshops and gift shops before we had Amazon.'

'Really?' Excitement gripped her. 'Do you have a copy?'

'Um . . . I don't think so . . . *why?*' He gave her a curious look.

'Oh, I . . .' Damn, why hadn't she thought before she blurted that out? 'Nothing important but I saw a copy in Joan's book-case when we were sorting through her things. I was interested, but now the book's not there. It's a lovely book and I think it meant a lot to Auntie Joan.'

He shrugged. 'I know of the book but I used to borrow mine from the library. Sorry I can't help you more.'

'It's fine. It's not a problem.' Scarlett tried to sound casual. She had been clutching at straws to think that Jude had somehow got hold of that copy of the book.

Luckily, he didn't press her any more on why she wanted to locate the book and in the next second, her jaw dropped as the main beach appeared, a vast expanse of glittering sand with cloud shadows scudding across it. Dogs chased after sticks and a kite surfer skimmed the waves.

'You like the view?' he asked.

'Wow. Yes, it's amazing.'

Jude jumped deftly onto the beach but she stayed on the rock, inhaling the sights and scents of the ocean. How beautiful Cornwall was, in all its moods. She really hoped she could make it her home. In the same moment, she thought of her father on his own at her other 'home' and her heart sank. Was he relieved or lonely now that his wife had left? Would their mum ever go back to him? Was Scarlett being disloyal to him – to Roger – to be so hell bent on discovering who her birth father was? The aching gap inside her gave her the answer. She had to complete the circle.

'Scarlett?' Jude murmured from the sand below her. 'Need a hand?'

She glanced down at him, waiting on the sand below. 'Thanks. It's gorgeous here. I'm just drinking it in.'

He smiled and held out a hand to help her down a final slippery drop onto the sand. 'You see – civilisation,' he said, pointing to a stone building with parasols outside on the headland.

After a coffee at the café overlooking the beach, they walked to the car and drove home.

Jude frowned when they turned into the drive of the manor. The source of his annoyance seemed to be Hayden Penberth, who was talking to Scarlett's mother outside the house. From the way she was standing with her arms folded defensively, the discussion didn't look like a meeting of old friends. Both turned at the sound of the wheels crunching on the gravel.

Anna lifted a hand in greeting and Hayden had a broad grin on his face. Whatever they'd been discussing, they seemed happy enough now.

'I wonder if he wants a lift home,' Scarlett said.

'I don't know.' Jude didn't seem thrilled and Scarlett's stomach swirled with mixed emotions about finding them together.

'Hi there, Scarlett. What a lucky man I am to have mother and daughter together.'

'Dad,' Jude cut in. 'Everything OK?'

'Why wouldn't it be? I was out for a walk and saw Anna in the garden so I decided to pop in and say hello to my new neighbour. We haven't seen each other for ages, have we, Anna?'

'No.' Her mum sounded civil enough, but there was a definite edge to the atmosphere. Mind you, Hayden put everyone on edge with his cheesy comments. Jude's relaxed mood had evaporated and he was tight-lipped.

'Anna told me you two lovebirds have been for a swim . . . at least, that's what you call it, eh?'

'Dad . . .'

Scarlett longed to melt into the ground.

'We went to the cove near Sennen,' Scarlett said, determined to crush any hints that they'd been up to anything else, not that it was any of Hayden's business. 'Jude lent me a wetsuit.'

'Really? He doesn't bother with one usually, do you, son?'

Jude looked like a volcano about to erupt.

'Wasn't it cold?' Anna asked, eyeing Scarlett closely.

'Not in a *very thick wetsuit*,' Scarlett insisted.

'You're a real water baby, by the sound of it,' Hayden said.

'Look, d'you want a lift or not, Dad?' Jude snapped.

Hayden smirked. 'Suppose I could do. Save me the walk home. Nice to see you again, Scarlett, and you, Anna. I expect to see a lot more of you now we're neighbours.'

# Chapter Fourteen

Ellie's torch swept over mud as she weaved between the puddles on her way to Cove Cottage. The lights of the cottage came into view just as the hood of her parka blew off.

'Argh!'

Why had she even bothered blow-drying her hair? Why hadn't she put it up, safe, like she usually did, instead of leaving it loose? With one hand on the torch and the other carrying a bag of food, she couldn't pull her hood up again, so she'd have to get wet.

The roar of the surf drowned out the drumming of the rain. The tide was high and white foam boiled up the cobbled slipway, throwing flecks of spume into the air that reminded her of coffee froth. She jogged the last hundred yards to the cottage and, to her relief, saw Aaron silhouetted in the doorway. She almost fell inside the tiny porch and straight into the sitting room.

'It's a h-horrible night. I must look like a drowned rat. Now I'm soaking your floor.'

Aaron took the bag from her. 'Don't worry about that. Why didn't you let me fetch you in the van?'

'It's four hundred yards away.'

He shook his head. 'You're here now. Let me take your coat.'

Ellie heard a dull roar then a crash as a breaker hit the rocks on one side of the cove.

'Jesus!' Aaron went to the window, looking outside. 'It sounds like the sea's about to swamp the place.'

'It's OK, the water won't reach here.'

'Yeah. I must be going soft,' he said sheepishly. 'I'd forgotten how bad a Porthmellow storm can sound. Then again, from Mum and Dad's place on the cliff, you can see the waves from high up and enjoy the spectacle. This is too close for comfort.'

She patted his arm, laughing. 'Don't worry, the cottage has never been flooded. The previous tenant – remember Reg Seddon?'

'Foxy's grandad?'

'Yes. He's ninety now. He moved to a sheltered bungalow near the football pitch. He told me that a huge wave had once broken the shed window, but he'd never actually been flooded in seventy years.'

'Oh well, that's OK then.' Aaron smiled, but Ellie was convinced he'd been genuinely rattled.

'Can I get you a drink?' he asked. 'White wine? Red? G&T?'

'G&T would be great, thanks.'

Listening to the sounds of glasses and bottles chinking from the kitchen, Ellie tried to relax and just see how the

169

evening panned out. She'd slept with a guy she'd only known for a few hours when she was young, but lately . . . lately . . . it had been two years since she'd had sex with anyone at all. He was a man who'd worked in the same bar as her in Brisbane and they'd eventually become an item. They'd even shared a flat for a few months before he'd become a dive instructor and moved to the far north. She hadn't realised how attached to him she'd become until he'd kissed her goodbye at the airport and said 'be lucky, lovely girl'.

Shortly afterwards, Auntie Joan had passed away and Ellie had come home. At the airport, Ellie had looked around at the families, the kids yelling and grouching, the exasperated, tired parents . . . and for the first time, had felt the tick tock of the clock. Thirty-nine was around the corner, forty not far over the horizon.

She shook the thoughts away. A virtual stranger who didn't even know his own plans was not the man to fulfil her vague dreams. How many times had she told herself she didn't need a partner or children to have an exciting, worthwhile life? Auntie Joan had done without either.

Yet, how different would it have been if her baby had lived? A pang of fresh loss clutched at her.

'Here you go.' He handed her a glass and brought a beer for himself.

'Cheers,' she said, taking a large sip of her G&T, hoping to chase regrets away for a while at least.

'Cheers.' He tipped the bottle to his lips.

Ellie was determined not to turn maudlin and she would not let the lingering fallout from her past dominate her emotions tonight. Although they'd chatted a few times over the past month, this was probably the first time they'd sat down alone with the specific intention of getting to know each other – whatever form that took. Some delicious aromas were wafting in from the kitchen, but Aaron didn't seem concerned about eating yet, so the talk turned to her travels and the places they'd been.

'I've been very lucky. I've travelled all over the world and now I live in a wonderful house I couldn't possibly afford in one of the most beautiful places on earth. I have my family, even if things aren't perfect. You?'

'Very similar to you.'

'Apart from the tanks, and being shot at, obviously.'

He laughed. 'Apart from the tanks and the bullets. But I enjoyed seeing the world, in all its states, good and bad, and I got out unscathed – physically, anyway, unlike some of my mates . . .'

'I'm sorry,' she said, intrigued by his turn of phrase. He implied he'd been scarred mentally – but perhaps it was impossible not to be if you'd been on active service.

He was smiling again and Ellie didn't want to darken the mood, so she sat back and listened, feeling more at ease by the minute.

'So am I, and I'll never forget them – but tonight, we're talking about the good times. I've met some fantastic people, all ages, men and women, and I'm privileged to have known them and to still know them. Look what I came back to? A family who drive me mad at times but are solid gold. I haven't seen anywhere near enough of them. Mum and Dad are getting

171

on and I feel I've missed so much of them, as well as my sister, Gemma, and I want to get to know my niece and nephew.' He hesitated before smiling. 'Now I've landed here in this cottage right at the edge of the sea, with Porthmellow around the corner. It's not a bad place. Compared to some of the places I've been, it's paradise.'

'I've stayed in some places that are meant to be paradise. Porthmellow might not be perfect, but it has its own charms.'

'So, there's no one to miss, no one who'll burst in on us, offering to beat me to a pulp?' he asked.

'No. I don't think so,' she laughed.

'Phew, that's a relief.'

Ellie smiled, wondering if anyone would dare to challenge Aaron Carman anyway, he was such an imposing figure. 'What about you? Am I safe?' she asked, with a smile on her lips, but slightly nervous of the answer.

'Apart from my thousands of devoted fans worldwide, sure.'

She gave a mock gasp.

He sipped his beer before continuing. 'No one who'll care to come after me,' he said.

'No one at all?' Ellie teased. 'I can't believe that.' Something compelled her to make absolutely sure, because after Julian Mallory, she never again wanted to end up involved with a man who was committed elsewhere. She didn't want to suffer that way, or be the cause of a break-up.

'Like I mentioned to you, there was someone for a while,' he said, looking down at his beer. 'We tried to do the whole long-term thing and even managed to live together for a few months on a base, but it defeated us in the end. It was too difficult, or perhaps she decided the downside outweighed the good parts. I don't blame her.' He returned his gaze to Ellie and shrugged. 'Army life is tough on all kinds of relationships, which is why, by and large, I've probably kept away from them.'

Until now? Aaron didn't add that, but she felt that it was implied. She knew where he was coming from.

'Travelling is hard on loved ones too,' she said, adding a smile. 'But at least I had the choice of where I went next.'

Aaron looked at her intensely. 'Are you saying you deliberately kept moving so you could avoid anything long-term?'

Wow. 'You're not the first to suggest that and I've asked myself, too, but I don't know.' He'd touched a raw nerve. It was partly true. Definitely true when she was young and still hurting badly after Julian and the termination, but she could have grown out of it.

'I don't know,' she repeated, shying away from revealing too much about her past with Julian. 'Do you mind the fact that there's no one to come after you?' she countered, putting the ball back in his court.

'At one time, I'd have said yes, I minded . . . but tonight, it feels like a good thing. A very good thing.' He rested his hand on hers. He smelled great. Crisp, clean. She was in deep trouble.

'You see, and sorry if this sounds serious.' She took a breath. 'But it's important to me. I'm not asking for anything heavy,' she smiled. 'After all, we've only recently met, but what I would appreciate is some honesty. There've been too many times in my life when I've seen that not being upfront ends pretty badly.'

He gave her a thoughtful look. 'You've been badly hurt by someone?'

'Yes, and the first time was my own fault – partly – but I vowed I'd never get into that situation again and, recently, I've seen what a lack of openness has done to the people I love. The past might not always come back to haunt us, but it never goes away. It lurks somewhere, hangs over us like a shadow, and it can reappear any time. So if there's anything I need to know . . .'

Aaron picked up her hand. 'Ellie, I admire you. You don't need to—'

The cottage shuddered and there was a loud clattering against the windowpanes. Aaron jumped up, instantly on the alert. 'Jesus! What was that?'

Ellie put her glass on the coffee table. The rattling came again, accompanied by a tremendous roaring of wind and surf.

She reached up and caressed his arm. 'Don't worry. It's only shingle tossed up by the waves.'

He sat down again. 'Wow.'

'It's nothing to worry about. We've weathered much scarier storms than this.' She smiled, amused by this big guy who'd faced down God knows what, unnerved by a few stones against the windows.

'Yeah. It must sound a lot worse than it is. What a wuss I am.' He laughed.

'I'm sure that's the last thing anyone would say about you,' Ellie said softly, sensing genuine fear behind the humour.

Seeming to relax again, he leaned in slowly and she lifted her face to his. Her body thrummed in anticipation. This would be her decision, come what may.

'Dinner . . .' she murmured.

'Can wait,' he said. 'But I can't.'

He kissed her and she put her arms around his back, savouring the muscle beneath his soft shirt. His lips were warm, the kiss gentle but not tentative.

'I'm a bit . . . rusty,' she said, her body telling her that there was no going back.

She felt, as much as heard, his laugh. 'I've been in the army for ages. How rusty do you think *I* am?'

She giggled in a most un-Ellie-like way, but she could forgive herself. This was hardly a normal situation. 'I'll make allowances if you will.'

Aaron lay back on the sofa, taking Ellie with him so she was sprawled on top of him. His hands rested on her waist before slipping under her top, his fingers warm against the bare skin above her jeans. They were big hands that spanned the width of her back . . . She could feel safe with Aaron, if she wanted to. She did and she didn't . . . but thrilled to the knowledge that it was her decision to be safe or not.

She lowered her face to his and kissed him again. His hands slipped further up her back, and flicked open the catch of her bra. Ellie murmured in pure pleasure and pressed herself against his body.

Shingle was flung against the windows again, louder, like the roaring sea was demanding to be allowed in. Aaron didn't flinch, too intent on exploring her body. The wind screamed around the rooftops, wailing like a banshee. But the house might have been swept away and neither of them would have noticed.

# Chapter Fifteen

'Ellie didn't make it home for breakfast, then.'

Scarlett's knife hovered midway between her toast and the butter. She'd been waiting for her mum's comment since late the previous evening when Ellie had texted to say she was staying over at Cove Cottage, complete with a winking smiley and a 'wow'.

'No, Mum,' she said, spreading the butter on the slice. It was mulled wine bread, left over from a loaf Ellie had brought home from the café. She vaguely wondered what Ellie might have had for breakfast.

'Hmm.'

Scarlett braced herself.

'She popped in to get her stuff first thing and then drove straight to work,' she said, without glancing up from her toast. 'I heard her but didn't actually see her.'

'Funny, I didn't even hear her.'

'It was dark. You must have been asleep.' Scarlett crunched

her toast as loudly as she could, guessing Ellie had crept up to her room in her bare feet, the way she used to when she was a teenager and home much later than she should have been. Scarlett used to lie awake, with a book and torch, waiting for the creak on the stairs and the sound of Ellie slipping into her room.

'Hmm. Well, she's a grown-up, I suppose. I want her to be happy.' With an even more significant 'hmm', her mum poured herself a cup of coffee. Scarlett managed to hold her tongue, even though it did seem more than ironic that her mother was offering advice on their relationships. She knew an ill-judged comment would be like throwing petrol on a bonfire and without Ellie to referee, she decided to switch the subject to a safer topic.

'Will you be staying for the Solstice Festival, Mum?'

'When is it?'

'December the twenty-first. That's why it's called the Solstice Festival,' she said, innocently.

Her mum rolled her eyes. 'Well, I didn't know they were sticking to the actual date. Hasn't there already been a big festival in Porthmellow this year?'

'That was the summer one in July, but this is the first Christmas event. It's obviously not going to be anywhere near as big, but it should be fun. Ellie's on the sailing trust stand – or rather on their new boat. I'm helping Jude with his foraging stall.'

'Really?' Anna asked sharply.

Scarlett was instantly on the alert. 'Yes. Why are you so surprised?'

'I suppose he seems like a nice enough chap—'

'*But?*'

'But I didn't think he was your type. He's quite a contrast to Rafa, who was so stylish and glamorous.'

'Yeah, well, much good style and glamour did me as far as he was concerned. Jude's a nice guy . . .' *And he makes me feel as if I can be myself, that just being me is enough*, she might have added but she didn't feel like revealing her deepest feelings to her mum, as she once might have done.

'Nice? Yes, he is a nice man, of course, but I'd never have dreamed you'd be into all that environmental and wild-food stuff he goes in for.'

'We're only friends, Mum. I've only known him a few weeks and, personally, I'm *glad* he's the opposite to Rafa.' Scarlett reached for the pot of bilberry jam that Jude had given her. 'To be honest, before I came here, I thought foraging was all hippy dippy stuff involving weeds and lethal mushrooms. Now I've changed my mind. It's fascinating and I've only had lovely food when I've been with him.' Apart from the pine-needle tea, she thought, with a shudder.

'Does he make a living from it – this foraging?' Anna asked.

'Not from the foraging alone. He runs courses and writes books on wild food, and he has a part-time job at the college too. He has a PhD in Botany. He's Doctor Penberth.'

'Yes, I remember now . . . Joan thought a lot of him. He's always seemed harmless enough and, as you say, you're only friends.'

Scarlett's hackles rose again. She didn't want to start a row but why was her mother so anti her and Jude? 'Harmless enough' and 'only friends' made their relationship sound like something out of the *Famous Five*. What if things went beyond good mates . . . ? In fact, she hadn't realised quite *how* much she wanted their friendship to go way beyond mates until now. The problem was, did Jude feel the same? Her confidence in judging male emotions, and emotions in general, had been shaken to its core lately. How could you really know what those around you were feeling, even the people closest to you, your own flesh and blood . . .

However, as her mother had brought up the subject of the Penberths, she decided to probe further.

'Did Joan know Jude and his parents well?' she asked, slathering jam viciously onto her toast.

Her mum shrugged. 'I'm not really sure. She used to let him roam around the gardens and I think she thought of him as a surrogate grandson, but I'm not sure if she was as close to the rest of the family. I can't imagine that Hayden and Fiona shared her interest in literature and the arts. Why do you ask?'

'No real reason, apart from the fact that Jude showed me a photograph of him down in the cove with his dad. You were there too. Jude was around five or six. Ellie and Marcus aren't in the picture though, and I wasn't even born, of course. Do you remember it?' Scarlett crunched her toast, knowing she'd ventured into dangerous territory but not caring.

'Good grief, I can't remember that far back. I used to come and visit Joan often in the summer. Ellie was probably playing with a friend and Marcus might have been in his buggy, out of shot. Where is this photo?'

'Jude has it in an album.'

179

'Oh . . .' She pursed her lips then nodded. 'Hmm. I have a vague idea when it could have been taken. Marcus was asleep and the woman who helped Joan with her manuscripts was looking after him at the manor while we all went for a walk. Ellie had gone to a children's party in the village.'

'Right . . . so where was Dad?'

'Abroad, of course. He was away a lot then.'

'Must have been hard for you to spend so much time without him.'

Her mother peered at her. 'Where's this leading? Are you implying that something happened when I was down here?'

'No! I'm not.' Scarlett was stung into pushing further. 'But did it?'

Scarlett could have bitten off her tongue. Her mother's eyes were bright with tears. Of shock or anger, she wasn't sure.

'I'm sorry, I shouldn't have asked,' she said, feeling the atmosphere between them crackle with tension.

'That's what family secrets are, things you don't talk about. You hide them away in a dark cupboard and hope they never see the light of day,' her mother said quietly.

'Until someone opens the cupboard . . .'

'I never thought that would happen.'

'The man though. My biological father. He might have come looking for me.' She wasn't going to let her mother off the hook, not now she was so close, closer than she'd ever been, to finding out the truth.

'Why would he? He's no idea you're his,' her mother said.

'Does he even know I exist?' Scarlett asked.

Anna hesitated. 'No. I've never told him.'

Scarlett snapped. 'So you *did* know him, then? You still *do*.'

Anna's chair scraped on the tiles as she stood up. 'Please. Stop this. It won't make an ounce of difference whether he knows about you or not.'

'But I'm his daughter. He has a right to know!'

'No. He shouldn't. He has absolutely no right to know about you whatsoever. As far as I was concerned, you were far more likely to be Roger's than his. And that is the *absolute* last thing I have to say on the subject. Forget him. I have. It won't make your life one tiny bit better to go hunting him down, and will make a lot of lives a whole lot worse!'

Anna snatched her plate up but knocked her cup over. Coffee dregs spilled on the table and splashed her skirt. 'Fuck it!'

Oh God. Her mother never swore so she must be upset, and not over some spilled coffee. Scarlett grabbed a tea towel.

'Shit, shit shit!' Anna cried.

Scarlett dabbed at her skirt.

'Leave it!' She batted the towel away. 'I'm sorry. I came here hoping to build some bridges with you both, but my presence is only making things worse. I can't take this.'

'Well, I'm sorry, Mum, but I can't take it either!'

Anna rushed from the kitchen, flapping her hand at Scarlett to keep back.

Scarlett clutched the sink, feeling desperate and ashamed. Well, that had gone spectacularly wrong. She hadn't meant to hurt her mother – oh, who was she kidding? She clearly had meant to hurt her and she was a horrible person. That was one of the worst things about the whole mess: it had dragged

181

so much nasty stuff out in all of them. It had *changed* them, for the worst and possibly forever.

Now she might have driven her mum out of her own house and made it more unlikely than ever that she'd get any answers to the questions that were tormenting her.

Floorboards creaked as her mum moved about upstairs. Scarlett was sure she could hear muffled sobs. It was barely nine o'clock and she'd already managed to make her cry. No matter how hard she tried to suppress the urge – the need – to know the circumstances around her biological father, she couldn't help wondering. The hurt and desperation bubbled away, so close to the surface all the time.

She tipped the toast in the bin, her appetite gone. She'd have to tell Ellie what had happened . . . or should she leave Ellie in ignorant bliss? Ellie deserved happiness, after that horrible business with her tosser of a tutor. Their mother didn't know about that either.

For the rest of the day, she tried to work, but one thing kept coming back to her, amid the guilt and frustration. OK, her mother had been angry and upset at Scarlett's outburst, and she had good reason to be.

But she also hadn't answered her questions.

Scarlett spent the rest of the day in her study until Ellie came home from work. It was a treat to see a smiling face because Scarlett and her mum had barely spoken all day. Anna had gone out to the launch of a gallery in Porthmellow, a relief to Scarlett and probably an even bigger one to her mum.

'Everything OK?'

'Yes.' She gave a tight smile. 'Well, not really. Mum and I had a bit of a moment.'

Ellie flopped onto the sofa. 'Oh God, no. What happened?'

'I don't really know. Somehow, we ended up rowing about him – my real dad – and she said she'd come here to try and make things up with me, but now she thought it was a bad idea.'

'Oh, Scarlett!'

'Yeah, I know. You leave us alone for five minutes and all hell breaks loose. I don't want her to leave, even though it's really hard to be patient with her.'

'I'll have to talk to her when she gets home.'

Scarlett sighed. 'No, I'll do it. I was the one who upset her and even though I feel angry and frustrated, it's up to me to persuade her to stay. I keep thinking about how she must feel and if, you know, if she's always regretted that night. I just want things to be right between us, but while she's holding back, I don't feel they can be. No matter how much I love her and Dad, there's this space inside me now that can't be filled until I *know*.'

Ellie listened. 'I wish I could do more to help. All I can say is give Mum time.'

'Yeah. You're right. You always are.'

Ellie shook her head. 'That's not true.'

'At least you had a good time with Aaron?' Scarlett asked, wanting to change the subject and avoid bursting Ellie's bubble further.

'You could say that.' A smile formed on Ellie's lips and grew into a grin.

'It's serious with him, then?' Scarlett couldn't be happier for her sister.

Ellie sighed. 'Not yet. I'm trying to keep it light but, yes, I really think it could be the start of something special.'

'Good. You deserve it. I hope he deserves you.'

She laughed. 'Like I said, I'm no saint myself.'

Scarlett smiled and teased her. 'After you didn't come home, and seeing the look on your face now, I've worked that one out.'

The mood brightened and they spent the rest of the evening talking about the Solstice Festival and watching TV.

When Anna came home around half-past ten, Scarlett jumped up to meet her at the door as soon as she heard the car. She'd barely got the words 'I'm sorry, please stay,' out of her mouth when her mother burst into tears and embraced her.

Scarlett bit back her own tears and determined from that moment on to do her utmost to try and be patient and wait for her mother to reveal who her father might be . . . but of course, that wouldn't stop her trying to find out by other means.

# Chapter Sixteen

As Scarlett walked into Porthmellow with her mother, she was struck by how quickly Christmas had taken over the town during the past fortnight. With the Solstice Festival only three weeks away, Evie Carman had invited Scarlett to a lantern-making workshop at the Fisherman's Institute. The finished Christmas lanterns were designed to hold tea lights and be paraded through the streets on poles by families before the solstice revelry kicked off.

When their mother had heard about the workshop, she'd been keen to go along too. Having been an art teacher, it was right up her street. Ellie – and Scarlett, if she was honest – thought it was a good idea for everyone to get out of the house and do something fun and festive together. Ellie had promised to drop by the Institute after her shift at the café.

The previous evening, Gabe Mathias had been invited to turn on the town's illuminations and the streets had been filled with locals enjoying the switch-on while the local silver band played Christmas carols. The jewel-coloured bulbs bedecked the quayside and narrow streets, brightening the dark afternoons as the shortest day grew closer. Porthmellow wasn't the bright lights of Brum, but it had its own quaint charm that made up for the lack of glitz and mega malls. She couldn't help picturing her dad's wry smile if he could see the quirky lights in the shape of luminous lobsters and crabs on the harbour wall. Scarlett considered texting him again to try to persuade him to come, but decided she'd run the idea by Ellie first.

Over the past two weeks, an uneasy peace had broken out at Seaholly, on the surface at least, with Scarlett restraining herself from any mention of the elephant in the room. She was on a deadline for several work projects anyway, with the holidays coming up.

A potent pong of glue hit Scarlett as she walked into the workshop. The room was alive with chatter and laughter as half a dozen families and helpers wrestled with the paper and willow twigs used to make the lanterns.

Spotting them, Evie Carman made her way gingerly through the chaos. 'Hello. How lovely to see you both!' she exclaimed, hugging Scarlett.

'Hello, Evie,' Scarlett said, a little awkwardly. Evie's enthusiastic greeting had attracted the attention of most of the room but soon everyone went back to their creations.

'Nice to see you, Anna.'

Her mum kissed Evie on the cheek and smiled. 'You too. How's the new knee?'

'Oh, doing nicely. It doesn't feel like my own but it doesn't hurt either, so that's a bonus. Now, if I can get my other one sorted, I'll be giving that Mo Farah a run for his money.'

Scarlett and Anna laughed.

'I'm glad your op went well,' Anna said. 'You'll soon be back to running around the beach.'

Troy joined them, still in his cap even though the hall was overheated. 'I see the professional's here,' he said. 'We need all the help we can get, maid.'

Anna laughed. 'You must be the only person who still calls me a maid, Troy, but thank you. This looks like fun.'

Scarlett glanced at the sea of wood and paper, thinking the opposite. Her mother was the one with the artistic talent in the family; Scarlett had barely got beyond the stick-man stage, preferring to express her creative side in words. Looking back, she'd probably decided that she couldn't possibly live up to her mum's skills, so she'd much rather make her own mark. How on earth she was going to produce a decent lantern from paper and a bit of twig was beyond her.

'Don't look so terrified,' her mother said.

'Oh, we'll help you,' Evie assured her. 'Look, if the little kids can do it, I'm sure you can.'

'I made this!' a ginger boy of around six held up a very professional-looking starfish-shaped lantern.

'That's fantastic,' Anna said. 'Look at all his arms.'

'It's a girl starfish,' said the boy, bottom lip jutting in disgust.

'I see. What's *her* name?'

'It's Rita, silly,' he exclaimed.

Scarlett and Evie held back laughter.

'Rita? Sorry, I should have known.' Anna touched the starfish.

187

'It's the name of the lady who runs the launderette. I like going in there. I'd like to climb inside one of the machines and see what happens when it goes round. I've got my own snorkel.'

Troy sucked in a breath. 'I don't think that's a good idea, son,' he said in a voice of doom. 'I know Rita and she wouldn't want to have to fish you out from one of her machines. You might clog up the filter or spin round so fast, you get washed away to nothing.'

Evie, Scarlett and Anna all burst out laughing but the boy stared at Troy as if he was an alien. His mum came to retrieve him.

'What's a filter? What would happen if I did go round and round in the machine? Would I really be washed away to nothing?'

'You've gone and done it now, Troy. He'll be driving his mum mad for the rest of the day.'

Troy chuckled.

'Shall we get on with some lantern making?' Evie asked, taking Scarlett's arm.

She introduced Scarlett and Anna to the workshop leader, who showed them how to start making a basic lantern frame. Some of the creations were quite elaborate: a robin, a snowflake and an angel were taking shape alongside the simpler designs like stars and bells. A small group were even working on an octopus. With her craft skills, Anna was soon in her element, sketching out a design and helping Scarlett cut and form the willow frame.

With her mother's help, and guidance from the workshop

leader, two hours flew by and Scarlett had amazed herself by producing a passable star. Anna had made a fish, complete with a fin and eyes.

'That's good for your first time,' Evie commented.

'Thanks.'

'Anna?' A red-cheeked woman in a turquoise kaftan spoke to Scarlett's mum. 'Fancy seeing you here. It's Hazel. Hazel Guise. You remember me? I'm Lawrence's eldest. Have you moved here permanently?'

'No, I'm just staying with the girls at the manor.'

'Your 'usband off the leash, is he?'

Anna smiled weakly. 'He's at home.'

'He'll be down for Christmas though, I s'pose.' A grin cracked Hazel's ruddy face.

'We haven't decided yet.'

'I was sorry to hear about your aunt Joan.'

Anna sighed. 'Yes, we all miss her a lot.'

'I bet. My dad would have been heartbroken if he'd lived to see her passing.'

'She was very upset when Lawrence died.' Anna turned to Scarlett. 'Hazel's dad was Joan's gardener and handyman.'

'Oh yes . . . I met him a couple of times.' So, this Lawrence was the man who Joan was supposed to have had an affair with.

'Poor Dad. He just keeled over one day when he was working in her vegetable plot. She was devastated. We all were,' Hazel said, her eyes glinting with tears. 'She was so very fond of him.'

Scarlett listened intently, wondering if Hazel knew what her father's duties included.

189

'I know. I am sorry.'

'Oh, it's been over ten years now but we still miss him every day. He was very close to Joan after my mum passed away.' She looked wistful.

'Sad to think there'll be no more parties at the manor,' she continued. 'Back in the day, your auntie loved a do. There was always champagne flowing and all sorts of glamorous people getting up to all sorts of antics. My dad wasn't a party animal himself, but he loved helping her set up the garden with tables and lanterns. He made sure the grounds were shipshape, though he reckoned not too many of the folk there were interested in his herbaceous borders, if you know what I mean. He always said you could hear the music in the town if the wind was right and my mum, God rest her soul, said he'd found some interesting stuff in his potting shed in the mornings after.'

Hazel glanced around her and lowered her voice to what she obviously thought was a whisper. 'A thong. Bright red it was, and not from Marks and Sparks, either. And a C-O-N-D-O-M.' She raised her eyebrows.

'Sounds amazing,' Scarlett agreed, eager to hear more from Hazel, though her mother was tight-lipped.

'Oh, it was! I never went but I overheard Dad telling some of his mates about it. Scantily clad folk running around the gardens, people smoking stuff you can't get from the corner shop and he told me that he'd once seen a famous film star with a cabinet minister in his potting shed.'

'Really? I didn't know Joan knew big celebrities,' Scarlett said, itching to hear every possible detail.

'She knew a lot of famous authors,' Anna cut in quickly.

190

'And they probably brought some friends, but I've certainly never met any movie stars or politicians.'

'No? Oh, well, things calmed down when Joan got older.' Hazel winked at Scarlett. 'I'm sure your auntie kept a lot of her wilder adventures secret from you two girls and your brother. Bet your mum has some stories of her own.'

'A lot of it was probably gossip too,' Anna said. 'Though I don't doubt your dad had some tales,' she added hastily.

'Oh yes, Dad never told me the actual names of the film star and politician but he dropped a few hints. One of them was in Mrs Thatcher's government and the star was some bloke who'd been in a Bond film with Roger Moore.' She giggled. 'Probably just as well I never went myself, or I might have got into all sorts of trouble.'

'Oh, look, Ellie's here,' Anna said with relief. 'It's been lovely to see you again, Hazel.'

'Yes, we must catch up and have a good gossip about the old days.' Hazel chortled and hurried off to join her grandkids around the octopus.

Ellie caught their eyes and waved.

Scarlett's mind swirled. Could her father have been someone famous? An actor or author or – God forbid – a politician. But her mum did seem very keen to shut Hazel up. There was no way her mum would have shagged a cabinet minister, was there? Though with so much booze swilling around, not to mention wacky baccy and wild antics, she'd started to believe anything was possible.

## Chapter Seventeen

Ellie walked in on a scene of heaven – or hell – depending on your point of view. A giant paper octopus dominated the room, surrounded by hyper kids shrieking and laughing. Others were darting about with lanterns on poles, almost knocking over each other and their families.

'Eh, mind my cap!' Troy shouted as a ginger lad almost sliced it off with a paper fish.

Parents were shouting at their offspring to 'calm down!' and a girl fell on top of another boy's lantern, leading to wails of dismay and a heated argument between the families.

'Hello!' one of the festival organisers, Chloe Farrow, greeted her. 'Mad, isn't it?'

Chloe's toddler granddaughter was playing with paper.

'Gan gan.' She offered a chubby fistful of paper to Chloe. 'Thank you, Ruby.'

Ruby offered the paper to Ellie next.

'I'm not sure Ellie wants that, darling.'

'It's fine,' Ellie replied, amused. 'Thank you, Ruby.'

Her dark brown eyes were so innocent and trusting. Ellie's stomach clenched. Ruby dropped the soggy mess into her hands. 'Oh, lovely. All warm and squidgy.'

Chloe wrinkled her nose in apology but Ruby chuckled in delight. 'It's almost over. Lucky you,' Chloe said.

'Looks like I missed the best of it. That octopus is something else.'

'Hmm. The Christmas parade will be fun but personally this whole pagan solstice thing reminds me a bit too much of *The Wicker Man*, though they don't burn the lanterns at the end of the ceremony.'

'You hope,' Ellie said, laughing.

'Hmm. We don't want this lot going up in flames. It's fun for the children before the rowdier stuff gets going.' Ruby let out a huge yawn. 'She's shattered and so am I. Think we'd better get off home now. See you again soon.'

Leaving Chloe to strap Ruby in her buggy, Ellie joined her mum and Scarlett.

'I made an actual lantern,' Scarlett said proudly, showing her a star.

'That is . . . actually pretty impressive.'

'Don't sound so surprised!'

'It's lovely,' Anna said.

Troy grumbled up, adjusting his hat. 'Bloody kids. One of them near brained me.'

'They're not that bad, Troy!' Evie admonished him with a roll of her eyes. 'Sorry, have to go. Hazel wants me in the kitchen.' Evie waved at Hazel and went off at a surprising pace for someone with an artificial knee.

'Little buggers. God knows what'll happen when we get these creations near naked flames,' Troy said, eyeing the hyperactive bunch racing around with their lanterns. 'Aaron did well to keep away. These kids would drive him mad.'

'Really?' Ellie was puzzled.

'Yes. I remember him saying on one of his trips home that he joined the army to get away from being saddled with a brood before he was twenty-five.'

Ellie laughed but was dismayed. She was hardly at the stage of discussing a family with Aaron but if he was so against kids, it was unwelcome news to her.

'You had two of your own, including Aaron, and they didn't turn out too badly,' she said, trying to make light of his comments.

Troy chortled. 'Aye, I did that, maid. Eh!' Troy cried out as the ginger boy bumped into him once more, knocking his cap clean off again. 'Mind me hat, you terror!'

Ellie retrieved it from under a table and handed it back.

Troy muttered something about 'little devils' before Evie beckoned him over to the kitchen area.

Scarlett joined Ellie again. 'Everything OK? Ready to go?'

'Yes, I think so.'

'You look tired.' Scarlett peered at her hard.

Ellie rolled her eyes. 'It's been a long day.'

'Lantern making's hard work and I'm high on the glue fumes too.'

'Have you and Mum been OK?' Ellie asked, thinking Scarlett looked happier than she'd seen her for a few days.

Despite the chaos, the session must have been good for them both.

'Yeah . . . No shouting, anyway.' They both spotted their mother, admiring the octopus, surrounded by excited kids.

'Mum looks happy,' Ellie said, with relief.

'She's in her element.'

'She loves kids.'

'Yes,' Scarlett said wistfully. 'Shame her own have given her so much trouble.'

Ellie shared a wry look with her sister, and while her mind was on children, it was in a different context. Troy's comments, however tongue-in-cheek they might be, had put a different spin on her relationship with Aaron. They had made her realise how hard she'd fallen for him, with little real insight into what he felt about the fundamental and vital things that mattered to her.

Scarlett nudged her. 'Oh, look. Aaron's here.'

Aaron waved from the door and started to make his way over. Ellie hadn't expected him and would, until a few minutes ago, have had to stop herself from doing a happy dance at the surprise.

Suddenly, shrieks filled the air as the ginger boy and two mates sent a pile of lanterns clattering to the floor. The kids who'd made them started crying and one boy lashed out at the ginger wrecker. Anna tried to intervene but the parents dived in, adding to the chaos. Ruby Farrow started to wail loudly, and another baby joined in with the chorus.

Aaron reached Ellie with his hands over his ears. 'Jesus, I'm glad I didn't turn up earlier. It's hell on earth in here. Kids, eh? Who'd have 'em?' he asked, wincing as the volume ramped up.

Ellie forced a smile but her heart ached as much as her jaw. 'Yes. Who?'

# *Chapter Eighteen*

As the first week of December rolled by at an alarming pace, the Porthmellow shops went into full-on festive mode. There was a carol concert on the quayside, and a festive farmers' market in the Institute with crafts and local foods. Jude took Scarlett to an illuminated National Trust house with stunning gardens that stretched down to the estuary. The blooms and trees were lit in jewel colours, the early flowering camellias and pale branches glowing in the lights.

It was beautiful and something she'd never have done back in Birmingham. If there was ever going to be a romantic moment, this was the opportunity, but Jude had kept things on a friendly level, never hinting he wanted to take things further.

Scarlett couldn't help feeling that every Christmas tradition or activity, small or large, had a bittersweet edge. It soon became clear that Anna planned to stay over at the manor at least until Christmas, which meant her father would be spending the day with Marcus and his family. Anna also announced she was joining the watercolour class in the village. While pleased that their mother had something to divert her from her worries, Ellie had told Scarlett that it was another clue that she planned on staying at Seaholly – and away from their dad – longer than they'd hoped.

Scarlett wasn't sure how she felt about Anna staying on. Part of her wanted everything to go back 'to normal', which could never be. Part of her wondered if her parents were better off making a clean break. As time passed, the tensions between her and her mother hadn't really eased, but with the three of them living together, she'd had to try to curb her frustration for everyone's sake.

Once upon a time, she'd been eager to hit the shops and festive markets with her friends, scouring the stores for the perfect gift for friends and family. Her enthusiasm for Christmas shopping had all but faded away this year, despite the novelty of being able to hunt for gifts in Porthmellow's quirky galleries and shops, but it had to be done. So far, Scarlett had bought some Cornish gin for her father along with a canvas print of St Michael's Mount by starlight, taken by a famous local photographer. She'd got a voucher for a meal at Gabe's restaurant for Ellie, and a framed painting of a seaside scene for Marcus and Heidi. For the boys, she decided to book a lesson with the sailing trust in the hope it would lure them down to Cornwall at some point and remind them of happier times.

She'd found some quirky bits and pieces for her swimming club friends back in Brum and hoped to get back there before or shortly after the holidays to hand them over in person.

However, as yet, she hadn't found anything remotely appropriate for her mum. Everything she looked at in the shops; jewellery, paintings and art, seemed loaded with links to Porthmellow.

She didn't want to inadvertently pick something that might remind Anna of her affair.

Buying something for Jude, of course, was almost impossible. She didn't know if he'd get her anything and besides, with his keen interest in the environment, she wasn't sure she should get him anything new at all. But giving him a 'second-hand' item, even if she could think of or find something suitable, seemed well . . . a bit *mean*.

He'd been busy with his end-of-term student assessments at the college, but they'd been out for a drink together and she'd helped him read the final proofs of his foraging book. They always laughed and joked and seemed to be so in tune, but so far he'd never attempted to take things further.

Perhaps, she thought, that should be their Christmas present to each other – it was the one she wanted most. A great big recycled box with a note in it saying: *Shag me before I go mad with frustration.*

She might have laughed at herself, but actually it wasn't that funny any more.

With only two weeks to the Solstice Festival, it was time to plan what they were going to wear. Even if Scarlett was hardly in the dressing-up mood these days, she felt obliged to make an effort for Jude's sake, and to generally not be a party pooper.

She and Ellie headed up to the manor's attic to scour it for costumes. They switched on the strip lights, illuminating boxes, bags and trunks piled up under the eaves. Auntie Joan had loved dressing up. Even towards the end of her life, she'd always donned a 'posh frock and bling' at the slightest opportunity.

Scarlett remembered the conversation over what Joan should be laid to rest in. Their mother had decided on Joan's favourite red silk evening gown, though Scarlett and Ellie had decided they preferred to remember her as she was in life, rather than see the body. Her father had gone with their mum instead. He'd been a massive support to her mum, with all the arrangements. He'd been the one dealing with the tough, emotional stuff . . . which made it all the more poignant that they were apart now. She decided to try and persuade him to come for Christmas again, even though she didn't hold out much hope of him agreeing now that Anna was definitely staying on.

Right now, however, she had a more immediate concern: her solstice costume – and Jude.

Dust flew as Ellie delved enthusiastically into crates of old lampshades, bric-a-brac, and even more books and clothes. Scarlett decided to broach the subject of Jude's reticence as they looked through the crates.

'I'm going out of my mind with frustration. I don't know what's wrong with him,' she said, closing the lid on a box of videos that should have gone to the tip long before.

'Maybe he's waiting for you,' Ellie suggested, peering into a stained packing crate.

Scarlett sneezed and had to blow her nose with a red and white spotted handkerchief she'd grabbed from a box. 'There's 'no way I'm going to make the first move and risk being humiliated,' she said, once she'd recovered from the sneezing fit.

'I do know how you feel. It was the same with Aaron.' Ellie pulled out a black jacket from the crate.

'So how did you – um – get over it?'

'We were in the shed. He was chopping wood . . .' Ellie held the jacket close, as if it was Aaron. She had a dreamy look in her eye. 'I don't know who made the first move. It sort of . . . happened.'

'OK. I get the picture.' Scarlett half-wished she hadn't asked. 'It's as if Jude is holding back from me and I don't know why.'

'It will happen. Jude strikes me as a shy, cautious guy.'

'Unlike his father,' said Scarlett, eyeing an impressive cobweb over Ellie's head.

Ellie curled a lip. 'Exactly. So be grateful he isn't another Hayden.' She held up the jacket; a riding-style velvet affair. 'How about this for the Solstice Festival? It's too small for me and anyway Drew wants us all to go as pirates.' She rolled her eyes. 'Yippee, I can't wait.'

Scarlett took the jacket. It had a musty smell, but actually, it was rather gorgeous, if she could fit into it.

'You'll knock Jude dead in it.'

Scarlett sniffed it again and wrinkled her nose. 'You might be right, but not in the way I'm hoping.'

They started fossicking in the crates again, but so far, the jacket was the only thing Scarlett could even remotely envisage wearing. Ellie had moved into the shadows, stooping under the eaves over an old-fashioned trunk.

'Oh my God! Look at this.'

She held out a tricorn, a striped red top and baggy black trousers. 'Argh, you scurvy knave! I'll keel haul the lot of ye if ye don't put that kettle on!' she growled.

Scarlett laughed. Ellie was lovely, trying to cheer her up like this. 'Argh, it's Long John Silver! I'm terrified.'

'I'll look ridiculous in these, but Drew will be delighted and the kids will enjoy it.'

Scarlett sneezed again. 'Shall we get out of here?' she said, her eyes watering from the dust.

Mission accomplished, they turned off the attic light and went downstairs to the warmth of the kitchen, bearing their finds. They looked over the costumes again in the kitchen.

'So you're on the *Marisco* all evening?' Scarlett asked, mug of coffee in hand. She was sure she smelled as musty as the jacket, which would have to go to the dry cleaners.

'Yeah. We're serving hot rum punch and turkey pasties. We'll get them in from Stargazey Pie because we're too busy to make them. Luckily, Tina has enough staff on at the Harbour Café because I can't be in two places at once. How are you and Jude getting on with the wild-foods stall?'

'I promised to go and help him tomorrow afternoon after I've got some writing done. He wants to sell his books from the stall and I said I'd keep an eye on things while he does a cookery demo. He's going to show me how to make figgy puddings from nuts he gathered during the summer.'

Ellie curled a lip. 'Yummy. Sounds uber-tasty.'

'They're delicious, actually, but I'm no chef, as you know.'

'Yes, but any excuse to spend time with Jude. He must really like you if he asked you to help him out.'

'Hmm . . .'

'You don't sound too happy about it all.'

'I am . . . but Mum's taken against him, not that I should care – but I do.'

Ellie leaned back against the worktop. 'Really? I hadn't noticed. But Mum's not keen on any man and I can see why.'

'Jude's lovely. Why would Mum dislike him?'

'I don't know, she doesn't seem to like the Penberths in general, especially Jude's dad.'

'I must admit he makes my skin crawl.'

Ellie mused for a moment or two. 'I know what you mean. He comes into the café for his lunch sometimes and seems to think he's the Brad Pitt of Porthmellow. Tina can't stand him, but she has to be polite. Some of the younger staff would like to chuck his food over him.'

Scarlett wrinkled her nose in disgust. 'Why? Has he made a move on them?'

'He's never *done* anything, or said anything that was blatantly offensive, but there's definitely something creepy about him,' Ellie went on. 'I feel sorry for his wife. Maybe it's his creepiness that Mum's picked up on, and she's known him a long time.'

Scarlett thought exactly the same. Hayden obviously once had a thing for Anna and still did. 'Jude doesn't get on with him either. He goes tense and clams up when his father is around.'

'He's probably embarrassed by him. Jude's so different, quiet and serious. Look, don't worry about what Mum thinks. Her view of romance is soured, and after what happened with whoever, she's bound to be right off flashy types like Hayden.

Let's concentrate on this festival. It should be fun, as long as we don't have a raging storm.'

Scarlett nodded and reached for a mince pie from the tin on the table. 'Ellie. Am I the only one finding all the Christmassy stuff a bit . . . difficult? I'm trying to enter into the spirit of it all but there's so much that doesn't feel right.'

'It isn't only you. It is different. It's hard. I'm going to miss Dad so much. In fact, I spoke to Marcus again last night. I was going to tell you.'

Scarlett was relieved that Ellie shared her feelings. 'And? Has he forgiven me for opening a can of worms?'

'He's coming round. He was always so close to Mum and Dad. It's hard for him to accept that we have anything other than the perfect family.'

'I guess so. Sometimes I think I should try to forget about it – about my biological father – and get on with my life. It's only me who wants to stir up the murk at the bottom of the pond. Maybe if I decide to move on, you and Marcus and his family, and even Mum and Dad, might be happier? Should I forget it, for everyone's sakes?' she asked. 'I should stop looking for him, for a start. It might heal the rift between us, if I accept the situation.'

'Can you even do that? Genuinely? Will it make you happy?'

'I don't know. Finding him might make me *un*happy, though. Mum seems to think so. But no matter how hard I try, I can't help wondering. The other day at the lantern workshop, Hazel was going on about the crazy parties here at the manor when

Mum was young. You could tell Mum was desperate for her to shut up, as if she had something to hide.'

Ellie put her mug down. 'What did Hazel say?'

'That there were famous people at the parties. Authors, actors, even a politician. This might sound mad, but what if my dad is someone famous?'

Ellie laughed.

'It's not that silly! If he is a cabinet minister or an actor, no wonder Mum won't say.'

Ellie fixed on a serious look. 'I'm sorry, you're right; it's not funny, but I doubt it—'

'It is possible, though.'

'I suppose so. It could be almost anyone.' She covered Scarlett's hand with hers. 'I can't imagine how confusing and surreal it is not to know, and I wish I had an answer. But until and unless Mum chooses to tell us, there's nothing more we can do.'

Scarlett sighed. 'You're right, of course.' She smiled. 'At least your love life is going well. You look happy, Ellie, and no one deserves that more. Dare I ask if there's a chance you might be moving on after Christmas?'

Ellie's brow furrowed. 'Me? Moving on? You mean out of Porthmellow?'

'No. Out of the manor. You are spending more nights with Aaron than here, so I wondered if you might move into the cottage with him?'

Ellie laughed again. 'Whatever gave you that idea?' She gathered up the mugs. 'I'm staying put. Unless something major changes I can't see myself leaving the manor anytime soon.'

Ellie put the mugs in the dishwasher so Scarlett couldn't see her face, but Scarlett could sense the tension in her body and hear it in the edge to her voice. Just when she thought everything was at last going well for her sister, it looked as if she had troubles of her own.

# Chapter Nineteen

Ellie met Aaron at the farm shop after work to collect a Christmas tree. She'd been delighted when he'd asked her if she wanted to help him choose one. Somehow, selecting a tree for someone else's home felt less laden with dangerous emotions than getting one for the manor. Besides, despite Ellie's gentle hints, her mum had shown no enthusiasm for having a tree at all so far, and Scarlett hadn't been much better.

Ellie thought it was a bit desolate, but it looked like Auntie Joan's decorations would stay in the attic this year. At least Aaron was keen. After so many Christmases on tour, he was determined to go full on now he was in his own place. Still, choosing a tree together felt somehow *significant*. It was the kind of thing that couples did for their own place, and made Ellie think more carefully about Scarlett's speculation that she and Aaron might move into the cottage.

Obviously, Ellie kept her musings on the subject well hidden as she and Aaron spent way too long picking over identical firs. They eventually settled on one and carted it home in Aaron's van. While he trimmed the trunk and fixed it into a base, she made up the fire in the cottage and brewed hot toddies. She helped him set it up in the corner of the sitting room and they sipped their drinks, admiring their handiwork. Aaron had sawn a good foot off the bottom, and hacked off some of the lower branches, but the tip still touched the ceiling.

The room was alive with the rich essence of the season – pine, woodsmoke, spices –and the honey-scented whisky filled her veins with warmth.

Aaron abandoned his glass on the coffee table and slipped his arms around her. 'I was right, that tree's way too big for this little room.'

Ellie smiled. 'They always are.'

'Not at the manor with your high ceilings. I ought to trim some more off, but I don't think I can be arsed to go out in the cold and dark – though I might have to cut the tip or we'll never get a fairy on top.'

She laughed. 'Do you have a fairy?'

'Hmm. I'm not sure. Mum insisted I have some of their old decorations. Apparently, it was the only way to persuade Dad to invest in new colour-coordinated ones. That's what she claimed, anyway. They're in the box on the table.'

'Great. Shall I fetch them?'

'Sure. They might be kind of vintage if they're Mum's cast-offs.'

'Sounds like fun.'

Aaron connected up the new string of lights he'd bought

208

from the farm shop while Ellie brought the box to the tree and set it on the carpet. She got down on her knees and unwrapped the creased and faded tissue paper and loo roll from around a dozen baubles. They were an eclectic mix of decorations from across the generations. A fragile faded penguin, which must have been fifty years old, glittery baubles from the eighties, and a mini rocking horse.

He shook his head, amused by the faded penguin. 'I remember some of these. I loved getting them out each year. I sent them the rocking horse from a visit to the States. I missed a lot of Christmases.'

'I missed a few too.' She picked up a cartoonish Disney snowman with a carrot nose. 'This one of yours?'

He caught sight of it. 'What the heck's that?'

'I think it's Olaf from *Frozen*. One of my nephews loved the film when he was little. He'd swear blind he'd never even seen it now, of course.'

Aaron rolled his eyes. 'That must have come from Gemma's youngest, Lyra.' He took the Olaf figure from her. 'Surprised Mum could bear to part with it.'

'Perhaps she doesn't know it was in the box?'

'Maybe, or she might have wanted me to have it as a reminder of the kids. I'll hang it on the tree and mention it to her when she comes over.'

Decorating the tree was never only about decorating the tree. Every piece held memories, of people lost and found and long gone. She and Aaron had unwrapped and hung around half the box's worth of baubles when Ellie found a small tin box that had once contained toffees.

Inside was an object wrapped in extra layers of tissue. The tissue was worn but it was clearly protecting something precious. She took extra care in separating the layers and came upon a chubby glass angel with tattered feathered wings and cherubic features almost rubbed away by age. Ellie smiled to herself, wondering how many Christmases the angel had watched over in her time.

Aaron saw her examining it and came over. 'What have you got there?'

She held the angel out carefully, still in her tissue paper nest. 'Top of the tree?'

He knelt beside her and let out a breath. 'Wow. My God, I remember that from when I was a lad. It goes up on Mum's tree every year. She might even have had that from my grandma.'

Ellie peered at its once-ruddy cheeks. 'It's beautiful. From an innocent time. I'm afraid to touch it in case it crumbles away.'

'It's lasted this long. It's probably tougher than we think.' He picked it up and examined it wistfully. 'You know, I've a feeling that Mum might have an ulterior motive in passing on these decorations . . . I think it's a hint for me to stay, giving me her treasures.'

'She's only keen for you to be happy.'

'I'm sorry about that. Mum's wonderful but she is keen to get me paired off.'

Ellie couldn't quite say the same about her own mother. She didn't seem very happy about Scarlett and Jude's relationship. She hadn't commented much on Aaron, although Scarlett had said that their mother had been 'pointed' about her spending so much time at Cove Cottage. Ellie could partly understand her mother's cynicism, given her recent experiences. Ellie thought of the contrast between the devoted Carmans and her own parents' situation. Then again, she had no right to make assumptions about their marriage. Who knew what they might have gone through and hidden from their own kids?

'Family means everything to her,' Aaron added. 'So you can understand why she can't wait to have us all together over the Christmas holidays, me, Gemma and her kids too, if I know Mum. Any excuse for a massive get together and a shrimp creole.' He sighed wistfully. 'I sure missed those while I was on tour. Mum's recipe is legendary.'

Ellie kissed him on the cheek. 'You can't blame her for wanting to have you by her side, after all the time you've been away.' She smiled. 'And shrimp creole sounds absolutely delicious.'

'It is. My grandad taught the recipe to my grandma. It was one of the few things he brought with him from New Orleans after the war.'

Ellie already knew that Evie's father had been a GI stationed in Cornwall during the Second World War. 'Did he ever go home?'

'Briefly, but he came back soon after for my grandma. They were much too in love to part and he didn't want to take her away from her home. Life would have been very difficult, if not impossible, for them in the States – a black American marrying a white Englishwoman. They'd have had to move far from his family for a start, to the north or west, because Mum told me my grandma and grandad wouldn't even have been legally allowed to marry in Louisiana until nineteen sixty-seven. So, he came to Britain and luckily he was allowed to stay and marry her.'

'I can't imagine it was too easy for them here either.'

'No, but they survived and thrived and times move on, thank God. It's been tough for my parents too, but Mum always gave as good as she got and my dad would have punched anyone who said a word against her. He used to do a bit of boxing, you know.'

'Wow.' Ellie could imagine Troy doing that. He was only a small man, but wiry and he must have been very fit in his youth. Aaron must take after his grandfather in his build, she decided, as well as in his service to his country.

'Your mum and dad are really lovely people.'

He smiled. 'Dad's a character but I love them both and they've always wanted the very best for me and my sister. Mum seemed so proud when I joined the army; always boasting to the locals about my job, but "now I'm home safe" she's told me she was heartbroken too. I'm very glad to be able to spend time with them, even at this later stage in their lives. Mum told me she and Dad were worried sick for me every day when I was posted somewhere tricky.'

Ellie was amused by the word 'tricky'. He must actually mean somewhere bloody dangerous.

'I can imagine why they were so worried . . .' she said gently, knowing she'd have been terrified for him herself.

'I didn't realise quite how worried they were. When you're

212

in the thick of it with your mates, focusing on the next day, hour, or even second, you don't have much time to think long-term.' He became thoughtful. 'Unlike now.'

Ellie opened her mouth to speak, but it was hard to ask a question that didn't sound needy.

'We've only known each other a few weeks, but I like being with you, Ellie. I hope you feel the same. I don't want to sound scary, but when you meet someone special, I think you know deep down, almost straightaway. I've seen and experienced enough to know that time is precious too.'

Ellie caught her breath. She'd only known him a couple of months, yet she had feelings every bit as powerful as when she was a teenager; racing heart, thinking about him all the time, analysing every word and look. However, she was also more analytical of her own feelings these days, torn between wariness and seizing the day.

She hadn't committed herself to a man so deeply – or even at all – since Julian. She knew just how big a deal it was to allow yourself to care deeply for someone, to fall in love with them. It was a huge risk and one she was already almost too late to stop.

'I like you. A lot. Settling down in one place is – was – new to me too, and Seaholly and Porthmellow mean a lot to me. I don't plan on moving.' The words slipped out easily yet still took her by surprise. She could finally acknowledge that Porthmellow was her 'forever' home now. 'Even if Mum sells up, I'd like to stay around,' she continued. 'I have to think of Scarlett too. If we have to move out of the manor, I imagine we'd share a place for a while . . .'

'Porthmellow got under your skin, eh?' he said.

'Not only the town,' Ellie murmured.

'I'm glad to hear it. I feel the same. You've got under my skin too.' He leaned in and kissed her softly.

Her heart beat strong and fast. She felt that in a few moments, the connection between them had deepened and she was ready to risk a little more of her heart than she'd thought.

'Aaron . . . this is difficult for me but I need to – want to – tell you something about my past. It's ancient history now but I'd like to get it off my chest. There was someone, you see . . .'

'Ah.' He gave a long slow nod. 'I sense there's a "but" on the way. A pretty big one.'

'Not necessarily, but I'd like you to know the circumstances. The someone wasn't recent – not that I've been a nun.'

'I'm glad to hear it.'

She laughed. 'I've had a few relationships in my time. Short-lived but enjoyable enough. Like you, I've spent most of my life focused on the moment. Maybe not the next second, but the next day or week . . . always knowing I'd move on and probably one day come home. But . . . way back before I began travelling, there *was* someone who was special to me.'

'I see.'

'I haven't seen him for years. Not since I was nineteen. He was my tutor at college and he was married.'

He exhaled. 'Feck.' Ellie was momentarily thrown off course.

'Did you think I was too nice for an affair?' she said, half joking.

'Nice doesn't have to mean you never do something you might regret. Wait, that sounds judgemental and it's not meant to be.'

'I do regret it. At the time I thought it was the best decision in the world. The only thing to do.'

'Hindsight is a wonderful thing, and don't I know it.' His tone had an edge, as if he understood how it felt to have regrets. Ellie waited for him to elaborate but he turned the focus back to her. 'So you fell for this guy. How did it happen?'

'It was everything you'd imagine. Julian said his marriage was in trouble, that he'd leave his wife. I believed it because I was besotted and I wanted to believe it. The blame lies with both of us. He had a young child. I slept with him. I got pregnant and he couldn't wait to get rid of me or the baby. I decided to have a termination because I couldn't see what kind of future I could offer the baby.'

'Jesus, Ellie. What a bastard. You must have been traumatised by the whole experience.'

'I was . . . and I couldn't stand to be near him again, so I dropped out of college and went travelling and, until last summer after Joan died, I carried on moving.'

He swore again. 'I'm very sorry. This bastard has obviously left a deep scar.' She felt a wave of genuine empathy roll from him and embrace her, and realised she was falling even more deeply for him.

She tried to sound philosophical. 'It's long healed and it was partly self-inflicted.'

'I don't buy that. You were a teenager and he was supposed to be in a position of trust. Sounds like he also fed you a pack of lies about his relationship.'

215

'Maybe, but I wasn't exactly a child and it wasn't a one-off. I slept with him a few times and I accepted his lies because it suited me.'

'You can't possibly know that,' he said.

'Until very recently, I thought those days were all behind me. It's now I've stopped moving around, in the quiet and the stillness, that I've let the past creep up on me and thought about the future.'

Aaron let the pause in the conversation stretch out before he replied, perhaps eager to pick his words carefully, given what she'd shared. 'I know where you're coming from. There are parts of my past I can't shake off, and now I've left the daily discipline and routine of army life, I've had too many moments to dwell on regrets and "what might have been". The past does come back to haunt us.'

Ellie thought of her own family's past: her mother's affair and of her own fling with Julian Mallory. 'We can't let it take over. Have to keep moving forward.'

'The guy. The *prof*.' Aaron injected the word 'prof' with so much contempt, Ellie had to smile at his protectiveness. 'Does his wife know about the two of you?'

'I've asked myself that many times and I've concluded that she *must* have known what type of man he was. I thought no one at college had found out about our affair, but I think that's naïve. I would be amazed if I was the only student – the only woman – he's had an affair with. I thought I was special until I told him about the pregnancy. Then I realised he was a liar and a fraud. Such a massive disappointment. So, secrets can come back to bite us when we least expect it. I vowed I wouldn't make the same mistake again. Maybe that's why I never stayed in one place long enough to get involved.'

'And now?'

'I'm still here after eighteen months. That's going some.'

'And I'm still here after two months, which is a bloody good start. I plan on staying around a lot longer too if you'll put up with me.' He looked into her eyes and kissed her. She knew how that kiss would end, and where.

A while later, lying naked under a rug in front of the fire, Ellie nestled in the crook of Aaron's arm and idly traced patterns on his chest with her finger by the lamplight. His caramel skin was hot and sheened in perspiration after they'd made love, and she could feel the beating of his heart as a pulse under her fingertips. She wanted to lie there and feel that pulse forever. In that moment, she realised that she was in too deep with Aaron to get out without a great deal of pain.

All the bad feelings of the past rushed in: the tears, the lonely nights, the disbelief and the sense of loss and betrayal. The grief when she realised that Julian was never coming back. The panic when she discovered she was pregnant and the unexpected grief of losing a baby she hadn't wanted. The abortion might have been 'for the best', but it had left her bereft and wandering in the darkness for so long.

Tears stung her eyes and without warning, spilled onto her cheeks. She gulped back a sob.

'Ellie? *Sweetheart?*'

Aaron's voice reached her but his words were a blur through the hot tears. She tried to push him away.

'Hey, wait. No.'

He held her arm, gently preventing her from getting up from the floor. It was all she needed.

He propped himself up on one arm and gazed into her face. 'Ghosts from the past?'

'Only one tiny ghost of what might have been.'

His face mirrored her pain. He gathered her to him again. 'I am so sorry, sweetheart. So very sorry.'

'M-me too.' The loss of Julian and his child, held back for decades, engulfed her. He held her while she cried, long shuddering sobs, tears wetting his chest as she clung onto him.

'It's OK,' he soothed. 'You let it out. It's OK.'

She let the agony and regrets of the past years pour out, not that she could have stemmed the flood now she'd allowed herself to grieve again. She'd never told a living soul about the loss and betrayal she really felt. Not even Scarlett knew about the baby. But Ellie had trusted Aaron with her deepest secret. He said nothing, simply stroked her hair and enveloped her in his strong, warm embrace. It was weird and she couldn't quite explain it, but she finally felt she'd reached a safe haven.

She didn't know how long it was before her body quietened and she rested her forehead against his chest, unable to look him in the eyes.

'Oh God, I've cried all over y-you. I am so sorry.'

'Don't you dare say sorry again. And I'll dry.'

Laughter bubbled through the tears.

'Here you go.'

He handed her a bunch of tissues from the coffee table.

She wiped her face and blew her nose. So romantic . . . but

then, she already knew in her heart that she didn't have to pretend with Aaron.

'Th-thanks. What am I like?'

'Like a normal human being. Like someone who's been hurt very badly and held it back for a long time.'

'I thought I'd left it behind long ago. The termination felt right at the time and it was very early. I told myself it was for the best, but I still felt as if I'd been torn apart. I didn't tell my parents and I only told Scarlett about the affair with Julian a few weeks ago. Now I'm older, I wonder if bottling it all up was a mistake.'

'For God's sake, don't think that. You do your best at the time. We've all gone over and over things we should have done. I know I have a hundred times. When my unit lost people, I asked myself if it was because of something I did or didn't do, no matter how small or loosely connected. I asked myself "why not me? Why am I alive and in one piece and a mate isn't?" I still do, but I've learned to silence the voices for a little while longer than I used to. I don't let them dominate my life all the time.' He looked down into her face. 'I don't want you to let bad memories take over either.'

'I won't. This was a one-off. I'm not sure where it sprang from.' She wiped her eyes again, a little ashamed of pouring out such angst to him. 'Thanks for taking it, for being here.'

'Hey, I might look tough but I'm a big softy underneath. I've had hardened squaddies and stiff-upper-lip officers crying on me. There's nothing you can throw at me that would make me run away.'

219

She laughed. He seemed to have his mum's empathy.

He kissed her. 'I'm not your cowardly, lying prof. I'm not going anywhere.'

Still magnificently naked, Aaron threw the rug off to put some more wood on the fire. He pulled some more cushions from the sofas and they sat, propped up against them, watching the glow and the baubles and tinsel shimmering in the soft light. The cherubic angel still had a sheen, even though her smile had all but faded away.

'You'll be with your mum and Scarlett all Christmas Day?' Aaron asked, stroking her hair idly.

'Yes.'

'I'm at my mum's with Gemma and her brood.' He grimaced.

She was instantly on the alert. 'You're not looking forward to that?'

'Like a hole in the head.'

Ellie stifled a squeak of horror but a grin spread across Aaron's face. 'I'm joking. I love them, even if the pair of them have an answer for everything. They used to send me letters and parcels, you know. Every box we got, there was something in it from each of them. Lyra drew me pictures – me shooting people sometimes, but I think she meant well. Ronan used to send me his Haribos. Sometimes the packets hadn't even been opened . . .'

Ellie burst out laughing, as much in relief as amusement. Aaron genuinely seemed to love his nephew and niece.

'Even when they got older, they'd write a funny card or send me selfies. They're great kids. Gemma's done a good job.'

'Sounds like it.'

'I hope I can be half as good a parent as she is.' He looked at Ellie and her heart felt full to bursting. 'One day.'

She didn't need to say anything. He'd given his answer and all her fears had evaporated.

'If you don't have plans, why don't you come over on Christmas Eve?' he asked.

'I'd love to.'

'Great. I can't think of a better way to spend it.' He propped himself up on one arm and looked at her. 'I meant what I said. I won't let you down. I'd never let you down. You mean a lot to me, Ellie, and I want us to be together. All I ask is that you trust me.'

'Trust you? That sounds serious.' Ellie tried to cover her unease with a smile. Aaron's words had stirred up a memory from long ago, and it wasn't a happy one.

'It is, because I'm serious about you. I want you to be part of my future and . . .' He paused to draw a soft breath before going on determinedly. 'I swear I'm going to do whatever it takes to make sure that happens.'

Ellie was taken aback. She wasn't sure what he meant by whatever it took, but she was convinced he meant every word. She took a leap of faith, gambling that she wouldn't fall head-long into the abyss, not with someone like Aaron. 'Of course I trust you.'

They got up and had dinner in front of the fire before they finished decorating the tree, laughing and reminiscing over the decorations, talking about happy times. Ellie decided that over Christmas, she would ask her mother about her plans for Seaholly Manor, although after this evening, she was seriously considering the possibility of a move into Cove Cottage with Aaron . . . but then what about Scarlett?

Ellie couldn't keep a grip on reality; she felt she was holding onto the string of a balloon, floating one minute, and getting bumped along the ground the next.

'*Trust me*,' he'd said, and she wanted to, but a tiny, unhealed corner of her soul held back.

Aaron was no Julian, and she was no lovesick teenager, and yet, they were the exact same words that Julian had said to her. Right up until he'd broken her heart.

# *Chapter Twenty*

Ellie was wrong, Scarlett thought, throwing back the curtains on Solstice Festival morning. It was calm and dry, with even a hint of blue in the sky over the sea. No storms, no giant waves and no force-ten hurricane. Phew.

Feeling more optimistic than she had for a while, she took her breakfast into the study and worked on the copy for a website for Zennor and Ben.

Since they'd dug out the costumes, Scarlett had been home to see her father for a few days and to catch up with her old friends. Her dad seemed to be coping well enough; he could look after himself, but it broke her heart to see him rattling around the empty house. Marcus and Heidi lived nearby and had him over for dinner or to babysit the boys, and he had his woodturning group and cycling friends, but he must miss Anna.

He also brushed off any invitation to come to Cornwall for Christmas, saying that while he knew how much she and

Ellie wanted them all to be together, it wouldn't feel right in the circumstances and he'd be better off with Marcus.

No matter how hard she tried, Scarlett was always subconsciously on the alert for any tiny sign that he might be treating her differently. However, in the current circumstances, with emotions still running high, it was impossible to tell what 'normal' was, or even remember how things had been.

*Funny how many things we take for granted*, she thought, on the long journey back to Seaholly Manor, *until our world is turned upside down*. She wondered again if she should move in with him . . . a feeling that had become stronger when she'd met up with her old swimming group friends in Birmingham. Now, back at Seaholly, she felt the same pull to her new home.

She'd never felt more torn in two.

Maybe, she thought, she'd feel better later when she threw herself into the festivities. After all, that's what it was for: a midwinter party of warmth and revelry to mark the passing of the longest night and the turning of the year towards the light.

She hoped so, because the fog that rolled in from the far west during the morning was anything but festive. At first it was merely a bank of cloud looming on the horizon, but now it was slowly crawling over the hill towards Porthmellow.

She worked through lunch before stopping mid-afternoon to help Jude get ready for the event. The harbourside was ringing with the sound of stalls being constructed but it seemed strange there was so much activity in the midst of so much stillness. There was hardly a breath of wind and, as it was low tide, the waves barely whispered onto the beach. All the rocks were exposed like giant jagged teeth, and mirror images of the clock tower were reflected in the rock pools.

By the time she had set up the stall with Jude, dusk was falling. As she drove home to get changed, she saw the mist had thickened in the valley, and she couldn't even see the house until she rolled onto the drive. The scene reminded her of one of Joan's novels, a historical romance about a gentleman smuggler and his aristocratic lover: *Lady of the Mist*. It was clear Seaholly had provided inspiration for her aunt's stories.

Ellie arrived back from the café while Scarlett was putting on her costume. It had taken a lot of research on the Internet, scrounging off family and scouring charity and pound shops. She'd wasted far too much time when she should have been writing, but she had to admit it had been fun.

The Solstice Festival was a celebration of some of the traditional midwinter and old Christmas customs that used to be observed in Cornwall. Jude had explained that it wasn't based on any single event, but that it was a mash-up of all kinds of traditions and basically an excuse for a bit of a knees-up with fancy dress, singing, drinking and dancing.

'Mock formal' was the loose term for some of the costumes, which had their origins in the poor people's versions of their rich neighbours' fashion. The outfits were an eclectic mix, some based on old pagan themes and bedecked with holly and mistletoe to reflect the season. Others referenced Victorian-style clothing and gothic elements. A quick google of the Penzance event had showed people in everything from Jester-style tatters,

225

to cross-dressing and wearing animal costumes. The one item that seemed *de rigueur* was a mask.

Scarlett's usual style was skinny jeans, sweater and Puffa jacket these days. It felt ages since she'd dressed up and she'd certainly never worn anything as flamboyant as the ensemble she'd laid out on the bed. Auntie Joan, who favoured long skirts and flowing dresses in vibrant colours, wouldn't have been seen dead in a pair of jeans. She'd probably approve of the costume though. Scarlett wished again that her aunt were here to see her.

She'd gone for an ankle-length black skirt with leggings underneath to keep out the cold. The charity shops for miles around had started displaying festival costumes for a few weeks now and she'd found a white blouse with a lacy ruff at the neck to wear under Joan's jacket.

The hat was a traditional type, which she'd found in a charity shop. Scarlett didn't even know how to describe it. It looked a bit like ladies' Victorian riding headgear: shorter than a top hat, and more like a bowler with a flat crown. She'd decorated it with holly from the garden to make it more Christmassy.

After tying her hair back into a ponytail, she went heavy on the kohl and added a splash of plum-red matte lipgloss. With the addition of dangly earrings, also cadged from Auntie Joan's collection of costume jewellery, she felt almost ready. Nothing seemed too over the top for the festival, but she wanted to look mysteriously gothic rather than like a clown.

Finally, she added a black lacy eye mask from a pound shop and fingerless lacy gloves. It was safe to say that she didn't recognise herself in Auntie Joan's full-length mirror. A vampish creature from another age stared back at her and practised an alluring smile, which made her real self groan with embarrassment. She tried a moody pout, but the result was more Victoria Wood than Victoria Beckham.

'*Wow!*'

Startled, Scarlett spun round.

Ellie stood in the doorway, hands on hips. 'You look absolutely stunning.'

Scarlett wrinkled her nose. 'Really? Not too over the top?'

Ellie came over to make a closer inspection. 'Not for a solstice festival. I saw the TV coverage of last year's event in Penzance and I think you've caught the look perfectly.'

Scarlett sighed with relief. 'Thanks, I was worried I looked like I was off to join the circus.'

Their mum walked into the bedroom and joined them by the mirror, appraising Scarlett with a smile on her face and amusement in her eyes. 'I used to have a jacket just like that.'

It was a while since she'd glimpsed her mum's lighter side: the 'old' Anna. Her mum touched the sleeve of her jacket. 'It reminds me of my New Romantic days. Very Adam Ant.'

'Is that a good thing?' Scarlett asked.

'I hope so. I thought he was the coolest man in pop.' Her mum nodded approvingly. 'The outfit really suits you.'

Ellie nodded enthusiastically. 'I agree. You look gorgeous, whereas my pirate costume makes me look about as sexy as Mr Smee from *Peter Pan*.'

Scarlett glanced at herself in alarm. 'I hadn't thought this outfit was sexy.'

Her mother's smile faded. 'You look very nice and in keeping with the event,' she said firmly.

Ellie smirked. 'I'd still like to see Jude's face when he sees you.'

Their mother was tight-lipped. Scarlett couldn't fail to notice the disapproval written on her face. Her mood sank a little, but this was definitely not the time to risk a scene.

'It's very kind of you to lend him a hand,' her mother said. 'I hope he appreciates it.'

'I don't mind at all. His mum and dad are busy with their own stall. That's why I'm helping him,' Scarlett said, trying to sound blasé, but annoyed by her mum's attitude towards Jude.

Ellie slid her arm around their mother, perhaps keen to defuse the situation. 'It's still not too late to go in costume, Mum, I'm sure we can find something for you.'

'I think I'll just go as myself, thank you.'

The grandfather clock struck quarter to five.

Scarlett took off the hat and mask. 'We'd better leave soon. People will soon be queuing to get into town. Mum, I suggest you set off as well because you could find it hard to get a space. The traders have their own parking.'

'Thanks, but I've got a lift with someone from my water-colour class so I don't have to worry about that. I'll go and get ready.'

After Anna had left, Ellie gave Scarlett's costume a fresh appraisal. 'You look knockout. No matter what Mum says, you'll slay Jude.'

'Hmm. That's not why I'm dressed like this. I didn't want

228

to look silly or stand out. Mum really doesn't seem to like Jude.' Scarlett sighed. 'Her view of romance must be screwed at the moment. I so wish it wasn't.'

'I know, lovely, but there's nothing we can do other than let Mum and Dad work things out between them.'

'What if it ends in them splitting up?'

'It'll be horrible, but our job is to support Mum and Dad as best we can,' Ellie said. 'I was wondering whether to arrange to go home to see Dad, or if we should try harder to persuade him to come here rather than stay with Marcus and co.'

'I can't see that happening, the way things are. Oh God, Ellie.' Scarlett felt a lump in her throat. 'How did life get so complicated?'

'Because however much we want things to stay the same, it's impossible. Aaron told me that no matter how many risk assessments you carry out, however much planning and training . . . when he went out on a tour, the sheer randomness, the cruelty and injustice of life was what disturbed him the most.'

'That's a horrible image.'

Ellie hugged her. 'It's terrifying, but he also told me how much he learned to value his friends and his family. We're what matter.' Ellie let her go. 'Sorry, I didn't mean to bring you down.'

'It's OK. I needed to vent. You really like Aaron, don't you?'

Ellie frowned. 'It scares me how much I like him and care about him. I think it's the first time I've felt like this since

229

. . . well, for a long long time and I . . . I don't want my world to suddenly come crashing down.'

Scarlett heard the doubt in Ellie's voice. 'Why would it, Ells?'

'Nothing specific, other than I don't feel I know him that well. I think he keeps some painful stuff hidden under that tough-guy image.'

'In that case you should ask him.'

'He says there's nothing I need to worry about. No skeletons in the closet.'

'Everyone has a skeleton.' She touched Ellie on the arm in reassurance. 'But Aaron strikes me as totally upfront and straight. I bet you're worrying about nothing.'

Ellie nodded. 'What about you and Jude? Any signs of him taking things to the next level?'

She sighed. 'I could let myself feel a lot more for Jude but something keeps holding me back and he's made no attempt to move things beyond friends.'

'I'm sure he will, or you'll take the initiative when the moment's right. Take it slowly then. It's early days, as Dad would say.'

*Bong.*

'Oh! It's five already.' Scarlett grabbed her hat and mask from the bed.

'I'll be right after you. See you at the festival. If I'm allowed a minute away from swabbing the decks!' Ellie called, on her way out of the bedroom.

Scarlett dashed downstairs and out to the car, vowing to arrange a visit to their father the next morning. She had to get through this evening first. No matter what she'd told Ellie, she was dying to see Jude's reaction to her outfit and dreading it too. Once again, her confidence wobbled. Would he think she looked ridiculous? Or would tonight be the night they moved beyond friendship to something more?

Scarlett thought that Jude was the type of guy who was quite reticent about women and might need clearer signals that she was interested in a relationship, but did she have the courage to make the first move? She would never know unless she tried, so she steeled herself to be braver if the opportunity arose.

First she had to make it safely into town, which was easier said than done as she drove through the swirling fog, having to focus hard on the road. She'd had to remove the hat and eye mask to drive but put them back on once she'd reached the traders' parking area.

When she summoned up the nerve to get out of the car, Scarlett felt terribly self-conscious. The only other people she could see were in boringly normal coats and bobble hats. They stared at her: but then that was to be expected. She spotted her reflection in a shop window and did a double take. Within a few moments, however, other creatures, even stranger than herself, began to emerge from the mist. A man in a tailcoat and top hat entwined with mistletoe and greenery was unloading a musical instrument case from his Land Rover. Three people in long robes passed her carrying fiddle, a drum and a tin whistle, and a man with a plague doctor mask called to her in a deep Cornish burr. 'Nice evening for it, love.'

More and more mysterious figures emerged from the fog

as she made her way around the harbour. She'd no idea who they were, but they were setting up stalls, carrying instruments, lanterns and strange sticks. They wore top hats, tricorns and bowlers, adorned with holly and fairy lights. Some had masks of woodland creatures, fantastic birds and beasts or simply eye masks like herself. There were people in Venetian carnival costumes or Morris-dancing gear. A few already had drinks in their hands and at one point she was wolf whistled at by a bear with a pint of Tribute in his hand.

The closer she got to the centre of town and their stall, the more relaxed and liberated she felt to be in disguise. In the fog and wearing her outfit, she'd walked right by two locals she knew who hadn't even recognised her. Most of the stalls were already set up, and their proprietors were busy arranging their goods and setting up gas bottles and generators for the hot food. Jude's stall wasn't far from Sam Lovell's van, and she'd made sure Jude had a great spot right in the heart of the action, and very close to the marquee where he'd be doing his demo.

The marquee used for the chef's demonstrations at the summer festival had been pitched again on the green area behind the harbour. Hot food and trade stalls were clustered around the harbour and all the pubs and shops were open late. Coloured lights adorned the lampposts, and some of the boats in the harbour were decorated with lanterns too. Festive music played from loudspeakers.

She hurried towards the stall, hoping Jude wouldn't mind she was running a few minutes late.

'Ugh!'

'Oh!' Scarlett sprang back. In her haste, she hadn't been paying attention and had run straight into a man in a highwayman's outfit. 'Sorry!'

'Are you OK?' he asked.

'Yes, my fault. I was on another planet.'

He lifted his black highwayman's mask and his striking green eyes met hers. '*Scarlett?*'

'Jude? I didn't recognise you!'

He seemed transfixed by her. 'Same. Wow.'

Her own mouth hung open.

He wore a fitted black velvet frock coat and an indigo brocade waistcoat. His blond hair was secured by a black ribbon and topped by a tricorn. A bolt of lust hit her. Her throat dried. He was clearly lost for words too.

'Wow . . . You look . . .'

'Bizarre?' Scarlett offered with a smile, hoping against hope Jude would deny it.

'Bizarre is most definitely *not* the word I'm searching for.'

'Thanks.' She grinned in relief and pleasure. 'So the costume isn't . . . too much?'

'No. Not too much.' Jude obviously needed a closer inspection from the way he eyed her again from top to toe. 'On the contrary, it's very eye-catching.'

Scarlett was giving his outfit an equally thorough appraisal. 'You look . . .' she began, and numerous words ran through her mind. *Dangerous, sexy, hotter than a thousand suns* . . . 'Um. *Different*,' she said.

'Different good or bad?' The glint in his eye was accentuated by the mask.

'Hmm. I think I'd say . . . good. Very good. I especially love the tricorn, but this whole dressing-up thing is seriously weird.' She laughed lightly, trying to dismiss the wicked scenarios involving being asked to 'stand and deliver' that were rampaging through her mind. 'The whole event feels more serious than a carnival – kind of wicked and pagan.'

Jude laughed. 'That's because it probably *is* meant to be wicked and pagan. I've had more time to get used to the weirdness of it than you. I've worn this costume to the Penzance festival a few times.' He smiled, though given his disguise Scarlett would have called it a 'rakish grin'. She tried not to focus on his black breeches tucked into leather riding boots.

'Anyway, I was on my way to find you in case you'd forgotten where the stall was in the fog.'

'I hadn't, but thanks for thinking of me.'

When they reached the stall, she found that he'd already done most of the arrangement, setting out his books and leaflets on his courses and vouchers among the mistletoe, holly and ivy.

He gazed down at her from behind the mask, the pleasure lighting up his eyes. 'I'm so glad you agreed to come, Scarlett. It'll be so much more fun with you here.'

Music filled the air and excitement rippled through her. This could definitely be the night when things took a turn for the better. Maybe her outfit had been a great idea, after all . . .

Jude lifted two coolbags onto the table, and delicious aromas filled her nose. 'Come on, let's finish setting out our wares. The first procession starts in half an hour and the punters will be here any moment now.'

# Chapter Twenty-One

'Arghh, me hearties! Who wants to see a real-life pirate ship? Who wants to walk the plank?' Ellie swished her plastic cutlass with a flourish at a family with two boys of around five and seven.

The smaller of the boys pressed closer to his dad at the top of the gangplank while the older one tried to drag his mother on board.

'Who'd like some hot rum punch and a turkey pasty?' Ellie asked. 'Want to come aboard for some tall tales and a taste of life on the high seas?' she said, addressing the timid boy. 'There's fruit punch and ship's biscuits for the children,' she added, leaning down. 'And the pirates aren't *really* that scary.'

The little boy shrank against his father. Hmm, he wasn't convinced, but maybe it was something to do with Ellie's eye patch and cutlass. His parents reassured him and he was persuaded to cross the gangway onto the *Marisco*. Ellie kept up the patter, luring people from the stalls to the boat and marshalling the queue to make sure the *Marisco* wasn't over-whelmed with excited visitors. She was delighted with the queue that had formed on the quayside, all waiting their turn to get on board.

No one seemed to care that the *Marisco* had never seen a pirate, unless you counted the odd city trader on some of the corporate team-building days. She was actually a Victorian sailing trawler, not a galleon, but still a majestic old girl, with her deep red sails and gleaming decks. Ellie had spent many hours down in the tiny galley rustling up hearty grub for hungry sailors and handing out ginger tea to the queasy ones.

Colourful lights were strung from the mast and over the decks, and a skull and crossbones rippled in the breeze. The *Marisco* was a real magnet for the festival visitors. The boss of the trust and skipper, Drew, had a permanent grin for the queues of people lined up to tour the boat. The marketing team were doing a roaring trade in bookings and gift vouchers. Ellie wondered how some people would feel opening up a present of a sailing experience on a vintage trawler. Christmas surprises, as she knew only too well, could have a mixed reception.

After half an hour, one of her colleagues arrived to take over on the quayside, so Ellie went on board. She was grateful for the change because standing around in the cold wind was making her shiver despite the thermals she had on under her pirate's outfit.

She headed down to the galley and put a fresh batch of pasties into the oven to warm, before heading back on deck to top up the urns of rum punch and spiced Ribena. She was decanting punch into recyclable cups when she spotted Aaron on the quayside and couldn't help drooling at the way he carried himself. He had an uprightness and an easy confidence that she assumed came from his army training.

It was hard to focus on her work, knowing she was going to stay over at Cove Cottage that evening, if she wasn't too knackered – she laughed at herself. No matter how knackered, she was sure she'd find a new energy for him. The past couple of months had felt like being a teenager again. Only better.

At the food stall, the queue was longer than ever. She was grateful someone else was taking the cash while she popped pasties in bags for a family.

A woman in a long red coat reached the front of the queue. 'Are these pasties gluten-free?' she asked.

'Erm, unfortunately not.'

The woman sniffed and flicked her long platinum hair over her shoulder. 'In that case, I'll stick to the drinks.'

'Fruit juice or rum punch?' Ellie said pleasantly as a silvery hair settled across two of the pasties. Great, they'd have to chuck those now.

The blonde hooted in derision. 'Rum, of course, I'm not a toddler!'

She moved away and a family group emerged at the front of the queue.

'Hi there. What can I get y—'

The words dried in Ellie's throat.

No, it *couldn't* be.

But it was and there could be no mistake, not even after almost twenty years. Even though he was older, with more grey than black in his hair, and lines around the cornflower blue eyes, she could never forget that slight but ever-present smile she'd once mistaken for kindness and sincerity. It was and always had been the smile of a man who was quietly but utterly certain that he knew better than everyone else around him.

Julian Mallory.

*Julian.* The name formed on Ellie's lips, unspoken. Her stomach clenched like a fist and she was catapulted back twenty years to the day she last saw him. He was the picture of self-assured respectability as he always had been, with his Barbour jacket, expensive watch, and his well-dressed, immaculately coiffed wife holding the hand of a little girl of around three or four.

'Two fruit drinks and a rum, please,' his wife said.

'I'm driving.' His smile was both rueful and disarming.

'Well, I'm not and I need warming up.' His wife smiled down at the little girl. 'How about you, Alisa? Are you as cold as Nana is? You'd like some Ribena?'

The little girl gripped her nana's hand tightly and nodded.

'OK. Two Ribenas and one of the hard stuff. Grandpa knows his place,' Julian Mallory said.

Ellie snapped out of her frozen state. 'Of course.' She smiled at the little girl, avoiding his eyes. Was Julian pretending he didn't know who she was, or had he genuinely not recognised her?

'Any food?' she asked, addressing herself to his wife. Even if Julian didn't know Ellie, Ellie recognised Sarah Mallory. She could hardly forget the woman whose husband she'd slept with. The man who had fathered her unborn child – who might have grown into a little girl like Alisa.

They'd patched up their marriage . . . or more likely it had never been broken in the first place. Not back then or since or ever. The aroma of the food and booze turned from appealing to stomach-churning.

'No thanks. We've already over indulged on the other festival stalls. There was a wonderful wild-foods stall. We tried some of the figgy pudding and bought a book.'

'Sounds lovely.' Ellie thought of Scarlett helping Jude out. Scarlett would have served Julian and Sarah in all innocence.

'How much do we owe you?' Sarah asked, while Julian beamed beside her.

Ellie snapped back to the present again. 'Oh, sorry. A fiver, thanks. My colleague will take your money.'

She handed over the steaming cups. 'Be careful, the fruit drinks are only warm but the rum punch is very hot.'

Sarah handed the fruit drink to her granddaughter and collected the bag of food. Julian picked up the rum and his own drink.

'Thank you,' he said, and as Sarah turned away, he exchanged a glance with Ellie, acknowledgement finally flickering in his gaze.

'Hope it goes well,' he said.

He hoped what went well? The festival? Her life?

A moment later, he was gone, leaving Ellie with a queue of customers to serve. How could she keep working after that? But she had no choice and stumbled through the next twenty minutes on auto-pilot while her mind seethed with emotion. Had he recognised her or had she been reading too much into that final brief look they'd exchanged? Had

239

she changed too much from the naïve young student he'd known so intimately?

She couldn't help imagining what might have ensued if he'd introduced her to his wife . . . introduced her honestly.

*'This is Ellie, one of my old students . . .'*

*'This is Ellie, who I said I'd leave you for. I told her I loved her and she fell for it, the gullible, silly girl.'*

*'This is Ellie, who I told it was "for the best" and "a brave decision" when she told me she was quitting her course to go travelling.'*

Mercifully, they ran out of food and drinks as the festival wound down and her colleague suggested they call it a day. By now, she was desperate to get off the boat and go somewhere she could be on her own and take a breath. Julian should have been consigned to the past but she'd vastly underestimated his power to turn her world upside down.

# Chapter Twenty-Two

Wow, talk about being thrown in at the deep end. Scarlett was floundering as people drifted past the stall with no more than a cursory glance or lingered at a safe distance in case they were pounced on. It was funny to see them deciding whether to approach, or the kids dragging reluctant parents up to the food. Jude had a large family-friendly poster by the stall, entitled 'Can I really eat this?'

He was bolder than her, engaging the families in conversation but soon Scarlett grew more confident too; offering samples to the waverers was an easy way to lure them to the stall itself.

Slowly, she began to relax into her role and enjoy the atmosphere. Strains of music drifted in along with the misty tendrils, and soon were joined by the town band playing carols. Kids shrieked and danced around, whipped up by the sight of so many weird and wonderful costumes. The smells were to die for. The fruity richness of Jude's figgy pudding and cherry brandy competed with the scent of hot chestnuts and the tang of the pie van opposite.

A woman in a studded leather jacket adorned with metal logos and badges passed the stall. She was trying to restrain a Rottweiler whose claws clattered as he strained to reach the stall.

'He-el, Sacha!' she boomed. 'Keep away from the puddings!'

Scarlett giggled as the dog almost snaffled one of the samples.

'No, Sacha. How many times do I have to tell you that human food is bad for your delicate tummy? But these silly people will keep leaving it lying around.'

'Who's that?' she asked Jude once the woman was out of earshot.

'Bryony Cronk.' Jude rolled his eyes. 'She owns the local dog-grooming parlour and emporium.'

Scarlett giggled. '*Emporium*? This place is priceless.'

'Haven't you realised yet that we're all barking mad?' Jude's eyes twinkled behind his mask. Scarlett almost melted in a puddle of drool. It was impossible not to fancy the breeches off him.

They attracted more and more visitors, who asked about the books and courses, chatted to Jude and tried the samples. Scarlett was alarmed to find that people assumed she was an expert too, so she did her best to answer the questions that she could, realising she'd picked up more snippets than she'd expected while out on Jude's foraging trips, reading various books or helping him in the kitchen. However, she had to refer anything tricky – 'Can I eat the funny mushroom

I found in my garden' – to him. She'd caused enough mayhem for one year, she thought wryly. You really had to be an expert to tell your chanterelle from your destroying angel or funeral bell, even if the names were a bit of a giveaway.

'It's great to see Porthmellow packed on a winter's night. We've already sold more books than I expected.' Jude's voice held quiet pride.

Scarlett replenished the pile of softbacks on the stall. 'They're keen on the free food samples too.'

He laughed. 'People are always up for free stuff. I've taken a booking for a foraging course and sold a couple of vouchers, but we could do even better.' He cast her another lingering look. 'Thanks for doing this.'

'I don't mind. I'm enjoying it so far.'

A few moments later, their attention, and that of the people milling around the stall and nearby, was claimed by the arrival of the Christmas lantern parade.

The parade was led by the town band playing what Jude explained were old Cornish Christmas carols. The younger children were carried or held their parents' hands while the older ones jigged up and down, carefully clutching their lanterns with the tea lights flickering inside.

'Oh, look, it's Rita the Octopus!' Scarlett burst out as the giant sea creature passed by, supported by several people.

'Do you recognise your lantern?' Jude asked her.

'Not sure yet . . . I gave it to Ruby.' Scarlett scanned the line of kids and parents for her 'star'. 'Oh, hang on. Yes! There they are.'

Ruby was in her buggy being pushed by Chloe while Hannah held the lanterns that Chloe and Scarlett had made.

'There's Mum,' she said, spotting Anna with her lantern, alongside a couple of people from the art class.

A few minutes after the lantern parade had passed by, the carols drifted away to be replaced by less familiar sounds. Through the fog came the deep boom of a drum, overlaid by high-pitched sounds of a fiddle, a tin whistle and a wail that reminded Scarlett of bagpipes.

The noise grew louder and soon the eerie music filled the air.

Bellows and roars echoed across the street and there was an acrid smell of smoke on the night air. Bells tinkled and the roaring grew louder. Fathers hoisted their kids onto their shoulders while others craned their heads to try and see where the mysterious sounds were coming from. People moved aside to clear a path as the parade came into view, heralded by jugglers swinging balls of fire and licking flames from sticks of fire.

Sparks flew into the air and parents grasped their children's hands tighter.

People adorned in festive greenery, papier-mâché masks, top hats, tatters and motley strolled by, playing instruments and waving at the crowds. Shrieks rang out as a fantastical beast decorated with holly and fir branches stopped in the cleared space opposite the stall. Tongues of fire shot from its side, accompanied by bellows and roars. Most of its minders had pints in their hands and seemed to be getting into the traditional and pagan festivities with a vengeance.

The creature was followed by members of the various groups of revellers from pubs and trade associations, known as 'guises', all in their solstice outfits. Jude pointed out a couple of people but admitted even he didn't recognise most of them.

'Well,' Scarlett said, raising her voice to make herself heard above the din. 'You certainly don't see this every day in the Bullring in Brum.'

Jude laughed. 'I bet.' He eyed her costume, a long lingering look that made her tingle all over. 'You're definitely part of Porthmellow now.'

After ten minutes or so, the parade had passed by and Fiona Penberth turned up at the stall. On the brief occasions that Scarlett had met Fiona, she'd seemed tense and embarrassed by her husband's comments. Without him around, she was definitely more relaxed, joking with Jude as he signed his books.

Jude left to do a short wild-food cookery demo in the food marquee, so Fiona helped Scarlett hand out the samples and answer questions. With her son out of earshot, Fiona seemed happy to chat away about him.

'It's great to see him so relaxed about the whole thing these days, compared to how nervous he was when he had to do a cookery demo at the summer food festival a few years ago, now he's a pro. Stepping into the spotlight doesn't come naturally, but I think he comes across well when he's talking to people about his love of nature.'

Scarlett smiled to herself. Jude's mum was obviously very proud of him. She was sure his dad was too, but there was so much unspoken tension between father and son that

Scarlett found it very uncomfortable to be in Hayden's presence. Jude clearly took after Fiona more than Hayden, in personality if not in looks.

When there was a brief lull in the queue of customers, Fiona lowered her voice.

'He's had some tough times lately, so it's great to see him happy again,' Fiona said. 'I don't expect he's told you about his fiancée, has he?'

The word hit Scarlett like a punch in the chest. At first, Scarlett thought she'd misheard.

'F-*fiancée*? I'd no idea . . .'

She faltered, desperately trying not to sound as shocked as she was. Jude had a fiancée? He had been engaged all along, which must be why he hadn't seemed interested in taking the relationship further.

Fiona rolled her eyes. 'Typical of our Jude. He likes to keep everything to himself. Actually, not too many people know about the situation – the real situation – which is amazing for Porthmellow.'

'He's never said anything to me.' It was a miracle she got the words out at all, her throat was constricted with shock.

'It happened a couple of years ago. He and a woman from the college where he lectures were mad about each other, or so it seemed. They planned to get married and she was about to move into the cottage with him, then she changed her mind. She said she was "suffocating" down here in Porthmellow and that she'd accepted a job in London.'

'So they're not engaged now?'

'Oh no. Not now.'

Scarlett let out a huge inner sigh of relief. The fiancée was an *ex* . . . yet still, she wished she'd known about her, before Fiona had dropped the bombshell. 'I had absolutely no idea. Poor Jude.' She tried to recover her composure, hoping Fiona hadn't noticed how stunned she'd been to think he might have been about to marry another woman. Still, she'd suspected a couple of times that Jude was hiding some hurt in his past, just not that it was something as big as a broken engagement.

'He was very smitten with her,' Fiona went on. 'He even offered to move but she was having none of it. She said he'd never be happy in the city – which was right – and then left him. He was devastated, especially after he'd offered to give up the place he loved to be with her.'

'I can't imagine Jude in London,' Scarlett said, astonished that he'd been so much in love he'd offered to make such a drastic move.

'Nor me, but he felt that strongly about her. It knocked him for six, I can tell you, but there was worse. Last year, not long before Christmas, he heard that she was engaged to someone else. It wasn't a happy festive season, I can tell you. We usually go to my sister's house and have a big family do together. Jude decided he couldn't face it – not with some of his loved-up cousins about – and told us he'd volunteered for the Lunch for the Lonely at the pub.'

Scarlett hoped Fiona wouldn't notice her cheeks reddening at the memory of that day, but Fiona blundered on anyway. 'That was where you met Jude for the first time, wasn't it?' she asked, with a smile.

'Um. Yes. It wasn't the best circumstances to meet anyone.'

'These things are sent to try us, love.' Fiona patted her arm. 'I'm sorry to hear about your mum and dad. Jude says they're going through a bad patch.'

'You could say that,' Scarlett murmured, feeling like she'd ridden a rollercoaster of emotions in minutes and was still dizzy from the highs and lows.

'Don't worry, I haven't shared the details with Hayden. He can be a bit insensitive.' Fiona pursed her lips. 'And that's putting it mildly.'

'Thanks,' Scarlett said, liking Fiona more by the second, even if she did feel uncomfortable about the reference to her parents' troubles.

'Anyway, I probably shouldn't have said as much as I have, but I wanted you to know that if you ever notice Jude can be a bit down and moody, that might be why. His ex left a deep scar on him. You know how it is. When someone we love and thought we could trust lets us down, these wounds cut much deeper than we think.' Fiona sounded as if she had first-hand experience of being let down.

'I do know what you mean. It can be hard to put your trust in someone again,' Scarlett said, thinking of Rafa, but more tellingly, about her father and mother. It sounded as if Jude's ex had at least been honest with him, even if it had been a brutal shock.

'Yes, he took it very hard because he's a sensitive, deep-feeling lad. Or man, rather.' Fiona sighed. 'On the other hand, I do think Jude's been much happier of late,' she went on, with a significant lift of an eyebrow. 'I wonder why that should be?'

248

'Probably his business going so well?' Scarlett shot back. 'We've been very busy tonight.'

Fiona's eyes glittered with amusement. 'You could be right, although I don't think it's the foraging that's put such a spring in his step.'

The loudspeaker crackled into life and the announcer started to speak. Scarlett instantly recognised Evie Carman's rich Cornish burr. 'Now, my lovers. Do we have a treat for you! If you haven't visited the food stalls yet, and you're looking for a Christmas present, why not go along to see Jude Penberth. Porthmellow's own wild-foods expert is about to do his stuff in the cookery marquee,' Evie purred. 'The luscious Jude will be rustling up some tasty seasonal delights from ingredients you can find in your own backyard – all for free!'

People immediately turned around, peering at the stall.

'We'll have a queue again soon!' Scarlett said, struck by Evie's description of the 'luscious Jude'. She wondered if Fiona was trying to match-make between her and Jude, not that it would be a hardship to be matched with him, especially in his tricorn and mask. The image sent a delicious shiver through her. Fiona had opened up a whole new side to Jude that Scarlett hadn't envisaged. If he'd been badly hurt in his previous relationship, she would have to be extra sensitive towards him. He must have felt very raw to decide he couldn't even face a family party.

Still, it was almost two years since the split, and a year since his ex had announced the engagement, so perhaps there was hope of him being ready for a fresh start again. At least she hadn't been engaged to Rafa, Scarlett thought, on her way to the festival marquee. If she was honest, she probably hadn't loved him, not in any deep and lasting sense. He'd been glamorous and fun to hang around with, but she now acknowledged that they'd never shared the same values or been destined for a long-term future.

Jude had helped her realise that and regain her old spark to an extent.

A while later, she saw him making his way back to the stall, exchanging a smile or a 'hello' with locals on the way. He looked absolutely gorgeous but, more importantly, at ease and happy in his beloved Porthmellow. Perhaps Fiona was right: he was now over his broken heart. There was nothing to stop them from getting together . . . a fuzzy feeling in her stomach reminded her of just how much she'd love that to happen.

However, there was no chance to talk because a dozen people had gathered around the stall. Fiona stayed on, helping Scarlett hand out samples while Jude talked to his fans and signed books. She heard him telling people how to create a nut roast from the chestnuts, hazelnuts and walnuts he'd gathered over the autumn.

Scarlett's own mouth watered and she could see the crowd itching to taste the sample pots and cups after seeing the demo.

He poured a ruby liquid into two tumblers. 'Something I prepared in the spring. Cherry brandy. If you'd like to try some figgy pud or brandy, feel free.'

Soon the queue snaked around the stall and they were swamped with adults wanting the cherry brandy samples.

'You've got them eating out of the palm of your hand, love,' Fiona told him, when he slipped behind the stall for a quick swig from his water flask.

'I wish,' said Jude, obviously embarrassed. Scarlett smiled to herself at his reaction to his mum's fulsome praise.

'Shall I hang around for a little while until the rush has died down?' Fiona asked.

'Thanks, Mum.' Jude kissed her, then mouthed, 'Thank you' to Scarlett before launching into the book-signing queue.

The next twenty minutes flew by, and eventually supplies of brandy and books were running low. Hayden texted Fiona and demanded she went back to their catering stand to help him, so she had to leave. Even though they were busy, Scarlett knew they'd have to get fresh stock in the next few minutes and alerted Jude.

'There's another box of books in the cupboard under the stairs at my cottage. I didn't think we'd need this many,' he said.

'We're almost out of brandy too.'

'You'll find a few more bottles and more recyclable cups on the worktop. It's my entire stock.' He grimaced.

'Think of the samples as a loss leader. We're doing so well,' she said, delighted to see him happy.

'Yes. Way better than I hoped.' Jude handed over the key and Scarlett wove her way through the crowds to the cottage.

She opened the cupboard under the stairs and found a bag containing a dozen copies of his book. It was heavier than she'd expected so she went to look for a strong bag that she could fit the bottles in. She recalled seeing an oversized jute carrier in the kitchen and had a quick rummage for it in the walk-in pantry off the kitchen.

As soon as she switched on the light she saw the jute, and went in deeper to retrieve it from the bottom shelf. But she must have dislodged another item at the same time, and there was a thud as the object fell onto the tiles. Scarlett bent down and fished a book from under the shelf.

Not one of Jude's foraging guides but a much older, smaller book with a title she recognised instantly.

*Treasures of the Cornish Seashore.*

Her heart pounded. This had to be the book she'd been looking for and Jude said he hadn't seen – but where was the card?

She looked down at the tiles but could see nothing, so she crouched down and felt under the shelves in the darkest corner of the pantry, and felt a thin piece of card that had obviously slid out of the leaves and across the tiles when she'd dislodged the book.

Slowly, Scarlett stood up, the card trembling in her fingers.

She read the message she'd seen once before, but had convinced herself she'd misremembered.

**Anna,**
**Thanks for a night to remember,**
**All my love,**
**H xx**

She took the book and card into the kitchen and laid it on the worktop. There was no doubt. This was the book she'd seen when they were sorting out Auntie Joan's stuff. The book that Jude had denied having. She recognised the faded biro on the card too, with its tiny triangle of bent corner.

She hadn't imagined it, then. It was real – but what was it doing in Jude's cottage, why hadn't he mentioned it, and why had he hidden it away?

Standing in the middle of Jude's sitting room, Scarlett read the card again, unable to stop her hands from shaking.

All the pieces of the jigsaw were slotting into place but until now she'd been too afraid to look at the bigger picture – or had dismissed it. Now everything added up and it made her feel sick. Hayden's comments to her mother and her misgivings about Jude . . . the beach photo with Auntie Joan and now the postcard . . .

She'd begun to think she'd misremembered the message, or even seeing the card at all. Now it was in front of her eyes in black and white. She could no longer fool herself. 'H' – Hayden – had had an affair with her mother. Why else would he sign the card with 'All my love'? Only lovers signed a card like that. Even Rafa hadn't used such an emotive sign-off in his emails and cards to her.

The only thing that gave her hope was that if her mother suspected her father was Hayden Penberth, surely she would have come out and warned her? That part didn't add up . . . It looked like her night of passion with Hayden wasn't a one-off either, but part of a full-blown affair while she was staying in Cornwall in the summer after Marcus's birth.

She thought of her dad, and how devastated he'd be when

– or if – he found out. She clapped her hand over her mouth. Oh God, did she have a duty to share her fears with her dad?

Immediately, she dismissed the idea. This most definitely was not her secret to tell, and yet the knowledge was going to weigh her down like a gigantic stone. She had to tell her mother.

But first, she had to go back to the festival and face Jude. And his parents. She had to steady herself with a hand on the chair. The shock was almost as bad as the one on Christmas Day, but this time, she was determined not to freak out. She took a few calming breaths, replaced the book and card and picked up the bags.

# Chapter Twenty-Three

While Ellie was clearing away the rubbish, she spotted Aaron making a beeline for the *Marisco*. Her colleague made a jokey remark about him, telling her she should take a break. Everyone in Porthmellow probably knew they were seeing each other by now.

Aaron strode on board, all smiles. Ellie took him to the water side of the boat, behind a roped-off section.

He gave her peck on the lips. 'Hi there. How's it going?'

Ellie mustered all her composure even though she was reeling from her encounter with Julian. She supposed there had always been a slim chance she might see him again, as he was from the area, but it had been so long, she'd let her guard down.

She would *not* let Mallory ruin her evening, especially an evening that included Aaron.

'Good. In fact, we ran out of food.'

'I'm not surprised. The smell is incredible. Shame I'm on duty, but maybe we can share a hot toddy later.'

'Yes. Maybe.'

Aaron's smile faded a little at her lack of enthusiasm. 'Only if you want to. It must be hard work being a galley slave. Bet Drew cracks the whip?'

'He tries, but I don't take any notice.' Ellie made sure her reaction was keener but Aaron was no fool and must have guessed something wasn't right with her. 'It's been a hectic few days. If I never see another turkey pasty, it'll be too soon.' Better that he thought she was only knackered.

He arched an eyebrow. 'I could rustle up a little something while you put your feet up.'

'You must be tired too, after being on security duty all day.'

'Not really. It's been a very quiet night. No dramas, for a change.'

'No.' She laughed weakly. Realising she was still wearing a tricorn, she took it off, which only drew attention to it.

'I love the outfit, by the way,' he said.

Ellie winked. 'You should have seen me with the eye patch.'

'I like it.' He waggled his eyebrows.

'Thanks.' She brushed his lips with hers, thinking how different he was to Julian. She'd begun to believe he might be a keeper.

'You know,' he said, a little more hesitantly, 'this is probably the worst time but maybe you'd consider not going back to the manor at all one day . . . after Christmas, possibly?'

*Not going back to the manor at all.* Wow. Was he asking her to move in with him? Ellie struggled to reply. She'd thought about it herself, but he'd blindsided her.

'Too soon. I knew it was too bloody soon. I always jump the gun—'

'No. No.' She took his hand. 'It's a very tempting offer. *Extremely* tempting, and we should definitely talk about it very soon. Let me get through Christmas first.' She smiled so he knew she wasn't rejecting his offer. 'It's been a turbulent year and the next couple of weeks will be difficult for the family. In the new year, ask me again. I mean it.'

He nodded. 'Sure.' He kissed her again, full on the lips and obviously not caring who saw them.

Julian had reminded her of how easily you could be mistaken about someone, and how agonising the fall to earth was when you'd put all your trust in one person. However, Julian was her past. Aaron was the present and very possibly her future, and she should focus on that.

Buoyed by a hope she hadn't experienced for years, she walked with Aaron onto the quayside, exchanging smiles with familiar faces among the traders. The festival was winding down. The fishermen's choir were finishing their pints around the brazier outside the Tinners' along with a few hardy visitors. Stallholders were getting rid of the last of their wares or packing up.

'Hello there.'

Aaron's parents hailed them from outside the Fisherman's Institute, which had been used as a base for the festival. No one could help warming to lively, funny Evie or Troy.

'Looked like you were doing a roaring trade on the *Marisco*,' Evie said.

'I hope you weren't overloading that vessel. I am a harbour

official, you know,' Troy muttered, but the glint in his eye told Ellie he was joking.

Evie batted him on the arm. 'Ignore him, he's having you on. The festival's done well, considering it's the first Christmas one.'

'No trouble to deal with, son?' Troy asked.

'Nothing to bother us, Dad.'

'No one would dare cause any problems with Aaron in charge.' Evie squeezed her son's arm. 'Who'd go up against him?' She half-addressed this to Ellie.

'*Mum* . . .' Aaron winced.

'Well, look at you. You're a professional. No wonder there was no trouble.'

Ellie had to smile at Evie's pride in her son and his obvious embarrassment. She was enjoying it too much.

Troy let out a cackle. 'You've embarrassed the lad in front of his lady.'

Evie glared at him. 'Now who's embarrassed them both! I am sorry, Ellie, my husband's speciality is putting his foot in it.'

'Shouldn't you two be getting home? It's cold,' Aaron said.

Troy spluttered. 'We're not decrepit, my lad. Not yet.'

Evie tugged at Troy's arm. 'I think they want us to leave them alone and I don't blame them.'

Troy smirked. 'Aye. I bet they do.'

'It's been lovely to chat to you,' Ellie said, sensing Aaron cringing even more.

'You too,' Evie said, 'and you should come up to our place for a meal, Ellie. Any time you like. I'll make my shrimp creole. It's a family recipe.'

Ellie glowed with pleasure at the invitation and hoped Aaron would be happy about it too. 'That sounds delicious.'

'No one makes it better than my Evie. Got it from her father.' Troy's voice was bursting with pride.

'In fact, why don't you come over on Boxing Day after the swim? We always have a bit of a family get together. Gemma and her kids will be there and a couple of neighbours. I know Aaron would love it, wouldn't you?' She turned to Aaron, beaming.

Ellie held her breath slightly, in case Aaron wasn't as keen as his mum.

'Course he would, maid.' Troy chuckled.

Aaron broke into a grin. 'Dad's right. I'd love it if you could be there, as long as you're not busy.'

'I've no real plans apart from the swim,' she said, hoping Scarlett and her mum would spare her. 'If you're sure, then, yes, I'd love to come.'

'Great. I'll get extra food in.'

'There's a feast planned anyway. The fridge won't take it.' Aaron laughed.

Ellie felt his fingers alight briefly on her wrist, obviously signalling he wanted to be off. After all the drama, she was ready to drop.

'Thanks again, both of you,' Ellie said to Evie and Troy.

'See you, son. We're off to talk to Sam and the rest of the committee before we turn in. Some of us have work to do.'

The Carmans went inside the Institute, leaving Ellie and Aaron on the steps.

Ellie shivered as he kissed her, full on the lips but briefly.

She didn't care . . . Then the rogue thought slipped into her mind that Julian Mallory might have seen them. She hoped he had, but by now, he'd be long gone to take his grand-daughter back to bed.

Thinking of the little girl, the ghost of 'what might have been' came rapping at the window momentarily but she refused to let it in. It wasn't too late for her. Aaron's parents and grandparents showed two couples devoted to each other and prepared to risk almost anything to be together. It touched Ellie deeply, and reminded her again that a long, happy marriage or lifelong relationship was more than possible – and that Aaron could be the man for her.

'Ellie?' Aaron slipped his arm around her. 'You seemed miles away for a moment.'

'I'm fine, just a little tired, that's all.'

'Not too tired for a "nightcap" at mine after we've both finished up here?'

The way he made a nightcap sound absolutely filthy thrilled Ellie from her head to the tip of her boots. 'Oh, I think I can manage that.'

His eyes lit up and he kissed her again. 'Great. Take care on the way home, sweetheart. I won't be long.'

'I will.' Ellie wandered back to her car, her weary body at odds with a mind still reeling over the night's contrasting emotions. Her encounter with Julian was shocking but had been blown out of the water by Aaron's invitation to move in with him. Tonight was a loud and clear message that she had to put the past to bed and embrace new opportunities.

## Chapter Twenty-Four

With a stomach tied into knots, Scarlett loaded the books into a jute bag and the booze into another and let herself out of the cottage. Her fingers fumbled with the keys as she locked the door and she forced herself to trudge back to the stall, bottles clanking in the bag. Her arms and shoulders were soon burning with the weight of her burden, even on the short distance to their pitch.

Families swarmed around her, laughing, shouting and doing 'normal' things and living normal lives like she had before she opened that stupid bloody DNA test. Now she felt like a bottle adrift in the sea, bobbing along at the mercy of the waves, with no idea where she was going to end up.

Earlier in the evening, she'd found the jaunty music of the silver band and folk groups fun, but now they seemed to jar and make her head throb. The smell of smoke, incense and street foods mingled, making her feel queasy. She longed to run right back to her car and drive home, but her rational side told her to stay calm and not make a scene. One dramatic entrance in Porthmellow was quite enough for one year.

She'd never felt so torn. No one in the Latham family had made her feel excluded, but she was horrified by the fact that she partly 'belonged' to another family – and the possibility that it might be Jude's family made her want to throw up.

When she reached the stall, she saw that her mother had arrived and was chatting to some of the people in the queue who were waiting for Jude to sign their books. The sight of them together made her stomach turn over again. Forcing herself to walk over with a semblance of a cheery expression, she lifted up the bag of bottles and put them behind the stall. Jude smiled a cheerful greeting. 'You found everything OK, then?'

'Yes. Everything was exactly where you said.'

'Great.' His eyes shone with gratitude. 'I don't know what I'd have done without you tonight. Since Gabe finished his demo, it's manic again.'

'I can see that. I had trouble getting through the crowds with the stuff.'

He took the book bag from her. 'Wow. This is heavy. I should have gone myself.'

'I was fine.' Scarlett was like an automaton.

Her mother finished chatting and came behind the stall. 'Hello, you look busy. I wanted to see how it's going.'

'Good. We've done well. Business has picked up a lot since Jude did his demo.' Scarlett took the bottles from the bag.

'I can see that. Can I give you a hand?'

'Thanks. There are some more little cups in that box under the table.'

While Scarlett uncorked the bottles, her mother laid more sample cups on the table. Scarlett's hands shook as she decanted the brandy into the tiny pots.

'Cold fingers?' her mum asked.

'Brr. Yes.' Scarlett clapped her gloves together. 'Maybe you could pour the drinks while I dish up the rest of the figgy pudding?' she asked.

'No problem.' Her mother smiled. In fact, she seemed happier than she had for weeks, which made Scarlett feel even more disconnected from the world around her.

She tried to focus on dolloping pudding into the pots, adding a little wooden spoon and handing it over to the crowds milling around the stall. Her mother was filling cups and dishing those out too.

'Doing well, eh? But people are always up for a freebie.'

Scarlett glanced around to find Hayden at the front of the queue. She couldn't bear to meet his eye and her hands shook.

'Cold hands, warm heart.' He winked at her and grinned. His eyes were hazel rather than startling green. Like Scarlett's own. She almost passed out.

Jude hadn't even noticed, he was so busy signing a book for some 'fans'.

'Oh, hello, Anna.'

'Hello, Hayden.' Her mother flashed him a smile but there was a chip of ice in her tone. Oh God, this was excruciating.

'You're looking as lovely as ever. How's me old mate Roger?'

His old *mate*? Scarlett cringed but her mum brushed off the comment. 'He's fine, thank you,' she said tightly.

'Not with you tonight? I thought now he'd retired, he'd have all the time in the world to spend with his lovely family.'

Busy dispensing pudding, Scarlett's toes curled, but her mother seemed to be handling things.

'He's sorting a few things out at home.'

'I bet he is. Probably down the pub most of the time. While the cat's away, and all that.' Hayden's booming laugh attracted the attention of some of the people in the queue. Scarlett wanted to tell him to shut up. Fiona had said she hadn't discussed their problems with him but had he worked out that her parents were estranged? It was possible, in a small place like Porthmellow. Rumours must be rife all over the town, particularly now she'd become more involved in village life and with Jude.

However wild their speculation, they would probably never come close to the truth. For once, she could see a major downside to moving to a small community.

When he came behind the stall, Scarlett could have sunk through the cobbles. Jude glanced up at them. The smile he'd had on his face while meeting the public vanished when he saw Hayden talking to her mum. He didn't seem to care that there was a queue of people waiting for samples. All Scarlett could do was grit her teeth and hand out the freebies, while listening to Hayden interrogate her mother. Did Jude guess that his father and her mum had had a fling and hidden the 'evidence' – the book and card? He surely couldn't suspect that their affair had resulted in Scarlett, or he'd have kept his distance from the very start.

'I suppose good old Roger will be joining you at Seaholly for Christmas?' Hayden said to Anna.

'I really don't know what our plans are yet, Hayden.'

'Well, if you're staying, we'll have to meet up for a drink. With the other halves, of course, if they can make it. Bring your lovely daughters too, if you like, although I expect they'll have their own plans. I know Jude will.' He guffawed and Jude shot Scarlett a desperate look.

Scarlett was desperate herself, but for other reasons. Hayden's comment made it abundantly clear that he had no idea that she might be his daughter . . . but that meant nothing. Like her mother, he'd probably assumed that she was her dad's.

Oh Jesus, this whole thing only got worse.

'Thanks for the offer, but like I say, we haven't confirmed our plans for Christmas yet.' Her mum's smile was forced and her patience obviously wearing paper thin. No wonder, Hayden made Scarlett's skin crawl and the idea of spending another minute in his company was nauseating.

He rubbed his hands together. 'Well, can't stay here gossiping with you ladies. Must get back to our van. Fiona will be doing her nut, I was only supposed to nip off for a slash, but I wanted to see how Jude was getting on. I'll catch you later. The party's over, anyway.'

Scarlett let out a huge sigh after Hayden left, although the postcard immediately sprang to the forefront of her mind again, making her relief short-lived. Her mother also left to see some of her friends from art class, so Scarlett went through the motions of serving customers. They sold a few more books and got rid of the rest of the brandy, but Hayden was right about one thing: the party was over. Within half an hour, all the families had gone home and only couples and groups who'd decided to end their evening in the pubs remained.

She helped Jude pack up the books, banners and paraphernalia from the stall, grateful that they were busy and there was little time for conversation as they ferried stuff to and from his car. He went off with a final load of kit, leaving the stall bare, and planning to come back only to take down the canopy.

Scarlett exhaled and sipped from a flask of water to try to steady herself. Even if the postcard confirmed that her mum and Hayden had had an affair, it didn't mean that he was her father. Although she was probably grasping at straws, because it was barely credible her mother had had flings with *two* different men.

She was glad of a few minutes to herself to try to tame her rampaging thoughts. Jude was away longer than she'd expected so she took the bag of empty bottles over to one of the large recycling bins a few yards behind the stall. She was about to post the first bottle through the slot when she heard the voices of her mother and Hayden coming from behind the recycling skip.

'That offer of the drink still stands even if Roger can't make it – or doesn't want to.' Hayden was as bullish as ever, and making no attempt to lower his voice. 'We could talk about the bad old days. Cheer you up a bit. I know something's not right between you and him or he'd be down here with you. You know what happened that time you were let loose on your own in Porthmellow.'

'And what would Fiona think about you asking me out for a drink?' Anna's tone was icy.

Hayden laughed. 'Fiona? She won't care. We're not joined at the hip, you know. She never minds me seeing an old friend, and anyway–' he lowered his voice but not by much '–what she doesn't know, won't hurt her. Silence is golden, eh?'

Scarlett's stomach clenched.

'Not always,' her mum muttered.

A car horn tooted and Scarlett missed Hayden's reply. She strained her ears to hear.

'You don't look a day older than you did at the beach party, Anna. You're still a very attractive woman.'

'Even if that were true, and I doubt it very much, I certainly feel much older,' her mum said sharply. Scarlett listened harder, the bottle still in her hand. 'We *both* are.'

'I often think of what might have been, between us, that is.'

'You'd be better off thanking your lucky stars for what you have.'

Hayden sighed dramatically. 'Oh, Anna, sometimes I think we ended up with the wrong people. You can't deny there was a spark between us. It's a shame we never had the chance to kindle it beyond that one time.'

'Once was more than enough!' her mother said.

Scarlett dropped the bottle on the cobbles. 'Oh shit!'

No one could fail to hear the crash and in seconds her mother was by her side.

'Scarlett! Are you OK, darling?'

Hayden sauntered up, a smirk on his face. 'Oh dear. Butterfingers.'

'She could have been hurt. Has the glass cut you?'

'No. I'm fine.' Scarlett tried to make light of the accident.

'Want me to take a look? I'm a trained first aider,' Hayden said.

'No! I'm absolutely *fine*,' Scarlett blurted. 'I'm more worried about the smashed glass on the cobbles.'

Jude jogged over. 'I heard the noise. What's happened? Scarlett? Are you all right?'

'Yes! Will people please stop asking me that?'

'We're only concerned about you, darling,' her mother said.

'I'm OK. My hands are cold in these silly gloves.' She held up her fingers. 'All I need to do is clear up the glass before someone is hurt.'

She crouched down, wanting to hide away from everyone and the reality of the conversation she'd overheard.

Jude knelt down next to her. 'Don't use your hands. I'll get some newspaper.'

'I'll find a brush from one of the stalls,' her mother said.

Hayden stood there. 'Anything I can do?'

'You can take the canopy down on the stall,' Jude said, glancing up at him, sensing his father's presence wasn't wanted. 'If you don't mind, Dad,' he added, a little less frostily.

Hayden shrugged and grinned. 'Anything to help my son.'

He strolled off. Scarlett straightened up, finally meeting Jude's eyes. 'Sorry, the bottle slipped out of my hands.'

'Don't worry about it. Accidents happen.' He was so soothing and eager to make her feel better; Scarlett could have wept. He was lovely in every way, so in tune with her, and she'd fancied him so much. Now, the very idea made her shudder. Perhaps the reason they'd had such a bond was

268

precisely because they were related. Hadn't she read some-where that half-siblings who had never known each other could fall in love when they met? Or was that total bollocks?

Her head swam and she thought she might throw up.

Her mum arrived with a yard brush and a brisk smile. 'Here we go. Just stand aside, Scarlett, and take a few deep breaths. You look awful.'

Scarlett was in no state to protest, so she watched as her mother swept the broken glass into the newspaper that Jude gathered up and disposed of in a bin. Hayden had taken the canopy off the stall and finally gone to meet Fiona, and soon after Anna went to meet her art class friend for a lift home.

Scarlett was finally alone with Jude and it was all she could do not to cry. She wanted to blurt out that she'd found the card and what she'd overheard between Hayden and her mother, but the implications of it were too horrible to give voice to.

Jude gave the vicinity of the stall a quick scan before joining her on the almost-empty quayside. 'Well, I think that's it. It's been an eventful night, much busier than I expected and a lot more fun. That's mostly down to you . . .' he added, and the light shone in his eyes. 'Thanks for your help.'

Now, hyper alert to his slightest change in body language, Scarlett had a sickening sense that he might be about to kiss her so she stepped back. 'No problem,' she muttered.

His eyes clouded with confusion, then he peered hard at her.

'Sorry. People are around,' she muttered and tried to soften her comment with a smile.

Jude glanced over her shoulder. 'And? Why would they care

about watching us? We're only talking, and it's none of their business anyway.'

'I'm probably being silly,' she said, telling herself she was being paranoid about Jude being about to kiss her. If he had been, he certainly wasn't now, judging by the edge to his voice and confusion on his face, and there *might* still be an explanation for the card and Hayden's remarks about the night he and Anna had slept together. She mustn't overreact, but nonetheless, she shuddered at the very possibility.

'Cold?' His brow furrowed in concern again. 'Do you want my coat around you?' He'd already started to take it off.

'No. No, I'm *fine*.' She stiffened, fighting the urge to get away from him, and the whole situation, as fast as possible.

He shrugged, obviously nettled by her terse response. 'OK. So I'll see you soon?'

'Yes, but I've got a client meeting in Exeter tomorrow so I'll be out most of the day.'

She saw his body tense as he realised how desperate she was to get away from him.

'OK. I'll call you tomorrow after you get back from your meeting,' he said, hesitantly.

'It could run on. I might be late home. Probably be knackered when I get home too after the drive.'

His eyes bored into her. She wanted to melt through the cobblestones. 'Then I'll wait for you to call me,' he said, his tone dropping about twenty degrees.

'Good plan.' She flashed him what she hoped was a friendly smile. Every moment in his presence was excruciating. Surely this couldn't be happening to either of them?

Once again, the urge to ask him about the postcard loomed in her mind . . . She wanted to admit her suspicions, but there was absolutely no way she could think of to broach the subject.

It seemed as if the unthinkable might be true. What if Hayden Penberth *was* her father and Jude her half-brother? And if her mother didn't want to say who her father was because she'd been high or pissed or both and *really* couldn't remember who she'd slept with, how would she ever know for sure?

'Scarlett. Are you sure you're only tired? Nothing else is wrong?' he asked.

'Of course, just tired. I've had a lovely time, but it's been a long day.' She gave a pantomime yawn. 'I take my hat off to you, these festivals are exhausting.'

His mouth lifted in a brief smile. 'And it's a very nice hat.' He nodded at the brim. 'The mistletoe is a nice touch.'

'Mistletoe?' She groaned inwardly. 'I'd forgotten about that.'

'Really?' He waggled his eyebrows above the mask, obviously taking her comment about only being tired at face value. 'Are you sure?'

Her body ought to have responded in that fluttery, deliciously painful way. Instead, she simply felt sick.

'Yes. Really. Look, sorry to be a party pooper but I need to get my beauty sleep.'

'I'm sure you don't. This is probably the worst time ever to say this. I can see you're knackered and stressed about tomorrow but I have to say this or I might lose my nerve. I had a great time tonight. All of that was down to you.'

Scarlett stifled a squeak of horror as Jude went on.

'These past few weeks I've felt happier than I have for a very long time. I don't need to spell out why that is. It's been hard to open up to the possibility of . . . of caring for someone else so deeply again. Now I know I've shut people out for far too long.'

He smiled again. She could not bring herself to speak, just stared at him, her lips parted in absolute guilt and horror. He took it as licence to carry on and took her hands.

'You've changed all that. I'd hate it if we missed our chance.' His eyes flashed sexily behind his mask, but Scarlett stood there as if she'd been turned to stone. She knew in her head that she fancied him and he was a kind, gorgeous, lovely man. She knew that in any other circumstances, she'd have said all those things, but these were the circumstances and – just for a moment – she thought he sounded exactly like his father.

# Chapter Twenty-Five

'Deck the halls with boughs of holly, fa la la la . . .' Ellie sang along to the carols playing in the Harbour Café the morning after the festival.

She'd come straight to work from Cove Cottage and had been helping serve up the breakfasts before laying out festive goodies under the counter, ready for coffee time. She carefully arranged stollen slices and mulled wine bread from the local bakery, along with a homemade strudel, alongside seasonal savouries. The aromas alone would make anyone's mouth water; piled on platters and cake stands right in front of the customers' eyes, they'd be sure to fly off the shelves.

Her boss joined her behind the counter, a fresh tray of mince pies in her hands.

'Wow, Ellie, you seem very lively this morning considering it was festival night last night. Whatever it is you're on, I'll have some.'

Ellie tried and failed to suppress a cheeky smile. 'I'm knackered, to be honest.'

Tina raised an eyebrow. 'Sleepless night?'

Ellie felt her cheeks heat up and took the tray from Tina. 'Do you think we've got enough mince pies?' she asked, popping the pies under the counter display.

'You can never have too many,' said Tina. 'And though it's none of my business, I think he's very good for you.'

Ellie thought so too and while she finished the pie display, Aaron was all she could think about. She hadn't had a lot of sleep, it was true, but most of that was down to good reasons, even if Julian Mallory had crept into her thoughts when she'd woken.

Tina went back into the kitchen to prep the sandwich fillings for lunch, leaving Ellie on counter duty. A group of ladies from the knit and knatter arrived and settled in the corner with cappuccinos and their latest project. They were the only customers and the slight lull gave Ellie a moment to think about Aaron's Christmas gift, which she'd had her eye on for a while in one of the harbour shops. She'd agonised over what to get him – if anything – and eventually settled on a very nice pen as she'd noticed he took an old biro to his business meetings. It seemed to be the right blend of thoughtful, personal and practical. She'd no idea if he would get her anything but she decided to buy it after her shift.

After the previous evening, she'd allowed herself to think of the longer-term future for the first time in a long while. Her roots really did seem to lie in Porthmellow now and the invitation to the Carmans' Boxing Day party was symbolic of their relationship moving on.

She was acutely aware that it would be her first family occasion with Aaron, and that his extended family would be there. It felt 'serious', and despite knowing and liking the Carmans, she was a little nervous. She knew she'd be under scrutiny, even in the friendliest way, but was also honoured they wanted to welcome her into the family. Aaron's face had almost cracked when she'd happily accepted, his grin was so wide. His pleasure made Ellie happy too, but reminded her that her own family wouldn't be together.

Ellie served a couple with mincemeat scones and ginger-bread lattes, and a family arrived for hot chocolates and mince pies topped with clotted cream. Gradually the café was filling up, and she'd just decided to fetch Tina from the kitchen and collect a fresh bottle of gingerbread coffee syrup when the door opened.

A woman lingered on the threshold as if she wanted to size the place up, leaving the door open behind her. A blast of wind, straight off the sea, rattled the window and lowered the temperature. She was striking and willowy, ensconced in a post-box red maxi coat and wearing black high-heeled boots. Her long, platinum-blonde hair had been left loose and was striking against the brightness of her coat.

Ellie wished the blonde would make up her mind and the knitting ladies were also darting disapproving looks in the stranger's direction.

The customer decided, closing the door behind her and approaching the counter. She glanced up at the menu boards and wrinkled her nose, the tip of which was magenta from the cold, making Ellie think of an exotic bird. Actually . . . that hair was familiar. Several strands of it had fallen onto the pasties at the festival . . . It was the woman who'd loudly demanded gluten-free pasties.

'Morning. What can I get you?' Ellie asked cheerfully, hoping that the café menu would meet the blonde's requirements.

The blonde glanced at the name badge on Ellie's uniform. 'You must be Ellie?' she said.

It was an unusual response to 'what can I get you?', but Ellie was used to all sorts. 'Yes. I am,' she said, still smiling.

'Eleanor Joan Latham?' the blonde repeated.

Ellie's skin prickled. 'May I ask why you need to know?' she said politely, noting that Tina had come back from the kitchen with a tub of salad. She guessed Tina's ears were waggling furiously as she arranged the stollen slices on the display.

'So you *are* Ellie,' said the blonde with a satisfaction that made Ellie's hackles rise.

However, she was a customer and Ellie was determined to be polite. 'Yes. Have we met? Is this anything to do with the festival?' she asked, trying to ignore the urge to ask what business it was of hers.

The blonde pursed her lips. 'Hmm. I thought Aaron might have mentioned me – but on the other hand, I'm not too surprised he hasn't.' She offered a leather-gloved hand across the counter. 'I saw you last night. I'm Liza. Liza Carman. I'm Aaron's wife.'

Ellie felt as if a lightning bolt had struck her. She managed to squeeze out two syllables. 'His *wife*?'

'Yes. And I thought I ought to inform you that I intend

to name you in our divorce petition.' Liza lowered her hand when it became obvious that Ellie was in no fit state to take it, even if she'd wanted to. 'I assume you're sleeping with Aaron.'

It was a statement, not a question. Ellie's throat seized up. The ladies from the knitting circle were no longer interested in their tree decorations, but had all homed in on the counter scene like meerkats. Their necks must be stiff from straining to hear, although Liza wasn't keeping her voice down.

'I can see I've shocked you. Perhaps I shouldn't have been so blunt. Aaron wants a divorce on the grounds of five years' separation and I was going to agree, but then I saw you with him at the festival and I thought to myself, why don't I make things far more interesting by divorcing *him* for adultery.' Her voice was infused with bitterness and hurt, but Ellie was in no mood to be charitable after being confronted in public.

'Hold on a minute!' Ellie found her voice. 'You can't come into my place of work accusing me of – of – things.'

'So, you're denying it?' Liza asked, her eyebrows rising rapidly.

'No. Yes. Look, there's no way I'm discussing any of this here. You'll have to wait until I've finished work. In fact, I don't have to talk to you about my personal life at all.'

'Ellie. Can I help?' Tina directed a laser stare at Liza. 'I'm afraid I'm going to ask you to leave, *madam*. I can't have anyone upsetting or harassing my staff.'

Liza laughed. 'Upsetting? I've only told the truth. I wouldn't dream of eating in a shitty little hole like this, anyway.'

Tina puffed up. 'Right, that's it. Please leave my premises immediately or I'll call the police.'

'It's OK, Tina. This is my fault. I'll deal with it.'

'Not until this *customer* has left the premises.' Tina really was magnificent, but Ellie wanted to curl up and die of shame. She was surprised the knitting ladies' jaws hadn't unhinged and clattered onto the floor. The other customers were all staring at the sideshow in horror and fascination.

'Don't waste your time. I'm leaving but –' she directed this at Ellie '– you'll be hearing from my solicitor. Aaron should already have heard. Given the obvious state of shock you're in, I suppose you didn't even know I existed until now.' She held up a hand to Tina, who had advanced upon her from behind the counter. 'It's OK. No need to summon PC Plod. I'm going.'

Liza swept out of the café, leaving the door wide open and Ellie behind the counter, frozen with shock.

Tina jogged to the door and shut it.

'It's OK, everyone, the show's over,' she said, walking over to the knitters with a cheery smile. 'Now, would anyone like a free top-up?'

The ladies nodded and their heads shot back to their knitting.

'Thank you, folks, I'll be round with the coffee in a sec,' she said to the other customers. 'No charge for the extra entertainment.'

She hurried back to the counter with the knitters' used mugs. 'Come on, into the back with you,' she whispered. 'Go and sort yourself out while I make these coffees and then I'll be in to see how you are.'

She gave Ellie a tiny shove, snapping her out of her trance. 'Yes, thanks. I'm so, so sorry—'

'Later,' said Tina briskly. 'Go on.'

In the staff room, Ellie struggled with her apron strings and in the end had to leave it on. She collapsed onto a chair. She couldn't believe what had happened.

*I'm Aaron's wife. I'm Liza Carman. I'm naming you in the divorce petition.*

Was Liza bluffing? Was she really married to Aaron? How could he have kept something so momentous from her? She'd trusted him, shared her biggest secret with him – and he'd lied to her and let her down.

A few minutes later, Tina marched in. 'That was more drama than we normally get in Porthmellow.'

'It's more drama than I ever want to be part of. I am so embarrassed about it.'

'No need. Tell me if I'm being nosy, but sounds as if you had no idea about her?'

'No . . . and I feel like the biggest fool on the planet.'

'Bloody men, eh?' Tina said, patting Ellie's shoulder. 'Although I'd have bet the café that Aaron was one of the good ones. The Carmans are such lovely people.'

'He told me a bit about his army days but left out the part about his wife.' Ellie thought back to Aaron's comments. Every word, every nuance of the conversation had to be seen in a new light, but she was still in too much shock to remember it all at this moment. But the fact he'd sworn he didn't have anyone in his life and asked her to trust him: those two facts were burned on her memory. 'What a bloody mess,' she murmured, fighting back tears of anger and disappointment.

Tina laid a hand on her arm. 'Do you want to go home and sort things out with him?' she asked gently.

'Thanks, Tina, but no. There's no way I'm leaving you short of staff today. The lunch lot will be in soon . . . and the sun's coming out so we might have some tourists.' Ellie scraped up a half-smile from somewhere. Even though every cell was screaming that she needed to get some answers from Aaron, she refused to leave her boss in the lurch on top of causing a scene in the café. Plus she needed time to try to cool down before storming in on him.

'OK, if you're sure. But take a bit more time to get yourself together. Make a coffee and have something to eat, then come out when you're ready.'

'Thanks, Tina, you're an angel.'

Tina laughed. 'I've been called some things, but never an angel.'

Ellie made a cuppa and once her hands had stopped shaking, she touched up her make-up and dragged herself back to the counter, still reeling from the spat with Aaron's wife. Not his ex, his *wife* – a word that drummed on her brain and made her head throb. There were half a dozen more customers in addition to the knitters who'd obviously stayed on in the hope of more entertainment. Christ, thought Ellie, taking orders and serving beside Tina, the whole saga would be halfway around the town by now via WhatsApp and Facebook. It might even be up on YouTube.

She was genuinely terrified that the Carmans or her own

family might have heard. Or did the Carmans already know about Liza? Ellie decided they couldn't, or why would they have been so innocently keen for her to get together with Aaron?

Surely, someone in the town would have known he was married, though . . . this was one of the questions Ellie was dying to ask him, but that would mean a huge confrontation.

Any answer he could give could never repair the total destruction of her trust in him.

# Chapter Twenty-Six

Even though she'd been exhausted by the festival, Scarlett had a rough night, churning over the dark questions that had been so scarily exposed to the light. She'd been up before her mother was even stirring and on the road in the chilly dawn to see her client in Exeter. It was very close to Christmas to be doing business but they'd wanted her to start work on the brief immediately after the holiday, so she had no choice. Jude hadn't been in contact, although she hadn't expected him to be after she'd brushed him off the previous evening.

A new thought had struck her: as Jude clearly didn't suspect that they might possibly be half-siblings, why had he taken the book and kept the postcard? It was a conundrum that no amount of churning would solve.

It was a relief to concentrate on her meeting for a couple of hours. However, the moment she'd finished, her troubles mobbed her like crows. She set off for home and stopped at Jamaica Inn on Bodmin Moor for a quick lunch. When she came out of the ancient pub, snowflakes were whirling in the air and the sheep were huddled by the wall, sheltering from the wind.

High up on the moor, the temperatures had plunged and her smart wool jacket was no match for the biting wind.

Something about the bleak isolation of the place as Christmas with its all its family associations approached strengthened her longing to be close to her dad again. She opened the boot and pulled out his ancient waxed jacket. It had been his idea to keep his old gardening coat in her boot just in case, but it had lain there for the past couple of years, never needed until now. Though it was cracked and mucky, she put it on over her jacket and got into the car again. Watching the snowflakes melting on the windscreen, she imagined a time when her life had jogged along at an easy pace well within her comfort zone. How quickly she'd been thrown into a situation that was so far beyond her.

She dialled a familiar number and listened to the ring tone. It went on and on and she was ready to cut the call when her father finally answered.

'Dad?' Even saying the word had become loaded. 'I almost rang off.'

'I was in the shed,' he said, slightly out of breath.

'You should take your mobile with you.'

'I go in there to get away from the thing.'

'Yes . . .' She imagined the scene. Her father at his lathe, sawdust in his hair, his feet covered in wood shavings. 'What have you been creating this time?'

'One thing and another.'

'Christmas presents?' she asked, noting his caginess.

'Might have been . . . Are you OK, love?'

Scarlett hesitated as the snow whirled around the car. She felt lost and cold when she wanted warmth and comfort. She needed her family back together, if not for a perfect Christmas, then at least for one with the hope of reconciliation. She took the plunge. 'Dad, will you *please* come down to Cornwall for Christmas?'

She held her phone tighter as the silence lengthened. 'I don't know, love.'

'Shall I come home, then?' she said, offering the lifeline she didn't really expect him to take.

'No. Your mother needs you.'

She felt desperate. 'So do you. I hope.'

'Of course I do but . . . look, I promised Marcus I'd stay with him and Heidi and the boys.' The snow was thicker now, she could hear the sheep but not see them. She had to get home in case the road over the highest part of the moor was closed.

'After Christmas, then,' she pushed, growing desperate.

'Yes. Afterwards.' He sounded more certain, which suggested that it was the festivities, or perhaps bad memories, that had put him off from joining them at the manor.

'Thanks, Dad. I love you.'

'I love you too, Scarlett. Is everything all right?'

'No, it isn't. I can't handle this any more. I know it must be bad for you, what happened. Mum finally admitting what she'd – what went on. I love you so much but I want to know more and . . .' She stopped. She couldn't tell him her worst fears.

284

Too late. Her father's hackles were up. 'What has she said?'

'Nothing. Mum's said nothing. I don't know any more than you.' She'd no idea exactly what her mother had told her father. They might be two different versions of the truth, or completely different. There was also the chance, of course, that Anna had told him nothing.

Snowflakes had almost covered the windscreen. Scarlett flicked the wipers and they cleared it away but, outside, the snow was a whirl of white. Ghostly headlights lumbered past the pub.

'Dad, I'm on Bodmin Moor and the snow's getting worse. I have to go.'

'Bodmin? In this weather?' He sucked in a breath. 'You take care, love. Text me when you get home. The news showed a blizzard sweeping in from the north. They said it could be really bad in mid Cornwall.' His tone had switched from sad and wary to warm and urgent. He was her father again, his only concern her. 'You should get on your way now, if it's safe, and, love, for God's sake stop blaming yourself for this situation. The responsibility lies with us. Perhaps not even with your mum. With me.'

'What? Dad. Why do you say that? It's not your fault.'

'It's never one person's fault. I'm not perfect, not by a long way.'

The snowflakes thickened. A gritter passed by, orange light flashing.

'Scarlett?'

'Sorry. A gritter lorry came past.'

'Then you should go home before you get stuck. Call me

285

later, or anytime you need help. I don't know what I can do from here but I'm always here for you, love. I'd do anything to keep you safe. I love you. Hold onto that, whatever happens.'

'Thanks, Dad.' Scarlett brushed away tears. Her father had provided no answers and made no promises, even raised more doubts, but the warmth of his love for her comforted her, even as her car wheels skidded on the slush.

She drove very slowly onto the junction for the main road, horrified at how much snow was on the dual carriageway. She might have already left it too late to get home safely, but she had to try, or risk spending the night at the inn. She crawled down the seemingly never-ending road, passing stationary lorries and cars that had become stuck on the steep sections over the moor.

She prayed she didn't have to abandon her own car and end up appearing on the local news as one of those reckless people who sets off into a raging blizzard when the police begged everyone to stay indoors. All she could think about was that her dad loved her – and that he'd said he was partly to blame for what her mother had done.

If this were true, then she knew both of them even less well than she'd thought.

## Chapter Twenty-Seven

Ellie stumbled through her shift at the Harbour Café until Tina sent her home half an hour early. A squall of sleet and rain had blown in, chasing most of the customers back to their holiday homes anyway. Darkness was falling by mid-afternoon, giving Porthmellow's deserted streets a gloomy, godforsaken air, despite the Christmas lights and decorated windows. For the first time since she'd moved here, Ellie thought longingly of the swaying palms and sugary beaches of a tropical destination. Perhaps it was time to move on . . .

Aaron had tried to call her an hour before, then messaged her.

**I need to talk to you, it's urgent. Call me.**

So, Liza had found him, then.

Ellie took the back alleys to her car, wrestling with if and when to return Aaron's call. The lights twinkled through the

287

gloom and a few flakes of snow drifted down but melted the moment they touched the cobbles. The snow had turned to rain by the time the car park was in sight, melting away like the faith she'd put in Aaron.

Her mother and Scarlett might be at home and she didn't want a slanging match with him there. As for Cove Cottage: what if Liza was there now?

The decision was soon taken out of her hands. Aaron was waiting for her by her car. He jogged up to her, but she hurried to her car and wrenched the door open.

'Ellie, wait!'

She climbed into the car and was about to shut the door, but he stood in the way. Ellie gripped the wheel and stared straight ahead.

'Please don't say you can explain.'

'OK, I won't, but if I don't, how are you going to get some answers to the questions you must have? I know Liza's in Porthmellow.'

She looked up at him while the rain soaked his hair and ran down his face. 'Have you seen her?'

'A short time ago. She turned up at the cottage.'

'Well, she got to me before you. She was at the festival last night and saw us together and she came into the bloody café, ranting and raving. She said she's naming me as co-respondent in your divorce.'

'I know. I wish I could have stopped her, but when her blood's up, she does things she regrets. She's impulsive . . . and very upset. She won't really name you. I know her.'

'You *know* her? You've never even said she existed!'

'I had no idea she'd come down here and do – this. I thought I had everything under control.'

'Control?'

He shoved his hands through his damp hair.

'Not *control*. I meant that I thought I was dealing with it. With Liza and me. It sounds much worse than it really is.'

'Not to me. Not to her. She was angry and bitter, from what I could see.'

'You have to let me tell you the whole story. *Please.*' His voice was a plea, his confidence had collapsed like a sandcastle under a wave.

Ellie steeled herself. 'Is she – Liza – at your place now?'

'Not now. She called me after she'd been to the café and met me at the cottage. She told me what she'd done. I'm so bloody sorry. She's gone back to her hotel now and she won't hassle you again,' he added hastily, as if that made things better. 'No one knew about our marriage, Ellie, not even Mum and Dad or my sister. Only a few mates from way back.'

Ellie couldn't speak. Nothing he could say would make things better.

'We can talk at the cottage, if you want to,' he said.

She hesitated, feeling that no matter what he had to say, it was pointless as she'd lost faith in him, but decided to hear him out anyway. 'I suppose we'd better get it over with.'

She made it to the cottage safely – miraculous in the circumstances. She'd had to force herself to concentrate on the five-minute drive, telling herself out loud to keep her eyes on the road, watch the bend, turn left – like a learner.

Aaron had gone on ahead and she followed him inside the cottage, noticing the glow in the hearth and two mugs on the coffee table, one half full.

'Can I get you a drink? Coffee? Whisky?' he offered.

'No, thanks.'

'Will you at least sit down? This could take a while.' Ellie let his fleeting attempt at humour wash over her. It would take a lot more than charm to defuse the fact she was ready to go off like an unexploded bomb. Realising how twitchy she was, she decided to sit down after all.

She chose the chair, leaving the sofa to Aaron. She couldn't bear to be close to him. 'I will have that whisky,' she muttered, thinking she could leave the car at the cottage and walk home to the manor.

'I think we probably both need one.' His absence, while he splashed water into the drinks in the kitchen, gave her a few minutes to try to calm down. Sitting here in the cosy warmth of a cottage where she'd enjoyed so much pleasure, it was hard to imagine that it could – had – all been blown apart.

Aaron set a glass in front of her.

'She's not planning on bursting in on your poor mum and dad too, is she?' Ellie asked, finding it hard to say Liza's name.

'Not yet. She doesn't know where they live, as far as I know. After the festival, she googled the *Marisco* and you came up as one of the staff so she knew your name. She managed to find out where else you worked from one of the hotel staff.'

'Oh, the bloody gossip in this place!' Ellie burst out, furious with Aaron, with Liza for stalking her and with the village grapevine in general.

290

'Liza can be very persuasive and charming when she wants to be, but that's not the issue, is it?' His tone darkened.

Ellie nodded. 'No. It isn't.'

'Before I try to explain . . .'

Ellie snorted in derision and took a larger sip of whisky than she'd meant to. It seared her throat and made her feel worse, so she pushed the glass away.

'Before I tell you about me and Liza, I do want you to understand a bit more about her. She sometimes says things she doesn't mean. Yes, she was furious, but I swear she won't name you. She's already said she was sorry she kicked off at you and told me she'll agree to a five-year separation, no-fault divorce.'

'Oh, that's all fine then!'

Aaron hesitated, probably hoping she'd calm down a little, but that wasn't likely with her emotions at fever pitch.

'Go on,' she ground out, desperate to hear what he had to say, even if she was sure it wouldn't make a difference.

'Please understand that Liza's very . . . volatile. She can be a lot of fun and she has a good heart but she can also blow up.'

She muttered 'You don't say?' under her breath, but he went on.

'We were never suited from the start. It was a huge mistake . . . and she's had a tough time. She was serious about some guy from the crew on her latest ship, apparently, and he'd told her he wanted her to quit the cruise ships and settle down with him. She turned down a new contract but a couple of days ago, she had a message from him to say he'd changed his mind. She's devastated, hurt and angry.'

291

'I know how she feels,' Ellie cried. 'And I'm sorry for what she's going through but no matter how bad she's feeling, there's no need to burst in on me like that.'

'We'd been planning to get divorced for some time but hadn't got round to it. I wanted to get on with finally making things official and asked her to come down here after Christmas.' He sighed. 'But when this bastard let her down, she freaked out, booked a hotel and headed straight here. She admits she wasn't in the best frame of mind when she tracked you down to work.'

'I'm sorry about that. Sorry that she's hurt, but even if the café had been empty, it wouldn't have mattered. The point is that you didn't tell me you were married. In fact, you openly denied there was anyone else in your life.'

'That's because there *isn't*.' He sounded desperate, but Ellie wasn't softened. 'Liza and I haven't seen each other for years. We got married in the States when I was nineteen and in Cyprus for some R&R after my first tour. I was – it was a bad time, a crazy time, and we hooked up after a night in a bar in Paphos. A week later we decided to go to Vegas to a wedding chapel.' He stopped and closed his eyes briefly.

'I realised that it was a crazy idea and we knew by the time we were home that we'd made a mistake. I went back on tour; Liza was working as a singer, all over the world. We meant to get a divorce but,' he took a breath, 'I guess we just never got round to it before.'

'Why the hell didn't you tell me about her instead of lying?'

'I didn't mean it to be a lie. I thought it would be less . . . complicated to sort it out myself and I was sure I could. Not

292

even Mum and Dad know. They'd hit the roof. Marriage is important to them, and it is to me too . . . commitment and loyalty are, though you may not think so at the moment. They'd be devastated to know I did it on a drunken weekend in Vegas. They're so proud of me. I love them and I don't want to destroy that. I didn't want to hurt you or complicate things when it was over twenty years ago.' He passed his hand over his eyes. 'I've been a complete and utter idiot.'

Ellie resisted the urge to agree. 'Why didn't you deal with this years ago?'

'Like I said, we just never got around to it, and us both being away such a lot didn't help. At first, we kept meaning to but then we lost touch completely. I knew I had to sort it out and I fully intended to. I managed to track Liza down through Facebook and saw that she was coming home over Christmas so I thought it was finally time to deal with it. Especially since I've met you and we had grown so close. I had no idea she'd suddenly decide to land here out of the blue.'

'The past comes back to haunt you, Aaron. That's the problem,' Ellie retorted.

'Yeah. Well, now I've learned the hard way.'

'Anything else I should know about while you're at it?' she asked, stinging from his revelations about Liza. She felt light-headed, with exhaustion and shock, and her head had started to ache again.

'Nothing I want to tell you about now.'

'Right. *Other* secrets.' It felt as if all the relationships around her were turning to ashes.

'Not secrets, so much as things I'm ashamed of. I've made plenty of mistakes in my time.' His tone was bitter. 'There are times I've got things wrong and I'll have to live with that for the rest of my days.'

*Mistakes*. Was he referring to his army career? Ellie knew that was unblemished; Evie had told her he'd even won a medal and now Ellie realised she'd no idea what he might have been through. She hardly knew him at all, but that hadn't stopped her from falling in love with him.

'None of this is relevant to not telling you about Liza,' he said. He straightened up and put his shoulders back as if he was facing a court-martial and ready to take all responsibility. 'And you're right. I *did* lie to you and I'm so sorry. It was the most stupid thing I've ever done and I'll do anything I can to make up for it and gain your trust again because, dear Ellie, I don't want to lose you. I love you, even though it's too late to say that now.'

His eyes glittered and Ellie's resolve wobbled. He seemed on the verge of tears: this big, strong man she'd handed her hopes of a brighter future to.

He *loved* her.

And she believed him.

A crack opened up in the wall of anger that was protecting her from bursting into tears. She'd made mistakes with Julian. Aaron had listened to those and been non-judgemental and kind.

She loved him too, yet that wasn't enough. He'd shattered her trust, and it probably was too late.

'I wish you'd been honest with me,' she murmured,

disappointment crushing her into the depths of despair. 'I can handle that you're married, that it was years ago, but what I can't deal with is that you didn't tell me. You lied to me when I asked if there was anyone else.'

'There isn't anyone else. I swear on my life.'

Ellie winced. The pulse in her temple threatened one of her occasional migraines and she sure as hell didn't need that on top of everything else. She wished she'd never said yes to the whisky.

'Liza is my wife in name only. There's nothing between us apart from friendship.'

'How do you know she thinks that?'

'Because it's true, and you know it too. Please, Ellie, give me some time and another chance.' He reached out for her but she turned away, wrapping her arms around herself defensively.

'I am so sorry I've hurt you. It's my fault. I should have told you. I would . . . you're the best thing that's ever happened to me. I didn't want you to think badly of me. I didn't want to tell you how lightly I once treated marriage. Not when I know you're a good person, that you value love and commitment. Not when you've been let down so badly before.'

'Don't blame me for this. It's not the way I am that made you lie.'

'It's not the way I am, either. Not then, not now.'

She shook her head, unable to form her turbulent thoughts into words. He didn't ask again, didn't plead – not that she would have listened anyway. The voices of shock and disappointment had drowned out any reason. She had to be as far away from him as possible.

'You know, there have been times when I saw things happen to mates and innocent bystanders . . .'

Aaron spoke so softly, Ellie had to turn around to hear. 'Times when I was only yards away. Instantly, before the dust had settled, almost in the fraction of a second *before* the flash . . . I knew it was all over for them.'

She stared at him, saw the resignation in his expression. 'This feels like one of those moments. There's no coming back from this, is there?'

'I – I need to go home. Be on my own. Please don't call me.'

'If that's what you want.'

'It's not what I want. It's the last thing I want, but right now, it's what I need.'

Her head throbbed sickeningly. She let herself out of the cottage and walked into the darkness, tears half blinding her. The moon came from behind a cloud, showing her the path to Seaholly Manor. The sea boomed behind her, foamy in the half-light. She heard the door close behind her. An aura of coloured lights formed ahead of her, appearing from nowhere in the half-light. She knew she was in for a migraine.

She had to get home.

She should have relied on her own intuition; been much more guarded, not handed him her trust and her bloody heart on a platter: *Here you are, Aaron, carve this up and feed it to the crows, why don't you? I'm gullible, trusting Ellie who loves being let down by blokes.*

She'd lost Aaron. She needed to be on her own, but then, she needed to go home to her family. To Scarlett, her mother . . . and to her dad, but he wasn't there.

Never had she felt the fragmentation of her family more than in this moment. Her whole world appeared to be caving in around her.

She had the terrible feeling that Aaron was right. There was no coming back from this.

# Chapter Twenty-Eight

It was after seven o'clock and pitch dark by the time Scarlett made it home. It had been a nightmare journey, with the snow only turning to sleet and rain when she'd got down to sea level and closer to Porthmellow. Her phone had died a couple of hours before and she'd left the charger at home.

The moment she pulled up, her mother appeared in the porch and dashed out onto the drive. She had the door open before Scarlett had the chance.

'Scarlett! What on earth has happened to you? We've been so worried about you. Why didn't you answer my calls? I expected the police to call me at any moment.'

'My phone battery died and I left the charger at home.'

Anna hugged her, almost squeezing the life out of her. It was the first time in ages that she'd had such a spontaneous, heartfelt embrace from her mum. She let the hug go on a second or two before they both stepped back.

'The weather looked horrendous on the TV. I was so worried.'

'It's been a bit difficult,' Scarlett said, playing down her journey. 'But some people have had things much worse. So many people have had to abandon their cars. I'm lucky.'

'Well, come in by the fire. You look frozen.'

'I'm OK. Honestly.'

'Is that your father's old gardening coat?'

'Yes. I needed an extra layer.' She walked in ahead of her mother and despite her weariness, burst into a smile.

'Oh my God, who got the tree? I didn't think we were ever going to get one.'

'Well, I thought it would be more cheerful and that you'd enjoy it. Someone from art class helped me to collect it in his van and set it up in here.'

'It's huge!'

Her mum smiled. 'It was all they had left, and while I had the offer of help, I took it.'

The tree was magnificent, almost touching the ceiling. Even though her mum must have used all Joan's decorations and a few extras, it could still have taken more, and patches were bare. Scarlett vowed to buy some more decorations to fill the gaps, she couldn't bear it to be unfinished.

While Scarlett was heartened to see the tree, she couldn't help thinking of how much her dad had always enjoyed going to the forestry centre when the Latham kids were young, and her parents still continued the tradition. She thought of the doubt and loneliness in his voice when she'd spoken to him, and her heart ached.

'I've almost finished decorating it.' Anna cut into her

thoughts. 'I hope you don't mind. It gave me something to do while I was worrying.'

'No . . .' Scarlett was struck by a pang of guilt. Her mother must have been very anxious about her. 'I'm sorry to have worried you, Mum,' she said, meaning it. 'Where's Ellie?'

'I don't know. She should be home by now and she's not answering her phone. Why don't you try now and let her know you're OK? Sit down while I get you a hot drink.' Her mother handed her the landline handset. 'I'll make one while you get changed.'

Scarlett hung her dad's coat up in the cloakroom and tried Ellie's mobile, but there was no answer. She must be with Aaron, Ellie thought, or off on a secret present-buying mission. Maybe Ellie had left a message on Scarlett's dormant mobile.

With her phone charging by the bed, she scooted into the shower, luxuriating in the feeling of being warm and safe after her exhausting journey.

She changed into sweatpants and a hoodie, while texts and WhatsApp messages pinged and beeped when the phone woke up.

Oh no . . . three texts and a call from her father, asking if she was alive. She replied quickly to say she was fine. There was one from Ellie that was hours old wishing her a safe journey then five from her mother . . . and one from Jude.

**Sorry to bother you. Just a quickie to see if you are OK because your mum called to see if I'd heard from you. I've seen the snow on the news. If and when you get this, text me to let me know you're home.**

So, even though he'd said he wouldn't bother her, he cared enough to break that silence and see if she was OK.

Jude was solid gold. She might have been a tiny bit in love with him before the festival.

She was safe at home but all her problems were still here. In fact, they loomed even larger. Lovely, gorgeous Jude deserved an explanation, however painful and horrible that would be. She was going to have to broach her fears with him . . .

She quickly texted Ellie back to say she was home, anticipating a reply if and when Ellie had a signal. Then she took her phone and charger downstairs and plugged it in next to the chair, reluctant to be far from it again.

Her mother walked in with a tray of steaming mugs and plates of food. 'Here you go. I warmed a few mince pies. I made them earlier so they might not be up to Ellie's standards. I cut a slice of Christmas cake too. It's not quite ready but I think you need it.' She smiled.

'Thanks, Mum.'

Scarlett accepted the tea, sipped it and the warm liquid filled her veins. She bit into the mince pie and tried to swallow it. She was starving, but now, safe and surrounded by the comforts of home, the adrenaline that had kept her going through the blizzard had evaporated. The twinkling fairy lights reminded her of previous Christmases with their innocence and blissful ignorance.

'You do like the tree?' Anna asked.

She nodded, crumbs and unshed tears clogging her throat. 'Ellie will love it, I'm sure.'

'I must admit I'm getting slightly worried about her.'

'She's probably with Aaron,' Scarlett said.

'Hmm.'

There was the crunch of footsteps on gravel.

'That sounds like her now.' Anna peered around the curtains. 'It is,' she said.

Shortly afterwards the front door opened and Ellie walked in. However, it wasn't the bouncy, smiling Ellie they expected, but an Ellie with a tear-stained face and slumped shoulders.

Scarlett met her halfway across the room. 'Ellie. What's the matter?'

Their mother hurried to her side. 'What's happened to you, darling?'

'Don't worry, I'm OK. Physically.' Ellie hugged her mother and shot Scarlett an agonised look. 'It's Aaron. I should have known better than to trust any man by now, I suppose. I just found out he's not who I thought he was.'

# Chapter Twenty-Nine

Even though she'd been dying to get home, Ellie's heart sank to her boots. Telling her mum and Scarlett was almost as bad as hearing the news in the first place and made her headache even worse.

'What do you mean, "not who you thought he was"?' Scarlett demanded.

'He's married. Getting a divorce, as a matter of fact, but it would have been nice if he'd told me about his not-so-ex. She waltzed into the café this morning and informed me she was his wife and would be naming me as co-respondent in the divorce.'

'No way! You're joking!'

'It'll be all round town by now.'

Their mother clapped her hand to her mouth. 'Oh, darling. This is horrible for you.'

Scarlett was instantly on the warpath. 'I can't believe Aaron would lie to you like that. I had no idea he was married!'

Ellie allowed herself a fleeting inner smile at Scarlett's loyalty before going back to the reality of a situation which no amount of righteous indignation would solve.

'Me neither. Nor his parents and sister. He married her – Liza – years ago after a whirlwind romance. They've been meaning to get the divorce ever since but lost touch while he was in the army.'

'What a cow to come to your workplace and humiliate you like that!' Scarlett declared.

'What a nasty thing to do,' their mother said. 'This Liza must be a real charmer.'

'In one way, I can hardly blame her, even though it was a shock at the time. She's just been let down by her latest boyfriend and she's a volatile character, according to Aaron.'

'She must be to burst into the café like that!'

'Yes . . . but she'd already headed down here for the festival, wanting to see Aaron and maybe use him as a shoulder to cry on.'

Scarlett let out a snort but Ellie was willing to be a little more forgiving of Liza now she'd heard what had happened. 'She saw us together aboard the *Marisco*, looked me up on the sailing trust website then asked around at the hotel and found out where I worked.'

'She sounds quite a character. You must have been very shocked when she turned up at the café,' Anna said gently.

'She's certainly a character but she was obviously in quite a state herself,' Ellie muttered before firming up her voice. 'Aaron reckons she won't follow through with naming me, but if she's as unpredictable as he says, who knows? And it's not the point. The point is he didn't tell me. He let me think he was free.' Voicing her hurt to her nearest and dearest opened the wounds all over again and reminded her of the yawning chasm that had been opened between her and Aaron. 'I've just had a massive row with Aaron about it. Sorry to put a dampener on the Christmas spirit.'

Ellie flopped down on the sofa next to Scarlett, and leaned back against the cushion with her eyes closed. 'You think your life is all going well. You find a place to settle and someone decent – special – to share it with, and then, kaboom, someone blows your cosy little dream sky high.'

She opened her eyes, realising the irony of what she'd said. The lights on the tree made her head pulse and feel sick.

'We all know how that feels,' Scarlett said quietly.

Ellie patted her hand. 'I didn't mean you, lovely.'

'Sounds like you need a large G&T,' Anna said. 'In fact, I think we all do.'

Ellie held up her hand. 'Thanks, but not me, Mum, I've got a splitting headache.'

'Do you want some of your migraine tablets?'

'Yes, please. Then I think I'll go to bed.'

Scarlett gave Ellie a gentle hug. 'Sounds like a good idea.'

Their mother got up. 'I'll fetch them from the kitchen and bring a glass of water.'

'You've had a shock,' Scarlett said soothingly. Ellie's head pulsed again and she wondered if she might throw up, but wanted to make sure her sister was OK.

'How are things with you and Jude?' she said to Scarlett. 'I haven't had chance to talk to you since the festival. I thought you seemed like you were having a good time when I left.'

'Oh, with me being out all day, I haven't spoken to him.'

'But everything's OK?' Ellie closed her eyes.

'Yes, of course.'

'Thank God for that. I couldn't stand it if you were miserable too. This family has had enough troubles with men to last a lifetime.'

# Chapter Thirty

Only two days to Christmas and it was shaping up to be almost as miserable as last year's, Scarlett thought, watching seagulls squabble over the remains of a turkey pasty on the quayside.

While her mother was queuing in the post office, she'd been wandering around the harbour. A local choir was singing carols, accompanied by some members of the town band. Holidaymakers admired the boats, sipping hot chocolates or even eating ice creams. It was a mild December morning and while some people were wrapped up, the kids were chasing around on the wet sand of the harbour. A toddler had a bucket and spade, his father helping him to build a sandcastle, dressed in cargo shorts and a fleece.

Scarlett smiled to herself: her dad had always insisted that while he was on holiday, he would wear his shorts. It didn't matter that it was raining or blowing a gale. He wasn't at work, and he refused to wear trousers. He'd have loved being here this morning in the December sunlight that bathed everything with a mellow glow.

It looked like that wasn't going to happen this year.

Heaving a sigh, Scarlett told herself to cheer up. The last thing Ellie needed was her acting like a wet blanket. Realising she was almost level with her favourite gallery, she decided to pop inside and splurge on a bracelet that Ellie had had her eye on for ages. Ellie deserved a treat. She'd been so shocked and hurt about Aaron's deception, and no wonder, even Scarlett herself had thought he was a nice, straight bloke – one of the good guys.

So was Jude . . . which was why it was tearing Scarlett apart to back off from him. She'd heard nothing else from him since last night, and had sent a quick reply to his text, letting him know she was home safe.

Anna waved from the opposite side of the harbour and Scarlett turned back to meet her halfway, only a few yards from the Harbour Café.

As she approached Anna, Scarlett's pulse quickened. There was only one way out of this situation: take her courage in both hands and ask her mother straight out if Hayden Penberth was her father. Immediately the thought of the answer being 'yes' made her feel sick.

Anna reached her, a smile on her face. She really had no idea how bad Scarlett was feeling, did she?

'Hello. What's that you've got?' she said, nodding at the gallery bag.

'Something for Ellie,' Scarlett replied. 'A bracelet she liked.'

'That's a lovely idea. Look, I've been thinking. Why don't

we grab a coffee at the Harbour Café and say hello to Ellie at the same time?' Anna suggested.

'Good idea,' Scarlett said, meaning it.

They'd barely taken a step towards the café when Anna stopped and frowned. 'Actually, why don't we go into the Seagull Coffee Shop instead?' she said, taking Scarlett's arm.

'Why?'

'It looks like it could be very busy in there today. We might not be able to get a table.'

Scarlett was puzzled. There *were* a few people lingering outside the café. A family with three young boys had gone in ahead of them; she could hear the parents begging their excited brood to calm down and be careful as they piled through the door. They were followed almost immediately by a couple with a baby buggy. The man held the door open so his partner could wheel the buggy inside.

'It might not be so busy inside,' Scarlett said hopefully, looking forward to a few words with her sister, to show support.

'I think it will be,' Anna said firmly, linking arms and steering her away. 'And besides, we don't want to interrupt Ellie in her work. She'll be rushed off her feet.'

'OK.' Scarlett shrugged, disappointed but not ready for any further conflict. Her eyes and thoughts kept drifting to Jude's blue cottage on the other side of the harbour. Her mother marched onwards, seemingly in a hurry to get to the Seagull Coffee Shop, which had plenty of space. They found a cosy corner and Scarlett gave their order before returning to their table to await the cappuccinos and festive treats.

'Hmm. I haven't been in here since it changed hands,'

Scarlett remarked, admiring the freshly painted walls and local artwork. The door swung open, and a family walked in, taking a newly vacated table not far away from theirs. Scarlett spotted a striking picture of Lizard Point that she guessed her mother might like. 'They've done a nice job with it, don't you think? There are some gorgeous pictures.'

Her mother was staring into space and didn't seem to have heard Scarlett at all. She reached out to touch her arm. 'Mum?'

Anna snapped back to the present.

'What's the matter?' Scarlett said in a low voice.

'Nothing. I – I must have been on another planet. I was thinking about Christmas Day.'

'Ah. Me too.'

'That turkey we ordered is far too big for the three of us.'

Scarlett swallowed a lump in her throat. 'You don't think there's any chance of Dad coming down?' she said, thinking better of telling her mother that she'd already asked him.

'I don't know. I'm not sure I want him to. Marcus says he'll have him until they go skiing after Christmas.' Anna smiled.

Scarlett was saved from replying by the arrival of the waitress with their order.

They chatted about the food and the gifts they'd bought Ellie, but Scarlett also had half an eye on the other customers. She wasn't convinced her mum had been staring as aimlessly as had first appeared, and was sure that something or someone in there had transfixed her mother. She scanned the customers again. There were a couple of locals she recognised from the town, including Evie Carman with some of her bingo pals, and Chloe Farrow with her daughter, Hannah, and little granddaughter,

Ruby. All had nodded and smiled as she and Anna had entered, making Scarlett realise how fast she was becoming part of Porthmellow life.

There were strangers, too, including the couple with the buggy who had gone into the Harbour Café but obviously changed their minds, deciding the Seagull was nicer. They weren't far away at all, and Scarlett could now see that they were probably a little too old to have a young baby. Even though the woman was very smart and glamorous, she had to be of a similar age to Scarlett's mum.

The man was still handsome, though in his late fifties. Scarlett thought his hair was suspiciously dark compared to her own father's. He reminded her slightly of Hayden Penberth, although Hayden's thick silver hair was a more natural colour. This man had finer features than Hayden and no year-round tan, as if he spent his time indoors.

She supposed he *could* possibly be the baby's father, but it was far more likely he and his wife – if it was his wife – were grandparents.

There was something about him that fascinated her; and made her want to look at him, though the slight ripple in her stomach wasn't entirely pleasant.

She thanked the waitress and turned her attention back to the cakes. Her mother sipped her coffee while Scarlett attacked her carrot cake with a fork. She hadn't eaten much since the festival but the smell of spices had re-awakened her appetite. Behind her, she heard Chloe and Hannah exchanging pleasantries with the visitors about the problem of getting children's buggies into shops and cafés.

'We tried the café on the harbour front but it was so busy, we walked straight out again,' said the older woman. 'I'd forgotten what a palaver it is to bring one small person out for a walk.'

'Tell me about it!' Chloe exclaimed. 'They need a whole entourage, don't they, Ruby?' Chloe laughed and the toddler giggled and said 'Nana!'

'This one needs her own caravan of porters,' the man said in a cultured voice. He and his wife carried on chatting to Chloe. Scarlett had heard on the grapevine that Chloe and her family had only recently been reunited after years of estrangement, and the joy in her voice was unmistakeable.

Scarlett shot a smile at her mother, who also knew the story, but Anna seemed distracted, poking at a morsel of cake with her fork.

'Is your strudel OK?'

'Hmm. It's lovely, but I'm not terribly hungry.' She smiled at Scarlett. 'Thank you for the treat, though.'

'Are you feeling OK?'

'Yes. Fine. Let's ask for a box and take it home. You could give some to Jude, if you like.'

'I could . . .' She lowered her voice. 'Jude and I aren't that friendly at the moment.'

'Oh no! I am sorry. I hadn't realised you'd fallen out.'

'I wouldn't say we'd fallen out . . . it's just something we need to work out on our own. Shall we go?'

Hoping she'd put off further questioning about Jude, Scarlett excused herself and asked for a cake box at the counter, taking it back to the table before popping to the bathroom.

312

She came out and almost bumped into the glamorous granny.

'Oh. I'm sorry!'

In the time-honoured way, they both apologised profusely and Scarlett stood back to let her into the bathroom before opening the outer door back into the café. She stopped halfway, catching sight of her mother and the baby's grandfather intent on each other. He was smiling, showing a dazzling set of teeth and murmured something but her mother shook her head and glanced away, her lips pressed together.

Anna noticed Scarlett watching them and snatched up her bag from the floor. Before Scarlett could make it to the table, she'd grabbed her coat from the back of the chair, knocking the table. It wobbled and the cake box slid to the edge.

Scarlett rescued it just in time. 'Wait, Mum, don't forget your cake.'

'Yes. Sorry.' Anna picked up the white box and dropped it in her bag. 'It's so hot in here. I'm going outside for some fresh air.'

She wove her way around the tables, muttering apologies without looking at the man. He exchanged a glance with Scarlett and smiled politely but immediately switched his attention to his wife, who had come back to the table. They started cooing over the baby.

Anna was some way along the quayside when Scarlett caught up with her, her back turned and staring out over the breakwater at the open sea.

'Mum, are you OK? You rushed out of there. Did that bloke with the baby upset you? I saw him talking to you.'

Anna turned, her face as white as sea foam. 'What? No . . . to be honest, darling, I don't feel great. It was so stuffy and oppressive in there. Can we please go home?'

'Oh . . . of course. You do look pale and it was very warm,' Scarlett said, worried that her mum was about to keel over. 'Come on, let's take it steady.' She kept close to her mother on the way to the car, worried that she might be unwell, but suspecting that Anna's desire to get away had more to do with the over-familiar, dark-haired grandfather than the overheated café.

# Chapter Thirty-One

Scarlett had an agonising journey home as Anna refused to say anything until they were at the manor. She was sure that there was a lot more to her mum's distress than feeling a bit under the weather. She had to leave her mother in the car while she collected the turkey from the farm shop. It all felt so grim, doing the festive traditions with her mother silently waiting outside.

She joined a long queue of people at the farm shop, all of whom seemed patient and jolly, accepting the free glasses of mulled wine. She had to make conversation with a couple of locals she recognised, pretending that everything was fine and discussing how many were coming to dinner, what they were having and so on until she wanted to weep with frustration.

While she queued, her mind kept jumping to the man in the café. He *had* upset her mother and she was sure it wasn't a random row.

Jude sent her a WhatsApp message that launched her mind into overdrive.

**Are you OK? Have I done anything to upset you? Are you still doing the swim on Boxing Day and coming over? I might have a small surprise for you.**

'Oh God.' Scarlett squeezed her eyes shut in despair. She couldn't keep Jude dangling like this. She had to ask her mother for the truth, whether to rule Hayden out, or in.

'Here you go, my lover. It's a whopper.'

The farm shop man handed Scarlett a box that almost made her stagger under the weight.

'Popped your veggies in a bag on top. Expecting an army, are you?'

Scarlett muttered a thanks, threw the man a weak smile and escaped. Even the bloody turkey mocked her: they'd surely still be eating it until Easter, it was so large, but she guessed her mum hadn't lost the habit of catering for a houseful.

She put the giant bird in the boot and got into the car.

Once they got home and the fridge shelves had been rearranged to accommodate the turkey, she took a cup of tea to her mum, who was sitting on the sofa staring out into the garden.

'Feeling any better?' she asked, despite guessing the answer from her ghastly pallor.

'A bit.' Anna's voice wobbled.

'Mum, what's the matter? I saw you arguing with that man in the café. What was he saying?'

'Nothing. We weren't arguing.' Anna left the cuppa untouched.

'Right.' A wave of frustration and anger broke.

'Mum, I'm sorry you don't feel very well and this is probably the wrong time but I have to say this. I can't keep it in any longer.'

'Scarlett . . .'

'No. Please let me finish because there's something bad – really bad – bothering me about Jude. About the two of us. I *really* like him but I'm worried that he might be . . .' She could not say the words out loud but she had to ask the question. 'If you can remember *anything*, anything *at all* about my father, for the love of God, you have to tell me. Because if it's Hayden Penberth, I think I'll have to leave Cornwall and never ever come back!'

Anna stared at her. 'Hayden?' she murmured.

'Yes. I need to know. *Please* try to remember, or if you do know, tell me. Or if you can, say it wasn't him. Tell me. Why else would you keep trying to warn me off Jude? *Was* it Hayden Penberth?'

Anna found her voice at last. 'Scarlett, I can promise you that Hayden is not your father. What makes you think he had or has anything to do with us?' she asked quietly.

'What? But he must be.' Relief washed over her, followed by disbelief. 'I don't understand . . . I was so sure he *had* to be.'

'He isn't. Why do you think that?'

'You've been so cagey about who you slept with at that party and you obviously don't like the idea of me and Jude getting together. When we were sorting out Joan's stuff here at the house, I saw a postcard written to you, hidden in a book. It mentioned a special night and was signed H. Then during the festival, while I was at Jude's I found the card in his house in the book.'

'*Treasures of the Cornish Seashore* . . .' Anna murmured, then frowned. 'Though I've absolutely no idea why Jude had it. Oh God, he must have seen it and read it and put two and two together.'

Scarlett's pulse beat hard. 'So it *was* from Hayden?'

'Yes. He gave it to me years ago when I was down here one summer. I hid it in the book, meaning to get rid of it but I forgot about it. It had nothing to do with the night of the party.'

'Is that true, Mum?' Scarlett demanded. 'Are you sure you didn't sleep with Hayden that night?'

'Yes. It's true. I swear it.'

'But what about the conversation I overheard by the bins?' Scarlett still wasn't convinced by her mother's explanation and refused to let go until she knew everything.

'The bins?'

'Before I dropped the bottles, I heard you and Hayden talking about the night you spent together at a party. What else was I to think, but that it was the night you conceived me?'

Anna let out a cry of anger. 'Oh my God. Bloody Hayden. I loathe that man. He is the source of so much trouble. I swear to you on my life that it isn't Hayden and I *do* know who I slept with.'

'Then, w-why have you lied?' she burst out.

'Because I'm ashamed and telling you would cause you – everyone – even greater hurt and anger than I have. It isn't him.' Anna covered her face with her hands. 'I'm so very sorry that you thought it even for a moment.'

Scarlett closed her eyes, remembering the look on Jude's face the previous evening and his desperate messages since. 'Oh, Mum, I pushed Jude away last night. He must wonder what the hell was wrong with me. Why do you hate Hayden? What did he mean when he said you'd had a night to remember?' Tears of relief stung her eyes, mixed with angry ones at how she'd misled herself. 'Did you actually *have* an affair with Hayden at all?'

'No. What kind of person do you think I am?'

She joined her mother on the sofa. 'I don't mean to be horrible to you but I'm desperate to know the truth. I spoke to Dad before my phone died yesterday. He sounded sad and he said . . . he said it wasn't my fault what happened, and it wasn't yours either, and he should take the blame . . . and I don't know what was going on between you and Dad at the time, but I'm guessing there were things happening on both sides. Stuff that none of us know about.'

Her mum took her hand. 'Hayden has always had a soft spot for me, but he's had a soft spot for a lot of women. I've never kidded myself I'd be any different. He is – was – a very attractive man, just like his son, though far more confident. He knows how handsome he is – or *was*. He's had several affairs; poor Fiona probably knows about most of them. Auntie Joan warned me off him the very first time she saw us chatting.'

Scarlett listened intently, filled with relief that her worst fears were groundless, but dreading what fresh secrets her mum was about to reveal.

'Way back before I met your father, when we were both single and very young – and I'm talking seventeen here – I had a very brief fling with Hayden while I was staying with Joan. Even in my starry-eyed youth, I knew deep down that it couldn't come to anything, but I was still heartbroken when I had to go home. Hayden seemed less worried and by the time I'd come down the following Christmas, he was already going out with another girl.'

She sighed.

'I put it down to experience and a few years later, I met your father and realised what real love is. It deepens and grows. It weathers many storms. It must do, or why would Fiona have stayed with Hayden through all these years and all his betrayals?' She patted Scarlett's hand. 'It's a storm that your dad and I are going through now.'

'Will you weather it?' Scarlett said softly, hardly daring to hear the answer.

'I hope so. I want to very much. Rest assured that I have never slept with Hayden, or dreamed of it, since we were teenage sweethearts.'

Scarlett sank into her chair. There was hope then that her parents would get back together. And Jude wasn't related to her. It was hard not to scream out with the sheer relief.

'So what was the postcard? That wasn't sent to you thirty years ago, was it?'

'No, it was sent to me a decade ago. It was Hayden referring to our youthful fling, and tormenting me. He can't resist reminding me – or any woman – that I was once one of his conquests.'

'He's such a creep!'

'And nothing if not persistent. I almost kneed him in the balls, to be honest. The nerve of the man. He didn't come right out and ask me to sleep with him, but he said I was free and single now, there was nothing to lose and we'd had such a wonderful night.'

'So why is the postcard at Jude's now? It was hidden away in a cupboard.'

'I have no idea. You'll have to ask Jude.'

'And tell him about the two of you?' Scarlett shook her head. 'I don't think I can.'

'It's up to you . . . look, I *do* like Jude. He's handsome and charming in a modest way, but I don't want you to be hurt, that's all. I've had a hard time accepting that my lovely daughter, who deserves the best of everything, especially after all that's happened, has fallen for the son of a man like Hayden.'

'I don't think you can inherit cheating genes, Mum.'

'Really? Actually, you can . . . I read about it, you see, since the test, there's good evidence that the tendency to be unfaithful can be passed on.'

'Mum! Surely you don't really believe one pseudo-science article?'

'No. I suppose not. But it's hard not to assume "like father, like son". You do know he broke it off with his fiancée?'

'Who told you that?' Scarlett asked.

'Hayden.'

'Why would he do that? It isn't true. Fiona told me what really happened and it was Jude's ex who dumped him and hurt him badly,' Scarlett told her. 'It's rubbish. Hayden's spreading lies.'

'Why would he paint his own son as the villain?' her mother asked. 'Unless it's true and Fiona's trying to protect Jude . . .'

'I don't know. Maybe he feels ashamed that any son of his might get dumped by a woman! He's arrogant enough to believe that.'

Anna wrung her hands. 'I think you must be right. Darling, I'm so sorry. I believed Hayden.'

Scarlett screamed silently in frustration. 'Why does Fiona stay with that horrible man?'

'Perhaps because the alternative is worse? Because she loves him and doesn't want to lose him? Don't let what's happened to me and your father, or Jude's parents, sour your view of marriage or love. I don't want you hurt like I was and I'm very sorry to have misjudged Jude. It sounds like you need to have a conversation with him.' Anna squeezed her hand. 'If you don't believe me about Hayden, we can do a test. It will prove that you're not related to Jude in any way.'

'There's no need. I don't want to do any more tests,' Scarlett said. 'I don't want this to turn into *Jerry Springer* . . . But you do know who my biological dad is?'

Anna nodded. 'Of course I know, but I promise that knowing will not bring you, Ellie or anyone in this family the slightest scrap of joy or·peace.'

She took a breath then started speaking.

'When Marcus was tiny, not much more than four months

old, your dad had to go and work abroad for a few months. So, I came down to stay with Auntie Joan. It was company for me and Joan said she loved having the little ones around . . .

'Things had been very difficult between your father and me and I think – I now realise – that I must have been suffering from post-natal depression after Marcus's birth, but at the time, I thought I was only tired and stressed. Your father . . . your father was away a lot and very busy. He was worried that his firm would collapse and he'd lose his job, so he had to take the assignment abroad. With Ellie and Marcus to look after, and I wasn't working at the time, he was terrified we'd lose the house. I don't think he understood how I was feeling and why. I didn't understand myself.'

Scarlett choked back a gasp of horror. She'd never heard anything about her mother's depression or their marriage problems before. 'Mum . . . I'm so sorry.'

'Don't be. You weren't even born.' She let out a sigh. 'I remember his words: "I'm working all the hours God sends to keep a roof over this family's heads. Do you think I like being away from home all the time? Spending my life in bloody hotel rooms, living out of a suitcase. No, I can't get another job. I daren't, not in this economy. I need to work harder than anyone else just to keep my job." He said: "If it's the baby blues, it'll pass. Go to the doc if you have to, but you'll have to put up with it."'

Scarlett couldn't speak but she *could* imagine her dad, in one of his morose moods, in another time, saying those words. She really had no idea of what had gone on between her parents.

'And?' she murmured, willing her mum to go on, even though she dreaded hearing the full story.

'While I was down here, there was a barbecue party on the beach and I was invited. I had no intention of going, but Joan said it would do me good to let my hair down and have a night off from the children. I didn't feel in a party mood but she said she'd love to babysit and I'd only be five minutes away. I could keep popping back to check on them any time. And I thought: maybe she's right, and this is exactly the thing I need to perk me up.'

Anna held Scarlett's hand. 'So, I went and I did pop back a couple of times but Ellie and Marcus had settled so Joan told me to go back and relax. I can't say I wish I hadn't returned to the party. I'll never regret what happened because if I'd stayed at home, I would never have had you, dear, darling Scarlett. And that's something I couldn't bear to even think about.' There were tears in Anna's eyes.

Scarlett's cheeks were wet but she daren't move.

'There were dozens of the younger villagers dancing on the beach. Hayden Penberth was there, of course, and he was flirting with me as usual.'

'But if Hayden isn't my father, who is?'

'His name is Julian Mallory . . .'

Scarlett reeled. Oh Christ, Ellie . . . not Mallory. Anyone but him.

'He was young then, not long out of his PhD and a junior lecturer at the local college. He'd been invited to the party with some of his students – he wasn't much older than them, I suppose. He said I seemed sad and we started talking. He was kind, gentle, cultured – he really *listened* to me and for the first time in a long while I felt like I was *me* again. Not a mother of two young children or someone's wife. *Me*. I told him how low I was feeling and he said he was having problems too. He said he'd recently found out his wife had been having an affair.

'I believed him at the time. I'm not even sure it was true now. His wife seems lovely and you saw her earlier in the café. He did remember me, and he tried to talk to me while you and his wife were in the loo. I realise now what kind of a man Julian is: cowardly and narcissistic. But back then he seemed fresh and sensitive – he made me feel like I mattered. But I didn't intend to sleep with him, of course not.'

Scarlett hid her face in her hands, wishing she didn't have to hear the truth but knowing she must.

'The booze flowed and the music played and people started to pair off and we, Julian and I, ended up on our own by the beach fire. It was such a beautiful evening. He kissed me. And . . . then I can't really remember because I was drunk or high or both, but I do know we had sex. I cheated on your dad.

'Afterwards, I must have passed out completely. The moment I woke, the shame started. Julian had gone: he'd left me on the beach, the coward. Although I was relieved that I didn't have to see him again. I crept home as dawn was breaking, and Joan heard me. I went upstairs to throw up and Joan came into the bathroom and asked me where I'd been. I told her I'd been smoking weed and drinking all night with one of the villagers.

'Nothing was said out loud, but I could tell she didn't

325

believe me. Joan was a sharp old bird. She'd had too many regrets of her own not to recognise them in others. She knew who'd been at the party and I think she thought that I was having a fling with Hayden Penberth.'

'Why didn't you tell us before?'

'Because I was ashamed and guilty and most of all, how could I tell you that Julian was your father? He ended up being Ellie's tutor and I suspected she had a bit of a crush on him. I even wondered for a while if she left college partly because he broke her heart, though Ellie wouldn't say.'

My God, if her mother knew the whole truth about Julian, Scarlett thought . . . But her main concern was for her mother. She was the product of an assault. Her poor mother.

She put her arm around her. 'Mum, if you *were* that drunk, then Mallory is a bastard. He should have made one hundred per cent sure you consented. You could have reported him to the police.' Scarlett wanted to blurt out that her mum wasn't the only woman to have been taken in by Julian, and have her life changed forever by him.

'It would have been my word against his, and I had been flirting with him. I encouraged him and well – it was a different time; you just didn't say anything in those days. I'd have had to admit I was attracted to Julian and that I couldn't remember the exact details. How would that have looked in court?'

'Oh, Mum. I'm so sorry for everything. For what that man did to you, for Dad not understanding how bad you were feeling and for bringing all of this pain to light and hurting you all over again.'

Anna smiled and kissed Scarlett's cheek. 'You know what? I'm glad you dragged it into the light. It's almost a relief, and I'm going to tell your father everything – and then Ellie and Marcus. I'll take the consequences of what I did.'

'You've already been punished enough, not that you should ever, ever think you need to be punished. I feel so angry for you!'

'It won't be a punishment to admit the truth. Nothing can be worse than living a lie all these years, though I'm worried your father might come down here and punch Mallory's lights out.'

'It would serve him right!' Scarlett declared, ready to march out and give Mallory a thumping herself.

'But I'd have to tell him the whole truth . . . I don't want him to think I'm shifting the blame onto him.'

'Dad must be so hurt and lost . . . he knows he's been part of it. He hinted as much to me on the phone the other day. But why does there have to be blame? Why does someone have to feel guilty?'

Her mother kissed her hair. 'You're right. No one should feel guilty but that's not how human nature works. I'm glad I've told you, and I know it sounds trite but truly, a burden has been lifted from me, one that's crushed almost every drop of enjoyment from my life lately.' She took a breath. 'Now, I just have to hope that your dad and I can move on from this somehow. I hope that we move on together, but I simply don't know until I've told him everything.'

Scarlett wanted to wave a wand and make it all OK, but had to accept that there might be no 'happy ending' for her parents. All she could do for now was whisper, 'OK, Mum,' and hug her mother again.

They'd barely parted when they heard the key in the front door. She waited for Ellie to call 'hello' but there was only the thunk of keys being tossed onto the hall table.

Scarlett tensed all over again. They had to break the news to Ellie and she had no idea how her sister would react – or if she'd tell her mother that she, too, had been so closely involved with Julian Mallory. Would the revelation that they'd both been taken in by Mallory help to heal her mother and her sister, or simply create new and wider scars?

## Chapter Thirty-Two

On her way back from the café to her car, Ellie looked in despair at the five missed texts, calls and WhatsApp messages from Aaron. It had been a hell of a day, serving up Christmas food and festive spirit to an endless stream of tourists who were down for the holidays and in the mood to party.

She'd smiled and exchanged season's greetings until her jaw ached and she never wanted to see another slice of stollen as long as she lived. It might be uncharitable of her, but any seasonal goodwill she'd had had shrivelled up like a balloon. She'd also been tense in case Aaron turned up at the café, and torn between dreading him appearing and hoping that he might fight for her, even though she could still not see a way of forgiving him. It was hardly likely, given that she'd left him in no doubt of her anger and shock the previous evening.

She reached home, relieved to see the lights on at the manor. This was one time when she was glad to have some company, even if it might mean answering more questions. What she needed right now was a sit down and a cuppa – or preferably, a large glass of something cold and white. She was sure that Scarlett would have a bottle chilling, unless she'd decided to go to Jude's . . . or perhaps not, given Ellie had a feeling that all was not well between them either, though Scarlett hadn't said so.

The sitting room door was pulled open by Scarlett, red in the face. Ellie was sure she'd been crying.

'What's the matter? Is it Jude?'

'No. Yes. Not really. It's Mum . . . and my father. My biological dad. I – I – you'd better come and hear for yourself.'

'Mum?' With a sense of foreboding, Ellie hurried after Scarlett into the sitting room, wishing that she'd found time for a heart to heart with her sister, and not been so preoccupied with her own troubles.

Anna was waiting by the fire, clasping her hands together and clearly agitated. Ellie's alarm bells clanged.

'Ellie, I need to tell you something.'

'We both do,' Scarlett said.

Ellie's heart pounded.

'It's about my dad,' Scarlett told her. 'And about Julian Mallory.'

She swallowed. 'Julian? What's Julian got to do with this?'

Mother and sister exchanged a look again. Ellie's mind whirled . . . what could Julian possibly have to do with Scarlett's father?

'Oh Jesus. I can't do this.' Scarlett put her head in her hands.

Anna sat next to Ellie. 'Earlier today, I – we – saw him in

330

town. I couldn't tell you what happened between us before and it's almost impossible now. How could I? Julian and I had a one-night stand at a party on the beach here.' She took a deep breath. 'He's Scarlett's father.'

'And it wasn't Mum's fault,' Scarlett hurried to add. 'She was hurt and depressed and drunk, and Mallory took advantage of that. He is a shit, a cowardly lying user – but you know that already.'

Ellie had listened without uttering a word. Numb was the only way to describe how she felt. Anaesthetised. Julian Mallory was Scarlett's father. Julian Mallory had been the father of her own lost child. How could she tell her mother that?

'You're very shocked. I can see why. He was your tutor. I think you had a crush on him. I was very drunk—'

'So drunk it was technically assault!' Scarlett broke in. 'And you had post-natal depression. I hate that man! I can't believe he's my dad.'

'Julian? *Julian* . . .' was all Ellie could say. 'Julian?'

Ellie was dumbstruck while her mother unfurled the story of what had happened that summer night at the beach. Scarlett was in tears and swearing . . . and the more her mother talked, the more vivid Ellie's memories became of another summer night, many years later. The flattery, the careful sympathy, the lies and the crushing realisation that actually, Julian Mallory didn't care about anyone but himself. His world revolved around Julian alone, he existed only to gratify his ego and his addiction to using people.

'You were in love with him at college, weren't you, Ellie?'

331

Anna asked. 'I heard the way you spoke about him and I guessed, even though you never actually said it. That was why you really left early, wasn't it? I should have warned you about him but I didn't dare. I was too ashamed and too proud to tell you what I knew about him.'

'Mum, don't you ever be ashamed. I fell for him too,' she said, horrified that they'd both gone through the same experience with the same man. 'In fact, I was madly in love with him. I thought he liked me too, but I was wrong, and so I left rather than face him every day. But I don't regret leaving, or knowing him or anything that happened because travelling has made me the person I am now, and I hope I'm able to understand what you're going through. Most of all, I'm determined that none of us should let Julian Mallory dominate our lives ever again.'

Anna let out a howl and Ellie reached for her, each comforting the other.

Scarlett joined them and they hugged each other. Anna was sobbing, but over her head, Ellie shared a look with Scarlett and made her decision. Now was the time to tell her sister everything; that Mallory hadn't only had affairs with them, but that he'd also fathered two children, only one of whom had ever been born.

It would hurt them both to share the secret, but she wanted there to be nothing left in the dark between her and Scarlett. However, as Anna's sobs subsided, she also knew that she could never tell her mother about the lost child. It would stay a secret. Her mum had suffered enough and some things were best left in the back of the cupboard forever, for everyone's sakes.

## Chapter Thirty-Three

Against all her expectations, Scarlett found herself humming 'Oh, Little Town of Bethlehem' as she hurried around the harbour towards Jude's house. The Christmas lights twinkled in the streets, and stars pricked the sky like tiny fireflies. Although the shops were closed, lights glowed behind almost every cottage window, spreading from the harbour, up the hillside to the cliff top. Festive music spilled out of Gabe's restaurant, the Net Loft, and huddles of locals were gathered around the door of the Tinners', pints in hand.

Anna's revelation about Julian had knocked her for six but there was another blow to come. After their mum had gone to bed with a headache, Ellie had told her about the baby who might have been her half-sister. It was fortunate that Anna was fast asleep or she might have heard the fresh round of weeping from the sitting room.

Julian was even more of a louse than she'd ever dreamed; but at least knowing he'd fathered her meant that Jude wasn't her half-brother. She now owed Jude a proper explanation about why she'd turned so cold towards him. She also hoped he'd be able to tell her how he came to have the postcard.

She'd stopped wishing that things – like the test, and Julian Mallory – hadn't happened. It was pointless to un-wish the past and all she could do now, as the year drew to its close, was look to the future and try to make that the best it could be for everyone close to her. That would be her Christmas gift to everyone this year: looking after them, soothing Ellie's loss, her mother's guilt and her father's isolation.

After she'd collected herself, she'd refused Ellie's offer of wine, told her she had to speak to Jude and driven off. She'd decided to simply turn up and surprise Jude, gambling that he'd be in.

His lips parted in shock when he opened the door. So did Scarlett's at the sight of him barefoot again, in jeans and a faded sweatshirt that brought out the green of his beautiful eyes. Nerves overcame her and she stammered.

'S-sorry I'm here unannounced, only I w-wanted to tell you something. Something important.'

'Yes. I'm here.' Jude sounded wary, and no wonder after the festival evening. 'You'd better come in.'

He showed her into the sitting room where a small tree twinkled with lights, and cards were hung from a string above the mantelpiece.

She'd rehearsed what she wanted to say, but now she was here, how could she possibly tell the whole truth about what had made her freeze him out? Without some explanation, she wouldn't be able to get an answer about the card, either.

334

The silence stretched out, only for a few seconds, but that was long enough to bring her nerves to fever pitch after the emotional day she'd had. Jude launched in first.

'Look, Scarlett, we haven't known each other very long but it's obvious that I like you and we're a lot more than friends. I *thought* we were a lot more than friends, but now that seems to have changed since the night before last.'

'Jude—' she murmured.

'Please, let me say this before I chicken out. We met under pretty weird circumstances, which must have been awkward for you. At first when you landed back in Porthmellow, I wanted to take things steadily as I knew things might not be perfect with your family and that you'd recently come out of a relationship.'

She listened, amazed as his words tumbled out in a most un-Jude-like way, sensing that she didn't dare stem the flow.

He shoved his hands in his pockets. 'I also need to tell you something else – about *me*. I've had a relationship go badly. I'm over it, but that kind of thing . . . leaves a mark. I was engaged a couple of years ago, but my fiancée left me without any real warning.'

'Your mum mentioned it at the festival,' she said softly.

He blew out a breath. 'Jesus. Is nothing private?' He frowned. 'Is that why you went cold on me at the end of the night?'

'No. God, no. It was nothing to do with that . . . but I do need to tell you why I wasn't myself – whatever myself means – and you see, that's the problem. You already know some of what happened at Christmas. There's more to it. Much more. I made a mistake and when I tell you what it is you'll think

335

I'm nuts, or you might be hurt and offended. It's very difficult for me to explain . . .'

'In my experience, it's better to be honest.'

She smiled to herself, thinking of how much she'd grown to like him, care for him and how badly she wanted to deepen every aspect of their relationship, not to mention, of course, take him to bed.

'I'm not always sure about that. In some ways I genuinely think some things are best left unsaid. I think that's how long-term relationships – partners, siblings, friendships – work but on the whole I'm in favour of honesty and getting things out in the open too,' Scarlett went on. 'Believe me, I *really* like you.' Scarlett cringed a little. It sounded so teenagery, but how else could she put it? 'And what I'm going to say has to do with that, with my mother and – with your father.'

'What?' He stared at her.

'You see, the real reason for all the trouble at Christmas was a DNA test . . . Ellie and I thought it would make a great present for the family but it only ended up tearing us apart. It showed that I couldn't be my dad's real daughter, which meant that my mother had had an affair.'

He hung back for a moment, obviously weighing up his reply. 'I'm very sorry to hear that. No wonder you were devastated . . . but, Scarlett,' he added gently, 'what does this have to do with my family?'

'For ages now, since before I even came here, I'd been trying to find out who my real father is and I discovered that he might have links to Porthmellow. Basically, on the night of the festival, for all kinds of reasons that I now know

I had the wrong end of the stick about, something . . .' She swallowed.

'About what?'

'I, um, came to believe that you and I might be related. That you might be my half-brother.' She rushed out the last words, cringing.

Jude considered for a few agonising seconds before saying, so quietly she almost couldn't hear above the waves, 'I see.'

'I can understand that it sounds mad, now, in the cold light of day. It's not true. Mum told me it isn't true.'

His face crumpled in confusion. 'So why on earth did you think it in the first place?'

'I overheard and misunderstood a conversation between my mum and your dad . . . and I saw a picture of them together around the time I was conceived.'

'Is that all?' he said quietly, still looking bewildered and hurt.

'I'd also seen a postcard in a book at the manor last year which I thought – and now know – was from your father to my mother. And the other night I found both in your pantry when I fetched the books.'

Jude's mouth fell open.

'Later I heard them talking after the festival and I must have got my wires crossed, but if you'd heard what I did . . . So I asked Mum what was going on – or what had gone on between them. She said that the two of them had had a brief fling as teenagers and that . . . and that . . .'

Jude folded his arms. His eyes glittered with hurt. Damn, this was going down like a lead balloon.

'And what?'

'I was wrong. In the end. I'd made a huge mistake.'

'Sounds more like a massive assumption,' he murmured.

'Yes, but it was all a misunderstanding. Put yourself in my position,' she said, feeling affronted that he was annoyed. 'I only found out that Roger – my dad – wasn't my biological father a year ago. Since then I've been desperate to know who is, and no one would tell me! Not Mum – for her own reasons – and so I started searching for him myself. You must at least understand that much!'

Scarlett was out of breath with stress again.

Jude was rigid with tension himself. 'So, you don't know who your father is and your mum wouldn't say. I get you must have been cast adrift, devastated, confused, but why automatically assume it was my father? Nobody's family is perfect. Don't forget that.'

'I didn't automatically assume . . . Don't act like this.' She let out a groan of frustration. 'I came here to make things better between us but it's made things worse for both of us. And you did have that book – which you denied knowing anything about – and the postcard in the cottage, so what else was I to think?'

Jude took his time about answering. 'And is that why you asked me about the book and stayed close to me? You wanted to find out if my dad was this guy . . . were you playing me?'

'No, I wasn't playing you!' Scarlett burst out angrily. 'That's not it at all. I genuinely like being with you, Jude, and I'm sorry I got it all wrong, but you also lied about that book.'

'Yes, I did. I shouldn't have but it was . . . personal. I'd always loved it and shortly after Joan died, after the funeral when you'd all gone back home, the house was empty for a while.'

'Before Ellie moved in?'

'Yes, of course, otherwise I'd never have done what I did. I was foraging in the grounds one day and I spotted a bedroom window wide open and banging in the wind. I was worried it might get smashed, so I let myself in with the spare key that was always left in the potting shed. I closed the window and noticed the bookcase . . .' Jude's voice faded, as if he was reluctant to continue, but Scarlett was dying to hear the rest.

'I knew I couldn't make the funeral, you see, and I was gutted, but I was giving a paper at an academic conference in the States . . . and so I took the book as a keepsake. Joan had always known I loved it and I decided no one would miss it, though that was wrong of me, I realise now. She was so kind to me, your aunt, when Mum and Dad were having one of their rows. I used to escape to the manor, lose myself in the grounds, sometimes she'd invite me in for a drink, or offer me cake, and we'd talk about books and nature . . .'

'I don't mind you taking Joan's book as a memento of her,' Scarlett said softly. 'None of us would have. But why did you keep it, and the card, and why didn't you tell me?'

'That's personal.' He pressed his lips together. 'I thought I knew you, Scarlett. I genuinely thought we might have something special together, an understanding . . .' he began. 'But I was clearly wrong. I – I think we both need to cool down.' He seemed on the verge of tears and opened the door to the hall.

Scarlett stifled a gasp. Jesus, he was actually throwing her out. 'So I've been honest with you and you're not even going to tell me why you kept that card?' she threw back at him.

'That's my business. Now, can you please just *go*?'

Even though Scarlett was embarrassed and sorry she'd hurt him, she had her pride and was angry with him for deceiving her about the card.

'I think that's a very good idea too,' she snapped. 'No, don't bother seeing me to the door. I can find my way. If you feel like telling me the whole truth anytime soon, you know where I am!'

She barged past him and into the hall. She didn't mean to slam the door behind her but the wind must have caught it and she heard it bang in her wake.

She made it to the car, jumped in and collapsed back against the head restraint, gasping for breath. Even as she caught her breath, the adrenaline that had kept her going for the past few hours ebbed away like the tide.

A tear trickled down her face, followed by another. They were tears of disappointment, but also of anger at Jude refusing to meet her honesty with his own. Why had he refused to say why he had lied about the card? She tasted salt in her mouth and everything went misty as the tears flowed out.

She'd thought Jude might be shocked and surprised, but not that he'd react so angrily and defensively. After he'd told her how much she meant to him, perhaps she should have saved her news for another time when they were both calmer; but he deserved an explanation. Oh, why did she have to go and put her size sixes in it, though? She should have been more cautious, held back more of her suspicions about his dad – or maybe plain lied.

Dealing with a brooding romantic hero wasn't half as exciting as it seemed to be in Joan's novels. Seconds later, regret doused the fire of her anger. Being told your father is a cheating snake is never going to make you happy. The truth hurt – and Jude was already bruised from his fiancée leaving him. Now she'd inflicted a fresh wound that might be beyond repair. But still, she was seriously wondering if she'd misjudged him, as much as he claimed he'd misjudged her.

# Chapter Thirty-Four

## Christmas Eve

Ellie recalled the previous year and how she'd enjoyed working in the café on Christmas Eve, feeling the buzz of excitement from kids and adults.

Since then, the year had brought a rollercoaster of emotions. Lows in the immediate aftermath of their family discovery as they tried and failed to broker a peace between their parents and with Marcus. She knew her father would be treated kindly by her brother, and even Heidi would do her best and the boys would love having Grandad to stay but . . . her dad liked to have all his family around him. With all their quirks, his family were comforting and familiar, like shrugging on an old pair of slippers. Scarlett had admitted he'd sounded lonely and lost when she'd called him, but their joint invitations to him had so far fallen on deaf ears.

Ellie was resigned to spending the day without him until she and Scarlett would return to the Midlands in the new year.

The New Year she'd be spending without Aaron, rather than moving in with him.

She thought back to their row, her shock and her harsh words. He'd tried to call her again but she'd ignored it, still working out whether she wanted to hear more explanations or excuses. Still working out if she could forgive him for the breach of trust. Besides, for all she knew, he might be working out the divorce with Liza. They'd probably want to talk to each other and she didn't feel like going near Aaron until Liza had left Porthmellow, whenever that might be.

The café shut at three p.m., much to the disappointment of holidaymakers still trying the door as she turned the closed sign on it. They wouldn't open again until December 27, and then they would close again after New Year's Day, when Tina planned on taking two weeks holiday in the sun. That's when Ellie and Scarlett had arranged to stay with their father. She wasn't sure what her mum was planning yet. The future was another country.

With a hug for Tina, Ellie left the café, clutching a gift from her boss. It was a bright day and here in the far west the sun hadn't quite set yet and a few shops were still open, with plenty of tourists scurrying to get last-minute presents. Ellie was gripped by a sudden urge to buy an extra gift for Scarlett and her mum. Something silly and fun to brighten the mood, just as they always did on Christmas morning. She also wondered what the hell to do with the pen she'd bought for Aaron – give it to her dad or Marcus, she supposed.

She popped into a small boutique and bought two pairs of hand-knitted fingerless mittens, one decorated with cats' ears, the other with a cheeky robin. They were ideal for taking photos or sketching out of doors, or, like Scarlett always was, scrolling through social media.

The shop owner wished her a happy Christmas, before locking the door behind her.

Ellie spotted two familiar figures a few shops down near the end of the harbour. That coat was like a red rag to a bull. Liza and Aaron were standing together in a narrow alleyway. Liza was laden with shopping bags and Aaron had a parcel in his arms. Liza was laughing up at him.

Ellie clapped her hand over her mouth. They'd obviously been Christmas shopping and looked extremely cosy together. In fact, they looked exactly like any married couple.

# Chapter Thirty-Five

It was turning out to be the least festive Christmas Eve ever, thought Scarlett, tidying up the sitting room after the drama and tears of the night before. Ellie had gone to work and their mother had left early on a final present-buying trip. The house was quiet apart from the ticking of the grandfather clock and even the distant roar of surf seemed muted. For everyone's sake, Scarlett had glossed over her troubles with Jude when she'd returned the previous evening. Mind you, she could tell that neither Ellie nor her mum were convinced; not with her face puffy and red, as if she'd swallowed a wasp.

This morning, the awfulness of last night's conversation had hit her again and she had itched to call Jude, but decided not to. She didn't know what to say that she hadn't said already. Half the time she was angry at his defensive overreaction, the other half annoyed with herself for triggering it with her insensitive comments.

Nothing would be served by another row and no matter

how shitty she was feeling, it was Christmas and she owed her family a smile and some effort. The sun was out so Scarlett forced herself to pull on her coat and get outside. She'd offered to make a special Christmas Eve dinner to cheer everyone up and decided to use foraged ingredients from the grounds, if possible.

The fresh air, and focus on her task, did calm her down a little, although it had the double edge of reminding her of happier days with Jude. Gathering the vibrant green leaves, she was amazed that the world was still alive and offering its bounty in the midst of winter. She'd pulled a paper bag from her pocket to collect some sea beet when she heard the rustle of the undergrowth.

Jude strode towards her in a reefer coat, a checked black and white scarf wound around his neck. He hadn't shaved and was obviously exhausted. If he looked that bad, she dreaded to think how she appeared after her restless night.

He nodded at the leaves in her hand. 'Are those for Christmas lunch?'

She answered warily. 'No, they're for dinner tonight. I'm not sure Mum could cope without her Brussels sprouts.'

'They may not be traditional but I think they're a lot nicer. My mum wouldn't agree either though. It's hard to let go of old habits and try something new.' He smiled warmly, stirring hope in her heart. 'Isn't it?'

'We could always start a new tradition . . .'

'Yes.' He came closer. 'Scarlett. I came to say I'm truly sorry for kicking off last night. I think I can sum up my shitty behaviour by saying that the truth hurts.'

'I was probably a bit insensitive. I do have a habit of putting my foot in it.'

'I hadn't noticed.' A fleeting smile briefly touched his lips. 'For a start, I'm sorry I accused you of wanting to be close to me because you were looking for your real father. It was an overreaction . . . you see, I have a habit of being a moody bugger so forgive me, and . . . as for my dad, you were absolutely right. He *has* had affairs, but not with your mother, I hope.'

'No. I'm sorry I even thought it, and that I'd thought for a moment you and I were . . . I'm still ashamed, but I was so sure it was your dad.'

'Don't be. Now I know you were searching for your father, I realise it's no wonder you thought that. I – I – was angry when you told me, but not at you. At him. At everything. Dad's not been the most loyal partner to my mum. His flings with other people have hurt her badly. They don't think I know about all of them, but I'm aware of at least three.'

'My mum and your dad did have a holiday romance before she went to uni, but they were both single then.'

'That must have been the late seventies, but the postcard doesn't look that old,' Jude said. He swallowed. 'I did keep and hide the card and I'm so sorry I wasn't honest. Forgive me, but when you asked about it, I panicked.' He grimaced. 'When I found the card and read the message, I had a pretty good idea that it had to be from my dad to your mum and what the implication of it might be, although I never made the leap you did.'

'Yes. Nothing happened, though. It turns out it was only your father . . .' She faltered, 'reminding my mum of the old days.'

347

Jude shook his head angrily. 'You mean he was trying to get her into bed again?'

She winced. 'He might have only been flirting, or winding her up.'

'I doubt it. I guess he's been trying it on over the past few weeks?' Jude asked bluntly.

'There's no chance of that happening.' Scarlett tried to be gentle, not wanting to light the blue touch paper again. Her heart went out to Jude even though she'd been angered by his reaction.

'On your mother's side, maybe not, but I wouldn't put it past him. Jesus Christ, he may be my father but sometimes, I think I must have been switched at birth. I know what he's like but I haven't always wanted to face up to it. I kept the card and I thought of confronting him with it, but he'd probably have lied. I was terrified he might have been carrying on a long-running relationship with your mother or starting it up again while she was estranged from your dad. I didn't want to accept the truth. Please forgive me, Scarlett.'

'It's OK. It's hard to face up to our deepest, darkest fears.'

'My dad has hurt so many people,' he said, swallowing hard.

'He can't be as bad as my biological father. I promise you that. I've even met him, although he has no idea I am his daughter.'

The line between his eyes deepened. 'My God, that must have been tough. Do you want to tell me who he is?' he added gently.

'I'm not sure I'm ready to share that yet. It was hard to

handle. Jude, you're the only person to know that I've found out who he is, apart from Mum and Ellie. I can't tell you his name yet because even my dad – Roger – doesn't know his identity. It's . . .' She hesitated. This felt surreal. 'It's a guy from the local area.'

Jude was too polite and sensitive to pry for any more details. 'I'm sorry. So is it worse now you actually know who he is?'

'I don't know. I can't make my mind up whether I'm relieved to know or not. I . . .' Scarlett had to tread carefully, not wanting to betray Ellie's confidence. 'I wish it wasn't this particular man. I haven't heard good things about him,' she said, knowing it was the understatement of the year.

'I'm very sorry you've had to go through this and that the answer, when it came, isn't what you would have wanted to hear.'

'That was always the risk I ran. Mum warned me all along it wouldn't do me – any of us – any good to know his name. I didn't understand why she said that at first, and then of course, well . . . you know why I wanted to know the truth. That's why I forced her to admit it wasn't your father, which was a massive relief.' Her face heated up at the assumption she'd made, but Jude listened patiently this time.

'But yesterday afternoon, my mum saw him in Porthmellow and she was so shocked, she decided to tell me and Ellie everything. That's when things got complicated because – well, because they *are*.'

'Come for a walk with me?' Jude asked.

She nodded. 'I'd like that.'

They walked down to the beach, side by side at first but

feet apart. They stopped to look as the wind blew ripples on the flat pools on the beach. She felt so small against the sky and sea, but Jude was closer now and she felt the tickle of his fingertips against hers. Without saying anything or even looking at him, she slipped her hand in his.

She was grateful for the warmth of his hand and the quiet solidity of his presence. She could have cheered for joy but sensibly for her, she thought, she only smiled and looked out to the horizon.

'Funny, but I always thought I'd want my father to know who I was, that he *deserved* to know about me. I wondered how I'd feel, not knowing I had a child, but now I'm not sure he *should* know. He isn't the kind of man to embrace responsibility, even though he has his own family and things are complicated . . . more complicated than I ever dreamed of.' She glanced at Jude. 'I can't share the details, but that's not because I don't trust you. It's because it's not only me who's involved.'

'You don't have to share anything. Say as much or little as you like. This whole business must have turned your world upside down. Sorry I haven't helped, acting like a total knob.'

Scarlett laughed softly, thinking of how different he was to Rafa. 'A man who can admit he's been a knob is refreshing. Last year I felt my world had caved in and when I started rebuilding it at last, it collapsed again.'

Jude's hands rested on her upper arms. 'I think this is the start of it staying intact. It won't be easy but you can move on, now. You'll work it out. Your family were strong before, you're the same people, you still love each other.'

'If Mum and Dad could be honest with each other, it would help.'

'There's no sign of that?'

'Maybe. Mum says she'll sort it out in the new year. We have to get through Christmas yet.'

'I can help with that.' Jude gathered her to him and they kissed. His mouth was warm and the kiss was all the sweeter after the bitterness of his last attempt at closeness. This time, she held him tight and long, making sure he broke the kiss first, but only so he could breathe one word into her hair.

'*Wow.*'

'I'm making up for lost time,' she said.

'Man, I hope so.'

'Would you like to come home with me?' The words fell out naturally. 'There's no one in at the manor. Ellie's at work. Mum's gone on a last-minute shopping trip and won't be back until later.'

'I'd love to. I'll help you prepare your sea beet, if you like.'

'Prepare my sea beet? I've not heard that one before.'

His eyes shone with sensual promise and real deep feeling. Scarlett wasn't sure it was love yet, but her own feelings were different to anything she'd ever shared with Rafa, or any man. She felt like she and Jude were knocking on the door of love, and it was opening . . . they only had to step through.

They walked hand in hand back to the manor and Jude followed her into the kitchen, where she put the bag of greens into the fridge.

Jude gasped when he saw the contents. 'What the hell is that? An ostrich?'

'It's an enormous turkey. You're welcome to come over and help us eat it tomorrow, if you like.'

'I'd love to but I'm helping at the Lunch for the Lonely at the pub and then I've got to go home for the family Christmas dinner.' He gave a wry smile. 'Now you know about my family, you know why I volunteer for it. It gives me an excuse to stay out of the way of some of the festivities. We have our main meal in the evening. My gran comes over earlier though, along with a cousin, her husband and her children. No one will miss me at lunchtime.'

Scarlett giggled. 'I'm sure they will. I'd join you at the pub but I don't want to leave Ellie and Mum, especially not this year.' She closed the fridge. 'It's going to be difficult, although nothing could be worse than last year.'

Jude held her. 'You'll get through it. You'll definitely do the Boxing Day swim, though? We all go to the pub afterwards and then why don't you come to the cottage with me? We'll both have earned some time to ourselves.'

'We'll probably be stuffed,' she said, already thinking of the vintage bathing suit she was going to unveil. Only a few days ago, she'd decided she was going to skip the swim after all.

'I wasn't thinking of wasting too much time on food,' Jude said, lifting her hair and kissing the nape of her neck.

The edge to his voice sent a shiver down her spine. 'Me neither.'

Scarlett led him upstairs to the bedroom. All her worries

faded to nothing as Jude carefully unwrapped her as if she was his best Christmas present ever. And, oh my . . . what followed in her bed blew away anything she'd ever read in Auntie Joan's novels – even the steamiest ones with the black and red covers.

# Chapter Thirty-Six

Ellie was first up on Christmas morning, having tossed and turned half the night; unlike Scarlett, who was still gently snoring when Ellie put the turkey into the oven. The vegetables had already been prepared and were sitting in a steamer on the Aga, while the farm shop parsnips, stuffing and pigs-in-blankets had been crammed into the fridge.

She wandered into the sitting room with a large cup of coffee. The tree had a smaller pile of presents beneath it than the previous year, of course. There were fewer of them, and no one had felt like going over the top anyway. Carols were drifting out of the radio, but there was no thud of feet as the boys thundered downstairs, no shouts from Heidi begging them to behave, no Marcus grumbling that he couldn't find his Christmas boxer shorts.

No Dad, standing on the patio, mug in hand, contemplating the peace of the garden before he had to join the 'fun' in earnest. Ellie recalled their conversation a year before.

'Are you ready for the fray?' he'd asked.

'The fray? We're supposed to be enjoying it. You love it really, Dad.'

'I love you. All of you, but Christmas . . . the jury's out.'

He'd laughed though and Ellie hadn't taken him too seriously. She wished he was here now so they could share a private joke. She would phone him later and looked forward to staying with him after New Year when the café closed. Spend a lot of time with him and try to get to know what he wanted. Try to build a bridge between him and Scarlett and bring everyone together again if it was possible.

However, the thought of leaving Porthmellow also had a bitter edge. She had once hoped to spend more time with Aaron. What would he be doing now, at home with the Carmans? Pretending, like she was, that he was OK, when he really wasn't? Was he with Liza? Ellie wouldn't have believed it until she saw them in town the previous day. It was more likely that he – and his family – were together. She wondered if he'd told them about Liza yet and how that might affect their celebrations.

The picture of Julian Mallory flashed into her mind, most unwelcome at any time and particularly today. He'd also probably be acting the perfect grandad with his kids and grandchildren. Maybe his dalliances were a thing of the past and he was now only concerned with keeping his skeletons – her and Anna – in his closet and acting the devoted grandpa.

'It's Christmas, but not as we know it,' she murmured.

'Ellie?'

Scarlett walked in, cradling a mug, still in a dressing gown. Their mother followed, in a new top, smiling. Ellie suspected she wanted to make the day as special as possible in the face of the odds.

'Shall we open the presents now or after breakfast?' she said.

Ellie glanced at the parcels, touched by her mother's efforts. 'After?' she asked, hoping that was the answer her mum and sister wanted to hear. It was so hard to know what they would prefer to do, but that was family life much of the time: walking a tightrope of compromise, all in the name of love.

'I'll make breakfast,' said Scarlett, disappearing into the kitchen and reappearing at amazing speed with a tray with three sundae glasses, with tall spoons in them.

Ellie whistled. 'Wow.'

'Ta da! Christmas breakfast granola!'

'This looks delicious,' her mother said. 'And very quick.'

'Made them last night and hid them in the back of the scullery. It's freezing in there.'

Scarlett's special breakfast perked them all up briefly, but no one was in the mood for Buck's Fizz so they settled on Christmas coffee from the hamper sent by Marcus and Heidi. The three of them sat in the sitting room, opening their presents while Ellie pictured the scene in Marcus's house. Was the atmosphere the same as here at the manor? Subdued and hardly festive, with the grown-ups trying to be happy and going through the motions for the boys' sakes?

Despite the absence of half their tribe, the presents were given and received with love and pleasure, perhaps even more

356

so than the previous year now that they felt more precious and personal. Ellie shed a few tears when she opened the wrapping on the bracelet that Scarlett had given her.

They cleared away the paper and checked the turkey again. Its rich smell filled the house. Everyone seemed eager for something to do. A sense of purpose . . .

Scarlett got up. 'You know what, I keep thinking about Jude getting ready for the Lunch for the Lonely.'

Anna shook her head. 'They don't really call it that, do they?'

'No. It's the Community Christmas Lunch but according to Jude, that's what Troy and Evie started calling it, and it caught on among the volunteers.'

'Who's going to it?'

'All kinds of people. Some are elderly, some rough sleepers, some students who can't get home for Christmas and a few foreign workers. Jude says they don't know who will walk in on the day. Maybe a mad woman who dropped a bomb on her family.'

Ellie smiled. Her mum hugged her. 'Or a wonderful daughter who's kind and a bit mad and still has her sense of humour despite everything.'

'Yeah. Call me Saint Scarlett.' Scarlett rolled her eyes. 'Thanks, Mum.'

Ellie laughed. Then there were a few seconds of silence. She looked at the gifts and the tree.

'You know, this is weird,' she said.

'It is a bit sad,' Anna murmured and the three of them exchanged glances. 'Tell me if I'm mad, but I have an idea.

We all know that turkey's far too big for us and we have far too much food so . . . why don't we take it to the pub and share it around?'

Scarlett's mouth opened in surprise, but a second later she grinned broadly. 'That's a brilliant idea.'

Her glee spread to Ellie, who nodded. 'It does seem like the perfect solution.' She laughed. 'Lucky we kept off the eggnog this year!'

Scarlett phoned Jude and headed off with the uncooked veg and trimmings while Ellie and their mother waited for the turkey to finish cooking. It had been put in so early that it would be ready before the pub served up lunch.

An hour later, she and her mother packed the turkey into the car and drove to the pub. A few people were out and about, enjoying a drink in the various inns before going home for their own Christmas dinners, and one of the restaurants was hosting a lunch. Families were out for a stroll, new scooters and first bikes wobbling on the quayside cobbles.

Ellie and Anna walked into the pub, with the foil-wrapped turkey in a laundry basket. It would have to be carved and served cold, but with all the piping hot trimmings and gravy, no one would mind.

The noise and colour as they walked in was such a contrast to Seaholly. Their quiet house was too big for three. It wasn't the turkey, presents and enormous tree that made Christmas, but the company, friends and family . . . even strangers. Never had she realised that so fully until now.

The pub was packed. The tables were laid for around forty people, she guessed, though that included the helpers. She recognised all of them, of course, among them Sam and Gabe, Zennor and Ben from the festival committee. Scarlett was laying out crackers and party hats with Jude. They were laughing and kept touching each other – unconsciously, probably. Ellie was happy for her. She deserved to be happy after the turmoil of the past year. Jude was a bright spot in her sister's life and they both needed some light, and no matter how disappointed she was by Aaron, she rejoiced for Scarlett.

Ellie and her mum announced themselves to Gabe and Sam in the kitchen.

'No Evie and Troy?' Anna asked Sam.

'Not this year. Evie's having a family Christmas with Aaron at home. Her daughter and family are there too. She's a cracking cook and she loves welcoming people.' Sam gave Ellie a knowing look. 'Are you going round tomorrow after the swim?'

Ellie was floored by the question. She'd been looking forward to the family event so much until Liza had landed. How could she skate over her disappointment? Despite Liza's reappearance, Sam obviously didn't know there'd been a rift between her and Aaron.

'Erm. I'm r-really not—' she stammered, flailing for an answer.

She was saved from a reply by a desperate shout from the chef. 'Sam! Any idea if someone got any cranberry sauce?'

'Sorry, 'scuse me. Catch you later,' Sam said, already part way across the kitchen. 'Coming, Gabe!'

# Chapter Thirty-Seven

Scarlett and Jude had been chatting to some of the guests while they tucked into nibbles and fizz. Anna had offered to drive home so her daughters could relax and join in with the party. Taking their Christmas down to the pub had been the best idea Scarlett and her family had had in ages. They'd found it fascinating and moving talking to people about the reasons they'd decided to join the lunch.

There were people who'd lost loved ones, others who couldn't get home for Christmas for various reasons, and a recovering addict who'd recently managed to get off the streets and into his own flat, but was still estranged from his relations. At least, thought Scarlett, she was still in touch with and knew she was loved by her family, even if they were splintered.

'Some of their stories put all our family problems into perspective,' she said while helping Jude load presents into a sack for the guests. They'd all been donated by local businesses.

'Yes, same here. You never know who's going to turn up or what their reasons are. Christmas is a very tough time to be alone.'

'Or to be with your family . . .' Scarlett said. 'At least no one's made such a dramatic entrance as I did last year.'

'There's still time. We haven't had the turkey yet.' Jude laughed. 'I'm glad you did make an entrance, despite the awful circumstances.'

'You must have thought I was mad.'

'No. Just lost. Everyone loses their way sometimes. Everyone can be lonely, even in the middle of a crowd – especially in the middle of a crowd. We don't know what life's going to throw at us and if our luck turns, we could end up here one day.' He gave a wry smile. 'Or choose to be here, like me.'

'At least you've ditched the elf hat this year. That's who I knew you as until we met again: the elf man.'

'Oh God, did you?'

She touched his ears. 'Yes, but don't take it too hard. I still thought you were uber-cute.'

'*Uber*-cute?'

'Not at first, of course. But you grew on me.'

Jude was about to kiss her when the music stopped, a fork tinged against a glass and Sam Lovell spoke up. 'Sorry to interrupt the merriment, folks, but I'm delighted to announce that dinner is served. Please take your places.'

Reluctantly, Scarlett peeled herself away from Jude, because it was an unspoken tradition that the helpers scattered themselves among the guests who might not know anyone. She chose a seat between a middle-aged lady from Porthmellow who'd lost her elderly mother earlier that year, and a Kiwi student who couldn't get home for Christmas.

The eclectic mix of people reminded Scarlett a little of the crowd at the swimming baths in Brum. She made a vow to keep in touch more often and go to the annual get-together they always had. The thought led her to introduce the topic of swimming to the conversation, and soon she'd persuaded both the older lady and a student to watch the Boxing Day swim, if not to actually go in for a dip.

Loud voices from the other side of the table came from a young woman in a metal T-shirt in conversation with a skinny young man with a straggly beard, gold earring and a fisherman's cap not dissimilar to Troy's.

'What are Bryony Cronk and her bloke doing here?' Scarlett asked Sam when she came round with bottles of wine. Bryony's contempt for community events was well known throughout the town.

'Apparently, she and her new boyfriend were looking for an excuse not to have lunch at his brother's place. Sacha hates the brother's pug and so the brother insisted Sacha had to stay at home all day. Well, you can imagine how that went down with Bryony, so they both volunteered to help. Not that they've set foot in the kitchen yet . . .' Sam said, nodding at Bryony who had her arms wound around her fisherman. Sacha lay under a table, gnawing a huge piece of rawhide that looked like something from a crime scene.

'I can't believe Sacha isn't barking or trying to snaffle the turkey,' Sam said. 'Though there's still time.' She smirked. 'So far, he's been bribed with a bowl of luxury turkey dog food and a massive dog chew.'

Scarlett laughed, feeling more cheerful than she had for ages, although she was always mindful of not having her father around, and of Ellie's unhappiness. Poor Ellie, she was trying to put on a brave face, as was her mother. She felt helpless again, but tried to think of all the people in far worse situations.

Crackers popped and 'ohs' and 'ahs' filled the room as Gabe and Ellie carried out platters of turkey and steaming veg and trimmings. Eventually, after the almost endless passing of serving dishes, everyone seemed to have groaning plates when the pub door opened.

A man stood in the doorway, looking around, unsure.

Scarlett turned and a few faces glanced over at the newcomer too, but most people were too busy eating or laughing.

Jude scraped his chair back. 'Oh, we have a latecomer. He looks lost.'

'I know exactly how he feels.' Scarlett stood up too. She put her hand on Jude's arm. 'I'll take care of him.'

She walked over to the door, her legs not quite steady. 'Dad?'

'Your mother said I'd find you here.' He kissed her and Scarlett hugged him, half afraid he might be a figment of her imagination.

'But . . . but when did you arrive in Porthmellow?'

'Last night. I stayed in a B and B. I decided I couldn't miss Christmas Day with you after everything that's happened this year.'

'I can't believe you're here . . . Mum said she'd gone on a secret mission yesterday. Did she know about this?'

363

'She might have. She called to see me yesterday.'

Scarlett glanced around the room, seeking out Anna and Ellie. They were standing together by the kitchen and even from across the room Scarlett saw their eyes shining. 'So, you've been to Seaholly Manor already?' she said, in wonder.

'Yes. I arrived shortly after you left. Your mum asked me to come round this morning and when I arrived, she told me you were all coming here. They persuaded me to come and so I thought: why not? I didn't want to disrupt your plans and I know how kind everyone was to you last year.'

'So you're staying with us tonight?'

He smiled. 'If there's room and you'll have me.'

'Oh Dad. I'll sleep in the garden if it means you'll stay.' She threw her arms around him again and he hugged her tightly. His embrace was almost too much to bear after so long apart.

'But what about Marcus? Don't he and Heidi mind you coming down here?' she asked.

'I've been able to spend plenty of time with him and the family lately, and when he heard I wanted to come down here to talk things over with your mum, he was right behind the idea. We'll meet up when they get back from skiing for a second Christmas.'

Scarlett nodded, grateful to Marcus and co. for understanding how much she, Ellie and Anna needed Roger's presence. 'Dad, there's someone I want you to meet.' She beckoned Jude over.

'Jude. This is my dad,' she said, aware of exactly how much those words meant. 'Dad, this is Jude.'

'Good to see you,' he said, shaking Jude's hand.

364

'Will you sit down to dinner with us, Mr Latham? We've only just started the main course.'

'If you're sure you have enough food, I'd like that very much. But for God's sake call me Roger.' He smiled.

Scarlett had half-expected her father to politely decline and say he was going back to the manor. Public events weren't his thing at all so she knew that he must be staying for her sake, which made her want to cry all over again.

'OK, I'll find you a place with the rest of the family, Roger.'

Her mother and Ellie waved at her from the opposite side of the table, and Scarlett showed her dad to the table. A few people gave them curious glances but soon went back to their turkey and cracker jokes. After all, the arrival of a stranger in the middle of Christmas dinner was nothing new or unusual.

'Thanks for coming,' Scarlett said while the chairs were shuffled to allow her dad to squash in beside her at the table.

'How could I miss Christmas Day with my daughters?' He squeezed her hand and Scarlett almost wept into the cranberry sauce jug being passed to her by the student next to her.

Her dad picked up a cracker, and Scarlett pulled it, the pop, as always, making her jump. Roger pulled out a pink crown and put it on his head.

Across the room, while her dad was helping himself to some sprouts, she caught Jude's eye. He was smiling and raised his glass to her. He mouthed, 'To you,' and she whispered back, 'You too.'

A couple of hours later, the Lathams were sent home, having been sternly prevented from staying to wash up after they'd helped clear away. Scarlett could hardly believe she could have had such a happy and uplifting time at a Lunch for the Lonely, but now she'd become hungry for some private time with her family.

The sun was slipping rapidly towards the horizon as Jude kissed her goodbye outside the pub. Her father was inside thanking the landlady and the volunteers for their hospitality, while Ellie and her mum had already set off for the manor.

She held Jude's arms, feeling happy but exhausted. 'Thank you,' she said to him.

'What for?'

'For being here. Just for being you and being here.'

'A pleasure. You have a lot to talk about. I hope it works out for you all.' He kissed her softly on the lips. 'Call me whenever you're ready.'

'I will.'

She let go of him, reluctantly, but knowing he'd be there for her whenever she needed him.

'Wait!'

He jogged after her. 'I guess you won't be doing the Boxing Day swim tomorrow now? I'll understand if you can't.'

Scarlett put her finger on her lips as if she was considering, then burst out laughing at his downcast expression. 'You try and stop me.'

She sat in her father's car watching as dusk fell over Porthmellow and the Christmas lights twinkled and the cottage lamps came on, giving the little town a fairy-tale feel. The stars came out in the clear sky over the sea. Her father didn't start the engine, probably aware, as she was, that now was their only chance for some private time before they were reunited at the manor with Ellie and her mother.

'Dad. It's so wonderful that you're here. There's nothing I – or Ellie – want more than for you and Mum to be happy again. But . . .' She took a deep breath. 'I don't want you and Mum to stay together – wallpaper over the cracks – just to have a perfect Christmas with me. None of us would want that.'

'There will be no wallpapering. The cracks haven't got any wider. In fact, I'd say they were narrowing. We want to try and rebuild our lives. Your mother came to me yesterday. We talked for a long time. I know what happened and who *he* is. I won't deny I was angry and upset all over again, but I also take my large share of the blame.'

'If I hadn't bought that bloody test, none of this would have happened.'

'Maybe. Maybe not. Perhaps we would have found out another time. In the heat of an argument . . . or another way. Too late to turn back the clock.' He picked up her hand and held it. 'You haven't split the family apart, love. You bought that test in complete innocence. It's because you loved me and Mum – all of us – that you wanted to make our Christmas perfect. The trouble is that nothing and no one can ever be perfect. The way I behaved towards your mother after she had Marcus wasn't even kind, let alone perfect. I was blind to anything except my job and making ends meet day to day, and I missed what she was going through.'

'Poor Mum. Poor you.'

'You're the one who's been at the heart of the fallout. I love you, Scarlett. I've told you before that I do. It was such a shock when I first found out about the test. It hurt all the more because I loved you so much. I'm deeply sorry for every single second that you didn't feel as loved by me as you did the day you were born.'

There were tears in his eyes.

She reached over and held him. 'Dad. Can you stop this, please?'

'Why?' he frowned.

'Because you won't be able to drive home if you start crying.'

'Your driving has always made me cry.'

'Dad!' She batted his arm and they both started laughing through their tears and they were still laughing as he drove them back to the manor.

# Chapter Thirty-Eight

L ate on Christmas evening, Ellie and Scarlett lounged in easy chairs in the snug. They each had a glass of Jude's cherry brandy, which he'd squirrelled away for the Latham family as a gift.

After they'd arrived home, they'd all talked together then left their parents alone in the sitting room. Marcus was fully aware of what had happened and so they had all Skyped him, Heidi and the boys. It had been a happier half hour than anyone could have hoped for. The boys were delighted that Nanny, Grandad and their aunties Scarlett and Ellie were all together and smiling. Marcus's relief at peace breaking out was obvious in his jovial manner, probably fuelled by lots of the good wine he liked to save for Christmas Day. Even Heidi had been smiling and on her best behaviour.

Ellie watched the glow of the snug fire, listening for the dull roar of the surf as the tide ran high up the cove. She wondered if Aaron was at the cottage or was still at his parents' place, or even with Liza, and if he was, was there even the remotest possibility of them getting back together? Seeing them looking so comfortable together in town had been a big blow. She'd also felt jealous, even though she'd told Aaron they were over.

'You know, sitting like this by the fire, we could be two old spinsters from Victorian times,' Scarlett broke into her thoughts.

'Nothing wrong with being a spinster. Auntie Joan had a fantastic life. She travelled the world, had lots of lovers and made enough money to buy this place doing what she adored.' Ellie smiled, grateful for the distraction from her churning mind.

'True. Let's raise a glass to her.' Scarlett chinked her glass with Ellie's.

'To Auntie Joan!' they declared in unison.

Ellie allowed the brandy to fill her mouth and slide down slowly. Its sweet taste had a surprising after kick.

She swished it around her glass, admiring the jewelled colours in the reflections from the fire. 'You can tell Jude that this is really very good.'

'Isn't it? Shame it's the last one. It was a Christmas present.'

'Weren't you supposed to be spending the evening with him?'

'He doesn't mind. Neither do I. I need to be here with you and Mum and Dad, and Jude is the first to understand that. Anyway, I'll be able to make up for lost time after Christmas.'

'You're happy here, then? Planning to stay?' said Ellie, noting the glow in her sister's eyes.

'Yes . . . even if Mum sells the house, well, Jude has offered to let me stay at his. Not that I'd ever leave you, of course.'

Ellie laughed, amused and touched by Scarlett's loyalty. 'That's a lovely thought, but if I were you and Jude asked me to move in with him, I wouldn't hesitate.' She knocked back a larger gulp of brandy than she'd meant to and gasped as the fiery liquid seared the back of her throat.

'What about you and Aaron?' asked Scarlett.

'What about me and Aaron?'

'Have you thought that maybe, you should talk to him? You said yourself he'd admitted he'd lied about the marriage and made a huge mistake in not telling you about Liza. Could you ever think about forgiving him?'

'Yes, I've thought about it.' Ellie's thoughts slid to her phone and the unanswered messages from Aaron. 'I need to think about it a whole lot more before I trust myself to speak to him.' She took a breath. 'Actually, I saw him with Liza yesterday.'

'Jesus, no. Where?'

'They'd been shopping in town. It was only a glimpse but he's obviously been talking to her.'

'Oh, Ells. Perhaps it was about the divorce.'

'That had crossed my mind, but unless and until I can bring myself to speak to him again, I'm never gonna find out, am I?'

'You need to do it, Ellie. It was horrendous when I had to tell Jude why I'd gone cold on him and, to be honest, I made a right mess of it. But it was better to get it out in the open, just like everything else between us all. It won't be easy, but think about going to see him. You'll never know if you don't try.'

Ellie smiled. 'Since when did you get to be big sister with all the good advice?'

Scarlett laughed. 'I'll make the hot choc.'

Scarlett went into the kitchen, leaving Ellie cradling the last of the cherry brandy. She was thrilled that Scarlett was happy with Jude and was coming to terms with the revelation that Julian Mallory was her father, as Ellie herself was trying to do.

As for her parents, they were at least together in the same room, when for many weeks they hadn't even been in the same county. They'd been honest with each other and were talking, so while this year was very far from a perfect Christmas for any of them, it was way better than the last one. Everyone in the family was in a better place, except perhaps her – having found Aaron and lost him. However, if that was all that life was going to give her family, she would live with that. She had to.

# Chapter Thirty-Nine

'R-remind me again why I ever agreed to this?' Ellie hissed to Scarlett, tugging her fleecy dressing gown tighter around her frozen flesh.

They were standing on Porthmellow Beach surrounded by other people who appeared to have gone completely bonkers. Some wore wetsuits, others were already stripped for action, jogging up and down in vintage bathing suits and – Ellie's eyes hurt – Speedos that should have been thrown in the bin decades before. Some of the flesh on display was epic, wobbling like a blancmange and paler than the bread sauce they'd served up with the turkey.

Scarlett flung her arms out and jogged on the spot. 'It's really not that b-bad. Jude says that the water is the same t-temperature as in early M-May.'

'Then why are your teeth chattering? Why can't I feel my toes? Or my fingers? Why the hell didn't I wear a wetsuit?' Ellie said.

'Because you don't own one and because you think they make you look f-fat. Which they d-don't.'

'It's better than looking like a plucked turkey!' Ellie declared, feeling goosebumps pop out on top of goosebumps.

'You don't. But the whole idea is to do it in a normal swimsuit. It's ch-cheating to wear anything else. You're lucky, you still have a lingering glow from working on the boat over the summer. I had to use a whole tube of self-tan and it's streaked down the back of my legs.'

It wasn't the cold that was making Ellie tremble, it was the prospect of seeing Aaron. She'd already spotted Troy and Evie taking people's names on a clipboard but Ellie and Scarlett had registered online before Christmas. Well, it had seemed like a good idea at the time . . .

Jude jogged over. He was wearing one of the fleece-lined surf ponchos favoured by surfers and wild swimmers. With his tousled blond hair and tanned limbs, he owned it and she could see why Scarlett was drooling.

'Morning! How are you? Ready for a dip?' He kissed Scarlett's cheek and beamed at Ellie.

'I've been brighter. I blame your cherry brandy.' She delivered her joke with a smile. Jude was annoyingly Tigger-ish but she couldn't fault his enthusiasm or the fact he'd made her sister smile again.

'I like the vintage look,' he said, flipping one of the flowers on Scarlett's swimming cap.

She touched the lurid pink cap and pulled a face. 'We almost got changed out of them, didn't we, Ellie? Mum found these caps in the loft. They were Auntie Joan's. I think she wore them in St Tropez.'

'I'm amazed they haven't perished after all this time,' Ellie said through gritted teeth. Wearing the yolk-yellow cap with its rubber daisies had probably been the second worst decision of her life.

Jude was obviously trying not to laugh too much, thought Ellie. 'You both look great. Lots of people are in vintage costumes. The hats will keep you warm and it's part of the spirit of the event.'

'Why aren't you wearing one, then?' Ellie shot back.

Jude raised his eyebrows. 'Couldn't find mine.'

She rolled her eyes. 'Fibber.'

Jude laughed. 'You don't know what I've got under my poncho,' he said in a cheesy voice.

'Yes, what *have* you got under there?' Scarlett lifted the hem.

'Laters, baby,' said Jude.

Ellie groaned. 'Oh, for God's sake. Will you two just skip the swim and get a room?'

'Sorry,' Scarlett said sheepishly.

Jude looked embarrassed. 'I'll see you in the water then. I'm meant to go in first to set an example.'

'Excuse me, I need the loo,' Ellie said, shaking her head, desperate to leave them to it, whatever it was. Being a spectator at a love match was excruciating, no matter how much she wanted Scarlett to be happy.

Scarlett's face fell. 'Oi! Don't run off now!'

'In this outfit? I'm hardly going far.' Ellie headed for the public toilet, waving a hand behind her. Mind you, she could go home, apart from the fact that she'd have to walk in a dressing gown and flip-flops. Their parents had dropped them off at the beach, which had seemed like a good idea at the time . . .

On her route to the loo block, she scanned the crowds of bathers for Aaron. There was no sign of him, so perhaps he'd decided to stay out of the way after all. A queue snaked its way out of the block, so Ellie waited. She would have felt ridiculous but there was a woman ahead of her with a yellow duck ring around her waist and a man queuing for the gents in a striped Edwardian costume and a hoodie.

When Ellie came out of the toilets, she heard Evie Carman's Cornish burr purring through a loudspeaker.

'Happy Boxing Day, my lovers! I hope you're all ready to take the plunge for the fifty-fifth Porthmellow Boxing Day swim. I'd like to thank the RNLI and St John ambulance for attending and hope none of you need their services. Now, before you all take off your clothes, I'd like to run through a few safety procedures.'

Ellie was about to move back to the beach when a willowy blonde woman in a scarlet coat made a beeline for her.

'Oh, Jesus.' That was all she needed: Liza Carman starting a catfight in front of hundreds of locals.

Liza stared at her. 'Wow, like the outfit.'

'I don't have time for this now,' Ellie said, walking away. 'Or ever.'

'Wait. Please. I'm not here to start a fight. The opposite in fact.' Liza trotted up to her.

'I need to get ready for the swim. You have five minutes.'

'OK. I can see that.' Liza smirked and Ellie almost turned her back and walked. 'This is important. I owe you an apology for what happened in the café the other day. I'm a passionate person and I speak my mind.'

Ellie gasped. 'You can say that again and I saw you with Aaron in town on Christmas Eve. You looked very cosy.'

'We'd only been shopping. Or rather, I'd been shopping and Aaron agreed to meet me to talk about the divorce.'

Ellie almost punched the air with relief. She'd convinced herself that Liza might work her way back into Aaron's life.

'How can I believe you?' she asked.

'You'll have to. I was out of order, but I'm happy to admit when I'm wrong. I was steaming angry and upset that morning – Aaron says he's told you I've just split up with Damian, my lying git of a boyfriend.' Liza stuck out her tongue. 'We were planning on settling down together and I decided I wanted a clean break with Aaron while I finally had some time off between contracts.

'I meant to contact him again and arrange to do it then I found out that Damian had changed his mind so I came racing down here, hoping for a shoulder to cry on.'

'Aaron's shoulder? Did you hope you'd get back together, then?' Ellie's hackles were up, fearing she'd been partly right to have her suspicions about Liza and Aaron.

'Not really. He'd wanted me to come down after Christmas anyway so we could finalise the divorce but I'll admit, I also needed someone to comfort me, a kind face. Someone who used to care for me, which he did. I'm not the most logical of people at the best of times and once I had the idea, I forged down here. I arrived during the festival, asked at the hotel and of course, the receptionist mentioned he was doing the security. Small place like this is as bad as a cruise ship for gossip . . . so I went straight from the hotel into the whole bloody shebang, hoping to see him.'

'You bought a drink from me on the boat.'

'Yes, but that was before I saw you together. I needed some Dutch courage. Not long after, I spotted you canoodling on that boat. I was jealous, I'll admit it. It all seemed so unfair: you two all loved up, while I'd been dumped and left with no contract and no bloke. I spent the night nursing my wrath, as they say, and then I took it out on you at work.'

'I'm very sorry about that, but it was hardly my fault,' Ellie said, trying to keep her temper in check. She partly understood what had driven Liza to act so vindictively at the café but she was very wary of her unpredictable moods.

'Course it wasn't and I shouldn't have been so spiteful even in the heat of the moment. If it's any consolation, Aaron's gutted that you've chucked him.'

'That's none of your business,' Ellie shot back, feeling that shivering in her bathing suit in a crowd of people was the worst possible time to have this conversation.

'It is though. I caused it by turning up here.'

'No. Aaron caused it by lying about you.' The loudspeaker purred into life again: Evie summoning everyone to the beach.

'I have to go.'

'Hang on! Much as I want a clean break from Aaron, it

was as much my fault as his that we never sorted it out. I carried on with my life, same as him, meaning to sort it until we both lost contact. I could have got in touch with him before somehow, I'm sure, but it never seemed important enough until I met Damian.'

'Great,' Ellie said clinging onto her civility by a thread.

'I really won't want to name you in the divorce, I was only being a bitch. Aaron says you're a nice person.'

'Gee, thanks.'

'Yeah well . . . I wanted you to know that I'm not going to make life difficult. I've told Aaron that I'm happy for us to get a quick divorce on five years' separation. I'm off to see my folks in a couple of days' time and then, if I can get another cruise contract, I'll be gone for months, but we're going to sort it anyway.'

'What does that have to do with me?' Ellie asked.

'It means Aaron will be free. So you two have no reason not to get together if you want to.'

Ellie shook her head. 'There's no chance of that,' she said, unwilling to hint to Liza that she'd even entertained the possibility of forgiving Aaron one day.

'You could have fooled me. He's in bits that you've dumped him. He's mad about you. Far more so than he ever was about me. I'm a bit jealous, to be honest.' Liza grinned but Ellie wasn't amused.

'Why did you get married in the first place?'

'We were young and stupid.' Liza's eyes bored into Ellie. 'I suppose you never did anything you regretted when you were young?'

'Erm . . .' Ellie shut her mouth.

'There you are then. But you're missing the most important thing. Give Aaron a second chance. I thought I was in love with him. He's a lovely, gorgeous bloke and a lot of fun. We first met when he'd had a shit time on tour. He likes everything to be perfect, thinks he should have it under control – so hard on himself, so used to dealing with stuff on his own.'

Everyone around Ellie was peeling off layers and doing star jumps ready for the swim, but Liza had her hooked. 'What do you mean?'

'I met him in Cyprus after he'd come back from Afghan. I heard what happened from some of his mates and from him. He had a really shit time that he's never even shared with anyone at home. Don't be fooled by that laid back, "I can handle it" facade, Aaron was a mess after his tour.'

'What happened?' Ellie shivered and pulled her robe tighter.

'He'll tell you if you ask him. I only know some of the details; but he was a junior officer and it was one of his first patrols, supporting a bomb disposal team. Out of the blue his mate was blown up by an IED right in front of him. Aaron was supposed to be in that spot but for some reason, he wasn't. It should have been him.'

Ellie immediately saw Aaron leaping to his feet when the stones had hit the window of the cottage. 'Oh God. I'd no idea. He hinted he'd had some awful times but I didn't know how badly he was affected.'

'His unit was on some rest and relaxation soon after and we met in a bar. I was young, up for fun, and he was a handsome junior officer. I thought he was the life and soul, really chilled out and right up my street, but one night in bed he woke up screaming and he poured it all out. The horror of it all.' Liza shuddered. 'I don't want to go into the details. I've had trouble getting them out of my own head, so God knows how he gets them out of his.'

Liza heaved a sigh and went on. 'Anyway, he told me that it had shown him how fragile life was and that everything could end in a heartbeat. He was based on the island for a while and a week later, we were married in Vegas. It seemed romantic and I thought I was in love, and hey, life's too short – so why not.'

'God . . .' Ellie could finally understand how they'd met and married after a whirlwind romance. She thought of Aaron and all the stuff he must have kept hidden, for all these years, never wanting to worry his family or open up the memories of those dark times.

'It didn't last,' Liza said. 'It wasn't founded on anything *real*, but that doesn't mean you and he won't last.'

Evie's voice came over the loudspeaker. *'Five minutes to the swim, my lovers. Please assemble on the beach!'*

'If you don't believe me, ask him, but I'd hate to think I'd fucked everything up between you. Please give him another chance,' Liza said.

'I – I'll think about it. But I have to go.'

'Yeah.' Liza pulled a face. 'Good luck. Personally, I think you're all out of your freaking minds, but each to their own. I'm off to my hotel for a large G&T by the fire.' She glanced around her in distaste. 'This town's barking mad.'

Leaving Liza tottering off to the town, Ellie stumbled back

381

to the crowd of bathers, who reminded her of chattering birds. She scanned the flock for Aaron but he was nowhere to be seen. Even if he was here, there was no time to talk now. She'd have to find him after the swim.

'Ellieeeeee!'

Scarlett's screech cut through the general hubbub, and Ellie waved. It was hard to jog in flip-flops, but she did her best. She reached Scarlett and to her amazement found her parents there too. Her father was taking off his jeans to reveal a pair of tatty trunks and her mum had just pulled off a sweater, uncovering a violet and orange fifties swimsuit.

'Where've you been?' Scarlett demanded.

Ellie was out of breath after her dash to the beach. 'Tell you later.'

'Mum? Dad? What are you doing here?'

'We couldn't miss the swim.'

Ellie gawped at her father, who had a pair of goggles on his head. His tanned arms and neck contrasted with his lily-white torso. 'You said you'd come and watch, not take part.'

Her mum smirked. 'Well, I've always hankered after trying it and your dad offered to join me. So how could I resist?'

'Is this a public show of family unity?' Ellie asked.

'Something like that,' her father muttered. 'Though I never agreed to freeze my bollocks off here.'

Anna slid him a look. 'You're not even in the water yet, Roger.'

'That's what worries me, that I'll have no balls left at all.'

'Roger!' Anna exclaimed. 'People can hear. Maybe we can get Marcus and co. in there next year so we have a full house.'

Their father snorted. 'There won't be a next year. This is a one-off. I'll be in front of the fire at the manor with a book.'

Scarlett and Ellie shared a look that needed no words. *Next year.*

A klaxon sounded and the attention switched to Evie once again. She stood on top of the slipway, mic in hand.

Ellie untied her robe as Evie boomed forth.

*'Right, you lovely people. The moment of truth has come! I'm going to start the countdown and when the klaxon sounds again, I want everyone to enter the water. Slow or as quick as you like but personally I prefer to get it over with and dive in!'*

Groans and ribald laughter followed.

Evie carried on talking, but Ellie's attention was elsewhere. Among the throngs of bathers, she saw a man with skinny legs taking off his sweatshirt. His mouth was downturned and his hair blowing in the wind.

*Julian* . . . though Ellie had a struggle to recognise him. He thrust the sweatshirt at his wife.

Oh God, had her mother seen him? Had her father?

'It's OK. I'm OK. Your dad saw him earlier. He's not going to throw him off the quay.' Her mum was by her side, holding her arm. 'None of us should let him spoil a single moment of our life. This is our day.'

Ellie hugged her mum.

'You're the glue that holds this family together,' Scarlett said. 'It's all for one or not at all.'

*'I'll be starting the final countdown in just a moment,'* Evie warned.

'What is this? Bloody *James Bond*?' her father grumbled, slapping his arms.

Ellie took a deep breath and shrugged off the robe, tossing it onto the picnic rug along with the rest of her family's clothes.

'*Ten . . .*'

Around her, everyone was jumping up and down, slapping thighs and arms, whooping and chattering. Julian was arguing with his wife . . .

'*Nine. Eight . . .*'

Scarlett was jogging on the spot. Jude was at the head of the bathers.

'*Seven, six . . .*'

'Jesus Christ. Why did I agree to this?' her dad muttered.

'*Five, four . . .*'

'Oh!' Aaron's head had appeared in the middle of the masses, staring at her, mouthing something she couldn't make out.

'*Three.*'

Ellie froze.

'*Two, one!*'

'*Braaaapppppp!*'

The klaxon blared.

Screams rang out and Jude led the way, splashing then diving through the waves. Scores of bathers followed, shrieking, cheering and swearing. Their father was already knee-deep, groaning as waves slapped against him.

Julian Mallory dithered at the edge, poking his lily-white toes into the water and pulling a face.

Ellie froze, stuck on the beach with Scarlett and her mother a few yards away, moving towards the water. Aaron was already out of his depth but treading water and looking at her. He raised a hand, beckoning her, but Ellie couldn't move.

'Ellie!' Scarlett ran back and took her hand.

Her mum joined them.

'Aren't you going in, darling?'

'I don't think I can.' She was transfixed by Mallory standing in the wavelets between her and Aaron.

Standing either side of her, they grabbed her hands. 'Ellie, come on! It's now or never. Don't chicken out!'

'Ready?' said Scarlett.

Aaron was wading back to shore towards her. He called but she couldn't hear what he said, yet somehow she felt it deep in her soul.

Ellie decided. 'As I'll ever be.'

'One. Two. Three, Goooooo!' With a warrior cry, the three of them ran forward. Ellie ignored the pain from the pebbles, then the icy shock of the water, holding on tighter to the hands of the women she loved most in the world.

'Way to go!' she heard from the water. 'Gooooo, ladies!'

Aaron was shouting, Jude whooping and their father yelling, 'Come on, you wusses!'

The first wave hit them and they screamed. The cold sucked her breath away, but exhilarated her. They were still holding hands, wading chest deep in the surf.

'Wave!' Anna shouted. 'Jump!'

They let go, jumped in unison, were taken up by the breaker and deposited down. The cold was biting, impossible to stand. Ellie struck out, thrashing at the water to try and get warm. She swam towards her father, who was bobbing up and down a few yards away. Scarlett and her mother were alongside her, splashing and swimming, shrieking with the cold and excitement.

'Fuckkkkkk!'

Behind them, a screech pierced the air, even above the waves. Ellie was out of her depth, so she stopped swimming, trod water and turned.

Mallory was yelling, arms in the air. A huge wave picked him up and he vanished in the white water. A second later, it spewed him onto the shingle.

Ellie allowed herself to float up and down with the calmer water beyond the surf.

Troy Carman and Bryony Cronk were ankle deep, hauling Mallory in like a stranded fish. He was spluttering and coughing.

The klaxon blared.

'*Oh no, people, looks like we have a casualty!*' Evie shouted.

The lifeboat crew reached Mallory but he waved an angry arm at them. Meanwhile Bryony's dog had started barking at him. Ellie saw his wife grab his arm as he tried to scramble to his feet, but he staggered and fell flat onto the shingle. Some of the swimmers were already out of the water, but Jude and Scarlett and her parents were still swimming and splashing each other.

A little further out, Ellie saw Aaron swimming towards her, with long powerful strokes. Ignoring the cold, she turned away from the beach and struck out to meet him. He was within his depth but he had to hold onto her once they reached each other, to keep her above the water.

'It's freezing in here. I m-must be out of my m-mind,' she said, her teeth chattering.

'I didn't think you were going to come in at all. Ellie, I am so sorry. I've made the biggest mess of my life and I'm going to regret it for the rest of my days unless you let me try to make it up to you. Please, please, give me at least some hope that I can start to make amends.'

His eyes held such a heartfelt plea, such agony that Ellie couldn't hold out any longer. What point was there in tormenting herself or him when she longed for happiness with Aaron, just as much as he clearly did with her. She wanted to hear more about what he'd been through and try to work through their problems, just as her parents had.

'I almost didn't turn up today either,' she said softly. 'But here I am. With you.'

'I can't believe it.' The hope on his face made her want to cry. He held her tighter as the swell lifted them up and down.

Ellie was turning blue. 'I s-saw Liza a few minutes ago. She told me a bit about what h-happened in Afghanistan.'

'What? I didn't ask her to. I don't talk about that.'

'I k-know but you can and you should. We both should. We should have no more secrets from each other. Ever.' She saw the relief in his eyes, and her heart swelled with optimism about the future. 'Now, c-can we please get out of here before one of us gets hypothermia?'

He laughed. 'Best idea you've had all year.'

He carried her until she could stand up, then hand in hand they braved the surf and waded towards the shore.

### THE END

# Acknowledgements

The two main people I'd like to thank for help with this book are Dave Hamilton – forager, historian and author of *Family Foraging*. Find him among the sea beet at www.davehamilton.co.uk and @davewildish on Twitter.

Also my daughter, Dr CJ, a lecturer and researcher in genetics and ancient DNA, who first suggested the spark of the idea on a Boxing Day family walk. I may have actually jumped up and down in glee as I realised that I couldn't wait to start writing it.

As ever, the process of getting that idea to finished page is a team effort, so thank you to the amazing team at Avon Books including my editors Rachel Faulkner-Willcocks and Tilda McDonald, copy editor Jo Gledhill, and the publicity, sales and marketing dream team of Sabah, Sophie and Dom who help to put the book into the hands of you, the reader.

Authors don't have colleagues and we spend so much time alone that we need friends and supporters to cheer us on and help us through the tough times. I'd like to thank in particular bookseller Janice Hume, Nell Dixon, Liz Hanbury, Bella Osborne, Sarah Bennett, Rachel Griffiths and Jules Wake for being simply awesome.

Finally, I'd like to thank my wonderful agent, Broo Doherty, and my family, especially Mum, Dad, Charles, James, CJ and John. ILY x